# Embrace the Lonely Heart

**Cathrine E Robinson**

*Sterling Hearts Publishing*

**Author's Note***

This novel contains subjects that may cause concern
for sensitive readers and is intended for a mature audience.
Included are topics discussing substance abuse; rough sex scenes;
abortion, relevant to the time period; murder, and body disposal.

Also, since the story takes place in Victorian England,
There are phrases that were common at the time,
and the British spelling of words,



ISBN: 978-1-7387156-4-0 (eBook)
978-1-7387156-5-7 (hardcover)
978-1-7387156-3-3 (book)

Cover design by: The Swoonies Romance Art by Holly Perret

Publisher: Cathrine E Robinson (Sterling Hearts Publishing)

# *Dedication*

***This book is dedicated to my family.
I love you with all my heart.***

*I would like to thank those who helped me prepare this novel: my many previewers for their input and encouragement, especially Linda Weldon of Weldon Equine Service for her knowledge of horses and their personalities. Deep gratitude goes to Ashley Robinson and Rebecca Lockyer for their editorial assistance and careful attention to detail and to Lynda Robinson Boyd, a lifelong student and teacher of foreign languages, who assisted in making sure that my French wording is correct. My deepest love is for my husband, Robert, for his encouragement and for helping me to always follow my dreams.*

*All ye come and give regard*

*To a tale of woe and wonder*

*Knight so bold t'was castle guard*

*Protecting one from plunder*

*Stalwart strong, resist the wrong*

*And be not torn apart*

*Take she to breast,*

*forsake the rest*

*Embrace the lonely heart*

# *Prologue*

**Northumberland, England**
**Camber Hall, 1862**

Sitting behind his heavy oak desk in the dark-panelled study, the current Earl of Camber Hall peered over his wire-rimmed glasses as his brother entered and casually relaxed into a tufted leather chair. "A dispatch has been received stating that Viscount Berwyke has died." He paused, waiting for a reaction. "You are now Lord Barwick, master of a decrepit estate, crumbling castle and future husband to a thirteen-year-old child. I'm not sure whether to congratulate you, or pity you."

***

Lauren Berwyke packed her few belongings into the musty-smelling trunk she and her governess, Mrs. Butterfield, had wrestled from the attic. Ellen Butterfield had guided her through the past years as best she could under the circumstances. Phillip Berwyke had been fortunate to find a dedicated and loving soul to care for the child after Lauren's mother passed from a fever days after giving birth. Lauren's father was in the depths of his indulgent lifestyle and wallowed in his self-pity. He cared little as his estate diminished, nor what his daughter had or did.

Over the ensuing years, with dwindling resources, household wages were decreased, and one by one the servants left to seek more lucrative employment. Ellie's years of toil to see to the care of the child and to make the large manse somewhat habitable, along with her advancing age, had whitened her hair and thickened her proportions. For the love she felt for the child, Ellie had stayed. She refused to see the little girl alone with no one to care for her. She did without and protected Lauren from her selfish father and her deceased mother's relatives, who occasionally arrived in the manse to rant and rave of feigned deception and hurts.

Lauren's mother, Elizabeth Etherington, had been forced by her stepmother into an arranged marriage to the aged Lord Barwick, a man three decades her senior. Agnes Etherington had seen it as a financial advantage to increase her own holdings through her stepdaughter. Surely, the pretty, young Elizabeth would outlive the aging Phillip Berwyke, especially since that one was inclined to drink himself to death. There was also an excellent chance that he could perish by way of a duel for his indiscretion at cards, and if that, among other things, did not cause his demise, there were different ways to see to her plans. All her schemes had come to naught when Elizabeth had succumbed to the childbirth fever.

At that time, the estate still had some value, however, with Phillip's careless management and vices, much of what the old Berwyke family had, was now long gone. They were an ancient family who had prospered and flourished, building the castle and a garrison closer to the coast to protect themselves during turbulent times. Now the walls were discoloured where massive paintings once hung. Furniture was sold to pay debts, and stables that had been envied sat empty. Even Lauren's little pony had recently been sold, though its worth had been dismal, except to her.

The old home showed signs of obvious disrepair. Without servants to care for it, out-of-reach cobwebs of intricate design covered the high corners of doorways and swung from dust-laden chandeliers. Only a scattering of threadbare chairs remained in some of the rooms to rest upon, while others sat empty, devoid of their one-time prestige. The many empty areas of the manse were shuttered, dark, unused and uncleaned. Wallpaper curled its way down walls while curtains hung limp, rotting and faded from the sun. Floors were dull and scarred from years of heavy boot traffic.

The tenants who remained on the land eked out a sparse living on the tired soil. They were unable to pay their full rent to the estate as little had been done to help them keep fresh bloodlines in the husbandry of the animals or assist in crop advancements. Scrawny chickens scratched in the dust, and weak, inbred animals roamed the fields.

Lauren closed the chest on her few possessions and dragged it down the faded, threadbare carpeting on the stairs. She and Mrs. Butterfield had been summoned to her father's barrister and told to bring their personal belongings along with them. A hired coach had been sent for the conveyance into town, and with dread and heavy hearts, she and Mrs. Butterfield clasped hands and stared morosely out the window at the passing countryside. The day was dull, grey and damp. Low clouds scudded lazily across the sky, which suited their mood. A mist hung in the trees as they jostled their way into town with thick mud sucking at the wheels of the well-used coach.

Mrs. Butterfield was left to nervously wait in the carriage at the solicitor's building while Lauren was ushered alone into the office. The grim look on Charles Kearney's face did little to ease her fears. He seated her on a tall hard chair and continued working at his ledgers, explaining that the parties named within the documents would arrive shortly.

He pitied the sorry state of the child before him. Her dress was worn and frayed. Too short and too tight on her little body. Skinny legs led to tiny feet pushed into worn, cheap boots. He had tried to have Barwick set aside funds for his only child to no avail. When the estate was mortgaged beyond any chance of the old lord making payments, Charles had gone to him to mitigate the damage. With no male heirs, Phillip had been forced, in a rare moment of lucidity, to consider the future of his only child and to a greater extent, a quick influx of cash to see to his vices.

Though barely known, Charles Kearney found a distant cousin after a search of the peerage. Charles was confident that the offer to become a Lord of the Realm would be accepted. Based on the information he had acquired, he had talked Berwyke into the choice. Once Berwyke learned of the relationship, he had heartily agreed that the second son of Camber Hall would succeed him as Lord Barwick upon his death. He was well aware that the family was wealthy and insisted on a marriage that would see to his child's future. Until such time, he demanded a large amount be deposited into his accounts for her current upkeep. He waited nervously to hear if the conditions would be accepted and could barely contain his surprise when it was.

Though funds had been forwarded to the estate to improve its condition and care for Lauren, Phillip had skimmed the majority of the money to see to his pleasures. Thus, due to the circumstances of a father caring only for his entertainment and debasement, here the mite sat, alone and afraid. Her face was pale, her eyes downcast as she twisted her hands in the threadbare material of her skirt. Too small to reach the floor, her legs swung in the air as she slumped on the seat.

The sound of a cane hitting the floor and the quick tattoo of footsteps sounded before the door burst open, slamming against the far wall to admit Agnes Etherington. Not one to display the gentleness of womanhood, she bore a proud forbearance. At sixty-six years to her tall slim frame, she held her nose perpetually upwards so she could easily look down on everyone else. Grey hair was severely pulled away from her hawklike features as pale, watery eyes glared at the solicitor. She stomped further into the room to stand before the desk, pounding the head of her cane on the solicitor's desk. Her perpetual black gown was not so much a statement of mourning as it was her preferred colour. The sweeping black feather on her bonneted head bounced once and quaked into submission of her will to tremble in her presence so she could speak.

"It is my understanding that Berwyke's will is to be read today," she annunciated in a cold, stern voice. "Why was I not summoned?"

Charles rose from his desk, removed his glasses and began to clean them with an impeccable white handkerchief. "There was no need, Mrs. Etherington, as you were not mentioned therein," he firmly stated.

Lauren had rarely seen this forbidding relative except for the times she had arrived to screech evil words at her father. She sank lower into her seat to create as small a target as possible as the steely grey eyes turned their focus onto her. The frightened child nervously fumbled with her skirt and cringed as Agnes' eyes narrowed, and she began her tirade.

"As her only living relative, it is only proper that she be left in my care. What was that useless Phillip thinking? We are her only surviving family. She should be given to us." Her calculating mind considered what the pitiful worth of the dilapidated estate would bring. However, something was better than nothing, and there was the coveted title.

"Arrangements have been drafted in the will to care for Lauren," Charles answered, adding with slight derision, "You are merely related to the child by marriage and not a blood relative."

Agnes squinted evil, narrow eyes at him. "I suppose you found a blood relative to take over the estate. I should have expected this much from you and Phillip. You meddle, and he never did anything for anyone other than himself. He killed my beautiful stepdaughter giving birth to this one." She pointed a crooked rheumatic claw at Lauren. "Why on earth should I think he would consider my hurts now and allow us to care for Elizabeth's child." She addressed Lauren directly in a wheedling voice."Wouldn't you like to come home with me and stay with your Step-Grandmama, dearest?"

Lauren remembered the ranting woman railing at her father whenever she appeared at the house. She remembered hands grasping at her, pinching her skin and hiding under furniture before Ellie came, hustling her out of the angry woman's wrathful path.

"No Ma'am," she ventured timidly, trying in vain to make herself smaller as she slid even lower in the chair. She would rather accept any option other than to place herself in Agnes Etherington's questionable care.

Agnes drew herself upright at the insult and could barely control the rage she felt as her plans slipped through her fingers yet again.

"I would have cared for you as my own, you little nobody," she seethed. "You have nothing now of any worth and will get nothing from me, ever, so do not come crawling for my favours. I would have cared for you. I offer a warm home, and you have the nerve to turn me down!" Agnes rose to her full height and glared at the girl. "I see your trunks packed and that old woman waiting in the coach. 'Tis a certainty that the new lord intends to turn you out of your home. Then you will be sorry you did not accept my offer. You're not but a reminder of what we once had. If not for you, Elizabeth would still be alive and Mistress of Barwick Castle. Maybe then, there would have been some worth left in that dreary piece of land."

Tears rolled down Lauren's face and fell to her chest. She sniffed and felt her face redden with her anguish. Her step-grandmother's words conveyed her fears of the unknown. Was she to be turned out of her home? Where would she go? How would she and Ellie survive? She felt the familiar guilt of her mother's death as she heard the words spoken. Throughout her life, she was sure she saw it in her father's dull eyes whenever he looked at her.

"Madam, your presence is not required here, and I bid you take your leave posthaste." The solicitor held the door open in an unmistakable gesture for Agnes to take her leave.

"I truly hope we never have to set eyes on your sorry face again. Ungrateful chit," she spitefully spoke as she stalked out the door, grumbling a muted expletive at Charles Kearney when she passed.

For Lauren, the dam had broken. Sobbing and sniffing, she felt wretched. Her mouth was turned down in a deep pout, her chin quivering as she tried to control herself, alas to no avail. Her eyes were swollen as she buried her face in her hands and cried out her anguish. Her unbrushed hair had come loose from the ribbon tying it and was a wild mass of frizzy curls. Try as she might, she could not control herself and heaved great sobs of misery.

This is the scene that greeted the men as they entered the close confines of the office. Lauren refused to look up as the solicitor made the introductions. At one point, a handkerchief was pressed into her cold hands, and she blew her nose loudly.

She barely heard the words of her father's Last Will until her name was mentioned. Her father had promised her hand in marriage to his heir. It was a condition of the inheritance to secure her future. He had considered what would happen to her after he was gone and perhaps even cared about her. She was not to be sent away. She would be allowed to stay, married to a man of his choosing.

It was then, through her tears, she saw a watery glimpse of her future husband standing beside her chair. He was so tall, she thought, looking up at him. His hair was wet, dark and hung over his forehead. His face was set with firm, angular features.

He had an extremely harsh, stoic look about him. The collar of his coat was pulled up high, restricting her full view, and he did not once glance in her direction. Charles had his full attention as that kind gentleman concentrated on reading the provisions outlined in the will. He had a hard look to the set of his jaw, which was covered by a short growth of beard, showing that he had not shaved for many days. To her young mind, he was so old! Her impression of him was that of being aloof, cruel and uncaring of her sorrow as he stared straight ahead, listening to the lawyer's words with an angry set to his features.

When the reading was complete, the short, rotund gentleman who had accompanied him into the close confines of the office, cleared his throat and began speaking the words of a marriage bond in a dull, steady voice. Startled that it was progressing so rapidly, Lauren felt a panic seize her. She wasn't ready to become a bride. All her fanciful childish dreams of a prince on a white charger rescuing her from a solitary life flew out of her head, and fear clawed at her belly. She shivered uncontrollably and was sure that in the next moment, she would deface herself and empty the contents of her stomach. She was sick, and there was a buzzing in her ears as Charles came to her side and nudged her to respond in the affirmative.

"You must adhere to your father's wishes, Lauren. It's the only way to secure your future."

In a daze, it progressed as she cried like the child she was throughout the procedure. She heard snippets of the conversation. The words '*until death us do part*' followed by '*convent*,' '*France*,' '*finishing school*,' and '*for the best, considering her age*.' In a haze of bewilderment, she was dismissed to be escorted by the solicitor across the room and outside to fall sobbing into the arms of a stunned Mrs. Butterfield.

Ellie Butterfield was given explicit instructions, nodding absently to the spoken words, and accepted a packet of papers explaining travel details, living expenses and all relevant information needed for a speedy departure. Once complete, Charles called directions up to the driver and their future was placed in the hands of another.

No time was given for questions to be asked or answered as the confused pair were drawn away from their home towards far-off London. There, they would board the ship that would sail away from their country and life.

Along the way, Lauren's tears halted. Her pressing grief was discreet, persistent and silent as the wheels turned, and the miles passed in a blur.

# *Chapter One*

**May 22, 1867**

The soft grey facade of *Abbaye Du Coeur Brisè*, located in the peaceful French countryside, was reflected in the interior of the wall that surrounded it. Early mornings were spent in prayer and reflection. Afterwards, the nuns moved silently as they tended gardens of vegetables and herbs. The students, quietly and with graceful deportment, attended their studies of proper elocution, how to sit and how to stand. There were periods of study in classical history and memorizing the current members of royalty, peerage and gentry.

The proper management of a great house was reviewed. The hiring and firing of household staff, the necessities of supplying the different areas of a mansion where hired men and women would care for the expensive furnishings, silver, china, and kitchen requirements. How to hostess a grand party, pen the invitations, who should be allowed on the guest list and where they would be placed at table. Most importantly, who belongs in society and who does not.

One's peerage was reviewed: exercise careful judgement in picking a mate, on rising no higher than your station less you be judged inferior by your new relatives, nor going below such station as to lessen your value. It was advised that a wife should always concede to her husband, never argue or complain.

Also, however seldom addressed, briefly and quickly, by a blushing, stuttering nun, were the intricacies of married life. The conjugal requirements, so to speak: never be unclothed in the presence of your husband, and always be a morally pure lady. The relations between husband and wife were to be performed under cover of darkness and purely for procreational purposes. It was ground into the girls that a true lady would hold to her own thoughts during this time and submit quietly and grudgingly to the baser desires of her husband. Her job in society was to provide an heir and be a perfect, socially accepted companion.

Later in the afternoon would be the more comfortable pursuits of languages, music, painting and needlepoint. Thus were the preparations for a life of entering into English high culture as a gracious and elegant Victorian hostess.

After a late dinner, they were allowed a brief time to read letters from home and write their own in return. Lauren did not send or receive mail as there was no one to write to her or send a post in response. Since she had been bustled off to France, no word had come from her solicitor nor her husband. A generous allowance for her wants and needs arrived faithfully at the beginning of every month. After paying the abbey for her board and lessons and giving Ellie her wages, Lauren spent the remainder on the clothes and accessories she would need if one day, she and Ellie were ever summoned back to England. The little maid had pushed her to acquire a sizeable trousseau, and

Lauren had come to appreciate the fine clothes she now wore compared to the rags she had owned as a child.

It was her habit to spend the evening reading news that was regularly sent to the convent for the English girls in residence. Often, the pages were filled with gossipy tidbits. Today was no exception, but for the one article she read, which had an uncomfortable ring of familiarity.

*Rumour abounds that a certain Lord,*
*whose young wife was hustled out of the country*
*and hasn't been seen in years,*
*is contemplating a divorce.*
*Has he taken up with a charming miss*
*from an excellent family?*
*Will this bring joy, scandal or despair*
*for the one who has set her cap to the handsome gent?*
*He being a man of considerable wealth*
*who has improved his lot in life*
*from the second son with no title*
*to a notable Viscount.*
*It seems he can easily afford the reckless behaviour,*
*but what of his new miss?*
*...and what of the wife!*

A coldness grew in the pit of Lauren's stomach. Could it be she the Tattler was discussing? Divorce! Never mind the scandal. She would lose her home.

Although she had been happy during her time here in the convent, it was not in her plans to spend the rest of her life living in cloister with the nuns, no matter how kind they had been. She had, during the past five years, learned to be a proper English Lady. In dress, talents, and deportment. A perfect china doll to be brought out and displayed but not to have an opinion or mind of her own. One of cool detachments. A perfect lady without emotion or zest. No highs, no lows, just a steady acceptance of calm, cleaving to the will of others.

Mrs. Butterfield had stayed by her side, honing her craft as a companion and lady's maid. But she was more than that. She was a confidant, a ready ear, someone who gave her opinion when needed and often when not. Lauren had not felt a necessity to employ another when Ellie Butterfield was and always had been by her side.

The time to leave was nigh, and leave she must. To seek out her elder husband and arrange a future. The choice would be to live without him, in which case a settlement would have to be arranged, and she would forfeit the comfort of the known and her beloved home. Or to live with him if she could adjust to a loveless marriage with the old, unfeeling man she remembered.

With this conviction, she passed the nuns in the quiet corridors with their hands folded in their habits and eyes lowered to the ground to seek the Mother Superior. In the distant confines of the convent, she could hear the choir of nuns softly singing their prayerful hallelujahs. Mother Superior, the woman who guided the souls of both nuns and girls given into her charge, was found in the peaceful setting of the garden. Sitting below the overhanging branches of a large oak with her rosary held in her hand. Her lips silently moved as she prayed her daily devotion. Her face was wrinkled with age, and her eyes betrayed a wealth of knowledge and serenity. She glanced up as Lauren walked towards her.

"*Ma Mère, un moment de votre temps, s'il vous plaît*"

"Dear Lauren, I can always spare a moment for you. What is it *ma petite*?" The kind aged nun smiled at Lauren.

"The time has come for me to leave and return to my home, for I fear I will have no home to return to if I stay any longer."

Mother Superior patted the wooden bench for Lauren to sit beside her. "The time comes with every student when they must leave this place and take up their position in society." She continued in her calm manner, "You have been with us a long time, and we have come to see a great change in you since your arrival as a frightened little girl. Truly, you have been one of our greatest achievements."

Speaking in a soft tone with Mother Superior, had a soothing effect on Lauren's disquiet, "I appreciate your kindness and patience with me throughout these years, *Mère Superieure*, and will treasure my time here. You have guided me well and shown me kindness and compassion.

"This is a sudden decision, and I wonder if you have thought it thoroughly. Will you arrive unannounced at your home and surprise your husband? What will you do if he is not there? Should you arrive first in London? What will you do when you get there?" She pondered on the many decisions Lauren had not yet considered.

"I will need to find my husband. He may still be at Barwick Castle." she furrowed her brow. "I'm not certain where he will be!"

"Parliament will soon be in session." Mother Superior patted Lauren's hand in a calming gesture, "This means he will have to travel to London, if he is not already there. It will take weeks before you will be able to arrange your travel plans. Consider carefully what I can do for you in your quest to return to England, and I will see what can be done to help with the details."

Lauren thought about all she would require to make the transition back to her home. With the season well underway by the time she returned, she would need to stay in the city instead of returning to her home in the country. It would perhaps be safer to first meet her husband in a crowded place instead of the isolation of her home.

"I will need assistance in arranging passage, furthermore, I don't know anyone who lives in London, so I will need accommodation for a short period of time. Do you think, with your knowledge of girls that have passed through these walls, you could help procure that for me?"

Rising and taking Lauren's hand, the peaceful woman guided her, in an unhurried sedate fashion, back into the convent so she could write the letters necessary to assist the young girl they had all grown so fond of.

"I have a very special friend who would be delighted to help you. I'm certain you will find her to be quite lovely."

"*Je vous remercie, ma Mere.* I value my time here and especially your instruction."

"We knew your time would come to leave us, and we will miss you, my dear. *Ta vie t'attend.* Your life awaits."

* * *

The rented house on the north side of St. James Square was an elegant surprise to Lauren and Ellie Butterfield. Servants hustled the trunks up the back staircase while Lauren entered through the wide front door opened by the barrel-chested butler with a formal flourish.

"Welcome, Lady Barwick. We have been expecting you and all has been prepared for your arrival." he stuffily pronounced, guiding her into the townhouse.

Inside the front entrance, along the wall, was a sweeping, lush carpeted staircase with filigreed gold leaf railings. The opulence was evident in everything seen and experienced. The interior was painted a robin's egg blue with white and gold trim from the chair rails to high baseboards and elegant crown moulding. Comfortable pale blue printed upholstered settees and chairs with dainty curved legs filled the morning room. Tables were placed in convenient spots to hold a cup of tea or a dish of delicacies. Tall leaded windows looked out on the bustle of the street, and underfoot, a thick wool Oriental rug created in a unique detailed design of flowers and birds softened the footsteps. Mother Superior had friends in high places.

"Well, my little Chuckaboo," Ellie quipped as they traversed the rooms of the townhouse. "If this isn't bang up the elephant, then I don't know what is. The convent was a quiet place to be in for the past few years, but I'll wager there will be a fine mafficking going on here in grand old London."

Lauren considered her words in silence, her stomach roiling at the thoughts running through her head. She fervently hoped that the rowdiness Ellie predicted would not be the future confrontation she would have when she met her wayward husband.

The household was managed with perfection by the butler and staff. It soon became a ritual that every morning, Lauren requested the team of horses hitched to the closed carriage for a drive along Pont Street, Grosvenor Crescent or Eaton Square, hoping for a glimpse of a man she could barely remember. The thoroughfare was a colourful display of civilized society as the ladies and their escorts, straight-backed and elegant, promenaded along the causeway, showing off their leisurely lifestyle.

After living in the colourless grey walls of the tranquil convent, the panorama of the bustling city was thrilling. The sights and smells of London, not all of which were pleasant, excited Lauren. Hawkers called out in the street, selling their wares as horses and carriages passed them by. It was a cacophony of tingling, throbbing life to assail the senses.

Gossip and rumour ran rampant as the elusive guest of the high-end townhouse kept to herself. Except for the occasional peek inside the lace-curtained conveyance when the breeze briefly blew back the curtains, Lauren did her best not to draw attention to herself, though there were few, if any, who would recognize her.

She had rarely been to London when her father came to sit in the House of Lords. His duties were well planned, and he had no time for the child; he had advised Mrs. Butterfield, so they had been left at the castle. Little were they aware that Parliament was not where he spent most of his time. More often than not, his equally dubious friends had been forced to search and remove him from the small community that had settled in an established slum of Limehouse in the docklands. It was an area of brothels and opium dens where Phillip Berwycke met his demons and succumbed to their power over him.

Though the sparse amount of time her father spent with her was much the same in the country, at least there, his access to the toxic drugs was limited. She could ride her pony and be out of the house away from him as he stumbled about the castle and fell into a drunken stupor to lay on the cold floor until he roused himself and went in search of another bottle to inoculate himself against acknowledging the waste he had become.

London was a dangerous place for any woman to be left unattended, even in the fashionable district. Though bobbies patrolled the streets, when night fell, miscreants lurked in the shadows looking for an easy lone traveller. Lauren was careful when and where she went and would not venture outside after sunset.

Ellie spent most of her day in the kitchen, where she had perched herself on a high stool to enjoy the relaxed atmosphere among the staff. She spoke deliberately, in her unique vernacular, about her mistress, tattling mercilessly and revealing harrowing stories of the aged husband and his ignominious attitude to his lady.

"He sent us away from all we knew and took over her house to do with as he pleased." She railed, holding them enthralled with her tales. "He's a skilamalink for sure, and I'll never trust him. An old lord, ugly and mean most likely," she condemned, elaborating with her own beliefs the impression Lauren had related on that sad, long ago day.

Ellie was finding it hard to let go of the grudge she held against Lauren's mysterious husband and felt no compulsion to protect his reputation. To her way of thinking, the staff of a great house always knew more about the family than even the family did, so what was the harm in spreading a few of her own beliefs? It would serve the old lord right for her opinions to reach his household.

On this bright day, a visitor arrived that whisked into the house, greeted the head butler familiarly and confidently inquired on the location of the current occupant. After being given directions, the elegant lady walked into the back garden, ordering a cup of tea and a plate of biscuits.

Lauren glanced up from the book she was enjoying to see a regal lady followed by a flustered butler.

"Madam, may I present the Viscountess Lady Grassett," he breathlessly announced.

Lauren knew she was renting the townhouse from the Grassett estate and could hardly refuse to receive her guest who was already standing before her and that one who actually owned the home. Standing herself and dipping into a pretty curtsy, Lauren greeted the Viscountess. "My lady, it is a pleasure to make your acquaintance. Will you sit here, or would you prefer to be indoors?"

"Here will do quite nicely, my dear. I've ordered tea and biscuits to be served, so we may as well enjoy the sunshine." Seating herself gingerly on a garden chair, she adjusted her light-flowing gown. She continued getting immediately to the point of her visit as she lifted a gold lorgnette and perused Lauren to gauge the worth of the woman before her. "You have been in London for well over a brace of weeks, and it's quite ridiculous for you to be hiding out in the townhouse. I know by correspondence with the abbey the reason you are here."

Lauren's eyes widened perceptively,

"Don't be alarmed that your Mother Superior spread any gossip; she's not that type. I believe I have a way for you to finally be in touch with your husband."

Lauren was quite willing to let Lady Grassett continue her speech as was her want. It seemed that it mattered little to the woman if Lauren spoke at all.

"Is it your wish to remain incognito as you seem to want to do?" she continued without waiting for an answer. "The gossips are having a heyday trying to figure out who you are and what you are doing here."

Lauren was impressed with the forthright attitude of the lady, much akin to Mother Superior's take-charge personality. "I did not consider that my presence would cause a fuss. London is a big city with so many people I thought I could quietly be about my business."

"Your clandestine behaviour has caused quite a stir among the *ton*. They must know, above all else, everything that is happening in the city. Quite a gossipy group. They wag their tongues like church bells and can't stand not knowing everything about everyone. Then what little they do find out, they pass on to one and all whether true or not."

The refreshments were delivered, and Lady Grassett poured the tea, offering Lauren a china cup and saucer, helping herself to a sugared cookie when Lauren declined.

"My family will host a ball at my son's home in four days. We had arranged for a masquerade, and I realize this doesn't give you much time to plan, but it will be the perfect venue for you. No one will be introduced on entry, and you can disguise yourself any way you wish." She took a sip of her tea and continued. "Because I employ everyone in this house, and they talk as much as the gossips, I have the upper hand to know that you have been taking carriage rides hoping to find Lord Barwick wandering about. That will never do. He's a very serious gentleman and is far too busy with his many business affairs than to be a man of leisure who mindlessly strolls about the parks and gardens of London."

Lauren considered that it was a different sort of affair that caused her concern regarding her husband, but kept to her own council and deflected to the lady's offer.

"This is very kind of you, madam. My decision to return to London was made quickly, and besides going home, I wasn't sure how I would get in touch with Lord Barwick." She smiled timidly. "I truly appreciate your loan of this house. I assume my husband now has a residence, but I wouldn't know where he is staying. Your offer may be the perfect opportunity to find him without causing too much of a fuss."

"The house was offered as a favour to Mother Superior. We became excellent friends when I was sent to the convent myself many years ago. I shudder to think of the time that has passed. It slipped by so quickly." She smiled, remembering the adventures of her youth, sipping her tea and swallowing a bite of her sugar cookie before continuing. "I don't understand your hesitancy in proclaiming yourself to Barwick." She assessed the young girl before her. "Listen to the advice of an old woman," she said. "Even one as young as yourself should not waste her time sitting alone in an empty house. You are lovely if you don't mind my saying so, and you and Barwick will make an excellent pair."

Lauren held her judgement of Lady Grassett's opinion of her suitability for her husband. She believed the woman would consider any older gentleman possessing wealth and a title attractive to one such as she.

The remainder of the afternoon was spent in pleasant conversation as Lady Grassett chatted amicably about this lord and that lady. She talked about her time in France when Mother Superior was a young teaching novice and the mischief they had gotten into. Lauren giggled at the thought that the serene nun she had known could be such a sprite. Lady Grassett was a true woman of character. She spoke glowingly about all, and not a mean word passed her lips.

# *Chapter Two*

Lauren began preparations for her costume the next day as there was no time to waste. The Grassett Ball would be mere days away. Hence, there was no time for a special outfit to be made. She would have to make do with what she had brought with her.

On the night of the ball, she dressed in her one and only Worth gown, a beautiful white tulle sewn with glistening crystals throughout the skirt. She overlayed it with a deep navy blue lace covering. When the crystals caught the reflection of the light, they sparkled through the lace, shimmering like starlight. A form-fitting navy bodice that matched the overskirt had a low scooped sweetheart neckline that dipped between her breasts and bared her back and shoulders. The corset was built into the bodice that was hooked tightly around her torso. Due to its brevity, it was constructed to reveal much of her flawless skin, making it appear that the top of the gown floated in place. It pushed her breasts upward to full perfection with no straps over her shoulder. On her head, she wore a white crescent-shaped halo that she had used in the choir at the convent. Her hair was pulled away from her face on the sides and pinned back with navy ribbons, allowing her curls to cascade down her back. Lauren wished she could wear her hair free more often instead of parted on her head and pulled back into a sombre knot as was the usual style of married women. A navy mask covered the upper part of her face, highlighting her piercing violet-blue eyes and long sooty lashes.

"Well my girl, you look grandly afternoonifed." Ellie stood back and perused the vision before her. "So what is it you're supposed to be at this high-flown affair?"

Lauren smiled at Ellie's abuse of the English language and spun in a tight circle, setting the crystal beads to sparkle in the light. "I'm the moon and the stars." She pointed to her headdress. "The halo is supposed to be the moon," She placed her hand on her stomach, "but with the fluttering I'm feeling in my stomach, mayhap I should have gone as a butterfly instead. It would have better suited my excited nervousness."

"Whatever you be, Darlin', you'll take the breath from everyone there."

The carriage pulled up to an impressive home alight with massive chandeliers. She entered the Grassett's ballroom and was immersed in a world like nothing she had ever seen before. Lady Grassett, who had become a true-to-life angel complete with huge white feathered wings, introduced her to her son and his wife. Agatha Grassett was an equally pleasant and pretty black-haired woman in a fairy costume with smaller pointed wings, a flowing colourful gown, and an upside-down tulip plopped on her head.

"It's wonderful to finally meet you," Agatha remarked. "The gossips are having a terrible time trying to figure out who you are and why you are being so secretive."

"There is no deep mystery I'm afraid, just a will to stay secluded for a time before I return home.

"Oh yes, Mother told us about your attempt to find your husband. He should arrive. Lord Grassett sent him a special invitation and insisted on his attendance this evening. Of course, we didn't tell him why. It should be a lovely surprise for him."

Lauren was not entirely sure whether her husband would find her presence, after all these years, a 'lovely surprise' or not.

The room was full of gaiety. There was laughter and dancing as guests, dressed as knights, jugglers, kings, queens, and an assortment of animals enjoyed the evening.

Lord Grassett wore a pirate costume and expertly spun her around the dance floor. He chatted through the steps on the attributes of Lord Barwick as if he willed her to appreciate the man she was married to.

"Brilliant in business and most skilled at cards. He must carry a four-leaf clover in his shoe, considering the luck he has at wagering."

The discussion did not sit well with Lauren as she had lost much in her youth by cards and wagers. When the music ended, she was swept into another dance by a rotund Greek god who wheezed around the dance floor and sweated profusely. Nevertheless, Lauren was entranced with the multiple dance partners who vied for a turn around the ballroom with her. Never in her life had she enjoyed an evening such as this, and she wondered if she ever would again.

A hush fell over the room late in the revelry, and as one, the guests turned in unison to the ballroom's double doorway on a raised dais. All the women dipped into low curtsies, and the gentlemen bowed deeply to the presence of a small group that had entered. The Prince of Wales, dressed as a beggar with a gaudily gowned woman on his arm, a Roman Gladiator and another companion dressed entirely in black, entered the affair and observed the assembly.

In the stilted silence, Bertie reached for a glass of champagne from a passing footman and raised it to salute the room. "Far be it for me to halt a grand party," he bellowed in an overly loud voice. "Continue on dear friends, that we may drink and make merry."

The chatter in the room rose as murmurs and talk increased once more. Discussions turned to the reputation of the newly arrived group, especially of their beloved Queen Victoria's errant son.

"From the look of the prince, I would say that he has already imbibed and made merry in several other ballrooms this evening," came the low tittering voice of the yellow-garbed canary beside Lauren.

Her companion, a gentleman in a tight cat costume that showed a heavily padded codpiece, agreed.

"The gentlemen in the company of the prince are not known for their discretion. The prince may not be known as a heavy drinker. However, since he married Princess Alexandra and was set free from the upbringing of his tutors and governesses, the Queen is beside herself with his fast behaviour and the company he keeps."

"So long as they are well-mannered to his degree of that state, sporting, and wealthy, he accepts them into his inner circle," spoke an elegantly feathered peacock.

"The prince is a rake of the first order. I hear he can be found in the bed of four different women on an average week," whispered a scandalized matron behind a gloved hand.

"Only four?" questioned a lion.

"On a good week, he's in the company of a different woman each night. They are commonly known as his troop. The man has an insatiable appetite for the fairer sex, and the princess pays no heed."

"No wonder he's earned the nickname of Dirty-Bertie," squeaked a mouse.

"Harriet Moncreiff is to marry Sir Charles Mordaunt this December, and it is said that she has caught the eye of the prince. Mordaunt has no interest beyond hunting and shooting, and she is a social butterfly flitting from one party to the next. Mark my words; it will end in disaster for her," piped a highland piper.

Lauren blushed at the comments spoken aloud by the guests. She turned from their conversation and noticed a woman in a blood-red Roman toga sashay towards the prince and his group. She wore her light blonde hair piled high on her head woven with ribbons of the same red hue. The dress outlined her ripe form when she moved and bared one shoulder. Lauren wondered if she wore even the barest shift under her dress because there was a definite wanton jiggle that took place under the cloth.

The woman smiled prettily at the black-garbed man and claimed his arm, pressing it against her ample bosom. Lauren assumed they were very well acquainted since he calmly accepted her demand for his attention. She couldn't help herself from noting that he stood out from the others, being taller than most. Broad shoulders tapered to a lean waist and long straight legs. From what she could see of his masked face, he possessed a casual elegance, a strong jawline and an aristocratic nose. Lauren gave herself a mental shake. She wasn't here to swoon over the handsome face of another woman's husband. She was looking for her own.

Lauren was approached by the Roman Gladiator, who pranced towards her. "I do not believe we have met fair maiden. Since there is none about who can make the introductions, I will do so of my own accord." He bowed low before her and clicked his heels together in a Prussian salute. "I am Lord Nicholas Emory, a favourite confidant of the prince." Attempting to impress her, he continued, "He holds to much of my advice in his affairs." Lord Emory reached for her hand, "You are far too comely to stand at the edge of a dance floor. I would be honoured if you would join me." He pulled her into the throng of dancers circling the room.

"You are fortunate to be held in such high esteem by the Prince of Wales," she answered politely as he waited pointedly for a response.

Not quite up to what he expected, Nicholas attempted to impress the beautiful woman again. Most young misses had been warned by their overprotected parents to stay clear of the Emory family. Rumours were spreading that they were facing severe money problems and delving into dishonest practices. With his father's insistence, Nicholas was doing his best to allay the gossip by his association with the prince. He was also searching for a rich wife who could save the family from ruin and be manipulated into accepting his '*quirks.*'

"I would be pleased to escort you to Marlborough House the next time Bertie and the Princess host one of their magnificent parties. The diversions present can be quite scandalous."

"That would be very kind of you sir, but I am a married woman."

"It would matter not," he suppressed a mild disappointment.

"I'm afraid it would to me!" she announced firmly.

Lauren considered the tall, somewhat prissy dandy. He had a sweeping orange feather atop his gladiator headpiece that floated to the music. His hands were soft and lacked a firm grip as they danced, and she worried that his gloveless hand on her back would leave a stain on her gown where he held her a little too closely. His steps were mincing, and his pouting lips were overly full.

She half listened to him as he prattled on about his importance in society. It did not seem to matter one whit to him that she was uncomfortable in his embrace and held herself stiffly in his arms. She counted the beats of the music and anticipated the remaining chords that would see the dance completed. When the music finally ended, she nodded her head in dismissal. "I trust you will excuse me sir" she announced as she turned and quickly left him to search for Agatha Grassett.

Returning from the dining room after a brief refreshment with the pleasant Grassett family, Lauren found herself beside a small group that included the couple she had seen earlier. On closer inspection, she found a strained politeness between them. The red-garbed woman seemed to simper in her willingness to please and remain the centre of attention with the darkly clothed man while he answered her queries in overtly polite yet brief responses. The Roman lady seethed in frustration as he gazed about the room or answered another woman's question.

"I was at the Germain's ball last eve and hoped you would appear." Drawing his attention back to her pouting face, she mewled in feigned innocence, "The younger son was very attentive to me, but my eyes kept wandering to the doorway to see if you had come."

"The prince demanded my company. I'm certain you were well entertained without my presence Margaret," the gentleman replied casually.

"Is that a hint of jealousy I hear in your voice, my lord? I would enjoy attending Marlborough House the next time the prince holds a function. Particularly with you on my arm," she gently chided, thinking of the notorious philandering prince and her excellent chance of catching his eye to reap the generous benefits he was known to bestow on his mistresses. This Viscount was a catch, a prize she was especially determined to snare, but time spent with the prince could reap bountiful rewards until this one was caught.

He looked over the blonde head of Margaret Edwards to the profile of the woman gazing at the dancers. Here was a woman who immediately held his interest. She was soft and elegant. He tried to place a name to her profile and found none he could remember. Margaret's words droned on in his ears as he was captivated by the slight figure standing near.

Trim and petite with soft curls flowing down her back. He noticed her head, held on a graceful slim neck, move to the music. The gown she wore revealed a shocking view of her bare back and shoulders. It dipped between the round mounds of her breasts, showing skin like honey, smooth and unblemished. When she turned to glance furtively in his direction, her piercing blue eyes, surrounded by the mask she wore, almost took his breath away. This was a woman in every sense of the word. One who was not afraid to show off her femininity and seduction in the sensual gown. Obviously, she was worldly and knew how to catch and hold the attention of men.

Lauren felt his warm gaze on her before she turned to look. Startling emerald green eyes held her pinned to the spot as he rakishly took in the view. She couldn't determine if she should be insulted by the open regard he gave her or flattered by his perusal. It was purely wicked. She felt rooted to the ground beneath his penetrating gaze and belatedly realized he had excused himself from his companion and, in a moment, was standing before her.

Bowing briefly, he took her small hand into his much larger one to kiss the back of it. Lauren felt his eyes piercing into the very core of her. A tingling sensation shimmied down her back, flipped into her stomach and quivered lower. A very unnerving response indeed.

"I find that I cannot wait for a proper introduction, my lady, and your beauty is not to be denied. If we can overlook propriety, I am Devlin Cavanaugh, and I hope you will not deny me the honour of a dance?"

This was a bold man. One who took for granted what he wanted. Lauren was out of her element with his self-assurance and the draw of his power. Mesmerized, unwilling to break the spell of his scrutiny, she assented with a slight nod of her head and moved into his waiting arms as if drawn to him like a moth to a flame.

They waltzed around the grand ballroom in complete synchronization one to the other, intensely studying unique expressions, their bodies responding to the music and each other. She fit into his embrace perfectly and responded knowingly to his expert steps.

Both were dressed in dark colours, her gown sparkling as he twirled her to the music. It was a sight to see. He was tall and sure, she petite, and following his lead as he dipped and moved across the floor, showing off her exquisite grace with the magnificent ball gown floating behind her. Many eyes watched them with appreciation, except for those of a red-gowned woman, who was not at all pleased, as they narrowed in a consuming rage. They spoke not, drinking with their locked eyes the inner thoughts of one to the other, taking their fill and wanting more.

When the music ended, he returned her to her place and smiled a rakish grin. "Thank you for the dance, my lady. I could spend all evening with you. However, I fear the other gentlemen waiting for a dance, would request a meeting at dawn for keeping you from them. I also believe it would savage your reputation if you have a care for it," he gave her a playful wink before releasing his hold on her hand.

His honey-smooth words caused another tingle to run up her spine. This was a man who knew his way in the world and accepted it with casual abandon. Lauren blushed at his compliment. When he stepped back and bowed to her, she was quickly approached by another partner who nodded amicably at the tall lord and, with a polite query, placed a gloved hand at her back to whisk her onto the dance floor.

The intrigued lord strolled about the area, inquiring and listening to whispered comments from those who believed they knew something about the woman. All the while, his warm gaze returned to her slim form as he watched eager bachelors and married men alike approach her, to offer and be accepted to dance.

"I hear that she is married to an ogre," some said with sure knowledge.

"She has been alone taking air in a closed carriage. Could it be that he refuses to allow her to be seen in public places?" whispered another conspiratorily behind a gloved hand.

"He must be old and doddering to leave her alone so much," declared a young swain.

"How cruel. To have such a lovely young wife and abandon her so," was the general consensus of those full of pity for one so young.

"Poor girl," they all sorrowfully agreed.

The revelry continued as night became the early hours of a new day. Lauren sought the fresh breeze to cool herself and take a moment to rest. Strolling out of the ballroom onto the balcony, she moved to the heavy cement balustrade. She removed her mask to cool her face in the evening breeze. Her feet were sore from dancing, and her heeled shoes pinched her toes, but she was titillated with the thrill she had felt during the party. The excitement of attending such a grand function left her breathless. Lady Grassett had found her at one point to let her know that indeed, her husband was here, somewhere, but had not been able to point him out to her when they had been scanning the crowded room together.

Lauren was enjoying herself so much that she didn't care that she had not yet been introduced to her husband, for that would surely mean an end to the gaiety. Most likely, he was liberally enjoying brandy with the other older gentlemen, playing cards in a smoke-filled room in the depths of the grand house.

Great cauldrons had been filled with wood and set ablaze, showing couples strolling among the garden paths or slipping behind the bushes for a moment of elicit privacy. Several guests stood at the railing, overlooking the scene below, talking in hushed voices.

A dark form pushed himself away from the wall he had been leaning against and purposefully approached her. He found himself enthralled by this wisp of a woman, which he found mildly amusing. Typically, his attention was directed at politics and acquiring wealth, which he had been most successful at amassing. He was never at a loss for female companionship when he wished it, and during his lifetime, he had rarely felt it necessary to form any long-term attachments. For the better part of this past year, Margaret Edwards had been trying to make herself available to him. He found her willingness to fall into his bed tiresome. He mentally considered her plump over ripe form to the one he had recently held in his arms. With Margaret, there was also the matter of the spreading rumours regarding her blatant promiscuity. He believed that if he were to take advantage of her offering, it would not long be held in confidence but loudly proclaimed from one household to the next, causing an uncomfortable scandal. He could ill afford an attempt for her to claim disgrace and be forced into a situation he had no desire to be in.

This trim madam, however, was already married and from what he had heard this evening, might be quite willing to be a discreet paramour and receive the attention she deserved. She appeared to be young, and her beauty was beyond his imagination. Something about her intrigued him and made him throw caution to the wind. He thought of her graceful movement, the feel of her in his arms, and the lack of modesty in her dress. The delicate features of her face, the soft gaze in her sparkling blue eyes. All things considered, he felt an excitement he had not experienced before and was reasonably optimistic in his pursuit.

Lauren heard his approaching step and cast a furtive glance at his outrageously handsome face. She felt an involuntary quiver of excitement pass through her body as he neared. She should squash this feeling immediately. But she did not. Perhaps it was the champagne, it could have been the darkness, or maybe the romance of the music playing in the ballroom made her feel like a woman and not a lonely girl.

"You have dressed all in black." He heard her seductive whisper, a voice like soft down falling from a bird in flight. "Should I be wary of your approach because you are the Devil?"

He was intoxicated with her silken voice, pleasant to his heightened senses. He smiled at her, showing straight white teeth in a boyish grin. A curl of hair escaped his immaculately combed hair and fell lazily down his forehead. "Nay, my lady. Your gown shimmers in the light, so if I assume that you are the heavenly stars, then I am the night sky." He moved close and inhaled the unique womanly scent of her. "I believe that makes us the perfect pair."

Lauren laughed, the sound like the chiming of bells. "You could have come as the Devil, but changed into the night sky just for that comment, sir."

"Are you unescorted?"

She turned to study him. "I am a guest of the Grassett family, and my husband is here...somewhere," she replied, somewhat taken aback by his abrupt change of subject.

"The man is a fool for leaving you unattended." He leaned an arm against the high railing while casually setting a foot on the bottom curb, tilting his large frame towards her.

Lauren felt dwarfed by his presence.

"If I were he, I would keep you by my side. There are far too many rogues about to leave such a one as yourself unprotected."

Lauren was beginning to wonder if he spoke of himself.

"Since your husband seems less concerned about your defence and has left you to the attention of others, perhaps you would allow me to offer my services," he suggested.

"Do I require protection, sir?" she softly whispered.

"Most assuredly, madam," he breathed.

Lauren was surprised by the path this conversation was rapidly heading towards. "Would your wife not be upset by your comments? She seemed unwilling to let you out of her sight, and I'm beginning to understand why."

The lord gave her a seductive smile. "If you mean Margaret Edwards, I'm not married to her, nor betrothed to any other. She is the daughter of Baron Edwards, a distant neighbour. Though it is true that I am married, my wife is abroad, and I have not heard from her in several years."

Lauren gazed at his handsome face, his dark brown hair combed neatly, curling at the nape of his neck except for the one errant strand that had escaped and hung roguishly down his forehead.

"Missing wives must be all the rage among the *ton*."

Devlin was not discouraged by her cool demeanour. "I understand that your husband is considerably older than you?" At her quick look, he continued with a slight shrug. "There is talk. Not much escapes the gossips."

"I don't believe I am alone in being married to an elder husband. It happens to a number of girls to be traded for land and position."

"Yes." He detected a note of bitterness in her voice. "A fate that is not fair to many young maidens, but has been the general practice for centuries. The answer, of course, lies in courtly love, or a more physical one by two discrete partners."

"Do you feel that this is a topic we should be discussing since we are both of us married?" Lauren expounded.

Though the conversation was taking on a life of its own and one she was unsure she could handle, she felt rooted to the ground. His presence was overwhelming, and she was enthralled by his nearness, the smell of his cologne, and the intensity of his gaze. She had never been looked at like this by any man, let alone one who showed an eager hunger in his eyes as he held her gaze. She felt susceptible to his power, physically drawn to him though he hadn't touched her.

"Since we are not free, nor even tied to our spouse," he continued, taking her silence as encouragement, "I would be honoured if you would consider the possibility of spending some enjoyable time together. To salve our loneliness."

Lauren's eyes widened at the implication of his speech. She might be naive, but she wasn't dense!

She had finally come to realize with crystal clarity what he had in mind. She was angry with herself for allowing the discussion to become so intimate. That he would consider she would allow such a thing.

In her outrage, her mind flew to any number of replies that came quickly to her defence. Her mouth opened to issue a retort, then closed since none that came to mind would be considered polite. The only thing she could do was leave this situation immediately. Spinning on her slippered heel, she stalked back into the ballroom, prepared to ignore him entirely and erase him from her mind. She put a hand to her face, feeling the heat of the flaming red blush from her embarrassment. The nave! How dare he!

Her progress came to a halt as Margaret stepped abruptly in front of the startled miss. With her closed fists sitting akimbo on her hips, she angrily confronted the woman who had the flushed appearance of having just left the arms of a most amorous suitor. Furthermore, she was fully aware of which suitor it was. She had searched the ballroom for the handsome rake she considered her current beau, and here he was chasing after another woman.

His steps were eager, following this upstart from the seclusion of the balcony where anything could, and probably did, happen. Her plans had included every scheme she could think of to entrap this fine wealthy lord into a compromised position, to give her the leverage she required to procure a betrothal. Even if he was married, the wife hadn't been seen in years, and no one could even say if she was still alive. He would be hers, and she was determined that no other woman would be able to snatch him from her grasp, especially after she had spent so much of her time and patience to bring him to heel.

Margaret focussed venomous eyes on Lauren, who appeared quite dishevelled and to her jealous mind, had a guilty look about her. The green monster sat squarely on her shoulders. In a huff, she brushed rudely past the exquisitely gowned woman, knocking her slightly off balance and settled herself beside the tall, handsome lord, claiming his arm in a vice-like hold, pressing it firmly against her ample breasts. She glared at the other woman and would warn her away from him in no uncertain terms before the night was done.

On spying the group, Lady Grassett, taking a spin around the dance floor, leaned against her partner's arm and tilted her head back to converse with them. "How marvellous Lauren, that you have found Lord Barwick. Devlin, your wife is an absolute treasure."

"Wife?" both Devlin and Margaret harmonized.

Lady Grassett quickly straightened and continued her dance, moving out of hearing range.

Lauren's eyes widened in surprise, and her lips parted in a gasp.

Margaret's eyes narrowed. "You liar!" she hissed. "How can you be his wife when no one here recognizes you or called you by your name except Lady Grassett? How did you secure an invitation? What proof do you possess? Anyone could claim Devlin if she were brass enough to think she could get away with it, and how perfect that you should arrive at a masquerade when it is that which you are attempting to play. A trick I say, on all of us." She turned to Devlin. "Any low-born actress could mince her way in here seeking your money and station. You can't possibly believe her. Why, she didn't even know you and had to have Lady Grassett point you out to her. You didn't recognize her either. Your own wife! How can that be? This is absolute madness!" Margaret's voice, which had started low and menacing, increased in pitch as she raged.

The other guests were becoming increasingly interested in the awkward situation presenting itself. Whispered comments were rapidly making their way around the room.

Spying Baron Edwards, Devlin motioned him forward. Extricating his arm from Margaret's grip, he set her firmly within her father's grasp as that one pulled her away from the melee. Baron Edwards admonished his wayward daughter beneath his breath, on presenting another spectacle of herself as it had not been the first time.

Taking a tight grip on Lauren's elbow, Devlin pulled her from the room back outside for a moment of privacy, eyeing those who stared with a dismissive gaze. So this was his wife. Not at all what he would have expected. He was certain that when the little miss returned from her life in the convent, if she returned, he would find a scrawny flat-chested maiden in a brown monk's robe with a plain common face. Nothing could be further from the truth.

"Madam, you could have been kinder in the telling of your identity and sought to meet in a more private setting," he scowled.

Lauren pulled away from him, rubbing her arm from the friction of his grasp. Staring into his angry face, she wondered at the image she had held all these years of an angry older man. He wasn't old at all. But he was definitely angry.

Her ire rose at the shock of the situation. "You sir, left me to bide my time in a convent in another land," she scoffed in return.

"You could have informed me that you had returned to England," he rallied.

"Shall I assume that if I had, you would have minded your manners and exhibited a few social graces?" she scolded. "All these years while I had been sent away from everything I hold dear, you played false and rutted like a boar with any bit of fluff that twitched her skirts at you."

"Madam, you have no idea what I have been doing since you departed these shores. I waited for you to send me word of your existence, giving you time and space to grow up and become a lady," he angrily threw at her.

"You certainly don't know how to treat a lady, sir!" She tilted her saucy face upwards and leaned towards him. "You propositioned me within hours of seeing me. You would have cuckolded yourself had I agreed to your rude, boorish request."

Devlin stared into the cold blue eyes that reminded him of frozen chips of ice and could do nothing but laugh at the situation. "Indeed, I would have Lauren, but at least we know that I am assuredly drawn to you. I would imagine that is, at the very least, a good start to this marriage of ours."

She stared in amazement at his mercurial moods. She would not stay in his presence a moment longer. The brute. The despot. Arrogant in the extreme to laugh at her. In a fury of unconcerned rage at the spectacle she would create, Lauren twirled on her slippered feet, her skirt swinging wildly around her legs. In a rebellious stomp, uncaring about the stares or whispered comments behind gloved hands as the coiffed heads of the guests rolled to and fro, discussing the events that unfolded, Lauren strode angrily through the ballroom and out the front doors of the manse.

# *Chapter Three*

The next day, those who had missed the delicious events at Lord and Lady Grassett's masquerade ball were regaled with a thorough description of all that had transpired. The lovely presentation of the guests in their fanciful costumes, the arrival of the prince and his small entourage, the music being played, and the delicacies to be found in the dining room for the late dinner. Left last was the deliciously scandalous confrontation with Margaret Edwards, Lord Barwick and the angry departure of the newly discovered Lady Barwick as she stormed out of the mansion. The tale was told and retold at every breakfast table of the London gentry and then carried below stairs by the staff who served them.

Lauren was mortified. Unaware of the gossip but sure that it would be forthcoming, she considered that she had wasted years of her life learning to be sedate and calm. A picture of perfection, she had studied manners and decorum. She had learned to be a model of femininity and an honour to her family. In one evening, every aspect of her learning had been dashed beyond compare. How could she possibly hold her head high in society again? She had not expected nor sought this attention. Her reputation was ruined. She had become a spectacle and a subject for the gossips.

Perhaps it would have been best if she had stayed where she was and not returned to England. Life was tranquil in the convent. Now she was married to a brute who did not care about her feelings and most certainly did not possess the decency to be embarrassed by propositioning his own wife. Lauren ground her teeth and buried her head further into her pillow. She covered her head with the blanket as if that slight protection would help make the world go away.

"He has the audacity to make suggestions in the rudest terms to a lady just met and continue to be hailed as a gentleman because of wealth, power, and the unfair advantage of being a man," she mumbled to herself.

Ellie entered carrying a tray with the morning's fare. "A card has arrived from your Lord Barwick," she announced while pouring the tea. She placed the pot on the tray and waited to hand Lauren the cup. "It says he'll be here this morning, so pull yourself out of your den and start the day."

Lauren groaned, sitting back against the pillows. "Things didn't go well last night."

"Don't you be selling me a dog. You found him didn't you?" Ellie handed Laurent the cup and, placing her hands on her hips, stared down at the miserable girl lost in the coverings of the bed. She reached for the blankets to fold them back neatly. "Are you saying that five long years of teaching you culture, refinement and the genteel art of womanhood didn't stick after one night out?" she shook her head from side to side. "You were always a willful child, but I thought we had buried her in perfect execution."

"Why would you think I was the one to cause problems?" she ventured, a look of hurt turning her delicate lips into a pout. "I met Lord Barwick. He's a debaucher of women! An evil rogue! A cad! Rude! A seducer of innocent women! I can't think of enough bad names to call him!"

She thought of his handsome face and proud bearing. His place in society would allow him to get away with his behaviour. For the hundredth time, she wondered how she had ever thought of him as a miserable, evil old man. Lauren sighed, miserable or evil, he was going to turn her life upside down. One thing was certain, she would not lose her heart to him. In fact, there was little fear of that. He had banished her from her home and then propositioned her in the most loathsome way.

To Lauren's way of thinking, they were starting this marriage with a definite absence of trust. Considering their meeting, she wondered if he could prove himself worthy of being a person she could abide by. Love was out of the question, just like it had been her entire life. She lost the love of a mother, was ignored by a father, and was now married to a man who would, without doubt, take many mistresses like the prince whose company he kept. Considering the handsome face and strong physic that it was attached to, there would be many willing women questing for the spot. The buxom Margaret Edwards at the front of the line.

"My poor lamb, there's ought you can do about it. His Lordship knows you're here and is coming to see you. Up you get. We must make you presentable to meet him. A grand look of confidence can help you set boundaries with the man.

Perhaps a contract of sorts because without an agreement, we have no place to go. Your home is now his." She became pensive, "He's not a dangerous sort, is he? Should I be afraid for you?"

Lauren thought of his quick laughter at her most horrifying moment. "No. I'm fairly certain he sees humour in the most base things."

Ellie wondered if Lord Barwick's interest in Lauren ran more towards the physical than the girl was accustomed to. With her cloistered upbringing, she would be caught off balance by any show of such affection, and any man would be taken by her classic beauty.

Ellie hurried about the room, laying out a morning gown that would show off her mistress to perfection. "Stop your dilly-dallying," she pulled back the covers to force Lauren to rise. "I won't be poked up by you not looking your best this day."

Ellie searched the wardrobe and chose a light cream lace dress with a sky-blue Lolita corset around the waist. It had a prim high ruffled collar that rose on her slim neck. The bottom of the skirt was layered and tied up with pale blue roses, and a swag rope of pearls joined one to the other. Like anything she wore, Lauren carried herself with an effortless grace. Ellie arranged Lauren's hair in the simple style of the day, parted down the middle and tied back in a full heavy knot. She was tucking a stray curl into place when they heard a footman admitting the guest.

Lauren's eyes widened in alarm.

"This is what we've come back to England for. You don't want to lose your home forever, and to have it; you must have him. Show him some of the bricky behaviour you had as a child roaming hither and yon. You're a fine woman with a good head on your shoulders. Now pinch your cheeks for a bit of colour, you're looking not up to Dick." After scrutinizing the girl, Ellie gently pushed her out the door. "Be off with you and get your life in order."

Devlin rose as Lauren entered the morning room. In the light of day, she was even more lovely than she had appeared by candlelight. Though high-necked, the gown she wore emphasized her small waist and full breasts. Her wide blue eyes were startlingly bright, her facial features delicate, the hands she clasped together finely boned and dainty. Devlin mentally rubbed his hands together at the sight of this beautiful woman who belonged to him.

She gave him a curt nod noting the fine grey trousers, silver vest and similarly lined black jacket. He wore his clothes casually and was undoubtedly a fine specimen in them. His handsome face was bronzed on a tall frame. His hair was long and slightly unkept, which gave him a boyish look. However, he was all man and exuded power: slim of hip with a broad chest and well-formed shoulders. When she seated herself in a chair instead of joining him on the settee, he smiled and rising, pulled another chair closer to her. Her cool demeanour towards him was taken as a challenge, and if there was one thing Devlin enjoyed, it was a challenge.

"Good morning Lauren. It is truly my pleasure to see you again." At her silence, he continued. "Now that I know you are in London, it is unfitting that you reside here alone, while I am located elsewhere. As I said last night, your husband, who we have now discovered is myself, would be a fool to leave you unprotected, and I, Madam, am no fool."

"Undoubtedly," she scoffed.

Devlin continued, unconcerned with her rancour. He would not be denied. "We gave the rumour mill enough to talk about last evening, so to squelch any more conjecture by them, I would like to take you to my family's townhouse." Sensing her reluctance in the stiffening of her spine, he quickly continued, "My brother and his family are currently in residence, so we will not be alone, and I will feel better knowing that you are under my protection."

"Sir, since arriving in London, the only person I've needed protection from is you!"

"Let us consider our discussion of last eve as a case of mistaken identity," he attempted to placate her mood. "In my defence, I did note what people were saying about your marital status. Rumour had it that you were married to an aged individual of ill repute. I merely thought that an arrangement between us would be mutually beneficial."

"Do you truly consider that a defence? Was not the conjecture correct that my husband is of ill repute?"

"I am a man Lauren and of an age long past wearing short pants, therefore, I do not profess to be ignorant of the ways between a man and a woman. Since I believed that my wife, you as it turns out, was unavailable and had been out of my life for years, there are basic needs that were being unfulfilled. Let us say that when I saw you, I became overzealous and perhaps a little reckless to have you."

Lauren was incensed with his explanation and scoffed, "Lord Barwick, the fact that you are unfaithful, and finding that out on our first meeting has left a remarkable strain on this relationship."

Devlin attempted a different tactic to deflect the current topic. "You could call me by my given name Lauren. We need not be so formal with one another."

"You attempted such informality last night sir, and I feel that a more formal address suits us for the time being," she sniffed.

Devlin leaned back in his chair and contemplated the lovely vision before him. He certainly had given her cause to be angry, but he was sure that he could change her opinion of him with enough patience and humour. He was not one to fall into any woman's bed. In fact, since he had become Lord Barwick, he had been exceptionally discrete about the few instances of female companionship he had experienced. There had been no lasting relationship, and those occasional instances had been mutually agreed upon and of short duration with no lingering animosity. Now, as he looked upon his wife, he felt an amount of guilt he had not considered at the time. The marriage performed years ago had felt like a cold, indifferent business arrangement. There was no emotion involved, no attraction between him and the child he married. Last night the sight of this woman proved a captivating allure to his senses. He was fascinated with learning everything about her. Winning her trust, though a current challenge, would be his most erstwhile pursuit.

"I concede to your hurt feelings and will do my utmost to prove my worthiness to you now that you are home. But considering what was being said about you and your husband, I received the wrong impression of how things really are." He leaned forward again and looked directly into her sky-blue eyes. "Exactly who did you tell, that you were married to an old ogre?"

They both heard a muffled guffaw in the hall before hurrying footsteps quickened away from the door.

"That would be Ellie." Lauren blushed. "She must have repeated my memories of you."

"I understand that our prior meeting must have been upsetting to you. Neither of us looked our best. I remember a frightened ragamuffin with frizzy hair and dishevelled clothing sobbing into her hands. You were terribly distressed at what was being forced upon you, but Lauren," he reached for her hands, taking them in his larger one and lowered his voice, "I didn't go around and proclaim it to everyone I've met since," he teased.

Lauren felt the heat of his hands warm her cold ones and changed the subject to her present problem. "We created a terrible muddle last night. I fear we will be the centre of gossip, and I have discredited your house."

His nearness was as disconcerting as it had been last night. She could smell the pleasant scent of his cologne and felt overpowered again by his significant presence. Lauren cast her eyes downward, removed her hands from his hold and folded them in her lap.

He remembered their first meeting when she had sat in the same position, but the memory stopped there. One could not compare the frightened little girl loudly sobbing and miserable to the lovely piece of fluff now in his presence. His large hand cupped her face and tilted it up so she could look into his eyes.

He spoke with sincerity, "There's nothing like a muddle to arouse the curiosity of the gentry. Trust me when I tell you that we will be sought after rather than shunned. The gentry will want to see what else we can do to amuse them. But Lauren, let us keep them suspicious, instead of giving them more meat to chew on. I propose we take on this town and show them a loving couple, happily married and in accord with each other. We'll be so boring no one will think ill of us, and those not present at the ball will not believe those who saw the ruckus."

She hesitated a brief moment. The time had come to set the agenda for her future. A space to get to know one another, to discover whether a union could be possible or if the need to separate would be best for all concerned. There was a physical attraction between them, but that alone was not a solid basis for marriage. They would have to discover if they were compatible, if they could abide one another. Could she ever learn to trust him, and would they be able to live a peaceful life?

"I will go with you as I must, but I have some conditions that will have to be agreed upon."

Devlin didn't think for a moment that life would be a bed of roses after the mess he had created last evening, and fully expected Lauren to devise terms for their arrangement. What he would have to agree to, might be interesting to see if it would stand the test of time.

Lauren braced herself to set the ground rules she would firmly insist upon. "I realize our marriage is not as yet a true marriage. You could force me to perform my marital duties, but I would like to get to know you better. Therefore, I request a titular marriage. One in name only for a period of time. I have been taught that I have no right to question your infidelities, but to have the matter thrown in my face is abhorrent. Prior to last evening, all I ever thought of you was that you wanted me to go away and possibly stay away."

Devlin decided to veer away from rehashing the first topic. "My dear Lauren. I sent you away to be educated. Would you have been willing at that tender age to become my wife in reality?" He paused, looking intently at her. "I think not, nor would I have wanted the gossips to spread the fact of our age difference which would have been much more pronounced then. The general consensus would have been young enough to wed, too young to bed. You may not have believed it, but the decision to send you to France was based on consideration for you. I must admit that in the time you were away, you have blossomed into the very definition of a woman. Indeed, you have far exceeded my expectations."

Lauren felt a twinge in her breast. How could this daunting man so easily affect her? Clamping down any kinder thought, and to protect herself, she replied with a hint of spite. "No doubt my Lord, you made that unmistakenly apparent last night."

"Ten years is a large age gap when one was as young as you were when we married. Now it is not so indecent. In fact, many women your age have found themselves married to much older gentlemen. Now, our age difference is not as noticeable."

"Yet indecency still reigns," she murmured.

Devlin let the point rest for the moment and stood to take his leave. She was his wife, under his protection, and currently, willing or not, she would abide by how he determined best fit with his plans for her safety and their lives.

"I will arrive early tomorrow morning. I would like to take a carriage ride around this old town to let everyone get a look at you. A cart will be sent for your trunks and maid. That should give her enough time to be packed and ready for the move."

The decision was made, and there was no need for further discussion. So it was decided, taken out of her hands, he had set an agenda for their future that would start on the morrow. To be shown off and presented as a married couple. Lauren's heart was heavy. Pretense and play-acting. Where would it lead?

* * *

Devlin had arranged everything flawlessly. Trunks that had been unpacked only a short time ago, were quickly packed again and loaded by the brawny youth that had accompanied the cart. Lord Barwick was taking over her life just as she had predicted. From this time forward, Lauren believed she would constantly be ordered about and have no say in her life. The idea continued to weigh heavily on her.

True to his word Devlin arrived by nine the next morning and was left cooling his heels as Ellie painstakingly dressed Lauren.

"Tis your first outing with your husband. This day we must make everything perfect. You were too long left to run wild, and I can do nothing now to get your waist the sixteen inches of some of the fine young ladies."

Stockings donned and boots buttoned, they began the morning ritual. Chemise and corset were in place, but the obligatory tightening of that garment after a ten-minute wait, and then again ten minutes later to achieve the tightest fit, took not only time but a toll on Lauren's comfort.

"Ellie, enough. I can barely draw a breath." she wheezed from the constriction around her torso.

Next, slipped over her head was a flexible hooped crinoline and a bustle bag tied around her waist to hold the massive train of her skirt from her rump, another lightweight camisole cover to protect the expensive outer garments and two petticoats to protect the dress from the hoops of the crinoline were pulled over her head. Finally, the pale pink skirt covered in vining roses was in place, and a matching day bodice was buttoned high on her throat. Thus the promenade dress was complete. Only other women of the wealthy set knew the trials of being dressed, not to mention the time spent each morning, afternoon and evening repeating the process. Her hair was pulled back atop her head, and heavy ringlets twisted down her neck to reach below her shoulders. A day hat of lace, flowers and feathers was pinned onto her head when Ellie stood back to assess the completed toilet.

"You look as fine as any of the high-class ladies of London who never set a slippered foot out into the fresh air of the country."

Lauren inhaled a breath, as best she could, to boost her courage. "We are about to face a major change in our lives Ellie. Do you think we are well prepared for what is to come?"

"If not my girl, we will just have to make it up as we go along." With that bit of advice, Ellie led Lauren to the top of the stairs, adjusted her gown to perfection and with a nod, sent her to meet her destiny.

When Devlin led Lauren out into a glorious day of bright sunshine, a sleek open barouche drawn by a pair of matching greys awaited them. She lifted the voluminous skirt and placed a dainty slipper on the footboard as he lent assistance holding her arm. Lauren tamped down the pleasurable feeling of his aid and immediately chastised herself for allowing him to have an effect on her each time they touched. The ostrich feathers of her bonnet brushed his face as she moved past him and settled herself on the soft upholstered seat. She flipped open a pink-lined parasol which gave her skin a rosy glow as the sun shone through it.

Before entering and seating himself beside his wife, Devlin cast a long regarded look at her profile and considered his fortune that he had been forced into marriage with this delicate woman. He knew of many men who had been coerced to marry unattractive brides to achieve land and titles for their families. Though he had considered himself among their ranks, he was pleased to find that Lauren had grown into the title of a woman so marvellously.

He was impeccably dressed, wearing a smooth black top hat, jacket, and trousers. A white pressed shirt lay under a tan-coloured vest, and a black tie was neatly folded around his neck, tied in a flat bow under his chin. He pulled on thin tan leather gloves as he leaned back on the seat beside her. They were a striking pair by the fact that they were complete opposites of each other. Masculine to feminine, male to female, husband to wife.

The boulevard was already crowded with the aristocracy taking their morning strolls as the carriage meandered around the streets and parks giving everyone on this fine day a chance to view them together. Gentlemen tipped their hats to the ladies while the women stopped to momentarily pass a comment to their contemporaries. It was a beautiful scene of gentility and grace. Even the dogs, their fur brushed to shiny perfection, in bejewelled collars and expensive leads, were on their best behaviour. The scene presented a perfect world filled with perfect people of impeccable manners.

The high-stepping greys were acknowledged and admired by many, as were the couple seated in the carriage. Devlin noted the admiring look of many men and the envy of some women as he and Lauren were greeted by the affluent.

They continued on their way with serene faces and obligatory nods.

"At the end of the season, I find myself looking forward to returning home. The grandeur and pomp of every situation wears on me in London. The pretended perfection of the households can't possibly be so absolute and unmarred by the normalcy of life. At least, you won't find that with my family. I'm afraid my brother has four rambunctious children who constantly escape their nanny and tear through the house like wild animals."

Lauren smiled at him, keeping the appearance of a newly joined couple. "It sounds quite chaotic and an experience I'm not at all familiar with."

"I'll do my best to protect you from them, but if the children surround me, you may find yourself on your own," he smiled into her violet eyes that sparkled back at him. He found the morning pleasing and the woman beside him perfectly so as well.

The barouche pulled up to an imposing facade of white stucco. London's fairly new, fashionable district was in stark conflict with its bloody past. Previously it had a reputation for crime and violence. Robberies and duelling had been prevalent until earlier this century when the 2$^{nd}$ Marquess of Westminster had asked Thomas Cubitt to design an estate. The current address rivalled Mayfair as *the place* to own property.

Devlin assisted Lauren to alight from the carriage and, pulling her hand through his arm, led her into the townhouse. The interior was decorated with the preferred dark colours of Victorian fashion. Dusky green walls with heavy tasselled red and gold curtains hung on the sides of the massive windows. Marble-grained pillars held the upper floors aloft. High above were wood ceilings with intricate designs carved into the centre, and surrounding the room, detailed scalloped edges of cornice moulding. Grandeur was evident from the structure to the furnishings of excess in the style of the day. Great overstuffed furniture made more for comfort than fashion was placed in groupings to promote a sense of family and conversation.

Marian Cavanaugh rose gracefully to greet them as they entered the parlour. Dressed in burgundy with a cream lace collar, her dark brown eyes crinkled at the sides as she smiled. Reaching out, she grasped Lauren's hands in hers and kissed her on the cheek. "My goodness Lauren it's about time we are able to meet you. Mama will be so disappointed she's gone home early, but she can only abide London for so long. She finds the throngs much too clingy and into everyone else's business for her liking." Looking past Lauren, she commented, "Devlin, don't just stand there. Go find your brother."

Devlin chuckled at their hostess, "As you may have surmised, Lauren, this is my sister-in-law Marian, who, as the Countess of a great house, is accustomed to ordering everyone about. Which is probably why my brother is hiding in his study."

"As if she couldn't find me there to give me direction," the Earl stated, clapping his brother on the back. It was obvious to the observer that Trevor and Devlin were closely related. Slightly shorter and a touch heavier but years older with grey hair showing at his temple, they were similar in looks and comportment. "Welcome to the family Lauren. You certainly gave Devlin a shock when you appeared at the Grassett Ball. It's a shame we were unable to attend. We would have enjoyed seeing the greeting he received," he winked at Lauren and smiled a mischievous grin. "At least Marian and I thoroughly enjoyed the retelling."

"I'm afraid it's not something I would like to repeat," Lauren said quietly, wondering how much of their conversation he had told his family.

"Nonsense, the gentry is too uptight for their own good. A bit of rumour and gossip adds spice to the family, just to show everyone that we do things unconventional for the fun of it."

"Indeed!" remarked his wife moving past the towering men to guide Lauren towards the stairs. "Let us get you settled into your room. We have a flurry of engagements planned since these are the last full weeks of the season. Your things have arrived, and Mrs. Butterfield is sorting everything to its place." She continued her friendly chatter to put Lauren at ease. "Breakfast will be served in the garden when you are ready since it's such a lovely day. I have a few things to pick up at the shops, and then we're accepting guests this afternoon to introduce you to everyone."

Lauren was led to a large bedroom where Ellie was opening the trunks. She quickly found the morning bodice that matched the skirt Lauren was wearing, this one with a slightly scooped neckline trimmed with pink rosettes. Relieved that only the top had to be exchanged for the second dressing, Lauren was able to put off Ellie's insistence on tightening the corset one more time as she was barely able to get her breath as it was.

Descending the stairs a short time later, she was greeted with a mixture of sounds from the dining room that abruptly fell to silence as four pairs of wide eyes, planted in cherubic faces turned her way. Giggling, they bounced to their feet. The little girls curtsied prettily, and the young masters bowed deeply though the youngest one lost his balance and did a little sidestep before righting himself again.

Devlin had been nearby waiting for her and came to the doorway to stand by her side. "Lady Barwick, may I present our nieces and nephews. From oldest to youngest, they are Master George," a blonde boy bowed his head in acknowledgement, "Miss Violet and Miss Rose," the little girls giggled behind gloved hands, "and Master Thomas," the curly-haired imp smiled broadly, revealing two missing teeth. "This is your Aunt Lauren."

Chatter began at once in a jumble of sound, from "Hello Auntie" to "Can you take us riding today Uncle?"

Their nanny, a tall, slim older woman similar in age to Ellie, returned to the dining room and barked out an order. "Shush yourselves! Tittering away all at once," she condemned them with a stern frown, "have you no manners?"

"Yes Nanny Grace," they subdued instantly, though the youngest one tilted his head and cast a sidelong glance at the matronly woman showing a spark of mischief. Nanny Grace assembled the children into a row, grasping Thomas' hand before he could scamper under the table. "Hallo Ma'am," she greeted Lauren quickly, leading the children toward the stairs.

Violet stopped on her way out and gave Lauren a tight hug around her hips. "I'm so happy to meet you, Auntie Lauren. You make it so we girls aren't outnumbered anymore."

"What did she mean by that?" Lauren quizzed, turning to Devlin after the children filed out of the room.

"You'll find out during family games. We boys can be ruthless."

She noted that his eyes crinkled at the sides of his handsome face when he smiled. She reminded herself not to be swayed by his good looks when she knew what his character lacked. Devlin offered his arm to Lauren, which was haltingly accepted, and they strolled through the house to the back garden, where breakfast was set for the adults amongst a briar of ruby red roses.

The meal was spent in friendly chatter as questions were asked and answered about growing up in the country.

"I was mostly left to my own devices," Lauren informed. "Ellie tried her best, but I was happiest on my pony from morning until dusk. There were the tenants and their children I could visit, but it was a lonely time for me."

"How terribly sad for you, but now you are part of a family, and since coming into it myself many years ago, I can affirm that the acceptance you will have here should ease any pains of loneliness you might still carry."

"Goodness," Lauren sighed. "I certainly didn't mean to be so melancholy and ruin this beautiful day. What of your childhood Lord Barwick? Did you have many tutors?"

"Enough. Our father was a very serious gentleman when it came to teaching us finance and world affairs. He was also a great deal of fun and loved to ride, hunt and fish."

"It was a younger Nanny Grace who was the disciplinarian," Trevor rejoined. "I felt the swing of her switch more than Devlin ever did. She mellowed considerably in between my youth and that of my puckish brother, who eluded much of her punishment."

Marian leaned towards her husband and brushed her hand lovingly against his cheek. "You poor darling, the firstborn always bears the responsibility of adulthood at such a tender age."

"I'm glad you understand the unfair advantage my spoiled sibling received and have pity for me, my dove," he laughed. "Nanny Grace often said he could charm a mouse out of its hole."

"I am fully aware of how lucky I was that I had the ability to disarm Nanny Grace," Devlin laughed. "She could wield a willow switch with the tactical ability of a marksman."

"Yes she could," Trevor agreed. "Considering that you were more mischievous than I, and had a habit of getting into trouble on a regular basis, I can only assume she couldn't catch you." Trevor focussed on Lauren, "Due to our age difference, Nanny Grace must have slowed down considerably in the ensuing years."

Lauren enjoyed the family atmosphere and the play of their conversation. She listened intently to the stories of the young pair of brothers. In the back of her mind, she considered that perhaps Devlin's ability not to have suffered consequences for the misadventures of his youth, is what led to his rakish reputation.

"If you are ready Lauren, we should be about our day. If you need anything, there's a lovely little haberdashery on Piccadilly Road. Devlin has an account there, so you can pick out something for yourself while I get my packages. I think we'll take the barouche again so we can ride with the top down and let everyone know you're part of the family."

Lauren realized that by this overt display of stepping out, first with Lord Barwick through the streets of London, and now with the Countess in the open carriage, they were lending the strength of the family name to her person. The indiscretion at the Grassett Ball could cause society to turn its back on a woman, especially in Lauren's case, as that happened at her first outing among the elite.

Marian treated her most kindly during their excursion and chatted amicably. "Did you enjoy your time at the abbey? I was sent to a girl's school in Scotland and missed my family dreadfully until my younger sister arrived."

"It was a major change in my life, and I was unhappy at first, but when I consider how my life changed, I came to appreciate everything I was taught there. It was peaceful, and all I had to worry about was learning the musical scale and what words were masculine and feminine in German and French."

"Languages! I never could understand that part of it," Marian commiserated.

"Being at the convent opened my world. Without the nuns, I realize how ignorant I would have been if I hadn't attended."

Their discussion turned to Marian's family, and life growing up as the oldest of seven siblings. Lauren giggled as Marian spoke of how she was allowed to assist with her younger sister's upbringing and the frustrations and follies of the little girls. Not having such an experience, and for the first time in her life Lauren could catch a glimpse of what having a family was like.

On the streets and in the shops, whenever a dowager or pert young miss approached them, Marian offered an introduction to Lauren. "Lady Dunlop," she greeted, "may I present our dear sister Lauren recently returned from France to take up her position as Lord Barwick's wife. The Earl and I are delighted that she is finally here, and we are able to welcome her home."

The ladies understood completely the honour being bestowed on the girl by the announcement. They offered kind acknowledgements of acceptance of the fact that the house of the Cavanaugh family, along with the Camber Earldom, would stand by their newest member.

Shopping complete, they returned to the townhouse to freshen their wardrobe. In the afternoon, a multitude of femininity arrived in all their excess finery. Cucumber or watercress sandwiches were carried by liveried footmen on tiered china plates. Tea was served from an elaborate silver service into delicate Meissen porcelain moss rose china cups sitting on matching saucers. Female voices filled the room as the billowing skirts brushed against each other, jockeying for the best position among the aristocracy.

Lauren stood in the light of an open window, hoping that a bit of the fresh breeze would give her the air she needed in the stifling heat of the room. As soon as everyone left the soiree, she would have Ellie loosen the stays of her corset.

Late in the afternoon, the room was becoming excessively hot as the sun beat through the windows of the overcrowded room. Lauren was having difficulty following the numerous conversations around her as they spoke of people she did not know. Her fan did little good, merely waving hot air into her flushed face.

She was looking around the room for a place to momentarily sit when striding purposefully towards her, came an infuriated Margaret Edwards. She had not yet cooled her ire at the so-called Lady Barwick. Her lips were set in a firm pout, and the intense brown eyes shot daggers at her. The dress she wore was a vivid green with a matching hat that clashed with her blonde hair and pale skin. In her wake was an older plump matron in a more sombre colour, but unmistakably her mother.

The pair stopped before her as Margaret snidely gestured to Lauren with a flick of her hand. "Mother, this is the upstart who is claiming to be Lady Barwick."

A gasp was heard from the ladies nearby.

Baroness Edwards insultingly perused Lauren from the tips of her toes to the top of her head. "My dear girl," she began, raising her nose into the air, "What a remarkable actress you are. I knew Phillip Berwyke, and you look nothing like him. What proof do you carry to provide us with, that proves you are who you say you are?"

A twittering arose from those present as heads rolled together, spreading whispered words throughout the room. A deeper blush rose on Lauren's face that this outrage would further taint her.

"It is said that I resemble my mother rather than my father. Did you know her as well?" She added, hoping to quell further discussion, "I have no reason to claim to be someone I am not."

"There's land, a castle and a rich husband in the bargain for that claim," scoffed Margaret.

A louder murmur grew from the gathered ladies. This was turning into an intoxicating melee of intrigue. It wasn't every day that they witnessed a burgeoning catfight between ladies of the upper crust, and they crowded close to improve their vantage point.

The Countess, hearing the commotion, as graciously as possible, moved her guests out of the way and regally took a position at Lauren's side, displaying the power of her station.

Linking arms with Lauren, she addressed the pair and those in hearing range. "Baroness Edwards," she acknowledged the elder, "Miss Edwards." she glanced at Margaret. "Of course, this is our dear sister Lauren. As you should know, she is the mistress of Barwick Castle and wife of my husband, the Earl's brother," she shamelessly name-dropped. "She has been away these many years studying in France and has just returned to us. In this house and without, my family acknowledges her presence as such, and we expect you and everyone else, to treat her with deference to the position she holds. If not only as Lady Barwick but as the wife of Devlin Cavanaugh."

A bobbing of the heads of other women present lent agreement to her statement.

"Then Lord Barwick played false with my daughter," replied the rotund matron. "He was seen with her at many parties and on numerous occasions."

"I am unaware of Lord Barwick calling on your daughter nor offering any promises which he was not in a position to fulfill. If Margaret cared little for her reputation and placed herself in his company at events, he was merely being polite to engage her in conversation or to ask her to dance. Surely she was aware that he was a married man," she looked at them pointedly. "It is her own foolishness to have allowed any rumour to be tattled of their mere acquaintance, and the behaviour displayed here will not be tolerated."

This time a muttering of agreement rose from the gathering.

"Lord Barwick has always been a most sincere gentleman whenever I spoke with him," a red-haired lady added to the conversation.

"His manners are extraordinary, and he is too much of a gentleman to consider a passing dalliance with any young miss," another agreed.

"His dancing is exceptional too," twittered another and blushed at the frowns she received from her distracted comment to the direction of the conversation.

Lauren was grateful that this lovely group of women were coming to her aid by commenting on the genteel manners of the rogue she was married to. If it meant no further scandal to her, she was most obliged to them.

Seeing that the subject was quashed and noting Lauren's face that had gone from flushed pink to a pale bloodless colour, Marian guided Lauren away from the Edwards declaring before they left, "Good day to you ladies. It was lovely of you to visit us."

She nodded graciously at the women who cleared a path for them."Come Lauren, I want you to meet Lady Benson," she said, dismissing the Edwards from the tight gathering as she guided Lauren through the room. "She's marvellous, and Mama's dearest friend."

Lady Benson, white-haired and aged, sat in a comfortable wing-backed chair and held court. A teacup in one hand and a dainty sandwich in the other, her admirers of young ladies, stood to rapt attention as she chatted on in good humour. The sandwich expresses her dialogue points as it rose, swung and dipped to the story.

"I see that many of the young single misses are all aflutter that they have not, as yet, made a match. The end of the season is approaching, and they are being hounded and harassed by anxious parents. In my opinion, they should all relax, and refocus their energy in the coming months. The girls should acquire a pet to keep themselves busy. Perhaps a cat, who will teach them, that like some of their future husbands, they will carouse all night seeking other companionship and illicit trysts, returning in the morning, bleary-eyed and too exhausted to be civil. Mayhap they should seek a sweet dog, who will stay by their side as those dear creatures will gaze at them with soft, loving brown eyes. That should teach them what to look for in a future mate. Oh if my family had been so advised, I would not bear the scars from that dreadful man I married. Take heed, my darling girls. Sometimes no marriage is preferable to a hastily arranged bad one."

The ladies contemplated her sage advice. It was common knowledge that this stoic woman had been in a dreadful marriage. If not for her family's wealth, her abusive husband would have continued to take harsh liberties with her person. Instead, the powerful family had taken the unusual step of removing her from the situation. They had been well aware of the marriage between George and Caroline Norton and the horrible abuse that lady had been forced to endure at the hand of her brutal husband. They would not see their daughter thrown down stairs and subjected to other such treatment. They instead provided her with a luxurious home and life of her own. She had been embraced by society because of their support and her charming wit. Meanwhile, her husband had been derided for his debauched evil lifestyle, returned to his country estate and had not been seen in polite society for many years.

"Aunt Eleanore, this is Lauren, Devlin's wife." Marian made the introduction at a barely held pause in the conversation.

"What?" her eyes grew huge. "Well girl, it's about time you came home and settled that man of yours!"

Lauren moved in front of the dowager and dipped into a deep curtsy, rising quickly as the breath squeezed in her chest, causing her equilibrium to spin.

"Just like you Marian, another beauty has joined this family. I assume that young rake didn't realize exactly whom he was sending off to France for so long when he married. All these years, he still considered you a wee young thing. Else he would have been sailing over the Channel to bring you back, I'll wager."

She gestured with her sandwich to the opposite end of the room, "Was that Fiona and Margaret Edwards causing a stir? She should never have thrown herself at Devlin. Others had the sense to know that he was committed elsewhere. There was no chance for them, regardless of what a handsome fellow he is. Had I been a maiden, I would have enjoyed the view, but the property belonged to another."

Finally realizing she held the dainty sandwich, she laid it on a plate and parted with maternal wisdom. "You have married into a wonderful family Lauren. I hold them in the highest regard, and they have been steadfast friends. From experience I can say that the Cavanaugh men are protective of their place in society, the land they hold and most especially to the women they love. I hope you will find happiness in your future, and provide this world with many beautiful children."

"Well," Lauren stammered, "I'm not sure, I suppose time will tell." She was flustered and put a shaking hand on her brow. The heat in the room and the renewed confrontation with the Edwards had worn on her. She couldn't draw a full breath, and standing in front of Eleanore Benson in the hot stifling room was becoming unnerving. Her legs were weak and began a slight trembling. There was a hollow sound to her hearing. She heard Lady Benson calling her name in alarm from a great distance and could feel her head tilt back and her wobbly knees folding in a faint. Hurrying footsteps sounded behind her, but she did not feel the strong arms that caught her as she collapsed. Sinewy muscles easily lift her against a solid chest.

# *Chapter Four*

Black lashes rested on her cheeks like butterfly wings that fluttered and finally opened for Lauren to see Ellie fretting above her, holding a cool cloth pressed to her forehead. Marian sat on the side of the bed and standing beside her, Devlin perused her with grave concern.

"You gave us quite a start," Marian said when Lauren tried to sit up. "No doubt the stress of the Baroness and Margaret's attack on you caused the vapours."

"I fear it's no more serious than requiring a loosening of my stays." She glanced quickly at Devlin, embarrassed by his presence. "I've barely been able to take a breath all day."

"I will leave you to your toilette Madam, confident you will feel better soon." Devlin stifled a smile, paused at the door and looked directly at her. "Rest assured Lauren, I consider you naturally slim and am pleased with your proportions. I don't desire nor am I impressed with the tiny waists squeezed into submission by artificial means."

Lauren blushed as he departed and stood on shaking legs for Ellie to adjust her clothing. "It seems that I am again embarrassing the family."

"How so?" Marian asked, "By swooning? Dear sister, I've seen ladies fall face-first onto the floor more than once. There was one time, at a very exclusive dinner party, that a friend fainted right into her soup! Yours was very graceful and with perfect timing in that Trevor and Devlin had just returned from their club. This way, all the ladies could see him rescue you. By this evening, you will have been a damsel in distress, and he will be flaunted as your knight in shining armour. There's nothing like a dashing saviour coming to the aid of his lady. It's good that Margaret and her mother also witnessed his regard for you. Mayhap it will teach them that they stand no chance for his favours. Not that they ever did."

Thankful that she could breathe after dressing for afternoon tea, Lauren was able to enjoy the warm family atmosphere. Either Devlin's comment about a lady's waist or the fact that Lauren had passed out cold was enough to stop Ellie from tightening the corset strings into an unbearable vice.

The family retired to the parlour for a short interlude with the children. Trevor and Devlin enjoyed a glass of whiskey while Marian and Lauren imbibed a light wine in slim long-stemmed crystal.

It was a pleasant scene as Violet played the piano, and Rose accompanied her vocally, singing in her sweet child's voice a fanciful ditty of fairies and princesses. George amused his younger brother by playing quietly with him on the floor, using metal soldiers, horses and artillery to enact war games. Sometimes the boys became overly exuberant when Thomas' loud "BOOM" set the battle scene of the occasional imagined cannon blast. They were heartily frowned upon by the melodious Rose as the adults kept their faces carefully poised instead of laughing aloud at the children's antics.

As the youngsters were sent to bed, the adults again retired to their rooms to change into full evening wear. Lauren found the constant changing of gowns to be tedious. In the convent, and also when she was staying at the previous townhouse, she would wear one dress during the day and change for dinner in the evening. Three or four different outfits per day was exhausting in itself. Her wardrobe was extensive, but she hadn't planned on requiring so many ball gowns. Her choices had mainly been for day use in the country. Thus, on this first evening out with the family, she once again wore the Worth gown with crystals sewn into the skirt. This time, no navy lace covering hid the fullness of the gown and the matching bodice with the low-pointed waist front and equally daring sweetheart neckline. Ellie pulled her hair out of the ringlets and styled the thick waves higher on her head, folding the curls into themselves in an elaborate coif.

This evening would see them travelling to five separate balls, each with crowds of approximately two hundred people. Lauren was praying that in the throng, she would be able to avoid another confrontation with the Baroness and her daughter.

Ellie handed her two red velvet boxes. "His Lordship gave me these for you. He bid you wear them this evening."

"Oh, Ellie look," she gasped after carefully opening the lids. Draped in the red velvet interior lay three strands of a pearl choker with a gold clasp. The matching pearl drop earrings set in gold filigree were in the other box.

As Ellie finished closing the clasp on the necklace, Marian knocked once and stepped into the room. "Are you ready to face the hordes?" she merrily called out.

Lauren was surprised to see that Marian had abandoned the dark sombre colours she had worn during the day and was adorned in a stunning gown of white satin with a flocked design spread over the expansive skirt. A satin shawl was draped across her back and held by the crook of her arms. "This material is so slippery I'm sure I'll lose this wrap and be sliding from one end of the carriage to the other."

"You look beautiful." Lauren smiled.

"As do you. Your gown is stunning, and the pearls are perfect, but let us go down to our husbands so they can tell us the same."

Trevor and Devlin stood by the front door, top hats in hand, dressed in similar black evening jackets that were short in the front and fell to tails in the rear. Snow white shirts with white ties around their necks were arranged in matching flat bows. Lauren could not deny that they made a strikingly handsome pair of fine gentlemen.

Those same men were equally impressed at the loveliness of the beauties descending the stairs. Both stepped forward in unison to offer their hands to their respective spouse as the ladies reached the bottom step.

Lauren felt the familiar thrill at the attention bestowed upon her by Devlin. She saw in his eyes an appreciation that she once again warned herself to be wary of, but at the same moment, found it pleased her greatly. To be courted by a man such as he, gave her a jolt of excitement that coursed through her veins.

"Thank you for the gifts," she said, touching her gloved fingers to the pears at her throat. "They are lovely, and I've never owned any jewellery before except for the small gold earrings I have always worn."

"We will have to remedy that fact, Lauren," he replied, appreciating how the choker emphasized her slim neck. "But there is an additional gift that should have been given to you years ago."

He moved his arm from behind his back to open a third ruby velvet box. Inside was a slim gold wedding band with three small sparkling diamonds embedded into it which he removed and slid onto her third finger.

"You were so young when we married. I had left home quickly to arrive at the barrister and didn't have time to purchase a ring, or even know the size you could have worn throughout your life. I hope this will never be removed from your finger."

Trevor and Marian smiled at the look of surprise on Lauren's face as she glanced into the serious one of her husband.

"It's beautiful my lord. I never expected such a gift and will treasure it always."

The night, the stars, the grand ballrooms and the well-dressed ladies and gentleman was enticing. Drinks flowed, music played, and in Devlin's arms Lauren felt like the most wonderful creature that had ever lived.

Lord Emory approached the group at the third ball. "A magnificent soiree, do you not agree, my lords, Lady Camber," he greeted Marian and turned piercing eyes to Lauren, "Lady Barwick, a particular pleasure to see you once more."

"Lord Emory," Lauren murmured.

"Barwick, you will allow a dance with your lovely wife? I've never known you to keep a woman all to yourself before." Nicholas reached for Lauren's hand.

"No other woman has been my wife," Devlin warned, moving to step between his wife and Emory. Though he had been placed in the man's company numerous times due to their association with the prince, Devlin had never learned to appreciate him. There was an undercurrent of deception that irked Devlin. One moment he acted like a buffoon; the next, a calculating gleam quickly disappeared from his countenance mere seconds after it was spotted.

Trevor felt the threat in his brother's calm voice and knew of the dislike between the two men. He was aware that they were occasionally forced into each other's company, and while Devlin did his best to keep Bertie out of trouble, Emory often encouraged it. Taking Lauren aside with his hand on the back of her waist, he interjected as he guided her onto the dance floor. "Terribly sorry Emory, but this dance has been promised to me."

Marian smiled dismissively at Emory and pulled Devlin away from the man into the swirling mass of dancers. "What does the prince see in that man Devlin? The family is rumoured to be dallying in unsavoury practices of late."

"The prince is a man in waiting. He has little to occupy himself and is overly concerned with a pleasurable lifestyle as he waits for the throne. Emory encourages this aspect and has similar if not more extravagant tastes."

Making their way to the different affairs, Lauren put the unpleasant Lord Emory from her mind. She couldn't put her finger on the unease she felt when he looked at her, but it was easy to see that her opinion of the man was felt by others and not just the Cavanaugh family. She thought instead of the magical evening, the grand ballrooms, beautiful gowned women and handsome gentlemen, especially her husband. She dreamed of Cinderella in the Grimm's fairytale book. Like Prince Charming, Devlin's attention had been focused solely on her. But there was midnight to come in that story when everything lovely had disappeared. After spending just one day with him, she wondered hopefully if she would, someday, have her happily ever after.

* * *

They returned to the townhouse as the clock struck the hour of three. Lauren woke Ellie and sent the sleepy older woman to bed once she had been loosened from the clothing she could not manage independently. She washed her face in the cool water of the pitcher left on the washstand and dressed for bed in the voluminous cotton folds of her nightgown.

She unbound her hair and brushed the knots from the long locks as she thought about the past day. This morning she had been taken from a solitary life into her new family. She had already been accepted and received their protection. The day had been busy and filled with meeting a new family and friends. Lauren experienced a feeling of being welcomed and part of a greater community. She twisted her hair into a braid, wound it around her head, and tucked the thick coil into the nightcap, as Ellie had her do all her life, so it would not be a tangled mess in the morning.

Devlin tapped quietly on the door, opened it slowly, and stepped into the room. He leaned back on the frame and eyed her suspiciously.

"Is there a woman in all that material," he asked, frowning at her neck-high, long-sleeved, loose-fitting nightgown. It reached to the floor, and not even her toes peeked out from the flounced hem. He had not expected this, considering her excellent taste in garbing herself. There definitely was nothing to get excited about or arouse the interest of the most ardent suitor in the yards of cotton.

"Lord Barwick, I thought we had come to an agreement regarding our marriage. You approved the conditions I proposed, and I will see you stand by your word," she replied uneasily, nervous at his appearance in her bedroom.

"I was merely coming to see to your needs in case Mrs. Butterfield had gone to bed. I assure you my offer of assistance is in consideration of extending any help you may require." He casually sauntered into the room. "Seeing you undress would have been purely my good fortune," he added devilishly.

Lauren felt unease with his assumption that he could come and go into her chambers as was his will. "My lord, I will not be swayed by your glib tongue. It is my hope that in time, if I can learn to trust you, I promise to be a dutiful wife. That all matters in our marriage will be deferred to you for the rest of our lives. But until such time, we will be together, yet not in any true sense of the word."

Devlin's brow raised in curiosity. "All matters will be mine to make Lauren?" he questioned.

"This is how I was instructed it should be. That you will have such power, as master of our household," she responded naively.

Devlin chuckled under his breath. He had serious doubts that for all eternity, any woman worth having would cleave to her husband's every wish. He was aware of what the etiquette books preached but had yet to find a woman alive who would meekly bow to the constant will of a husband, unless that husband used brute strength to force his will upon his family. Devlin was not of that bend.

"Promises have a way of being broken Lauren, as does learned behaviour. Don't give away too much of your spirit."

She was startled by his comment and continued in the vein of what she believed. "I have been taught that I have no right to question you, your judgements or your infidelities," she said, adding softly, "but that doesn't mean that I have to like it."

"I understand perfectly what the books young women read expound and what you may have been taught in the convent. However, you may find that life does not follow written rules or religious teachings. I will do my best to be considerate of your beliefs." He moved to the bed and folded back the soft quilt, motioning for Lauren to crawl between the sheets. "I have agreed to give you time Lauren, and I will hold myself from expecting the consummation of our marriage in the near future." He pulled the covers over her as she settled into the bed. "But you are my wife, and I will handle you as such. I suggest you let your guard down and allow yourself to take pleasure in my company as I will yours. Having you near today has brought me considerable enjoyment, and I look forward to all the indulgences to be had in a marriage."

"Physical desire cannot hold a couple together my lord. Does it not take a melding of ideas, plans, and goals?"

"It does. But physical desire is the first sense that draws a man to a woman. And Lauren, I am most certainly drawn to you."

She pulled the blankets tightly up to her chin as though the material would offer her protection from his smouldering gaze. Was he expecting payment for the gifts he had given her, she wondered?

Devlin saw the wariness in her feeble attempt to protect herself. She speaks of goals when my most earnest goal is to feel her arms around me and more, much more. Devlin felt like a damn fool for his first attempt to get her into his bed. Now he would have to depend on his perseverance to win his own wife's affection. He admitted to himself that the current situation was of his own making. If patience was required, he would see his to its limit. Bending down to her, he gave her forehead a brotherly kiss below the ridiculous nightcap. That would be the second thing to go before he had her in his bed. The ridiculous nightgown would be the first. He longed to feel the softness of her curls in his hand as he cupped her head for a more passionate kiss. As for now, he would curb his longing and wait for his opportunity to press his desire to its fullest with her complete cooperation.

"Good night, wife," he said, standing erect.

When the door closed on his retreating figure, Lauren contemplated the man she would eventually have to submit to or walk away from. She couldn't deny that he and most especially his family had shown her extraordinary kindness. Her mind was in a tumult. Such a man as he would wield a tremendous amount of power over her. She would constantly be ordered by his rules and have no say in her life. Not only could she see the physical strength he possessed, but his manner reflected a bold confidence in himself. It was a husband's authority that would govern his wife and children. Having no concept of what married life would hold, she wondered if she would be lost in his demands.

* * *

While Lauren's childhood had held Ellie's teachings, for the most part, she had been left alone day after day to amuse herself. She had ridden her pony, swam in the ponds, played with the few tenant children her age who were not busy with their chores, and in the quieter moments, read the books she had hidden in her room before the more expensive ones in the library had been sold to pay yet another gambling debt of her father. She was ignorantly unaware of what to expect in a bonding between two married people. She had never experienced the love of a mother, and her father had been consumed by his demons and had no time for a little girl. Ellie had guided her throughout her life, but she also kept a strict line of propriety between them. She had not taken the place of Lauren's mother, but as a trusted, kind governess. Until yesterday, Lauren had not seen how a married couple acted in each other's company except for the hard-working tenants whose lives had been filled with poverty and constant toil.

The day had been a wonderous adventure. Two short days ago, she had been alone with only Ellie. Today she had a family. Though she had no idea what real love was, she yearned for it. To have someone who would hold her above all others, care for her, want her, and only her.

She wondered how she would know what she was looking for. How would she know when she found it? And would Devlin be content with only her in his life?

# *Chapter Five*

A soft light misting rain was falling in the morning, giving the family time to spend at home, since very few would venture out for their morning strolls and risk ruining their expensive clothes.

Marian had gifted Lauren with needles, thread, hoop and a piece of needlepoint cloth she had purchased the day before at the haberdashery. Lauren was busy with lead, outlining a pattern to sew as Marian read to the children seated before her on the floor. Nanny Grace quietly played on the pianoforte at the opposite end of the room.

Trevor worked on his accounts at the big desk in the study down the hall when the front door opened, admitting a wet Devlin and a gust of misty wind. Handing his coat and hat to the butler, he entered the domestic tranquillity of the parlour as all eyes turned to him.

"It's a soaking rain this morning," he said shaking his head, flinging droplets of water from his long hair on the children and, due to her close proximity, Marian.

The peace and silence was broken as they all squealed in outraged surprise. The children jumped to their feet, laughing boisterously to attack their favourite uncle. Picking up the smallest, he tossed Thomas into the air before catching him again to hold him upside down by his right leg. Thomas's arms swung wildly, causing his little body to rock back and forth. Violet grabbed his arm as Devlin raised Thomas and he pulled her upward, her legs dangling and kicking in the air. Rose sat on his shoe and wrapped her legs around his ankle and arms around his leg, holding tight as he attempted to walk forward. George attached himself to Devlin's other arm and the muscle flexed as he lifted the older boy into the air. The giggling screams of the children were infectious as Marian and Lauren joined the laughter.

However, the no-nonsense Nanny Grace had seen enough. Clapping her hands to gain the attention of all, including a chagrined Devlin, she glared at them with hands clenched on her hips. Devlin lowered his arms to place the children back to earth and set a red-faced Thomas to his feet. Rose stood and quietly folded her hands behind her back.

"Out," she commanded the children.

They turned in unison to march from the room. Nanny Grace sniffed and stamped her foot in a rapid tattoo as she placed a condemning glare at Devlin. "You're a bad influence on the lot of them," she lamented, shaking her head.

Her attempt to stalk angrily past him was interrupted as he grasped her arm, pulling the older woman into his embrace and lifting her off her feet as he twirled her in a tight circle.

"You're not as mean as you pretend to be," he laughed.

Her black skirts flowed around them when he stopped, setting her back onto stable footing. Trying to look stern with the barest hint of a smile showing, she addressed him with a wagging pointed finger. "I've always said they misspelled your name when they gave it to you, for you've always had the Devil in you. Get it into your head now that I won't be caring for your wild bairns. The lot of them will be more of a handful than I'll be taking on in my advanced years. Get yourself a bull trainer with a strong whip." With a quick glance of pity at Lauren, she stomped out of the room.

"You do enjoy getting her dander up, don't you Devlin?" Marian asked.

"Nanny Grace's not as hard-nosed as she tries to portray," Devlin quipped.

"She swears you'll send her to an early grave," she set aside the book she held and leaned back into the comfortable seat. "Where have you been that you decided a ride in this weather was worth risking your health?"

"I've arranged an appointment for Lauren this afternoon at a dressmaker."

Lauren raised her brows at his statement. "I don't require any new clothes, my lord. I have multiple trunks as it is."

A twinkle sparkled in his emerald eyes. "Permit me to spoil you my dear, I noticed some garments you will require."

Lauren understood the gleam in his eyes when she attended the dressmaker's shop. She soon realized that what was ordered was much more for him than for herself. Two new corsets, one of black lace, and the other of blue silk, were made to seduce rather than just perform the necessary duty. The finest lingerie in soft shimmery lucent satin, semi-transparent silks that were lightweight and cool to the touch, incredibly soft natural cotton satin with a smooth feel against the skin and sheer, transparent organza with shaped motifs that subtly caught the light with a hint of sparkle.

The nightgown designs he had chosen were eye-opening, to say the least. A transparent blue, form-fitting bodice with billowy sheer sleeves and a long flowing skirt, slit on the side to reveal a full length of leg was one such design, as well as an emerald green satin nightgown that clung to the curves, tied at the neck with an extended length of matching ribbon and backless to below her waist.

Lauren felt her face redden as the seamstress happily chortled on about the designs, choices and the number of garments ordered. Fine robes, one lightweight and another for cooler weather that could be worn about the house, were also included and were the only items ordered that would provide modesty.

With promises of delivery before they soon headed to the country, Lauren wondered if her face was still aflame as she climbed back into the carriage.

* * *

A dinner party would provide the evening entertainment. Only sixty guests would be attending the more intimate affair. The dress would not be as formal for the ladies as were the ball gowns, since bare arms at the table were not in good taste.

Devlin guided her into the parlour with his hand placed possessively on her lower back. She felt a tingle down her spine at his warm touch and one more time, stomped her reaction down with a firm will, thinking of the ordered items of the afternoon and the fact that they had been designed for his pleasure and most probably her seduction. She quickly realized that his slightest attention and touch affected her almost immediately. She was finding herself increasingly incapable of being aloof in his presence. She warned herself that no matter how he made her feel, he was a professional when it came to women, while she, a mere innocent novice.

As they entered the opulent home of their host, she noted the reaction of some of the ladies present. Their warm coquettish looks at her husband were obvious. Few were dismayed when they noticed the woman at his side. Would she forever see the hungering looks he received from other women? Devlin was aware of the attention from the fairer sex. He had felt it most of his adult life and knew that it was partly due to his wealth and standing in the community. He dismissed the raw, open invitations of a few more daring women in the gathering. His prey was his wife, and no other met her standard nor stirred him as she did. He had one goal and would see the game to its end.

Moving about the room, Lauren was able to chat with the female friends of the family she had met. No mention was made of the previous day's debacle between her and Margaret, nor what was witnessed at the Grassett ballroom. As the evening progressed, Lauren began to feel a prickling of unease as though someone was watching her. She nonchalantly glanced about the room to see if Margaret Edwards or her mother were in the crowded space. Thankfully they had not been invited or had not accepted the invitation. Still, the odd feeling persisted.

The hostess called dinner, and the guests strolled as couples into the dining room. A massive formal table was set with flowers, gleaming silver, crystal and china. The glimmer of the candelabras set a warm glow to the room and were placed along the length of the table. Footmen stood to attention along the wall and moved forward to pull the chairs out to seat the guests.

Lauren noted Lord Emory speaking with an older man who appeared out of place among the finely groomed gentlemen. He was lean towards thin but had a protruding paunch that spilled below his chest. Short scruffy black whiskers sprinkled with grey, in need of a closer shave, were placed on sallow cheeks, and his hair of the same hue was a tad messy, as if he had just risen from a night's rest. Aside from that fact, he was well-dressed in formal attire. She found that both men continuously stared at her each time she looked in their direction.

The hostess flawlessly directed the flow of conversation as she first addressed the gentleman on her right. All ladies then turned to their right and spoke to the person seated there. When the hostess finished one subject with that gentleman, the conversation continued to the person seated on the left. Thus began the ebb and flow of the guests turning one way and then swaying the other like leaves in a soft breeze.

They discussed politics, affairs of the day and once again, a titillating conversation on the behaviour of the Prince of Wales, who could not avoid the scrutiny of his excessive behaviour. Lauren kept her opinion to herself as those around her made mention of the '*portly pepperpot and his good time girls.*' She wondered at Devlin's close connection to the prince and if his taste in women was at all like the prince, who it seems, didn't distinguish between harlots and duchesses, be they married or not. The discussions were shocking to the girl who had spent the past few years in a convent.

Retiring at the end of the meal, the ladies were directed back to the parlour as the gentlemen smoked their cigars, drank their brandy and indulged in never-ending talk of politics. Once settled, the women chatted amicably. Discussions ranged from returning to their country homes, their children, and their problems with servants. The unwillingness of the younger generation to work in service, when they could increase their livelihood in the newly forming industries. They rarely considered the regular manufacturing hours compared to the long tiring span from dawn to well past dusk these same men and women toiled in their magnificent homes for meagre wages. The ladies thought their unfaithfulness, no matter the reason to leave a life of service, a terrible attitude of the staff.

"I spent days with the girl, teaching her to learn her trade and serve me faithfully. Then, when everything was running smoothly, she married the footman. She wanted to have a family of her own. Can you imagine? Uncaring and ungrateful! I fired both of them on the spot."

The older women in the room commiserated with her woe, understanding her upset with the thankless attitude of the servile youth of today. It was hard for them to imagine why anyone would turn down the chance to work in a fine home for the upper class. The younger women present seemed to be of a different frame of mind as they too wished for a satisfactory marriage and family, but at the same time, they realized that they would require many servants for their future homes to cook and clean up after them.

Devlin stood at the side of Lauren's chair when the men rejoined the ladies. She noted Emory and the unkempt man making their way toward them and fervently hoped Nicholas would not engage her in conversation.

"Barwick," he called a trifle too loudly, "will you be betting on the Fiery Cross to win the Tea Race again this year?"

"I will not," Devlin replied. "Although the ship has served me well since '61, I'll leave the betting to other gentlemen this year so they can have a chance to win. The clipper is a fine vessel, and except for '64, I have done well removing a great sum from other participants." He nodded to several gentlemen who in good nature, returned his acknowledgement.

"I hardly think you would suffer overmuch on the loss of your purse should your luck turn," replied the scruffy individual as he puffed up his boney chest and linked his thumbs in the side collars of his jacket, attempting to portray a knowledgeable mien.

Devlin felt the continued talk of betting to be somewhat distasteful in front of the ladies and attempted to put an end to the conversation. "This year Trevor and I have invested in the cargo of the auxiliary steamer the Erl King. We believe she will make the trip in record time and beat all the sailships to port. I have put aside any wagers on the race and am concentrating on providing the lovely ladies here with silks and trinkets to purchase in the varied shops they like to attend."

The women in the room twittered with each other about the charming Lord Barwick, who would be so considerate to think of improving their daily shopping experiences.

"I think you will be disappointed," Emory confidently continued as he placed a daintily shod foot forward and rested a hand on his hip. "The 'Erl King' is still in China's port and hasn't yet started its journey home. With the wind at their backs, the clippers will surely outrun the steamer."

"I believe you will find, even with her late departure, the added benefit of steam to her sails will push our shipment to arrive in London long before the others. It will be the first cargo in port and carry over a million pounds of tea in her hold."

An in-depth conversation ensued on the merits of the tried and true compared to the upstart new vessels. Lauren could see by the passive looks on some of the ladies' faces who sat close enough to follow this topic that its content didn't interest them in the slightest.

"I see that your wife has returned." the scruffy blowhard changed the subject. "She has much changed from the last time I saw her, but I would recognize the colour of her eyes anywhere. They are exactly the same as her mother and grandfathers were."

He commented with a hardness in his voice and Lauren suddenly realized his identity. John Marlow, her mother's step-brother and son of Agnes Etherington. Lauren felt an involuntary shiver of fear, though outwardly she did her best to remain calm.

"Can you not give your Uncle John a proper greeting Lauren?" he leered at her.

"Forgive me sir, it is only now that I realize who you are," her voice cracked.

John studied her delicate features, so like her ancestors. Elizabeth Etherington, the daughter of his mother's last and richest husband. She who had locked her doors and stayed in her room to barricade herself against him. John and Elizabeth had played a cat-and-mouse game for months after Agnes married her father.

She had been quick and clever, eluding his attempts to get her alone, until his mother had gotten wind of his plans and forced the girl to marry the aged Phillip Berwyke. Agnes had explained to John her plans to have Elizabeth outlive the old wastrel and then give her over to him. Thereby the title and land would be theirs. Money from the estate of Dougal Etherington and every other husband of his mother, who had mysteriously met their demise, had played a role in accepting them into society. But they were the *nouveau riche,* whom the upper class continued to look down their regal noses at. They were grudgingly invited to the smaller, less influential affairs, but there it ended. No great house of the English elite would admit them.

Lauren remembered the times when this man had come to her home on the pretext of speaking to her father. She remembered him trying to entice her to come close, to sit on his lap or handle her in passing until Ellie had witnessed his touching and cajoling nature. Henceforth, if Ellie could not remove her from his sight the maid stayed near when he visited and always held a broom, fireplace poker or other such weapon.

Devlin witnessed the exchange and noted Lauren's unease. He felt the vibration in her body through his hand resting on her shoulder. Stepping beside her, he helped her rise from her chair and moved her noticeably out of John's reach. Gesturing to Trevor, he formally announced to the room, but most directly, to John Marlow, "If you will excuse us, the hour is late and we must take our leave."

Trevor heard the exchange between Lauren and Marlow, noting her nervousness. He gathered Marian to make their goodbyes to the host and the hostess, ever gallant and gracious, bid all a polite farewell.

With Marian holding Lauren's cold hands in the coach, she related her relationship to John Marlow and Mrs. Butterfield's opinion of the man. She had been a very young child at the time and could only remember snippets of events, but she certainly remembered Ellie's judgement of his character. She could not stop the dread that overcame her when she realized his identity.

* * *

The remainder of the season was a whirlwind of events. Morning carriage rides or walks in the park were a daily occurrence as they met the haughty men and women who could indulge in this leisurely ritual. Afternoons were spent following Marian as she shopped in one store or another, gathering what was needed for the country estate or ordering new garments for the children, Trevor, and herself.

Marian urged her to make her own purchases, but without knowing what she would find when she returned home, Lauren had no idea what would be required. From what she remembered, it would take many carts of everything from the shops to fill the empty castle.

They visited in the afternoons or received guests at home. Multiple balls requested their attendance each night, and they did their best to attend as many as they could. On the more quiet nights, they enjoyed a musical comedy at one of the many theatres operating in the city. Devlin was a perfect escort, attentive and gentlemanly. Lauren noticed that he held her a little longer, gazed at her a little softer, and smiled at her a little brighter, each day. She found herself pleased with his closeness, content that, for the moment, there were no other demands on their union.

All went according to the morals and customs of the gentry, and as each day passed, the late nights and early mornings began to take their toll on Lauren, who had been accustomed to going to bed early and getting a full night's sleep. Balls rarely ended until three or four in the morning, and the promenade started at nine followed by breakfast. Then there was a clothing change and visit where a light luncheon might be served. They returned home for another clothing change for an outdoor concert and tea time. The evening entertainment followed a fourth change of clothing.

Lauren was exhausted. Before attending an event, she had become startled while soaking in a warm tub. She very nearly fell asleep slipping low in the deep water. She was so tired, she was sure that if she did not remove herself, she would fall asleep and Ellie would arrive to find her drowned.

On the last evening out, they were seated closely together in a raised box at an opera. Devlin had his arm resting on the back of Lauren's chair, and instead of sitting ramrod straight as was her norm, she leaned back against the chair and relaxed, unable to support herself in any other position. Soon the German words to the soprano's voice dimmed as her head dropped slightly forward. She pulled it back quickly as her eyes flew open, but it wasn't long before she couldn't stop her eyelids from drifting closed. Her head dropped back to rest softly on Devlin's arm. There it stayed as his attention was drawn from the act on the stage to the much more interesting view of her delicate sleeping face, soft in repose. He judged that she had become more secure and comfortable with his presence while in his family's company. Within a few days they would be travelling home, and then they would be alone. Devlin was looking forward to the change of venue. He wanted to show her what he had done to her home and hoped she would be pleased with its new appearance, having little doubt of the fact since the change was vastly improved from how she had left it.

Her breathing grew deeper, and Marian giggled as a slight sighing breath escaped between Lauren's lips. "Your wife is purring," she whispered to Devlin.

"I'm pleased that city life has worn her out," he whispered. "I have a true country girl who will be happy with that preferred life." He placed her head so she rested more on his chest. Her mouth closed, and she muttered what he considered a seductive hum deep in her throat. She moved her arm to rest a hand in his lap, which had an immediate influence on him as he felt a familiar tightening in his loins. He squirmed slightly in his seat, uncomfortable that this slip of a girl could affect him so in such a public place.

The final applause woke her as the theatre lighting grew brighter. Glancing about in embarrassment, Lauren sat up, mumbled an apology to Devlin, and joined in the tribute.

* * *

The next afternoon saw the arrival of the garments Devlin had purchased. They were handed off to Ellie, who was shocked at the scant designs and folded them neatly away, muttering under her breath the follies of youth and the brazen nature of her new lord. Lauren was sure she heard "*shameless,*" "*indecent,*" and "*outrageous*" a few times as well. "That man of yours is a gal sneaker for sure," Ellie snorted. "With a giggle mug hiding his plans for seduction. He'll surely be aiming Cupid's shaft at your little butt."

Lauren, familiar with Ellie's propensity for colourful phrases and her still cool attitude toward Devlin, smiled behind a serene face.

"Ellie, I swear you are a grammatical assassin. Sometimes even I don't understand what you're trying to say."

"Well, let me tell you plainly then."

"Never mind," she raised her hand to stop the woman, "I understand enough."

Provided she could come to trust Devlin, the idea of being courted by the attractive man was thrilling. The garments he had chosen were wickedly revealing and caused some consternation in her modest mind.

Thankful that they would spend their last day in London at home with Trevor, Marian and the children before heading home, Lauren dressed in a comfortable gown, finally free from Ellie's attempts to tighten the corset. The fact that it was by Devlin's word pleased her immensely.

They sat at a small table playing a game of cards that elicited howls of anguish as the children had to pick up extra cards when they were close to discarding their last one.

"Are you cheating Uncle Devlin?" Violet inquired, eyeing him suspiciously.

"Excuse me miss, but if you were a gentleman, I would see you in the glen at dawn for calling me a cheat," he exclaimed as he let a card slip from his sleeve.

The lively group groaned and complained as they tossed their cards onto the table to signal the end of the game as Devlin held his arms out in mock surprise.

"I swear, I don't know how that got there," He pulled another from behind George's ear. "I don't know how that one got there either, so you see, young George is the real cheat."

The late afternoon saw them move to the grass beyond the rose garden. The boys set and won a game of croquet as their boots were made more sturdily than the girl's slippers. This gave them an advantage when it came to placing their foot on their ball and striking it to send a resting opponent's ball from the course. The girl's aims were taken with more care and less speed lest they strike their foot.

A merry group assembled in the parlour as boys and men hauled in the dining room chairs and pushed the furniture out of the way to set the stage for musical chairs. Ellie had formed a close friendship with the Cavanaugh governess and sat beside Nanny Grace, who positioned herself at the pianoforte and pounded out a marching tune as children and adults took turns around the chairs.

Surprisingly, Marian nudged Trevor just enough as he lowered himself onto an available seat to set him off balance as she quickly slid into his now vacant place. Trevor, off guard, found himself striking the floor as he became the first out, to the amusement of the female team.

"So this is how the game is played," he gruffly challenged, standing and rubbing his bruised posterior, if not his ego. "It would please me if you would remember, that unlike some, my bottom is not as cushioned as a matronly female."

"Argh! For that statement alone you deserve the wounding," Marian feigned anger.

Marian lost the next round to a quicksilver move by George to come in from the side instead of the front on an end-placed chair. Thomas was next out since he had trouble climbing up onto the seats, and was allowed to lay on one instead, but there were none to be had when his little legs rounded the curve on the last note. Rose was next because she was laughing so hard at her father, who was still concerned about his bruised rear end and complaining of the ache.

The competition was getting fierce as Devlin eyed Lauren devilishly. She was determined to last longer than her husband in the game. Nanny Grace would take a one-beat pause in the music but continue playing on to unnerve the competitors. When the music stopped, there was a mad scramble for the three remaining chairs. George and Violet easily slid into the chairs facing the door, and Lauren was sure she could reach the one in the opposite direction ahead of the bulk of her husband, only to find herself seated fully in his lap.

He quickly took advantage of the situation and reached behind her knees to raise her legs, tipping her back to cradle her in his arms. "Victory is mine, vixen," he proclaimed. "You play more fairly than Marian, but I saw the challenge in your eyes."

Lauren giggled as she tilted in his arms and reached behind his head to secure her position. She had no desire to fall and join Trevor, who was still rubbing his bruised behind. It was a thoroughly pleasant experience to be seated on Devlin's lap with his arms cradling her. She could feel the solid beat of his heart as her own did a little skip in her chest.

"Kiss her Uncle Devlin, kiss her," the girls cried seeing their sport.

Their eyes locked, and it seemed that only they existed in the room as he lowered his face to hers. His lips met her soft partly open mouth in a tender kiss that brought her senses alive. The scent of his masculinity filled her being, and she felt the strength in his arms as he pulled her close. Lauren was disappointed that the moment lasted only a brief second due to the audience of onlookers, but it had a warm sensual effect on her.

"That's not how Daddy kisses Mother," Thomas announced.

Standing, Devlin let Lauren's legs slide to the floor and shushed the child. "You shouldn't be watching Daddy kiss Mother, you wee sneak-about."

Lauren blushed and cast a quick glance at Marian, who had a shadow of a knowing smile touch her face.

Eventually, George was the master of the game as the children laughed and joined in the tussle that ensued between he and Devlin to claim the last chair.

Lauren had thoroughly enjoyed the past weeks held in the hearts of this loving family. Violet had sat close to her side as she stitched her needlepoint, and Thomas had crawled into her lap on more than one occasion for a cuddle and sticky kiss before scampering away again. Rose had shown an interest in learning to draw the flowers, butterflies and bees as Lauren had sketched quietly in the garden. Though he tried to act formal, as the eldest sibling, George had often taken her hand to aid her from her chair as a perfectly gallant gentleman would.

But mostly, she had watched the casual affection between Marian and Trevor. The silent communication of a glance, the warm, pleasant enjoyment of their company. The fun and joy they shared with their children. This is what she had never experienced but also what she wanted. If only she could trust Devlin to give this to her and forsake all others.

The morrow would see them leave the comfort of an extended family. They would be alone with their union and see to the true beginning of their compatibility as husband and wife.

# *Chapter Six*

There had been tears from the little ones as they waved goodbye to their adored uncle and new aunt. Trevor's four in hand pulled the well-sprung barouche over the tarmac and congested traffic of London to the Euston Station, passing under the towering Greek-styled archway over the entrance to the trains. Two hotels sat on either side of the massive pillared arch. The Victoria had basic needs for the second and third-class passengers, while the Euston on the east side was elegantly designed and catered to the rich who mingled on the front step waiting for a carriage to drive them into the station.

Hundreds of people scurried into the building as Devlin led Lauren into the great hall. A high coffered ceiling and sweeping staircase rising to a platform, extending upwards on either side to circular landings only to turn back to the centre and rise again to the second floor. This was the central feature in the throng of humanity who were either excited to arrive in London or happy to leave it.

Ellie had travelled in the luggage cart that had left London days before them, wanting no part of entering the iron beast who would swallow her whole and fly at an alarming pace along thin bars of steel. The cart was stacked high with Lauren and Devlin's trunks as well as carefully rolled carpets and tapestries Devlin had purchased for the castle. He had insisted on sending along rolls of whitewashed canvas and paints for Lauren's hobby, pleased with her talent of bringing her vision to reality through her art. They would spend two nights on the road and bed down in local inns along the way. This left Lauren in the care of Marian's maid, who had packed an overnight case to see to her toilette. Lauren dressed in a simple plaid outfit made of sturdy material to withstand the rigours of travel. This was the same garment she had worn on the ship from France, and there would be no need for a change of clothing as the compartment she and Devlin would share on the train lacked even the slightest bit of privacy.

Devlin collected their numbered and dated pasteboard tickets and taking hold of Lauren's bag, offered her his arm as they moved towards the platform and the waiting train. The enormous black engine sat on the tracks under a wrought iron roof, its stacks belching out great white plumes of steam, blowing like a winded bull as it rested against the boarding platform.

They were led by a uniformed boy along a centre hallway to their first-class compartment. Opening the door for them, he stood aside as they entered. Tipping his hat, he explained all the rail line had to offer in the form of dining, other facilities and their location. Devlin reached into his wallet to remove a heavy coin which he tossed into the headpiece of the porter.

Comfortable plush purple velvet benches sat facing one another. A windowed upper wall would allow them to watch the passing scenery as they made their way north.

"I've never been on a train before." Lauren nervously laughed, excited at the prospect of trying the modern conveyance.

Devlin attempted to calm any fears she had. "We'll be travelling at up to thirty-five miles per hour. When you consider that a horse walks at only eight miles, you may find it thrilling initially, but you will get used to it."

"I think it was an excellent idea for Ellie to go with the cart. She doesn't trust too many modern inventions."

"I did offer to purchase a ticket for her," Devlin chuckled. "She told me in plain English, for a change, that she was not interested in travelling in the belly of an iron dragon."

"The map in the station showed that there are about three hundred miles between London and Carlisle," Lauren paused momentarily as she did the math in her head. "If it will only take a little over eight hours to travel the distance, why must we spend a night on the train?"

"There is no direct route," Devlin explained. "We will be stopping at numerous stations for some passengers to leave and take on others. Also, depending on the terrain and bridges, our speed may slow to that of a horse, which will also extend the time needed to get home."

"Oh, of course. I didn't consider that. The ship to and from France didn't make any other stops at ports along the way, so it was a direct route and easier to calculate the difference between time and distance, barring any weather," she teased, smiling at him.

A shrill whistle blew, and a vibration ran through the cars of the train. Lauren felt the jarring pull of the locomotive as it strained its forward motion, taking up any slack between each of the cars as they were moved along one to the next, each time giving a tug on the connections as Lauren held onto the armrests of her seat.

Soon trees and houses whisked by at a dizzying speed. When a roadway followed along the rail line, they would often see boys on their ponies or men on horseback racing along the roadway, trying to keep pace with the chugging train. Lauren laughed and waved at the whooping lads, who raised their hats and waved back. Devlin was captivated by her excitement and watched the play of emotions cross her delicate features.

They visited the freshly decorated dining car with its green and white diamond-patterned carpet, leather chairs and white tablecloths. The tables were set with gleaming silverware and china plates serving the delicious fare that could be found in any of the fine dining establishments in London.

Dusk had settled outside the windows, and Lauren could no longer avoid returning to the cabin for the night. She had taken an exceedingly slow time to eat her meal, taking lengthy pauses between bites to gaze out at the countryside. Her eyes darted to the few occupants still seated in the dining car but found no way to engage them in conversation to avoid the inevitable fact of spending the night with her husband.

Devlin pulled Lauren's chair back for her to rise, "Are you ready now to go back to our box, or would you like to order another dessert or linger over another glass of wine." Lowering his voice in a conspiratorial whisper he teased, "Shall we try to bump into a steward or conductor at this time of the evening to have a lengthy conversation to improve our knowledge of the train schedule?"

"No my lord," she lied, wishing he was not so aware of her reluctance to be alone with him. She wasn't sure if she was more frightened of what he would do…or what she would want him to do.

"It's not like we will be sharing a cot," Devlin chided, "though our proximity will be close throughout the night. I fear it will lack the comfort or privacy for anything other than sleep, should we be able to find that blissful escape on the narrow benches, regardless of how softly they are covered."

He took her hand as he led her to their compartment in the gloaming dusk. His steady grip assisted in keeping her balance as the swaying train rocked from side to side on its journey northward. Blankets and damp cloths for washing had been provided in their absence as they took their seats across from each other.

"You will be more comfortable if you take off your boots," Devlin said as he bent to retrieve her foot and place it between his spread legs to untie the laces. He slipped her boot off and rubbed the dainty stocking foot leaving it to rest on the edge of his seat before reaching for the other foot. Performing a like service, her feet dangerously close to touching where his legs met, Lauren became flustered and felt the rising blush as she pulled her feet back to place them safely on the floor.

Devlin scrubbed himself with the damp cloth and watched the dainty strokes as Lauren applied hers to her delicate skin, then used a corner to clean her teeth. Devlin reached for the cloth and set it on a ledge keeping her small hand in his. He leaned his forearms on his thighs to study the ring on her finger and fought a strong urge to take her in his arms. He had been careful these past weeks not to press her for more than she would allow. The few tender kisses each night when he entered her bedroom to accustom her to his presence, had done little to ease the growing tension he felt in her company. His wife, his property, to have and to hold. He could imagine the fighting she-cat he would find on his hands if he voiced his raging sensual thoughts aloud. He turned her hand and brought it to his lips to kiss the palm, touching his tongue to its centre. "Good night wife," he murmured.

Lauren felt the heat of his lips go through her hand, up her arm and settle somewhere in her chest as she closed her fingers, unconsciously trapping the kiss in her grasp. She lay down on her bench, curling her knees up to fit on the space, and pulled the blanket over her shoulders, feeling the rhythmic motion of the train as it lulled her to sleep. The morrow would see her home. A place of joy or a place of sorrow, would the new day see?

Devlin wedged himself into a corner and rested his long legs along the seat. The small space would not allow for his tall frame to lie fully, but seated in this manner gave him an excellent view of his sleeping wife as he listened to her soft purrs. He considered himself both lucky to have her for a wife and miserable that he could not enjoy the pleasure of her. He felt his eyes close as he contemplated ways to improve his odds at wooing his wife, and with those imaginings running through his head, he joined her in sleep.

Devlin greeted Carl Yaegar, the coachman who had arrived from the Barwick estate, along with the four proud and muscular Friesian horses. Their black mane and tails, long and silky, billowed out behind them as their muscles stretched to pull the heavy well-sprung carriage. The sun glistened off their slick, shiny coats as they lifted their feathered legs in a mile-eating trot. Pleasing greenery and fresh breezes had replaced the soot and smoke of the train as they travelled beyond rolling hills and thick forests.

Eventually, Lauren began to recognize landmarks. They crossed the stone bridge over the River Eden and soon passed through the little town of Berwycke with its familiar shops, taverns and towering medieval church. She leaned forward, looking out the windows, and an excitement grew in her, for soon she would be home. On reaching Barwick land, where once the tenant homes had been in a terrible state, she noted pretty thatch-roofed cottages and litter-free front yards. Fat healthy cattle and sheep grazed on the hillsides of neatly hedged fields.

As they turned up the long drive to the castle, Lauren heard the crunch of fine pea gravel that replaced the sucking sound of muddy ruts that had been evident during her departure. The expansive lawns were well manicured, and neatly tended flower gardens planted in a riot of colours bloomed on either side of the lane. Finally, they stopped before the familiar grey stone facade.

The ninety-eight-room castle was small compared to other British castles, which had been built to hold a garrison of soldiers within its walls. Lauren's ancestral home, though still a fortress, was more of a private residence with the military fortification established closer to Solway Firth. An arched portico led to the front door, and two towering round turrets curved upwards on either end of the structure. Bay-fronted lead glass windows set with diamond-shaped glazing bars gleamed in the sunshine, and like beacons, welcomed her home.

Along the walkway, the staff had come outside to stand at attention in their black and white liveries. Devlin reached up to swing her down from the carriage and introduced her to the butler, a stiff older man who ruled the day-to-day operations of the household.

"Lauren, this is Winslow, who will be reporting to you on the household management, and his wife, Mrs. Park, our housekeeper."

"It is a privilege to have you home Lady Barwick and an honour to be at your service." Winslow turned to address his employer, "Welcome home Lord Barwick. The estate manager would like a word with you at your earliest convenience tomorrow morning."

Devlin accepted the appointment with a nod of his head and placing his hand on her back, led Lauren towards the double front doors. They were opened simultaneously by a pair of footmen, and the revealing panoramic view of the interior, caused Lauren to gasp in astonishment. Her world suddenly tilted as Devlin scooped her into his arms and stepped over the threshold.

"A wedding tradition I have thus far been unable to perform Lauren. I believe it is custom that a bride should first be carried into her home," he radiated a charming smile showing gleaming white teeth.

"Due to the tradition that a bride would not go willingly into her husband's house," she queried with an air of composure she did not feel being held in his arms.

Devlin's brow arched. "I assume you are quite willing to enter into your home, so it must be that I am protecting you from evil spirits that linger in doorways, if one believes in those things."

"Sounds like something that Ellie would agree with," she laughed.

Set to her feet in the front hall. She looked around this new wonderland. No longer drab and grim, it had been transformed magnificently. Across from the tiled front hall faced the grand staircase. Gone were the worn carpet and chipped wood risers. In its place, dark stained oak lifted straight to a landing and, like the soaring wings of a bird in flight, stretched upwards on either side, continuing in an arch to the second floor. The polished wood gleamed, and an unmistakable scent of beeswax filled the air.

"Would you care to freshen yourself first or look around?"

Her eyes sparkled with excitement. "Devlin, it's so beautiful, please show me around."

He raised an eyebrow at her and smiled broadly, realizing for the first time that she had called him by his given name. "So you do know my name. I was wondering if I'd ever hear you use it."

"Are we going to stand here and discuss how we address each other, or will you show me what you've done to the house?" she smiled prettily, pulling at his hand and dancing further into the interior.

Devlin was captivated by her enthusiasm and led her toward the hallway on the right. The parlour was wallpapered in warm gold and brown above dark mahogany panelling that reached three-quarters up the wall and was topped by a thick chair rail. The massive fireplace mantle held a long low bouquet of fresh white flowers that released a tantalizing fragrance, with crystal candelabras on either side of its ends. A Bechstein grand piano dominated one corner, and brown upholstered seating was grouped in the centre of the room with a patterned gold and brown Persian silk rug.

They passed from there towards the back through double-hung doors of etched glass to the formal dining room and its long table, hutch, and buffet. Not a dust mote or cobweb was in sight. Further down the hallway, her father's former smoking room now held a more intimate table and buffet for small family gatherings.

The ballroom, with three massive hanging chandeliers, was at the back of the house and leading off of it was the conservatory, now filled with plants and flowers, giving the room an earthy floral smell. Sparkling clean windows ran along the sides of the elongated room, and stained glass windows circled upwards to a point in the roof, sending prisms of light and colour dancing onto the floor. The broken windows and smashed pots that had been in Lauren's fractured memory of the shattered home were nowhere to be seen.

A billiard room held the necessary accoutrements to keep the male species content along with a well-stocked bar and three card tables covered with a green felt. In Devlin's study, with the mount of a fourteen-point buck placed behind his heavy desk, were dark green curtains pulled back by silk tassel holders that covered the windows from floor to ceiling. The library once again housed hundreds of books lining the interior walls. The light was bright, shining through a wall of similar floor-to-ceiling windows displaying a panoramic view of the lawns across from a covered porch. A stylish ornate secretary with a fold-down desk sat before the furthest window. This would be where Lauren would address her correspondence and administer the purchases for the daily needs of the house. The walls bore red flocked wallpaper against a gold background. A cozy red settee and gold wingback chairs were grouped comfortably against the interior wall with a warm red patterned carpet on the floor.

Overall the house had been transported from sadness and gloom to stately elegance. It showed a definite masculine bend with large furnishings and dark colours on the walls and the stain used on the heavy wood panelling. Since a very masculine man had made the choices, it suited the long-standing abode.

"I am amazed at what you have done. Five years seemed like a lot of time away from my home, but considering the work required to set it aright, it's amazing what you have accomplished. You must have had many workers here for years to complete the renovations. The house was so dreary when I left, and it's like a fairy castle now."

"I give you leave to change anything you wish, as you may not care for everything I've done."

"I wouldn't think of changing a thing. You've spent a great deal on refurbishing, purchasing all the furniture and paying the workers. It would be a terrible waste if I were to change what is already here, and your taste is excellent."

"I am pleased that I have a wife with a care for expenses, but you needn't worry overly much about a few variations here and there."

"You must excuse me if I believe being thrifty is a virtue. Considering how I grew up in this house and the condition it was in when you arrived, I am astonished at its present state."

Devlin observed her happy mood, grateful that he could give her this gift. "It's only a house, Lauren." Devlin observed her cheerful disposition, "I hope that you will turn it into a home," he vowed.

Gazing at her with those mesmerizing green eyes, Lauren was sure that Nanny Grace had been correct. She was sure he could charm a nun out of her vows with his warm look and prettily said phrases. But she also couldn't deny how she felt when he looked at her.

He had been an attentive husband, a perfect escort, witty and polite, but it had been just over a month since he had propositioned her before realizing who she was. He had more to prove to her before she would be at his beck and call.

Mrs. Park led her up the staircase to a large bedroom as Devlin followed. Ellie was in the dressing room, seated on a stool in front of a mirrored table, unnecessarily directing a pair of young girls on how to hang dresses and where to place the accessories in a large wardrobe.

On spying Lauren, she called out, "The old place has a fine new look to it, my girl. It's bang up to the elephant, and your father would be green with envy if he saw it today. I wouldn't be telling him my own self, but this new lord has a rich eye for things." She added with a chuckle, "It's like putting butter on bacon."

Devlin came to stand by Lauren, "I was concerned you would be exhausted by the long trip, but I see you've survived it well," Devlin greeted, finding humour in her wide-eyed look of astonishment.

"Aye Milord," she recovered quickly and looked only minimally chagrined. "It was a fair bumpy trip, but the young lads took great care of me, and it's a rare pleasant treat to have the help of these fine girls to assist me with the unpacking," she motioned to the girls, who were reaching into the depths of the trunks.

Gazing about the room, Lauren noted the deep ocean blue walls and heavy ornate furniture, which was almost dwarfed by the massive canopied bed set on a dias.

"Is this your room my lord?" she queried anxiously.

"It is, and though I am anxious for you to share it with me," he winked, "there is another bedroom on the far side of the water closet you can use for the time being." He motioned for her to precede him.

Lauren was surprised as she stepped through the indicated doorway. She passed into a small room that had not been there before. Along the outer wall stood a sizeable deep porcelain tub skirted with wood. Taps could be turned to allow it to be filled with both hot and cold water. Across from it, on an inside wall, stood a washstand with a flowered pitcher and bowl, and behind a screen in the outer corner of the room sat an unbelievably extravagant inside commode.

Lauren worried at the expense involved in installing these expensive fixtures into the old manor, but at the same time, was thrilled at what a luxury they would be and could barely wait to wash the dust off her body from the days of travel.

The bedroom she would use was smaller than it had once been. The water closet used up some of the space, but it was prettily decorated, from the brass bed to the sheer lace curtains at the windows. Here too, was a notable change. It was no longer an empty room, deprived of the furniture that once was used by family and guests in days gone by. The walls were painted a warm Prussian blue, similar to but lighter than the colour in Devlin's room. A silky white coverlet lay smooth and inviting on the bed, and a white desk and chair trimmed in gold sat before an oval mirror.

Her father's ruin had come about by the loss of his funds through gambling and exceedingly poor management. Would Devlin be able to sustain his fortune considering the cost he had expended to turn the mansion into a modern marvel? Did he also spend without care? Jewellery for her, this house, the luxurious carriage, excellent horses and the staff, from butler and housekeeper to footmen, cleaning girls, kitchen help and gardeners. Lauren felt a niggling of fear and vowed to do what she could to keep her expenses to a minimum.

She soaked in the relaxing tub that eased her tense muscles from the jostling of the coach and the stress of being alone with Devlin. The bath was a moment of bliss as the warm soapy water enveloped her. She could easily become accustomed to this enjoyment and felt a wonder that she was not only home, but in a home that was exactly like the fairy tales she had read and dreamed of. She changed into a light coral and cream summer gown, relieved to discard the heavier travel garment and feel clean and refreshed. Descending the impressive staircase and running her hand along the smooth polished railing, she couldn't help but feel like a princess in her new surroundings.

The evening dinner was perfect in every way. Elegantly served with an attentive staff and enjoyed with a considerate companion, Lauren couldn't recall a more delicious evening from the moment Devlin had taken her hand as she stepped into the hall to the relaxing stroll as they wended their way arm in arm through the floral gardens at dusk listening to the sounds of the crickets calling in the dark.

Having discarded the heavy folds of the cotton nightgowns she had worn in the convent in favour of the wicked ones Devlin had purchased, she slid into the green satin nightdress that clung to her body and exposed her back, dropping to just below her waist. The evening was warm as she sat in her room before the mirror brushing her long shining curls. Devlin entered silently and watched her as she stroked the brush along the silky strands. Her back, smooth and straight, with dimples showing at the bottom of her spine. She bore a rosy hue from the heat of the evening, and he longed to make her, in all actuality, his wife. To feel that perfect form beneath him.

Lauren quickly pulled her robe up her back as she saw his movement towards her and mildly questioned her choice of nightgowns this evening. "Did you want something my lord?" she queried in nervous anticipation.

Devlin debated his answer, for he certainly did want something of her. Would the first night in their home be the time to bring up the subject of this marriage of theirs? He thought better of it.

"Are you not yet used to my nightly visits to your room? Or is it because we are no longer in the company of Trevor and Marian, and I have you all to myself in my evil lair?" he teased.

"I think it is wise to be cautious whenever you are about Devlin," she murmured.

"Due to my wants? Or your own?" He noted the alarmed look in her eyes and relented his pursuit. "I merely came to wish my wife a good night," he said, lifting a lock of her hair and smoothing it between his fingers. He lifted his gaze to meet her eyes in the mirror. "You are so very beautiful Lauren. I'm amazed that you have become the treasure I see before me when I think of the frightened little girl I married."

"Continue this conversation, and you will soon see a frightened big girl," she warned.

"I hope it will not take you too long to forgive me for the indiscretion of wanting a woman who is, in all reality, mine!" Devlin ground in frustration. "Could you not take it as somewhat of a compliment that I was so enamoured of your beauty that I approached you in that way?"

Lauren was immediately indignant. "I believe it was only pure luck that it was I, your wife that day, otherwise, I would have found you in a compromised position with another woman! If I had arrived a day later, would I then be cast out of my home because you had chosen someone else who had tweaked your fancy?"

Devlin realized his blunder by touching on the subject of the dreaded proposition. "Lauren, I agreed to give you time, and I shall, but you do realize that we are properly married. A husband has his rights and eventually, you must cleave to them. Your virginal denial of those special moments between a man and a woman can further hold them apart, while a sharing of that tender time instead will draw them as one." He relented on furthering his terse argument, seeing the set of her stubborn jaw.

"I will wait for you to settle it in your mind to trust and enjoy all the aspects of married life. Unto the best of my ability, I give you leave to come to me when you are ready to perform those wifely moments, as I do not wish to force myself upon you before you are prepared." A glint showed in his eyes, and Lauren was amazed at how quickly he could transfer from anger, to calm, to rakish humour. "Nor do I want to miss an opportunity should I wait overlong," he added, lowering his head to move the robe out of his way as he kissed her neck just below her ear.

The touch of his lips sent a shock through Lauren as unconsciously, her head tilted towards him at the sultry contact. His view dipped to where the tiny buds of her breasts strained against the satin nightdress and where his touch longed to linger.

Plucking the nightcap from her table, he lifted his eyes to gaze at her reflection. He smiled, knowing how his kiss had affected her.

"Goodnight Lauren."

# *Chapter Seven*

James McCormack strode into the hall slapping a leather crop against the side of his pant leg in irritation. Tall and slim with short-cropped hair, he had a sinewy body from long hours in the saddle attending to his duties regarding the animals, records and tenants on the estate. Devlin had brought him to work with him in restoring the area. James' father occupied the current position of estate manager at Camber Hall. Thus, being of a similar age, they had spent much of their youth together. Their relationship was casual and friendly. James had requested the meeting with Devlin to report on the rash of unexplained mishaps that had recently taken place. The mayhem had been costly to the tenants and was intolerable in its waste.

"It's malicious damage Devlin," he used the less formal greeting in private. "A sheep here and there, a good sized calf from the Hartford farm and old man Patterson lost three goats. All in the last month. The animals are killed during the night and then left where they lay. The most worrisome event was the fire started in a hay field. The blighter hid himself in the woods when a cart came along, and they were unable to find him after the flames were extinguished. I worry that a blaze will be set to a cottage one of these days."

"If there's no rhyme nor reason to judge where the guilty party will turn up next, the only solution would be to pen what animals the farmers can overnight, or hold them in fields closer to the cottages. You could ask if any of the older lads are willing to ride from dusk to dawn, but then they won't be able to help their families attend to all the chores during the day, so there's no solution in that if the perpetrator can't be found soon. If it continues, hire some men to make a nightly tour of the roads to see what they can find. Pass the word along to keep a close watch for smoke, mischief or unusual behaviour."

* * *

A daily routine of domesticity was quickly established. Devlin and Lauren would spend a quiet breakfast before the sun rose as Lauren was slow to wake at such an early hour and rarely felt bright and cheerful until long after her breakfast was complete. Devlin suggested she remain in bed and have the morning fare delivered to her there. However, since she was, as yet, not performing the duties of a true wife, she would rise with her husband at an ungodly hour to begin the day with him.

In the early mornings, she passed through the house as the maids opened curtains and pulled wide the shuttered windows. Their day was filled with cleaning and dusting, rubbing beeswax into panelling and furniture, sweeping, and keeping the huge manse in perfect condition under the watchful eye of Mrs. Park, who demanded only the best from them.

After Devlin left in the pre-dawn, he rode about the estate to inquire among the tenants as they started their workday to see if he could address a need or problem. Lauren returned to her chambers, and if Ellie was not in attendance, she would crawl back beneath the covers to drowsily await her.

Mrs. Park would discuss the menus for the coming day and suggest items that would require purchasing. Devlin had done an excellent job of making the house suitable for a lord and his lady but had not been interested in the necessary items that were needed to host guests and parties. To a man's eye, there were the basic requirements. To a woman's eye, there was decor and decoration, and Mrs. Park cheerily advised Lauren on their needs.

In the afternoon, Devlin would be about the grounds in leisure pursuit, often with James McCormack if that one had completed his duties. They would avail themselves of fencing, archery or shooting while Lauren read or painted with her oils on the canvas. She would sit in the shade of the old oak trees to sketch the view before her. The flowers of the garden were drawn with great detail or quick sketches of Devlin and James as they parried, thrust or cut with their blades, legs spread, hands raised or dropped as they moved in dance-like fashion in their fencing motions. The young wife took particular notice of the play of muscles beneath her husband's clothing.

On days with inclement weather, Lauren could be found in an unfinished room that she had taken over to paint from her sketches. The lighting here was neither too bright, with full sunshine streaming into the room, nor too dark from the shade of the trees blocking the light. Devlin had watched the art come alive with skill and colour and often commented on her talent.

Evenings saw them spending time together as Devlin attempted to teach her to play the complicated game of chess with all its strategic troop maneuvering. She would grow frustrated with the complex moves and cunning play, moaning dramatically in defeat. Often, when he was moving about the house or working in his study, he would stop what he was doing to listen to her soft melodic voice accompanying the tinkling of the piano keys in the parlour.

As each day passed, they grew more comfortable in each other's company, and Devlin wondered if she would ever come to his bedroom of her own accord. It was difficult to see her in the mornings with her tussled hair flowing below her shoulders and a sensual sleepy look about her as she floated down the stairs as lightly as thistledown. He longed to reach for her, pull her into his waiting embrace, and end his monkish lifestyle.

* * *

Lauren and Mrs. Park entered the kitchen belowstairs to compliment Mrs. Osmond, the plump cook, on the fare she and Devlin had enjoyed since arriving home. The cook staff immediately rose to their feet, stopped their work and gaped at the new lady of the house who had deigned to come into their midst.

"I'm happy to meet all of you and wish to compliment you on your extraordinary talent. I don't want to intrude on your preparations, please continue."

"Leanne," called Mrs. Park to one of the kitchen staff, "Could you get Lady Barwick a chair and a nice cup of tea? Perhaps you have a few biscuits, Mrs. Osmond?"

"Of course, they've been freshly baked this morning," she said and nodded her head towards the pie cupboard situated near the large cast iron ovens. Leanne withdrew a tin of shortbread with bits of sugar sprinkled on the tops that glistened in the light streaming into the room. She placed a kettle on the stove to heat the water, pulled a Wedgewood teapot from its place on a glass-enclosed shelf, slipped a tea strainer into it, and brought a plate of cookies to the table where Lauren had seated herself.

This room, like the others in the house, presented a miraculous transformation. Like the neat woman who oversaw the kitchen, everything was in its place. An entire wall held gleaming copper pots, pans and moulds shaped in flowers or curved fish, hung by their handle on hooks. Cupboards were full of covered and open china bowls. Different sizes of platters leaned against a plate rail, and all sizes of plates and utensils were within handy reach.

The back door was left open to catch a fresh breeze. In the distance was the fowl pen where plump brown and black chickens scratched in the dirt and chased bugs. One of the kitchen girls was helping the rag and bone man load his cart with the cast-off scraps he would sell to the paper mills, glue factory and fertilizer manufacturers and off to the side was a building that housed the big boiler that heated the water for the kitchen and upstairs bath.

Inside there was a yeasty, homey smell to the place. The soot stains above the fireplace, and greasy walls near the stove had been scrubbed clean. Ellie entered the room and plopped herself in a comfortable rocking chair set in the corner.

"Another fine day it be and one to bring our Lauren down to visit with the kitchen staff," she proclaimed. "I'm supposing that will see Mrs. Osmond relinquishing some of her delicious tidbits, and we don't have to sneak them out of the cupboard." She laughed at the stern look she received from Mrs. Osmond.

"Are you causing trouble here Ellie?" Lauren admonished.

"No, no," Mrs. Osmond replied, good-naturedly not looking up from the dough she was kneading, "We like to have a bit of fun here, and your Mrs. Butterfield has some grand tales to tell us of living abroad."

She failed to mention the tales of woe that had been imparted. They had all shaken their heads and commiserated at the sorrows Ellie had told of what Lauren had endured throughout her young life. It made them have a sense of kinship with their lady. Though she was born with the title, hers had not been a luxurious life. She had lived in conditions similar to their lot, except in a grand house, impoverished though it had been. They had seen the home's condition when they came here to begin to work and knew what the young miss had overcome.

Mrs. Osmond placed a clean tea towel over the dough in a large bowl and set it on the warm stove. She poured the tea and passed cups around the table, taking one over to Ellie, who rocked in her chair. The conversation continued as they sat around the work table, with Mrs. Osmond explaining recipes and different punches she could offer when the house was thrown open to guests. It was a warm and comfortable atmosphere.

Ellie's scream broke the contentment, followed by the splintering sound of her cup and saucer shattering on the floor. Spinning her head to see what had caused the commotion, Lauren noticed a sudden movement in the dark corner of the room. She stared aghast as the quick scurrying motion of a mouse chasing a roach that had come out from under Ellie's chair darted along the wall.

Leanne noted the direction of the furry figure and scampered after the mouse, broom in hand swinging wildly.

Ellie held her hand over her rapidly beating heart. "I can't abide the wee nasty creatures," she exclaimed.

Lauren asked the stoic cook, who sipped her tea as though this was an everyday occurrence. "Mrs. Osmond, is there a kitchen cat in residence?"

Mrs. Osmond replied, setting her cup down. "We bring them in from the barn, but they high tail it right back out when the door is opened."

"There's quite a pest problem in the kitchen," Mrs. Park added.

Ellie apologized to Leanne as the young girl assured her that the mouse was gone and bent to retrieve the broken cup.

Lauren looked down at the old wood floors with wide spaces between the boards. "It was gruesome to be in the kitchen at night when I was a little girl. My father could hear my screams in his study." She shivered at the memory of the creeping, crawling insects that rose from under the floor as dark descended. "When I was at the convent, the nuns placed sodium borate and sugar in saucers and left them in inconspicuous places. If you could do that for a few weeks, it should kill the bugs. I will discuss with Lord Barwick a plan to lift these wood boards and replace them with tiles. The sanitation should improve immensely."

Assuring herself that Ellie was comfortable with another cup of tea and an extra biscuit, Lauren excused herself and sought Devlin in his study.

He looked up from his accounts gratefully as Lauren entered the room and stood before his desk. "Madam, the sight of you is genuinely a pleasure to behold, especially when accounting figures are all I have seen this day.

Lauren noted that he often complimented her prior to any discussion and smiled at his charming words. "My Lord, a serious matter in the kitchen requires repair. It may cost a heavy expense to replace the floor, but there has always been a bug problem with crumbs falling into the cracks of the wood."

Devlin set his quill into the inkwell and leaned back in his chair, giving her his full attention as he motioned for her to take a seat facing him. "I don't believe I've been in the kitchen to see the state it was in, so I commend you for your attention to this detail. What is your proposal?"

Lauren seated herself on the edge of the chair and leaned forward to discuss her plan. "The wood needs to be completely removed and burned. A hard surface would be best, tightly laid, so either tile or slate with a grout filling any spaces. This would have to be ordered, and then workers brought in to lay them. I will do my best in the choice of material to keep the costs as low as possible."

"Lauren, you seem overly concerned with the state of our finances. I assure you that replacing a kitchen floor will not see us in the poor house."

Lauren felt it prudent to address her insecurities. "My Lord, you must understand my hesitancy to spend your money freely. You are a man of leisure, the tenant situation has improved greatly from what I saw on our journey home, but their rents can't possibly pay for all the expenses you have incurred on the estate."

"Let me set your mind at ease, Lauren. I am not your father. I do not waste money, nor do I have a gambling problem, though, at times, I will wager on a venture or two." He looked at her steadily and explained. "The estate is doing very well, and this year should see us almost break even financially on its administration. What I am paying to help the tenants succeed will be returned to us in their rents. Some of them are looking forward to building larger homes for themselves and renting out parcels of their holdings to their own tenants. This prosperity, in turn, will be good for us and the economy of the area."

Lauren continued to express her concern. "But even in years to come, the tenants cannot support all you have done here."

"True, but before I became Lord Barwick, I was already investing with a great deal of success in many ventures. I am a second son and knew that the wealth from my father's estate would pass on to Trevor. Father guided me in learning all I could about investments, luckily, an industrial revolution is happening. The world, my dear Lauren, is changing more now than ever before. It's leaving behind antiquated ideas and living conditions. Machines are doing in hours what once took days." He emphasized his point by pulling at the material covering his chest. "My shirts would take a tailor fifteen hours to make and can now be completed in one using a sewing machine. Your dresses can be finished in a day or two."

"So you invest in tailors and dressmakers?" she questioned, confused by his financial decisions.

"No," he smiled at her innocence. "I invest in the ships that bring tea and silk from China, cotton that is finally arriving again from America. "There was a bit of a dry spell in that regard due to their civil war and blockades set up by the Union army. These goods are being delivered to the textile mills that turn the silk and cotton into material. I invest our money in the dreamers of this world. Those who invent the machines that manufacture the goods, power the nation and make life more liveable for all. Though the landowners are against it, a railway system is being built throughout England to easily see the country produce and animals to the markets of London and other large cities that will arise from the industry. This will be good for the country and our tenants, who will not have to drive the animals and have their condition deteriorate on the way to markets as they do now. So you see, with their rising wealth, so will ours rise. Furthermore, I have invested in building the different types of train cars, so our benefit will be twofold."

Lauren saw Devlin in a new light. She considered that she was indeed married to a brilliant, resourceful man.

"Oh, well then, I'll pick out a pretty tile to put in the kitchen," she smiled charmingly, "and I need a kitten."

"You need a kitten, or you want a kitten," he asked, bemused.

"I need a kitten for the kitchen," she laughed, "The mice will soon outnumber the staff, and Ellie is terrified of them."

Devlin walked the mistress of his house around the path and down to the stables. The old rotten and leaning barn had been torn down, and in its place was a facade almost as impressive as the house. Inside the cool interior, Lauren's heels clicked on the spotlessly clean herringbone-laid brick floor. The four Friesian horses leaned their heads out their stall doors, eyeing them patiently, waiting for a touch. Lauren caressed their soft noses as she passed. Further along, she was dwarfed by two massive Belgian mares that were used to plow the fields and pull heavy carts. Standing across from them were the smaller cart horses, and at the end of the long hallway, separated from the rest, was Devlin's riding horse, a superb example of Arabian horseflesh. His classic head was held proudly aloft, and he eyed her suspiciously from above. When Devlin neared, he lowered his elegant black head towards him and nickered softly.

Devlin reached up to ruffle the mane. "Daniyal is a little standoffish, but once he gets to know you, he can be very friendly."

Lauren looked into the knowledgeable eyes of the horse as he glared his assessment at the slight figure of the woman standing beside his master. "I will reserve my opinion of him until such time he decides to show his friendly nature. Danny, did you say?" The horse snorted his dismissal of the girl and tossed his regal head.

"Daniyal. It means handsome boy in Arabic. The breed has something of a reputation for being difficult or for preferring one person over any other, but the Bedouins brought the original Arabians into their tents to sleep with them so they can be gentle if they choose to be."

Lauren cast a doubtful look at both master and horse. "My lord, if I'm not willing to have you in my bed at the moment, the last thing I would want there is this giant beast."

Devlin laughed at her trepidation of the horse.

"I'm glad you added at the moment Lauren. It gives me cause to look forward to when I am invited into your bed or see you in mine."

At her shaming look, he took her hand and guided her to a corner of the barn, "Come, let's find you a kitten. Perhaps its claws won't be as sharp as your own."

# *Chapter Eight*

As the days turned into weeks, Devlin was finding it more challenging than not, to keep his hands off his wife. Dismissing the footman from holding her chair at mealtimes, he found himself, unlike the servants who stared straight ahead, doing the honour so he could gaze hungrily at her decolletage. She had become more accustomed to his casual handling of her person. Still, the monklike goodnight kisses did nothing to ease his manly desires, especially when she wore the revealing lingerie he had purchased. At least she had not asked him to return the frilly nightcap. Would this beautiful wife of his ever be relenting in his presence? He longed to awaken the sensuality he was sure she would possess. He had glimpses of her pleasing nature while in the company of his family, but since they had come home and been alone, she had thrown up a wall of cool politeness to him. He wanted a wife, not a refined stranger.

Passing along the portico towards the front doors, Devlin glanced into the library windows. He spied Lauren reading while reclining against the arm of the chaise. Her right knee was bent with her foot flat on the seat while her left foot was braced on the opposite arm of the chair. She looked thoroughly relaxed, comfortable and unaware of his presence as she displayed a length of finely proportioned calf and slender stockinged foot from under the risen hem of her dress. Devlin was most appreciative of the display.

Entering the house and passing quickly through the hallway, he strode into the library to see, instead of the lounging nymph, a dignified picture of quiet composure. Demure and ramrod straight, she held her book in folded hands and turned a serene face to him, smiling a pleasant greeting.

Lauren was not immune to the sight of her husband. She felt her heart flutter each time she looked at his well-hued proportions. His hair, lightened by hours in the sun, was long in the back, reaching just below his collar. The ever-present wisp of a curl hung down his forehead, no matter how many times he brushed it back. His face had darkened to a rich bronze that emphasized the deep green depths of his eyes. Without a jacket, his broad, muscular chest was evident through the fine lawn material of his shirt. Powerful shoulders and chiselled arms were well-defined, and Lauren found herself longing to be held in their embrace. The immaculate white shirt was tucked into a flat waistband of tan trousers that lowered to strong straight legs in tall black boots with brown tops, and she had to force herself not to sigh as she gazed at him.

His announcement that she must go to him when she was ready to fully become his wife had held her in a worrisome position. Would she seem wanton? The thought was horrifying! There was no denying that she enjoyed her perusal of his appearance, and she was not unaffected by his attention. His tender kisses when he left her bedchamber each night were having an effect on her. She yearned to do more than receive a light peck on the cheek, and when he kissed her neck, little rivers of desire coursed down her back. Her thoughts returned to the ministrations of the nuns, to partake of the intimate duties grudgingly, and she wondered how she would be able to do that.

She still could not pluck up the courage to go to him with those teachings gnawing at her brain. The contradiction between how she felt in his presence and what she was taught to feel was deeply concerning. She could not disassociate her emotions. How did other women act? What thoughts ran through their heads to take their minds from the waves of pleasure and stop the tingling response of their bodies? Was she just experiencing fear of the unknown? Would she disgrace herself?

He had done so much to improve her lot in this life. His attention had been on her and her alone these few weeks that had seen them attend the village, church, parties and host the odd guest here and there. He was a man who deserved the attention of his wife. But it was her desire for him that held her in reserve. Would he think she was a woman of no morals considering how he made her hunger to learn more about the relationship between a husband and wife?

Concerned with the direction of her thoughts, Lauren stood and moved to place the book back on the desk. Devlin came close and took her small hand in his, turning it to look at the delicate palm. Where he touched, Lauren felt the warmth of his fingers on her skin that sent the now familiar tingling through to her breast.

"Are you happy Lauren?" he sighed with a hint of sorrow.

"Yes Devlin, why would I not be?" she answered calmly.

He continued haltingly, picturing in his mind the child she had been. "After I sent you away, I was often stopped by the tenants as they questioned your absence. They regaled me with stories of a free-spirited child, unharnessed by societal norms due to an inattentive father. They told me tales of watching you riding astride and racing your pony across the moors, of passing their carts under trees to see you sitting up on the branches with your bare feet and legs swinging to and fro."

"My lord, you certainly don't expect me to climb a tree now, do you?" she queried uncertainly.

"I wonder if the stories I heard of you as a child were false," he contemplated, "because I cannot find that sprite in the woman I see before me."

Lauren could not believe that he was questioning her undisciplined childhood to the way she conducted herself as an adult. She stared blankly at him for a moment before explaining, "My father took that little pony away from me and sold him for a pittance of the value I placed on him. You ask me if I am happy, and though I readily replied, I truly do not know. What is happiness? Was it being ignored by a father? Growing up with little direction? Was it then to be married to a stranger and sent from my home? Now you dare question where the wild youth of an unkempt child has fled!" she finished on a strident note.

"Is there not more to you than a woman of cool detachment? Always polite, always perfect?" he ventured, feeling his temper rise.

She was incredulous that he should question her so, and her ire grew apace with his. "Did not the passing years and the nuns turn me into the woman you wanted?" she railed at him.

"I agree that you have become a beauty with impeccable manners, but you returned as an ice queen holding court in my home and keeping me at arms length. Look, but do not touch the grand lady," he argued, fury flashing in his sea-green eyes.

She whirled on him indignantly, and the servants scattered to other parts of the house as their voices rose. "I was sent from my home to live with strangers in a strange land. You wanted a porcelain doll did you not? Someone to take out, play with, and put on display, then return to a shelf until the next encounter with the high and mighty nobility?

Their anger grew as they continued, nose to nose, their breath mingling with the bitterness of their accusations.

"You were not sent away to turn into someone without feelings or a care for her husband," he barked.

Lauren sucked in a deep breath as she raged in return. "Am I not talented in the ways of a proper lady? I can sit and mind my manners. I can speak three languages, turn a cloth into a fine needlepoint design, paint a landscape, play piano and sing. I have been instructed on how to run a household." She felt the heat of the argument burning in her, turning her blue eyes into a stormy tempest.

Devlin's frustration grew. "I have explained before. You were sent to France to be taught the necessities to enter society and in consideration of your tender age."

Lauren ignored his words as she made her point. "All the while, I have learned to crush any independent thought that may run through my head or not dare question the word of a superior, or a husband. I am what you have made me!"

"It was not I that told you not to think and feel! Lauren, you are no longer a child, and I want a wife." He blundered on, "It is your duty to provide this household with children and in the commission of that obligation, there are certain functions that must be performed. You requested time, and I have given it to you. How much more do you require?"

The blue eyes darkened further like an encroaching storm. Specks of violet burned in intensity as the lids partially closed, and they narrowed resentfully. In defiance of the words he threw at her, she jeered at him in disdain. "Then throw up my skirts and do the deed here, Lord Barwick! Give me no more thought than the beasts in the fields if you must. A duty you call it? Have you no thought to my feelings? I have been auctioned off to my father's heir with no regard to my wants."

"There was no auction Madam, as there were no others who would have accepted the requirements to inherit this crumbling mausoleum."

Lauren's hands curled into fists as her anger grew. She wanted to lash out at the world for every hurt she had ever suffered. For the lack of love in her life and her inability to choose her destiny but instead be treated like chattel, something owned, something that society restricted.

Lauren raised her arms to strike his chest and beat at him for all her wounds and injuries to her innermost soul. She found instead her wrists grasped by his powerful hands. He held her with a force of steel. Angry face staring into angry face. He wanting, she denying.

Devlin lowered her hands, held in the vise of his and moved them to behind her waist. Her head tilted back as she tried to resist with feeble struggles against his superior strength. He felt the soft heaving breasts come into contact with his chest, and her legs brush the length of him as he pulled her toward him.

He lowered his head in a brutal kiss, drawing her will from her with his searching mouth. She could feel his strength and heat as it emitted from the close contact of their bodies. She was amazed at his swiftly mounting passion as she felt a growing hardness pressing against her belly. She could smell the scent of man fill her with a desire she struggled to resist. His mouth tilted on hers as his tongue forced her lips apart to delve into the depths of her mouth.

It was a scandalous sensation as his tongue sought hers and played a game of chase. His hot kisses moved to her cheek, her temple, along her forehead and over her closed eyes. He traced his tongue over her ear, and she moaned softly as his mouth mapped its way down to the base of her throat, kissing the tender spots that sent shivers throughout her body. He continued lower still to kiss and nibble at the mounds of her breasts.

At some point, he released his grip on her wrists, and of their own accord, Lauren felt her arms rise to reach along his neck, where his hair fell over the collar of his shirt. She thrust tentative fingers into the thick mane to hold him in the place where he was, sending delicious sparks of pleasure throughout her being. Even with the restriction of the corset, she could feel her nipples draw and tighten as he reached a hand into the space to hold the tender flesh and tease the hard beads.

Lauren's world was quickly spinning out of control. She gasped as he released her breast from its confine, and his mouth covered the swollen peak. Like a wave rolling along the seas, a flood of passion wrapped her in its depths and sent her tumbling into the far reaches of desire.

Devlin was mindful of this precious jewel he held in his arms. The softness of her skin, the scent of her perfume like flowers after a freshening rain. She filled his thoughts as his mouth searched and suckled at her breast. He felt a tightening in his loins and longed to lift her in his arms and be done with her hesitation and reluctance to share his bed.

If not for the damn promise that he would wait for her to yield her all to him, it would be done in but a thrice of moments. He wanted to pick her up and carry her up the stairs regardless of the looks he was sure would end in the tales spread among the staff. Blast a house full of people!

He had to end this before it became impossible to do so and destroy the meagre trust he had established with Lauren. He wanted more than one anger-inspired toss with his wife, and to take her in this way would be the undoing of the patience he had thus far extended. His mind was forced to ensure that their angry words would not end with her on her back with her skirts thrown over her head, as was his want.

Tamping down his roiling desire with a will of determination, Devlin raised his head and looked down into her closed eyes. Long dark lashes were resting against flushed, rosy cheeks. Let her ponder this moment and set it in her mind, of what can come of a more intimate relationship, he thought.

He set her upright and released her, stepping back as she half-opened those luxuriously sensual eyes and raised a hand to cover her moist breast. Devlin watched the display of emotions cross her face as she looked at him in wonder for a long moment. Sensual desire slowly turned to alarm at the wanton behaviour that he had invoked in her.

Spinning on her heel, she lifted her skirts and ran from the room, not stopping until she reached the safety of her room. As she threw herself onto the bed, she felt ashamed of the feelings Devlin had awakened in her body. Confusion railed in her head. How would she be able to show herself as a modest woman if he could draw her out of herself and set wings like a captive bird released from bondage to soar in riotous glee over mountains?

* * *

The heat of summer settled on the land. Fat livestock feasted on the green grasses and flourished with the knowledge and help Devlin and James had imparted to the tenant farmers. They had instilled the practice of crop rotation. Instead of leaving the land fallow, the farmers planted turnips to grow in the winter. The crop was deep-rooted, assuring the plants could gather minerals unavailable to shallow-rooted forage. Clover fields fixed nitrogen from the atmosphere and added fertilizer to the tired old land when it was turned back into the ground. It became a more arable light soil for the fodder to support the increased livestock numbers, which in turn, further added to the fertility of the soil by the increase in manure.

Instead of the inbreeding practices of producing inferior animals from the accessible weak stock they owned, the farmers had been able to outcross their animals with the higher quality breeds of cattle, sheep and goats Devlin had brought onto the land. Only the best progeny had been saved for breeding, and now those animals were being line-bred to produce the superior qualities of their breed. The change in just five years would continue to improve with the carefully established breeding practices.

James McCormack was ever present, riding from farm to farm, registering the pedigrees of the animals the estate was producing in his books. These records would keep the lines clean and ready for choosing the best of who a beast should be bred back to.

Where before there had been short-legged rough sheep, the fields now grazed three hundred pound white faced rams with heavy locks that twisted into spiral spears of long lustrous wool. Along with the solid Lancashire cows Devlin owned, he also imported a brown and white Dishley Longhorn bull that pushed the limit of a thousand pounds. Its bulk and the curving horns growing around the face, had given the farmers a fair amount of trepidation at the aggressive-looking animal when they brought their cows into his field for breeding. There was great relief when the hulking beast proved himself friendly enough. They took full advantage of his impressive progeny that produced superior beef and richer butter and cheese for their families to place on their tables and sell at market.

The tenants knew a burgeoning prosperity long overdue. A few brick farmhouses were being planned by the most industrious of them, and the families were generally healthier with less of a mortality rate among their own. The new lord had seen to their welfare and spoke to them often about their needs and plans, giving sound advice where required.

Most had been enriched by the new management with new ideas and had eagerly taken the offered advice and expounded on it. Yet there were those few who had been content with life under the old lord. They had not been interested in working to attain a better life through hard labour, preferring to lament on their misfortune and their unwillingness to lift a finger to improve their situation. They were the downtrodden, those who had given up and were content with their filth and drudgery, provided the ale they consumed flowed into their gaping maws. Tired and worn wives performed the strain of everyday life as they toiled to provide for their children. Their husbands swigged an ever-present tankard of ale as they ordered them about and gave little assistance. The weary women carried one babe on a sling tied across their sagging breasts as another grew in their bellies, and they knew no peace.

Lauren visited these women with offerings from the kitchen of Barwick Castle. She handed them baskets that included small kitchen implements, treats for the children Mrs. Osmond had sent, along with soap and towels. She spoke to Devlin of their hardships and had bolts of cloth and threads delivered so they could turn the material into new clothes for their families. The mothers appreciated these offerings and stayed up long into the night stitching the new garments. They started to look tidier and cleaner. Many of the husbands noted the improved condition of their family and seeing the benefit, began to show an interest in improving their holdings.

Devlin and James made a concerted push to encourage the men to take up their responsibilities. They spent weeks, which led to months in the endeavour. To those who marked even a slight interest, they offered praise and cheered any improvement as one would a child learning to walk. The baby steps saw an ever-increasing proficiency that was achieved.

Todd Harrington was not of a like mind to those of his friends who were becoming more hopeful of gaining a better life. He was doing just fine with the few coins he stole from any drunken sot he came across, and so long as they had eggs and gruel to fill his belly and the occasional choice piece of meat, he was content. However, with many of his contemporaries laying aside the daily consumption of ale, those occasions where he was able to lift the pennies from their pockets were becoming few and far between.

There was one he could count on who had hired him in the past to perform the less savoury duties of a landowner. The coin received from those transactions had weighed heavier in his pocket than any he had been able to obtain from the poor tenants. Of late, his acquaintance with the pair had proven most lucrative, and he received ample enjoyment in creating problems for the tenants who mindlessly followed the administrations of the new lord of Barwick Castle.

Agnes Etherington was unconcerned about how he performed the business dealings she set him to as long as her intentions were fulfilled and he didn't ask any questions. She was not overly worried about the great dumb hulking man thinking for himself and left her son to deal with him when it became necessary.

# *Chapter Nine*

The Glorious Twelfth of August was quickly approaching, when many of the elite would arrive at Barwick Castle for the hunt. The household staff were in a flurry working from six in the morning and finishing past midnight. As they did every morning, all curtains and window shutters were opened to let in the light of day and the house was swept and polished. Due to the influx of guests that were expected, the house would be brought up to standards far beyond the ordinary, which were already incredibly high. Mrs. Park was determined to have the old house shine like never before. This would be the first time Lord and Lady Barwick would open the doors to several of their friends and family who would be spending days and nights at the castle. As a single resident, Lord Barwick had not felt a need to entertain on such a grand scale.

The staff also had pride in the estate and how it was managed. No accompanying servant, from a lesser or greater house, would see a reason to snub the protocol of this ancient castle, whose lineage went back many proud generations, regardless of the last lord.

The present lord and his lady could trace their ancestors to medieval times. Devlin's family had anglicized from the Gaelic Irish surname of Caomh, meaning gentle or tender, which genetically, it seemed, had been passed down throughout the generations and settled in the current lord. Though the castle name had been changed throughout time from Berwycke to Barwick, Lauren's family had continued with the original surname until this generation, when it died on Lauren's wedding day.

There was always trepidation among the staff when a new lady was to enter a household, and those hired to care for Barwick Castle had mainly come from Devlin's family home. They had worried that when she arrived, there was a chance that she would be harsh and demanding, scornful of their attempts to please her. The Barwick staff had gladly accepted Lauren immediately and considered their lot in life above other servants. They found her easy to please with a ready smile and a kind word to all. Lord Barwick was a magnanimous master who, unlike other houses, allowed days off and generous wages comparable to those earned by the factory workers in the cities. He had proclaimed that to keep them content in service, they should be well compensated to stay in their positions. As such, they set their minds and talents to dust every nook and cranny, from floors and walls to the sparkling chandeliers and everything in between.

Newly dipped beeswax candles were placed in the lamps with cleaned round crystal or silver bobeches placed at the base to catch the melting wax. Rugs were rolled and taken outside to be beaten by the strong arms of the stable boys and left to freshen in the air before being returned to the house. The gardeners tended the lawn and flowerbeds in full bloom, bursting forth in a profusion of colour.

Beds were changed, and rooms were aired. Welcoming baskets of scented soaps, lotions, small treats, bottles of wine and crystal stemware were left in the bedrooms for the guests to use and enjoy. Each piece of silver, which ran to the hundreds, was washed and polished to a high sheen, and even the quarters on the top floor received a thorough cleaning for the incoming servants.

A brace of days before the partygoers were scheduled to arrive, Lauren was lending her talents to repair a bit of lace that had come loose from the side of a pillowcase when Devlin strolled casually into the parlour.

"Could you spare a moment of your time Lauren?" he asked, trying to conceal a secretive smile.

Lauren laid her sewing on the chaise as she stood. Devlin appreciated every aspect of his graceful wife. She seemed to float towards him. Her movements were so soft and precise. Taking her hand, Devlin pulled her to the front door.

"Close your eyes," he insisted before opening the portal.

Lauren cast a brief glance of suspicion over him before she complied. With the warmth of the sun on her face, Devlin cautioned her to mind her step as he led her onto the sweet-smelling grass and instructed her to hold out her hand. She felt him place something small in it, followed by the wet nuzzle of velvety soft lips reaching into her hand. Opening her eyes, she was greeted with the large brown eyes and long lashes of a beautiful chestnut mare sporting a long white blaze on her face. A brilliant smile and squeal of delight was Devlin's reward.

"She's yours Lauren. You'll need a mount for the fox hunt."

In her joy, Lauren threw her arms around Devlin's neck and rose on her toes to kiss his lips without thinking. "Oh Devlin, no jewels in the kingdom are as welcome a gift as she." Realizing her forwardness and the muscular arms that reached around her back, she pushed gently against his chest. "What is her name?" she asked as she turned again to stroke the soft, smooth neck to hide her confusion at her behaviour.

"She's Camber's Witching Willow, or just Willow, which is not quite so formal," he stated, pleased with her reaction.

"She doesn't seem like a witch at all," Lauren spoke softly to the mare moving her hand to the soft muzzle.

"She had her name changed when she was a filly because, like a witching stick, she found every puddle of water to roll in after it rained." He bent to run his hand down the elegant forelegs.

"I haven't ridden in so long. I hope I remember how to keep my seat and not embarrass myself by landing in the dust."

"Then I suggest you start slowly and stay close to the house. I will be happy to go with you whenever you wish, or if I'm unavailable, take one of the stable hands so you stay safe."

* * *

Unable to contain her excitement, the next day, Lauren dressed in the dark blue riding habit with bright red collar and cuffs Devlin had supplied along with the horse. Hurrying to the stables, she entered the cool dark interior and led the mare from her stall, hooking her to the cross ties. She rubbed Willow's slick coat with a curry brush before Carl came in from turning out the Belgians.

"Excuse me, my lady, I didn't realize you were here. Let me brush the mare for you."

"Don't bother yourself," Lauren replied, running the bristles over the mare's round hindquarters. "I prefer to get to know her a little bit better, and by doing this simple chore, I'm hoping we can become friends before I take her out for a ride. Perhaps then she will pity me if I seem inept," she glanced over the tall back of the horse. "Will you be able to accompany me? I can't seem to find his about anywhere."

"He rode off just a few minutes before I took Bertha and Bess to the field."

"If you point to his direction of travel, perhaps I can catch up with him and save you the bother."

"Oh it would be no bother to accompany you my lady, but he was taking his leisure, so you should come upon him shortly." He threw on a blanket and tightened Lauren's sidesaddle on the girth of the mare.

With Carl offering her a leg up, she adjusted herself to the new form of riding sidesaddle, and wasn't sure she felt comfortable to take Willow into more than a leisurely walk.

"I'll take care until I'm more assured of my ability," she waved as she rode off.

Lauren and Willow meandered down the path passing beyond the fields where Bertha and Bess stopped chewing on the timothy grass to whinny and stare at the passing pair. They soon entered the cool shade of the wooded glen and followed a gurgling stream as the water flowed over the ancient rocks strewn in the waterway. Tall oaks held chirping birds that grew quiet as they moved deeper into the forest.

Lauren paused at the crest of a slope. Below the roadway was the pond that had formed over centuries from the tumbling water as it flowed over the stream's waterfall. In that pond was the naked form of her husband as he swam towards the shower of water. The masterful strokes of his muscle-hewn arms reached and dipped into the water, propelling him forward as the tight muscles of his legs kicked in tune with the opposite movement of his arms. In between both, Lauren's eyes were drawn to his firm, muscular back and slim, well-formed buttocks.

Devlin disappeared into the waterfall as Lauren sat in indecision on what to do next. She should turn around and return to the barn, but her virginal curiosity bid her stay. He was magnificent. She wanted to examine, without being seen, of course, more of this salubrious man.

In less time than she expected, Devlin was easing himself out of the pool as Lauren sat her horse transfixed by his raw power. Bulging muscles on his arms were complimentary to the broad chiselled definition of his large moulded chest with dark, damp curling hairs. Her eyes lowered to his lean, rippled belly, where a trail of dark hair led a path downward. Lauren felt the molten heat of a blush pass through her as she realized Devlin had noticed her staring at him. His rising erection had caused her to look straight up into the verdant eyes that held hers.

Seeing her discomfiture, he bent to collect his shirt and drew it over his head, hiding from sight the figure of unexpected pleasure Lauren had gazed upon. She turned to peruse the more cooling view of the foliage, closely studying the intricate pattern of the bark on a tree as Devlin led the Arabian to her side and mounted him.

"Enjoying your ride?" he chided teasingly.

Lauren turned a deeper shade of red at having been caught ogling her husband. "I am! I was! I mean...yes," she flustered.

Devlin laughed a great bellow. "Relax Lauren, all you see before you is yours." He affirmed and leaned licentiously towards her, "Especially me."

***

The next day they rose later than usual. Devlin had no pressing duties and let Lauren sleep as he knew they would be busy over the next while with the frenzy of planned activities. The afternoon saw the lord and his lady welcome the string of guests pulling up the drive on horseback or in carriages with their mounts trailing behind. The front drive was filled with excited voices in the mingling crowd. Separate coaches of servants were directed to the lane leading behind the house to haul the heavy chests full of clothes up the back stairs. James directed the traffic and kept order in the hectic chaos. Inside, Winslow oversaw the black and white garbed footmen with impressive timing to lead the individual guests to their rooms and quickly descend to repeat the process with the next arriving couples.

Trevor and Marian arrived, followed by their servants and a shooting brake. The open country vehicle was capable of holding sportsmen and their dogs as well as guns and game in the slotted boot. In this instance, it held the foxhounds Devlin was borrowing from the Camber kennels. Sensing an end to their journey, the dogs were exercising their voices in braying discordant harmony.

Trevor clapped James on the back in greeting and bellowed,

"Get these dogs settled before we all lose our hearing. It's bad enough when they're on a scent in the open, but they're echoing off the walls in the cart."

"It's good to see you again my lord," James laughed. "There's a place set aside for them off the stables. I'll see to it immediately," he efficiently directed the driver of the cart and hurried the departure.

Though Lauren had been anxious about her duties with a large household of guests, her nervousness disappeared with the arrival of Devlin's family. Trevor reached up to swing Marian to her feet and then lent a hand to an older woman who appeared in the doorway.

"Mother insisted on coming to meet you Lauren," he proclaimed as the dignified woman slipped her arm into his. A cane in the other hand lent her support as she moved forward in a rustle of light beige taffeta.

"I daresay I'm not as decrepit as I first appear alighting from a carriage, but I swear the coachman hit every bump and rut in the roadway to get here," she admonished the driver, who sheepishly shrugged his head lower into his jacket.

Lauren offered Devlin's mother a deep curtsy. "Good afternoon Lady Cavanaugh. It is a pleasure to finally meet you."

"Good heaven's child, get up and address me as Marian does. I prefer Mama." She moved closer and offered her cheek for Devlin to kiss. "I had to travel this distance since you didn't seem willing to bring Lauren to me," she scolded.

"How else would I have gotten you here to see the estate," he smiled a reply.

"You young whelp, these old bones of mine rattle enough as it is. Now lead me into the house. I could do with a stiff drink." She turned to Lauren's look of surprise. "Doctor's orders dear. Purely medicinal."

"It took her a good hour of her time and a heated exchange to talk the doctor into issuing the prescription." chided Devlin holding back his mirth.

Lauren smiled at the teasing banter of her family as the Dowager Countess blustered in feigned anger. "I spent that time with the good doctor to talk him out of prescribing laudanum. I want to keep my wits about me while I am still in possession of them. Since your father died, I am allowed few vices, so my darling children, don't try to deny me this one."

The few mingling guests stepped aside for the passage of the grand dame and her entourage. Once ensconced in a comfortable chair where she could be the centre of attention, the dowager waited patiently for a flavoured brandy to be set beside her. Taking a delicate sip, she closed her eyes and murmured, "Ah, ambrosia, an excellent healing elixir. Very good for the circulatory system."

The family exchanged secretive looks as they indulged their mother. At her age, she let propriety go to the devil, and they all felt that she deserved the right. Her life had been long and dignified in her service to her station. If she chose to flout convention in her advanced years, she was entitled to do so.

"Let us take a look at our new family member." She passed a slow perusal over Lauren. "Tremont and I came here when we were newly married for the funeral of your Grandsire. Your father was already leading a wild life and running with a fast crowd. After his father's tragic death, the burden of responsibilities was thrust onto him quite suddenly."

"I was unaware of this. Father rarely spoke of his parents," Lauren prodded, "I would like to hear more about my family if you have other memories."

"Your father was a distant cousin of Tremont, so you and he were related. I remember feeling very sorry for Phillip. He seemed terribly upset about taking on the duties required. His interest ran more to gaming and other amusements. He never cared for his tutors or studies," she ventured. Lauren could sense that the memories she was probing were unpleasant as a pensive look came upon the aged face.

"This, of course, was long before he married your mother," she brightened, insisting, "and seeing the lovely child before me, I can only be happy that the outcome of his life gave us you. You are every bit as lovely as Eleanore told me you are."

"Thank you Lady, uh, Mama." Lauren smiled at the dowager's nod of approval. "I find myself quite fortunate to be considered one of your family."

Diana Cavanaugh waved off Lauren's comment with a flourish.

"It is as it should be," she quipped, taking another sip and holding the crystal out to Devlin for a refill.

The mingling guests were offered refreshments as the parlour grew noisier with their admittance. Drinks flowed, and acquaintances from London were renewed. A happy group met for dinner later in the evening, enjoying the exotic dishes prepared for the guests. Lauren had drafted handwritten place cards with a scrolling design and set beside the French menus. Courses of soups, fish, and Fricandeau of Veal with a brandy gravy, served with vegetable-filled pastry envelopes, were plated on the fine Wedgewood china. Grapes from the vines and cheeses made from the rich milk of the cows and aged in crocks procured from cold cellars were served and eagerly consumed. An assortment of fruit with individual rich puddings completed the meal, attesting to the skill of Mrs. Osmond and her staff.

Rising from her seat, Lauren gestured for the ladies to leave the dining room to the men and their brandy. The women sipped cordials of a low-alcoholic chocolate liqueur and played the game of 'The Minister's Cat' before Marian had to think hard for the letter K. At the same time, the other ladies giggled, assuming victory was in the making.

Smiling around the room smugly, Marian announced, "The Minister's cat is a kipper-eating cat."

The dowager gave up as soon as her turn arrived with the letter X making a great deal of her unfortunate choice of seating for the play of the game. "Had I been younger, I could have easily jumped up and exchanged seating with a lady of quicker wit," she drawled.

Once the gentlemen joined the ladies, all were entertained by the acting and gesturing involved in a game to guess an animal, phrase or person without speaking out loud. It was a hilarious group as the very distinguished elderly Lord Ferndale, in a contorted pantomime, attempted to have the revellers guess a portion of a lullaby and mimed a baby falling from a tree.

The house grew silent as all fell to their beds, exhausted from a day of travel, good food, and merriment.

The following day the men gathered in the dining room for a hearty buffet breakfast of breads, eggs, sausages, potatoes and strong coffee laced with whiskey while their wives lounged in their bedrooms and were served a light meal of scones and jam with tea on trays.

The afternoon saw all gathered to ride or be driven to the moors. Ladies, in their gaily decorated hats and summer frocks, were offered chairs and blankets and dined on a lunch of pretty sandwiches with pink or blue bread as a light sparkling wine was offered and poured by snub-nosed footmen. Special care was taken to either sit in the shade or conceal their fair skin from the sun with fashionable parasols.

A friendly, chatty group spoke of relatives near and far and the horrors of the war that had raged in the Americas. Of relatives who had died or been left with burned-out homes and the ravages both North and South had suffered.

"My dear uncle's family has been wiped out. Not one son is left. Their beautiful home was destroyed, and his only daughter up and married a Yankee. The horror! Now none of their friends will have anything to do with them." A pitying silence was followed more eagerly as the subject turned to fanciful discussions of their English families and the social scene.

"Jane Hornsworth has finally caught herself a fiancé," stated a matronly woman. "This is her fifth season, and her dear Papa was sure she would never leave his house."

"I hear her beau is from a fine family," replied Marian.

"They operate several businesses in London selling imported rugs and furniture," quipped Lady Ferndale. "It's a terrible shame she could not find a husband from the *ton*."

"She had her heart set on a number of the wild impoverished rogues in the elite, but none but Nicholas Emory would offer. She had her father terribly worried about her lack of choices, but in no uncertain terms, he had refused Emory."

"I believe she was hoping for Devlin to notice her as well," a young lady spoke and received a quick pinch from her mother, "But that was, of course, before he married you Lauren," she added hastily, rubbing the sore spot.

"I say there were several misses that had their caps set on Devlin Cavanaugh when he was unattached," remarked Lady Ferndale, "what with his good looks and impressive family." She smiled at Lady Cavanaugh.

"That was all in the past," insisted that grand dame. "Both of my sons have settled down quite nicely, and their choice of wives is exemplary." She directed the attention of the gathering to her daughters-in-law. "Marian has gifted me with her sweet care, and I adore my grandchildren. George is studious and will take over the duties one day with as much promise as his father and his father before. We are confident that Camber Hall will remain in excellent care for future generations."

"You and Papa set a fine example for us to follow." Marian smiled and tipped her head at her mother-in-law.

"As for Devlin," the dowager continued, "the choice may have been made for him, but he did agree to the terms, and we are privileged to claim that Lauren has joined the family. We look forward to what their union will produce."

Marian glanced at Lauren, who returned her look with a trembling tug of her lips. Marian saw the unease on Lauren's face and was aware that the couple were still in separate bedrooms and doubted that they had consummated their marriage as of yet. There was an air about them that was not conducive to a more intimate relationship.

Lauren couldn't help the blush that infused her cheeks as the talk focussed on her and desperately changed the subject. "What was Devlin like as a young boy? He and Trevor spoke a little of that time when we were in London."

"The same as any lad," Diana Cavanaugh contemplated, remembering when she was a young mother and the fine young men she was guiding to adulthood. "He tended his studies, played hard, argued his point, and would get frustrated when as a little fellow, he tried to compete with his older brother. He was ever mindful of his father's wrath when Tremont had enough of his over-achieving and laid down the law." She smiled, considering the strong-willed boys so like their father. "He was a faithful friend and brother who fought hard to win and be his best, but he was mischievous to a fault and nearly drove Nanny Grace mad with his shenanigans. Even so, the woman doted on him, much to Trevor's chagrin," she smiled and glanced at Lauren, "I'm sure you've heard that Trevor always complains about the fact that Devlin escaped much of Nanny's punishment."

"I did hear about that from Trevor" Lauren laughed. "And I saw Devlin's merciless teasing with Nanny Grace. She did her best to try to be angry with him, but it was easy to see how he manipulated her."

As talk turned to the other women's children, Lauren considered how Devlin had bestowed on her all his care and attention since they first met. He had given her so much of what she never had before. She saw how other women looked at him in London, but his focus had stayed solely on her. He had been considerate of her person, obliging and supportive of any decisions she had offered once they returned home. When he had come upon her painting a brown monochromatic scene of trees and hills on a plain light wall in a long hallway, he had watched the scene come alive. He complimented her profusely on her imagination and ability, standing back and admiring her composition as she completed the project. Her thoughts of Devlin drifted softly away, like a feather floating on a breeze, as Marian came to sit beside her.

"Don't mind talk of Devlin," she whispered. "I've seen a change come over him since you arrived. He's very determined to please you, whereas before, he could be standoffish with women."

"I would have imagined that he had escorted many women and was quite familiar with more than a few."

"As far as I know, he was never serious with any of them. His interests were predominantly focused on business. Once he knew that someday he would inherit your father's estate, he set out to learn what he could of its condition. He was aware that it would require a substantial investment to secure its future. So you see Lauren, years ago, long before he had met you, he had set it in his mind to build all this for both of you."

Lauren looked at Marian's steady gaze and realized that Devlin had instigated a worthy plan to make all she saw in her home and on the land come to fruition. She felt a warmth take hold of her as the harsher feelings she had for her husband were melting slowly away.

The men were stationed some distance from the picnicking group. James McCormack stood at a tall rough desk a safe distance from the action to record the hunter and the number of birds killed in his game book. He wrote the names of the guests who would be shooting as they stood ready with their guns behind the brush barricades. This would be a driven shoot instead of the rough one where the beaters would drive the game into the air. A heated discussion had ensued during the morning breakfast among the hunters on the best breed of dog for grouse hunting, with many of the men praising the dogs they owned, be it setter, pointer or retriever.

Some lauded the lightning reflexes of the setters as they covered, with shotgun speed, the distances required for flushing the game.

"My old Glory, in her youth, could outrun any of the other dogs in the field," stated a burly gentleman as others agreed.

"Aye, she was a whip-fast one," another guffawed, recalling the swift dog, "but sometimes she was so quick, she'd pass the empty spot the bird would land after it had been shot and have to turn around to pick it up once it hit the ground."

Many raised their voices to praise the unhurried diligence, steadfast and level-headed pointers.

"No matter how long you keep a good bottle in a dusty vault," one owner compared his dog to well-aged brandy, "the moment you imbibe too freely, it hits you like a hammer. That was my Bolt. He'd spend the winter stretched before a blazing fire, but the moment we were in the field, he was off to do his job unmindful if you were prepared or not."

The retriever group firmly believed the obvious, that none other than the retriever, with its easygoing disposition and friendly nature, could be out-hunted on land or in the water.

"If I miss a shot completely, my darling Brace will find any unharmed bird in the field or on the water, catch it up and bring it to hand, telling me with her lovely brown eyes that I am the greatest hunter to ever venture onto the dales; even if she had to do the job herself," quipped Lord Ferndale. "If only my wife looked at me with such devotion and offered such praise, my life would be perfect."

A band of beaters were employed to walk over the sloping fields towards the first shooters, separated behind their blinds by a goodly distance. The whirring sound of wings announced the birds' arrival as a steady clutch of reddish brown grouse with their black tails and white legs flew in front of the brush that covered the shooter's position. The blast of guns and the smell of powder filled the air with James noting, in his ever-present book, the hunters' trophies, if not by sight, then by their whoops of success. Between shots, there was plenty of time to wait for another opportunity to sight their targets.

It is not that the brothers avoided at all costs to discuss the subject of their relationship with their wives, it is just that it would not have occurred to them to do so. To query another relationship would be to question the integrity of how they conducted their family. So even though Trevor was aware that his brother was still sleeping apart from a most delectable wife, and the fact that Marian would question him incessantly on any knowledge he had of the situation, their conversation ranged from the safer topics of laws and politics to the thirty-pound salmons caught in The River Tyne.

Once the downed or wounded birds were collected, an excellent ale was passed around amid hearty congratulations and proud boasting. The second group of men took their place, and the process was repeated with the birds in flight coming from the opposite direction.

Returning to the castle, James saw to the cleaning and hanging of the multiple carcasses. The guests had all agreed to offer the days bounty to the tenants, so many a good meal of the fowl could be shared among those who were not, by conventional custom, allowed to hunt.

The evening meal was another fanciful gastronomic expression from the talented kitchen, which received high praise from the sated guests. Great care had been taken to rearrange the seating from the previous dinner. The guest would be carrying on the flow of conversation with new partners to avoid a stale rehashing of yesterday's topics.

What followed dinner, as the ladies were joined by their husbands in the parlour after their brandy, was a collection of the musical talents among those gathered. The evening entertainment began sedately with long elegant fingers moving over the ivory keys as the classical pieces of Mozart and Beethoven were played. Modern songs were sung as the evening progressed and the hours lengthened. Devlin and Trevor took it upon themselves to assist the footmen, to ensure that the guest's glasses were liberally filled with whiskey for the gentlemen and wine for the ladies. Late into the night, a group of somewhat inebriated gentlemen, including the host and his brother, participated in the entertainment. The men rolled their eyes, the women knew not whether from the drink or the raucous sea shanty they were singing. The staccato beat of their feet stomped to a rousing tune in time to the lyrics:

*Pirates behold*
*There's a tale to be told*
*of a wench and a buried chest.*
*On an island so bold*
*as the story is told*
*it'd kill any fool in the quest.*

*Merchants take heed*
*lest your fortunes all bleed*
*For Ramsey the pirate looms near.*
*He's a scoundrel at best*
*ye'll be put to the test*
*When his belly holds liquor and beer*

*Ladies forsake*
*for your virtues at stake*
*as women have so much to fear.*
*Old Ramsey flirts*
*to get under your skirts*
*and bring forth a young buccaneer*

The prudish Victorian values were dashed as the elicited shrieks of laughter and the shaming looks from the wives to their mates made the evening an enjoyable end to the day of fresh air, exercise and plenty of drink.

# *Chapter Ten*

Fox hunting was the bastion of the privileged. A sport exclusively for the upper class who were determined to keep the tradition pure from the newly enriched who desperately wanted to be included and accepted as equals. The strict dress code and etiquette were always followed, and the morning had aged to a late hour as the guests took longer to rouse. Before the sun rose to its full height, the field of riders mingled atop their mounts on the front lawn, awaiting in groups for the start of the hunt. They were offered one or two glasses of whiskey or light wine to help ease any lingering effects of the previous evening.

The obedient hounds were brought around the house by the red-jacketed Master of the Hounds and his group of whippers. In his navy blue jacket and white trousers, Devlin stayed beside Lauren to help keep her and Willow calm among the dogs wandering underfoot. Tension filled the air as the excitement pitched. The aged Lord Ferndale was as eager as any of the younger, more athletic gents to be off.

"I'll stay with you on the third flight," Devlin directed. "The pace will be slower, and we'll go around the jumps instead of over them. Willow isn't conditioned for the rigours of the hunt, and I don't want you getting hurt since you're not yet accustomed to riding sidesaddle."

"My Lord, if there were a fourth flight, I would follow behind them. I insist you ride where your talents suggest and accept the fact that I am fully aware of my limitations and will enjoy the day at my leisure. I feel no pressing inclination to show off what little confidence I have in my ability to stay in this saddle with a more aggressive ride."

Devlin thought for a moment to consider if her suggestion was sound until Marian joined them.

"I'll stay with Lauren," she insisted. "I've already been jostled mercilessly and have no need to get pushed around by the over-eager young gents in the second flight who are hell-bent on proving they should move up."

"Be careful," he admonished them both as he moved to the front of the field to join Trevor.

At the sound of the Huntsman's horn, the dogs trotted on with riders following. The first job of the hounds was to find the foxes as they lay hiding in the rough brush. The dogs would pass from covert to covert as they were recast over the area until the scent of a fox was discovered.

The sun had long passed its zenith before the first cry of the hounds were echoed by the pack as they scented the quarry. The leisurely pace of the field then picked up through brush and growth as the skilled riders raced over the land following the extreme flight of the dogs. The riders and their athletic horses jumped the gates, logs and hedgerows. It was the most exhilarating, yet terrifying experience Lauren had ever witnessed.

After some time, not only had the third flight moved ahead of them, but the forward group of riders were no longer in Lauren and Marian's view. The flight had ventured far afield and turned to a reverse course. The riders were on a circuitous route returning close to their location.

A broad creek had halted their path as they searched for a more shallow part of the waterway to cross. Finding a narrower flow, though still quite deep, they decided they could jump the gap. Marian's successful attempt gave Lauren courage as she watched the horse and rider easily fly over the space to turn on the opposite bank and offer encouragement.

Whether Willow felt Lauren's hesitant trepidation or just for the sheer joy of the moment, instead of jumping over, she decided to jump into the middle of the creek. The sudden stop jolted through Lauren and tipped her off balance loosening her foot from the stirrup. The last moment of view saw her feet sailing straight into the air as her back hit the water, knocking her bonnet forward onto her face as she sunk into the depths of the creek.

Hampered by the sodden weight of her riding gown, Lauren struggled to rise against the flowing water. Gaining her feet, she pushed back her soggy bonnet to see Willow shaking her head at her mistress' riding ability and eagerly pawing and splashing at the water with her hoof sending more waves onto Lauren.

"Are you hurt" an alarmed Marian quizzed.

"Only my dignity," Lauren answered as she reached for the reins, holding them tightly as they heard the baying calls of the dogs heading in their direction.

Spotting them through the brush, Trevor and Devlin veered from the front of the hunting party and raced to their locale. Jumping from his still-moving horse, Devlin waded into the creek reaching for her. He gently grasped Lauren's arm and guided her towards the slippery bank.

After a quick assessment that she was not injured, he announced, "I believe that though your riding could use more practice, your dismounts are abysmal."

She snorted at his humourous play. "My lord, should we not extricate ourselves on the side that leads home so I do not have to embarrass myself again."

He looked at her dripping condition, and fearing only slightly for his ruined boots, dragged the pair of them and a horse truly named for her joy in finding any watercourse, back into the depths and out the other side.

After backing away from the creek, Marian and Trevor jumped their mounts successfully onto the embankment. Devlin whistled for Daniyal to come to him. The stubborn Arabian looked at the group on the opposite bank and eyed them suspiciously, considering his options. In a high-stepped prance and a majestic flare of his tail, he took the only course that seemed reasonable and, with a mighty leap of his powerful hindquarters, sailed effortlessly over the divide, turning with a snort to Willow as if to say…*and that is how it is done*!

After assisting a sloshing and much heavier Lauren, due to the waterlogged weight of her gown into the saddle, Devlin sat on a log and poured the water from his boots.

"Never fear Devlin," Trevor laughed, "cows get wet all the time, and their leather stays just fine." Turning to Lauren, who looked absolutely miserable with her loose hair, wet and dripping onto her face and shoulders, he commented, "At least, since you are a newcomer to the sport, you won't suffer the fox's blood drawn on your cheeks. But you will owe the Huntsman a bottle of wine for the fall."

* * *

Lauren soaked in a perfume-scented bath before dressing for the hunt ball. Her riding habit, which had chilled her to the bone on the ride home, was difficult to peel off in its damp, clingy state and had been taken to the laundry to see to its cleaning. Colourful soap bubbles broke and danced on the surface of the warm water as Devlin stepped into the bathing chamber to shave.

He noticed her immediately and decided to continue into the room nonchalantly instead of offering his apologies for invading her bath and retreat from the scene. After all, he thought, this would be the typical actions of a married couple, and aside from pressing her into more intimacies, he would slowly partake of anything she could be coaxed into allowing.

"You look more delectable in your bath than you did in the creek Lauren, but then you were wearing unsuitable clothing for a dip in the water," he teased.

"Keep in mind that I do not require rescuing from my bath, so keep your distance," she chided primly and surprisingly found herself smiling at their play, enjoying his attention.

"I could offer to scrub your back."

She turned her head to make sure that he stayed at the washstand. "See to yourself my lord, Ellie will be returning shortly."

"There are far too many servants about. Should I fire the lot of them and keep you all to myself," he scowled.

"I already went through that scenario. We would soon have calloused hands and bent backs from performing all the chores that need to be done in this great house. Thus Devlin, I suggest that you will have to suffer the inconvenience of a busy household."

"I bow to your experienced knowledge, wife," he agreed as he turned and removed his shirt to wash and shave.

The broad back rippled with muscles drawing Lauren's soft gaze that she quickly averted when Ellie returned to the room.

"Milord," the old maid gasped at viewing her employer's undress. "I didn't expect to find you here."

"Be about your duties Mrs. Butterfield. I'll be finished soon enough," he reasoned, lathering his face.

Ellie grumbled under her breath something about the vast display of skin to be found about the old manse and held the towel so Lauren could exit the tub. Devlin watched through the mirror's reflection as his water nymph rose gracefully from the tub to be enfolded in the large towel. Her skin glistened as the water ran down her slim legs. This was the most of Lauren's form that he had seen to date, and he was held spellbound at her unclothed beauty.

From what he could see beyond the held towel, her breasts were high and well-formed, her waist naturally narrow. He was pleased that he was correct in his assumption that she did not require the tight cinching of a corset that some girls were forced to attain through artificial means, nor did she have the exaggerated wasp-like shape women were left with from years of abuse to their natural form. Her hair was a thick mass that naturally curled down her shoulders when Ellie slipped a towel over the wet locks and gave assistance to get the girl from the slippery tub.

Lauren stood on a drying mat placed on the floor as Ellie towelled her mistress with a soft cloth to remove any dampness. With razor poised and ready, Devlin gruffly gave himself a mental shake. Pulling his gaze from the image in the mirror, he chided himself to be more mindful of what he was doing. He had no desire to slit his own throat with the sharp blade.

Lauren and Devlin were dressed and at the bottom of the grand staircase to greet their descending guests in their best finery.

Elegant gowns, and gentlemen in tails, mingled on the main level of the house forming groups to discuss the fabulous days past. The fine horsemanship of some during the hunt, to the skill of the Huntsman and the Camber hounds. The topics ranged from the difficulty of the course and the enjoyment of the jumps and barriers, as all agreed, it was an excellent challenge. They quieted as Lauren stood on a step in the hall and rang a small bell to gain the attention of all.

"Master Huntsman of Camber Hall," she called out. "I bid you attend sir." The summoned one came to stand before her. "As one of the fallen in the grand sport of riding to the hounds, not to mention that my rather dampening position was witnessed by all present as they passed, it has been conveyed to me that I owe you a bottle of Barwick estates finest wines." She paused for effect and looked around at the guests, who were amused by the comments about her afternoon mishap. "You could say that I go to great depths to offer you an excellent choice of our best bottle." the guests laughed at her quip, "Devlin assures me that this dusty bottle I now present to you, in all humility, is highly rated." Applause followed her short speech, and she joined the laughter as she handed over the bottle.

The Master, with great aplomb, replied, "I must admit Madam, that you do go to great lengths to purvey your vintage, and you have my deepest thanks."

Through a network of motions from the staff, the musicians started playing in the ballroom. The music wafted throughout the house as the guests made their way along the wide side corridors to the back of the castle. They stood along the edges of the dance floor as Devlin and Lauren entered last, moving to the middle of the large room to stand facing each other.

Lauren had chosen to wear a dark blue off-the-shoulder dress with embellishments of tan lace forming pointed petals from her waist onto the top of her skirt. A wider lace of the same colour flowed around the dress on the lower three quarters, ending in a lace flounce that swept the floor. Devlin was resplendent in a formal, stiff white shirt with a black jacket and trousers. He bowed to his lady as Lauren replied with a deep curtsy and stepped into his waiting arms. The musicians picked up a lively waltz that had them gaily twirling about the room. When Marian and Trevor began to dance, the signal was sent that saw the floor filled with couples who joined the motion of the music.

Devlin smiled into Lauren's upturned face and complimented her. "You have outdone yourself these past few days. Your grace and execution of seeing everything run smoothly went without flaw, and I congratulate you on a job very well done."

"I will admit that it was enjoyable, and most of the credit will have to go to the extremely capable staff you hired who rescued me from any errors I would have made. However, I must say that in just three event-filled days, I'm fairly exhausted from the late nights and busy schedule. I seem to prefer the quiet country life we lead and long to put my feet up on a stool and just sit," Lauren laughed. "Does that make me sound like an aged dowager?"

"Should you age like my mother, then I look forward to years of amusement and a touch of alcohol in our future. Then perhaps the staff will have to take on more of your responsibilities," he teased.

"I swear your mother could be well into her cups and still perform these duties impeccably and not give a moments thought to whether her opinion was right or wrong and do so with ease."

Devlin laughed, "Regardless of whether her opinion is correct or not, she wouldn't give a whit."

"I love your family," she stated without thinking.

Devlin stopped himself on the precipice from what, surprisingly, had almost blurted from his mouth. Did he truly love her? It was what he had nearly said as he gazed at her warm, incredibly blue eyes that looked at him with trusting simplicity. He would have to ponder on his musing and consider if love could arrive so suddenly and with such ease.

The dance ended as they spied Lord Ferndale, making his way toward them to claim Lauren for the following musical number.

"Go dance with your mother," she murmured to Devlin as Lord Ferndale accepted her proffered hand.

* * *

Last-minute refreshments were handed to the departing guests as the waning morning saw many thanks and congratulations on a successful hunting party. Calls were extended for future visits, and promises were made and accepted.

Lauren felt a weight of sadness clutch her heart as the dowager and her family descended the steps and made their way to the waiting coach. The events of the past few days had renewed a kindred sense of belonging that she had longed for. Lauren struggled to hold back tears as they hugged and kissed their farewells.

"We won't be gone for long," Marian advised. "The distance between our estates is not so far to travel that we cannot visit more often. The children were beside themselves that they were not allowed to come this time, and Devlin has invited all of us to return at the end of October."

Trevor looked into her teary eyes and hugged her close, whispering into her ear so only she could hear, "Treat his heart well Lauren. You may think of him as invincible, but like all Cavanaugh men, we care deeply for what is ours."

The Dowager Countess Diana Cavanaugh patted Lauren's hand in farewell and drew herself to her most regal height to address the driver before accepting Devlin's assistance into the coach. "Frederick," she stated emphatically. At the first rut that sends us careening into each other, you will find yourself in the carriage, and I will take over driving us home! Is that clear?" She sniffed her nose into the air and gave a disgruntled snort.

The chastised coachman lowered himself on his high seat to make as small a target as possible, in the event that her ladyship chose to berate him further. "Yes Ma'am," he proclaimed, not for a minute thinking that she spoke in jest.

# *Chapter Eleven*

Dead trees, with their branches reaching like gnarled fingers to the dull overcast sky, occasionally broke off an appendage as the passing coach lurched along the dusty lane. The overgrowth of yews obscured the lower portion of the manor house. Sticky tendrils of the English vine-covered windows hung unattended as if seeking to return to ground from the protruding sills.

Inside the shaded estate of Agnes Etherington, the aged crone sat in her mansion like a spider in her web. The imposing figure contemplated her newly arrived son as he lounged in the chair before her. His left leg, slung over the worn armrest, moved in a mesmerizing back and forward motion as a glass of whiskey hung loosely from his long-nailed fingers.

"Margaret has been unsuccessful in her endeavour to lure Barwick into her bed though I swear a man would be an unmitigated fool to believe her claims of virginal ravishment once the deed was done," the old woman complained.

John Marlow assessed the familiar evil menace that shone in her narrowed grey eyes. He observed the lined face of his mother, which had the look of crushed leather. The visage displayed more deeply lined wrinkles instead of smooth flesh.

"I hear Margaret had two confrontations with Lauren Berwyke in London and came out poorly in both," he recalled. "It appears that in the short time Lauren has been in England, the little mouse has the backing of the Cavanaugh family who accepted her without reserve. Because of that, the elite has given her their heartfelt approval."

"So she's a Cavanaugh now. It makes no difference whether she hails as Berwyke or her married name. She will suit our plans just fine. There was always the possibility for Lauren to return, so instead of Margaret wheedling her way into Barwick's world and hoping that the girl would stay in France, we will have to change our strategy. One way or another, the Barwick estate and the title it holds will be ours. Where we failed with Elizabeth and Margaret, we must succeed now, especially since the value has increased immeasurably with Cavanaugh's wealth."

"What are you going to do with Margaret, and her mother, your plump unhappy niece?" he snidely added.

"Margaret serves no purpose to me now. She's as much of a disappointment to me as Fiona. When I think of all the time I wasted arranging for that one to marry Edwards and take over his estate, there she is, still under his control. The only enjoyment I receive from that situation is that Edwards is completely miserable with his wife and daughter." She drummed her long crooked fingers on the table. "Margaret arrived here yesterday stating that she missed my company and longed for a visit. She still wants to prove her worth and that she can have Barwick, but he is lost to her."

The incessant drumming of her fingers continued. "Edwards holdings are forfeit to us, so our only hope is that we are victorious with Barwick. We are spending far too much money to keep up the pretense of wealth. You are not helping the situation with your wild lifestyle in London. The money from Dougal Etherington is dwindling, and there are no suitable rich widowers I can find for myself to wed."

Marlow glanced up at his mother, assessing her worth. She may think that she was still capable of luring a man to her bed, but that possibility he decided, had long ago waned.

"We must get to Lauren and convince the brat that I am a loving Grandmother," she plotted.

"And how do you intend to talk her into believing that?" he scoffed. "Were you not in a fit of rage after Phillip died, and you couldn't snatch her then?"

"She was a child. I'm quite capable of talking her into doubting her memory."

"I believe you can Mother, just like you talked your way into marrying all your husbands and then played the grieving widow to the magistrate at their untimely deaths."

"You could have done a better job of finding a wife to thicken the pot as well." Agnes squinted her watery old eyes at her son. "No woman of any worth will have you with the reputation you have garnered. Know you this, my fine offspring, Barwick's land must remain prosperous after we dispatch him, or we will rue the day when we have nothing."

***

The house was dark and quiet. Only a skittering of mice could be heard in the walls as they went in search of sustenance in the form of the bugs feasting on decaying wood. John Marlow skulked down the hall to his cousin's door, the tender, plump form of Margaret Edwards. He chuckled as he thought of the moments to come. Stealthily his nails brushed against the wood as he reached for the handle opening her door. Without making a sound, he tread into her chambers, noting the reclining ample form in the bed. She lay on the far side facing him, her wide hips rising below the coverings, her breath coming slow and steady.

Sensing his presence, her eyes opened. A feral gleam showed, and a sensual smile beckoned as she rose onto her knees. Her long ripe breasts swung like bells as she crawled naked across the bed to come to him. Purring like a lazy cat, she reached beneath his robe to grasp his flaccid penis. John grasped a handful of her tangled blond hair in his fist and painfully pulled her head back.

"Ever eager my dove," he growled as his erection rose at the hurt he was causing her. "Then take this, take all of it." he pushed his erect member into her waiting mouth as she pulled and sucked at his cock.

His tight grip on her hair rocked her head in a rhythmic motion. He shut his eyes and pictured in her stead the finer features of Lauren Berwyke, so like Elizabeth, who had slipped through his fingers long ago. Margaret pulled and pinched at her nipples until they formed elongated peaks. Reaching between her legs, she thrust her fingers into her dripping cavern, stroking the wet labia as John laughed.

"You're an impatient slut aren't you."

He flipped her onto her stomach and roughly pulled her back against him, kneading her round full rump. Lifting her towards him, he spread her wide before pummelling into her without mercy, pounding into the yielding wet flesh. Margaret's hands grasped handfuls of the coverlet as his invasion tore into her. Tiny stinging rips in the soft flesh mounted her excitement as the nicks of pain proved his need for her. She was flipped onto her back so he could squeeze and pinch at her full breasts, moulding them like soft clay. She lifted her legs so her heels rested on his shoulders, and she felt the maximum ramming force of his entry as his scrotum, slung low like those of a well-used and aged bull, slapped against her ass with each thrust.

Her breath was expelled in grunts with each harsh pounding and thrust of his hips. He gripped her white throat with his hand, squeezing with just enough force so she could not get a full breath of air. As her world spun and stars blinked behind her closed eyes, she climaxed in pulsating rhythms, tightening the walls that held his organ in place with violent spasms. He emptied himself into her gaping yaw, pausing his strokes after the shudders of his ejaculation ceased.

"Your Lord Barwick wouldn't know how to handle you." he wheezed from the strain of his spent play. "In his most vivid imagination, he would not understand what you want, Bitch," John smirked at the angry glare in her eyes. "He thinks all of womanhood as being good and kind," he sneered, lowering his face inches from hers as she smelled the stale cigar smoke-laden breath emitted from his open mouth. His tongue, stained brown, licked along her face from chin to brow, leaving behind his stench on her pale skin, marking her as his.

"You know that I am good. Just not in the way he believes a woman should be good," she purred confidently. "When I have him, I will still have you."

"Content yourself with me, Margaret," he chided cruelly, straightening himself. "He won't set aside his wife for the likes of you. When we have Barwick's wealth, I will keep you tied to a bed and use you at will."

"You know I will do whatever you ask, so long as you spend enough coin to spoil me."

"I've spent enough on you." he balked

"You've spent enough *in* me," she jeered.

"I most likely have, and there is plenty more to come, my little whore." He placed the middle finger of his hand against his thumb and cruelly flicked her exposed, pointing nipple.

Margaret's mouth opened in surprise as her hand raised to hold the smarting breast. Instead of crying out in pain, she brought her pink tongue out to curl around her lips, a seductive smile lifting the corners of her mouth. She showed him her enjoyment of the pain he inflicted in the sparkle of her eyes.

He pulled himself out of her and folded the robe around his paunchy middle, tying the belt loosely. Staring down at her, she yielded the sight of her bruised and swollen womanhood to his view as she lay with her legs spread wide, open and exposed. She was assured that she could give him what he wanted, for she desired the same treatment of master and slave. Dominant and submissive. Of particular exquisite torture were those times when they had gone too far, and she had to conceal the injuries from her mother.

"Kiss me before you leave," she taunted.

John sneered at her with contempt, having no further use for her at the moment. "Why on earth would I do that?"

Turning, he strolled out the door, erasing her from his mind as he left the room.

* * *

Agnes Etherington dressed carefully for the meeting she had set herself to. All her plans were dependent on the visit she would have as she faced Lauren Cavanaugh for the first time in years. She adjusted the veil on her black bonnet and made her way to the coach, noting with disgust the threadbare sleeve of her coachman, as he assisted her into the carriage.

Winslow approached Lauren as she stood in her studio dressed in a simple gown that was covered by a paint-stained smock. The light was perfect as she blended the oil colours. Before her, she confidently applied crossing brush strokes to the top corners of a white canvas to begin a large painting she planned to hang in the hallway in due course. There was a definite dearth of paintings of ancestors displayed as Phillip had sold those that once hung on the walls. Though why anyone not related would have purchased her ancestors' images, Lauren was unsure.

"Lady Barwick, a Mrs. Etherington has come to see you."

Lauren turned wide eyes to the butler, the brush held still in mid-stroke, leaving a solid splotch of colour where blending was required.

"Oh?" she squeaked, images forming quickly of her step-grandmother and the turmoil they instantly created.

"She is in the parlour Madam," he informed, noting her pallor.

"Where is Lord Barwick?" she questioned.

"He has gone with James McCormack and should return later this afternoon."

Lauren stared at the brush in her hand. The enjoyment she had looked forward to, spending quiet moments with her imagination and paint, was rapidly being replaced with another matter. She tossed the brush into an open jar of turpentine. Removing the smock to hang on the back of a chair, she followed Winslow down to the parlour. Before entering, she glanced toward the butler to see his concerned perusal as he noted her unease. She brushed at her skirt and smoothed her hair, not so concerned about her appearance, as to extend the moments before the meeting. Drawing a deep breath and squaring her shoulders, she entered.

Lauren felt a trickling jolt of fear as the same narrow watery eyes she remembered raised from the intense perusal of a costly Spode candy dish to fix on her. She was exactly as Lauren remembered. The slim build, dressed in black, the way she held her head high. Her thin lips were pursed, her nose tilted upwards as if she could detect an off smell. She still carried her cane with the head of a raven as its handle. The dead glass eyes remained unseeing.

Lauren stood grounded to her spot, momentarily unable to move forward or run from the room. She hoped the trembling that seized her could not be detected. She was a grown woman in her own home. She stiffened her spine, and on wobbly legs, forced herself forward. She struggled mightily to show an outward calm she did not feel at the sight of the long-feared Agnes Etherington.

Agnes noted in surprise that the girl wore a simple gown, that any middle-class drudge could have owned. Certainly, she had no taste in dressing herself, or Barwick wasn't as generous as she had assumed. Agnes had decided that her servants could go about in threadbare clothes to save a few coins, but her own wardrobe was of the finest quality. She noted how Lauren had changed in other ways over the past few years. No longer was a frightened scraggly child in front of her but a woman who would turn any man's head with her delicate features. She held herself with more confidence than Agnes was willing to see in the chit.

Agnes felt the familiar anger as she looked at her. Lauren possessed the estate she had long coveted for her own. With a will born on the wings of deception, Agnes crushed an overt violent urge to physically strike the girl. To have Lauren show due respect as a younger member of her family, she noted with a growing rage that the young girl didn't honour her with a curtsy.

The matron would not have considered the fact that she was the commoner and Lauren, the lady of the manse, who possessed the title that went along with it. With a firm grasp on her temper, Agnes overpowered her desire to see the girl grovelling before her. She owned all that Agnes coveted, and to that end, a play must be enacted.

"My darling Lauren," she gestured, the words like bile in her mouth. "I am so pleased to see you again after all these lonely years when I was so concerned about your welfare. I did not know where you had gone or even if you would return, and my poor old heart wept for you."

Lauren was startled. "You will excuse me, Madam, that I remember our last meeting quite differently. I believe you said you never wanted to see me again."

"Dear heart, you must be mistaken," she wheedled. "You are the only link I have to your sweet mother, who was my treasured stepdaughter. Why, she was part of my family, and I knew a joy beyond compare when I married your grandfather Dougal. I realized then the close bond one could have with a daughter, after I only had the one child for so many years, and he a lad. Perhaps your memory plays on you."

Agnes motioned for the girl to sit beside her. Instead, Lauren moved to a seat facing the woman, and again, Agnes felt the snub of the girl to sit some distance away. She continued her ploy as Lauren rested her hands on her knees to still their shaking,

"I was devastated when we lost our beautiful Elizabeth. It was merely my horrible grief that you have mistaken for anger. After all, you were little more than a babe before I stopped calling on Phillip. I couldn't bear the thought of being here," she gestured with her hand to encompass the room, "in this house, where my beloved daughter died."

Astonished at Agnes's recollection of past events, Lauren was unmoved by her words. "I have very few memories of you, Mrs. Etherington, and those that I do, are not pleasant to me."

This was not the tact the aged matron was hoping for. To her mind, the girl was being obstinate and unreasonable in accepting her impressions of the jaded truth. "Surely you must realize how heartbroken I was when your mother died. Don't blame my upset as anger if you heard me raise a voice to your father. I despaired so at her passing, but now I have you, and it would please me greatly if you would allow me moments to call on you, to prove the love that was buried when your mother left us, or perhaps you would like to visit me in my home."

She could tell by the stiff way Lauren held herself that her ploy was failing. "Allow me in my old age to show you how much Elizabeth meant to me." she mewled, adding for the girl what she herself would consider a significant incentive. "You do know, that when I am gone, all the jewellery that once belonged to Dougal's first wife will be bequeathed to you in my will. It is a most impressive collection."

Lauren was not swayed by the offering, nor the presence of this interloper. She stood to direct the woman from the house, putting an end to the discussion. Lauren was unnerved by Agnes' foreboding presence and the memories invoked. As she walked to the front door on trembling legs, a reluctant Agnes had no choice but to follow.

Hurrying steps from the back of the house heralded a flustered Ellie as she propelled herself with haste to the entry. Her elbows swinging, head bent, and skirt swishing behind her, she looked like a bull in the midst of a charge. Before Ellie's angry glare and forward motion launched into a female geriatric rumble, Lauren directed her attention back to her step-grandmother. She firmly ushered her out the door opened by Winslow, whom Lauren realized, had stationed himself nearby after noting her upset at the summons.

"Thank you for coming to see me today Madam. I will consider your request," she addressed formally, giving no hint of warmth to her proclamation.

No further promises were made as Agnes turned withering eyes at the advancing Ellie Butterfield. That little woman had often stood in her way when she would have directed her wrath at the child instead of the father.

With a regal bow of her head, she left with her words hanging in the air like the gurgling mucus dripping down the back of her throat. "I do hope you will give careful consideration to my words dear Lauren. After all, I am all you have left of your family."

When Winslow firmly closed the door, Lauren released an audible sigh and held a hand to her quivering stomach.

Ellie was bristling like a spiny hedgehog. "I came running as soon as I heard that old witch was on the premises. That podsnappery old windbag! What was she snooping around here for?"

She offered to have a loving relationship with me," Lauren ventured.

"The woman wouldn't know the meaning of it! You would be wise to give that determined old crow a wide path. She assumes airs she has no claim to, and that should include anything to do with you. I know how you feel about Lord Barwick's fine family. Stay close to them and forsake any connection you have to Agnes Etherington and her evil whelp."

"Calm yourself, Ellie. You are more family to me than the people who married my grandfather."

"Yes, I am. You're not kruger-spoofing. That old woman won't be selling me a dog with any of her practised speeches."

Lauren gave her a queer look, not quite sure what she meant by those particular phrases but assumed it meant that Lauren was speaking the truth and Ellie wouldn't be accepting any lies. "I appreciate your arrival when you heard who I was entertaining in the parlour. I'm sure your presence hastened her on her way." She smiled kindly at the older woman adding, "The way you flew up here, I feared for her safety."

Standing stoically at the door to ensure he heard the carriage pass down the gravelled lane, Lauren turned to Winslow and placed a hand on his arm. She was comforted by the fact that he had remained near. "Thank you, Winslow, for staying close. I have terrible memories of my mother's step-family. That you did not leave me alone with her was most appreciated."

Winslow cleared his throat in acknowledgement of her kind words. "Anytime I may be of service my lady, you can depend upon my aid."

The disquiet Lauren felt by the visit continued. It brought to mind images long forgotten. She remembered being shaken and struck. Of hands reaching for her as she huddled in tight dark spaces hoping to hide from the angry wails and screeches echoing in empty rooms and of Ellie, pulling her to safety and carrying her away to the far end of gloomy halls.

The carriage carrying Agnes Etherington from the opulent castle with lush green manicured lawns and carefully tended gardens fairly rocked with the rage emanating from the departing figure.

What she had seen in the castle had mesmerized her greedy thoughts of riches beyond the wealth she had garnered from all of her past husbands. She was not foolish enough to believe that the meeting had gone as well as she had hoped. Ellie Butterfield was still watching over Lauren and had puffed her way towards them at the end. She had interfered more than enough times before, and here she was again, flapping her feathers like a mother hen over her chick.

Agnes did not consider herself a patient woman. However, in this instance, patience would have to be considered if her plans were to do away with Barwick and have her son force the wench into marriage. From what she had seen, she estimated that the estate was worth considerably more than she had imagined. It brought to mind that when the land held but a paltry amount of useable coin under Phillip's guidance, there was no comparison to today's increased riches, sitting there, waiting to be taken. She voraciously calculated the wealth of the place. Riches far beyond her imagination and the power she could influence with it. They would have the title, and then the elite of London society would be forced to accept them.

Agnes cackled in the confines of the coach. To see lords and ladies pressured to include them in their midst would be a treat indeed. If not for all she had worked towards with devious plots and meticulous planning, she and her brat would still be living in the brothel where she had given birth to him in squalid, filthy conditions. No face would come to mind of which one of the sick, twisted dregs of society who had paid for the use and abuse of her body had fathered the boy. He had proven his worth as a child, gaining them additional coins for their survival by entertaining men whose inclination leaned towards depravity of the young, to learning the art of pickpocketing. He grew up as mean and evil as his matron. Plotting for himself and what he could get had served them both well.

Agnes had escaped the slums by first proving her worth to a dumpy cruel lord, who had taken her for his plaything. After stealing what she could from him, he had been dispatched in a rubbish-strewn alley by a trusted friend. The money then had been used to set herself and John into a comfortable home in a small town where she began to scout the local business owners for her next prey. A recently widowed merchant had been deep in grief when she found him and offered her sympathy, as well as spread legs to forget his pain. After a lengthy illness, caused by the arsenic she had included in his nightly tipple, he had died in agony. She sold his business from under his children and moved to a better, larger house in another town. This continued with three more husbands until she found the elder Dougal Etherington. By then, her beauty had begun to fade, and she became a loving companion and caring stepmother to his daughter Elizabeth.

It wasn't long afterwards that Dougal was taken with a gnarling pain in his abdomen. This time it was a ruptured appendix and not the poisonous brew she usually delivered to her spouse. Dougal was in the process of establishing investments that would see their wealth grow exponentially, so his value as a living husband was still in vogue. Unable to conduct business, even though she had spent hours administering to him to keep him alive, it was obvious that he would die before the contracts were negotiated and signed. He suffered in abject misery, and his last words were issued in delirium as he calmed, reached out his hand as though he was taking hold of an unseen presence and peacefully called out his first wife's name.

Agnes spent little time worrying about an afterlife and who she would find waiting for her on the other side. She cast about for another scheme to enrich herself and set her plans on the nearby Barwick estate. To her dismay, she discovered John had ideas of his own for the virgin Elizabeth. Agnes quickly broached a marriage contract with Phillip Berwyke to ease him in his senior years and sent the girl properly into her marriage with the Lord of Barwick Castle. She nearly pulled her hair out of her head when Elizabeth followed her father to the grave shortly after giving birth to a progeny of Phillip.

Plans, laid and destroyed nearly two decades ago, had a way of coming to roost like an errant crow set off course by a weathered gale. One way or another, Agnes schemed, she would achieve her goal.

# *Chapter Twelve*

Devlin returned to the castle later that afternoon to a hovering and still bristling Ellie Butterfield as she attended Lauren. He could immediately see the sparks flashing in the older woman's eyes as she railed against a visitor who had arrived unannounced.

Milord, you must umble-cum-stumble, and I won't beat about the bushes in the telling. That evil old witch came here on more occasions than I can recall to bubble around the old lord. No sir, the wickedness of that crone pours out of her. She would have laid her evil hands on Lauren given half a chance."

"Ellie, when you get worked up like this, no one can understand you," Lauren tried to assure her. "Everything is fine now. We have Winslow and the footmen here and are well protected. Devlin is home, so we are safe."

I don't trust them, my lord." Ellie fairly snarled. "They're up to no good, not either of them. I never trusted the old bat and her wicked offspring and would advise you not to as well."

Devlin felt like he had walked into a powder keg and was totally confused. "Whom are we referring to?" he questioned, trying to get the story straight in his head.

"None other than Agnes Etherington and John Marlow," Ellie squawked. "She came professing kinship to Lauren and was simpering on about undying love for the girl. I saw the love she had for her on more than one occasion when the old Lord was in a drunken stupor. She'd a' soon belt the girl as she was wanting to beat the old lord. Instead, she flayed him with her tongue, calling him all sorts of foulness while I hid Lauren away and out of her reach. They be a skilamalinkin bunch with a host of secret shady doin's."

"Soothe your feathers, Ellie," Lauren gently chided. "It's over. She's gone and hopefully won't return." She placed a comforting arm around Ellie's shoulders and led her to the door. "Go get yourself a nice cup of tea, and rest assured that we are safe here."

Ellie glared at Lauren, and with a shake of her old head, reached a hand to caress her cheek. "You're a darling sweet girl Lauren. I'll go and trust the master here to take care of you, but it doesn't mean I'll be forgiving anyone, and stop my worrying." She shuffled off to the back of the house, her feet softly echoing down the hall.

"Perhaps she truly wants a relationship with me," Lauren explained after Devlin questioned the details of the visit. "Though I have awful memories of her, cannot people change? She is the only link to my grandfather."

"By marriage," Devlin avowed.

"Yes, but your family is related to me by marriage, and I adore them."

"I daresay my family has never acted in any fashion that it seems your step-grandmother is accustomed to."

"No," she avowed, "not at all. I can't imagine them doing so."

"I bid you to take care then Lauren," he said, handing her a small glass of a strong brew noting a slight shake to her hand as she accepted the cordial.

"I will my lord. I find I'm still a bit upset by the visit myself though I tried my best not to show it to Ellie. The memories it evoked are not at all pleasant."

Devlin decided that word would be passed to the gardeners and burly outside stable hands to be aware of the comings and goings of visitors to the castle when he was not in attendance. He trusted that Winslow had already made mention to the footmen. Word quickly spread that the mistress had been affected by the confrontation, to be on guard, and on hand, the next time company came to call.

***

The hour grew late, and the house settled into sleep as the moon cast its shadow to pass over the land. Quiet and darkness filled the empty corridors, and an owl could be heard softly hooting into the night.

In Lauren's mind, a chill fog rose from a nearby swamp, covering the house with its gloom. The moon's pale light shone through the barren branches of twisted and gnarled trees. Bats, with outstretched leather wings, flapped and squeaked their echoing calls as they hunted the insects for their midnight meal.

A horse appeared in the distance, starting as a vague dark shadow in the mist as he drew ever closer. His pounding hooves threw up clods of earth as he dug into the ground pushing with might to reach where she stood, alone and shivering with nothing to protect herself. Her gossamer flowing nightgown shone like a beacon in the swirling mist, easily pinpointing her location. The rider, cloaked in a black flowing cape, lifted from the rearing horse that pawed the air to join the flight of the nocturnal mammals with a banshee cry. He swooped to the top of the castle and crouched there like an ancient evil gargoyle, waiting, glaring at her with shining, hollow eyes. The beast slithered to the edge of the eaves and launched himself at her as she turned to run with all she possessed. She cried out and panicked as claw-like hands reached out to pull at her hair and her clothing. She was desperate to keep her feet moving as quickly as she could, so the monster would not cover her with its evil presence. With a scream torn from her throat, she felt herself falling into a deep dark void as hands clutched at her arms, holding them in an iron grasp.

"Lauren! Lauren!" Devlin pulled her into his arms to wake his screaming wife.

Her eyes flew open, wild and frightened. She could still feel the heat of the beast's breath on her back as she quickly scanned the room for it. With a cry of relief, she threw her arms around Devlin's neck and held him close. He could feel the trembling of her body as he held her.

"It's only a dream. You're safe," he gently murmured.

"Don't let me go," she cried, weeping softly against his chest.

He held her tightly, this gentle woman who lay in his arms with quiet sobs. He rubbed her slender bare back feeling its smooth texture until her crying ceased. "Will you go back to sleep now?" he lifted her chin and wiped the tears away with the sleeve of his robe.

She worried at the thought of him leaving her in the empty dark room. Fear drew her brows apart as her eyes opened wide. She didn't want to be alone, afraid, unwanted. She needed to feel his arms around her. Someone to hold onto and release all her real and imagined horrors to.

"Don't leave me alone," she begged him.

Devlin looked into the frightened tear-filled eyes of his wife, so young and tender. He considered her as she had been as a little girl, ignored and unwanted by the one man who should have stood against the world for her and offered her his protection. He felt a need to be her shield against her fears, a warrior to fight for the value of her love and her life.

Lifting her into his arms, he carried her into his room. Her arms stayed clasped around his neck. "Your bed is too small for the both of us. I offer mine so I can stay with you. Allay your concerns Lauren, I only wish to hold you this night and protect you from the demons of your nightmare."

He lowered her into his bed and was mildly surprised when she offered no resistance but curled into a tight ball. Deciding he'd be wise to leave his robe on, he lifted the blankets over them and rested his chest against her back, offering her his warmth. Moulding his legs to hers, he covered her with his arm.

She felt warm and secure in his muscular embrace. She listened to his deep, steady breathing as she felt the rise and fall of his chest, warm and comforting against her bare back. His arm was a solid anchor to hang onto.

She had never slept with another body, let alone one so large and imposing. The close contact was reassuring, and she felt snug in the shelter of his arms. The terrors she had felt slowly melted away as her eyes shut, and she drifted into a dreamless sleep.

Devlin attempted to reclaim that same slumber, but the slight figure of his delectable wife curled in his arms was a distraction he could not drag his mind from. He had been many months without a woman, and her soft form was affecting him though he tried only to consider her care, and not his desires. His robe was open where her back touched his chest, and he could feel the even breath fill her lungs and then exhale as she slept. Her soft round breasts lay but the thickness of her satin nightgown from his hands and her little bottom fit neatly against his stomach. His thoughts drifted down her body and how his hand would feel to discover the warmth he would find there.

Mentally shaking his head and turning his mind elsewhere, he forced himself with a strong will to consider other less pleasurable pursuits, like crop rotation or having Daniyal reshod, but then he thought of the breeding of Daniyal to Willow and the Anglo Arabians they would produce which brought him full circle to his own breeding and the children he and Lauren would produce. Devlin groaned in despair. He wasn't an animal, he scowled. Could he not just hold in his arms, for a few hours, the woman who consumed his thoughts throughout the day and his dreams at night? He heard her murmur in her sleep as her breathing deepened, and he pulled her closer. He enjoyed the feel of her in his arms and vowed that he would do all in his power to have her in his bed sooner, rather than later, in a more pleasing way than to protect her from her dreams.

Had he not proven himself to be trustworthy these past months? No other woman caught his eye, nor did he desire any other. Since the moment they first danced and he held her in his arms, she had been what he craved. His misfortune in his quest to have her, had forced this damnable wedge between them. He hoped it would soon be resolved, and she would come to him before he, in smouldering frustration, broached the subject again, which only irked her temper.

With her snuggled against him, he willed himself to relax and take what pleasure he could in the moment. She was in his bed now, and perhaps she soon would be again in a more wifely fashion.

As the shadows lengthened in the fields and forests, he finally found the succour of sleep as his mind cleared and he drifted into slumber.

The next morning in the still-dark room, Lauren opened languid, sleepy eyes and momentarily wondered where she was. Her head lay on Devlin's shoulder, and when she lifted her head to search his face, she found his intense green eyes already upon her. She blushed a deep scarlet realizing that she had turned to him in her sleep and that her arm rested on his furred chest. Her knee was drawn and rested intimately against his hips, and there was a definite bulge under the robe that pressed against her thigh. When she attempted to pull away, his arm tightened to hold her in place.

"Good morning Lauren. I often wondered if having you in my bed would be so enjoyable." he continued with an erstwhile gleam in his eye, "I find that indeed it is. I can only hope for more moments like this one and perhaps shared intimacies."

Before Lauren could reply, a yelp of fear sounded from the adjoining room. "Aiyeeee, my lord, come quick! They've taken her! Lauren, my girl, where have you gone?" Not waiting for a response, a white-faced Ellie dashed into Devlin's room and halted abruptly.

"I beg your pardon!" she squeaked, noting the embraced couple. "Master Barwick, um, I had no idea. I, uh, excuse me." Ellie didn't know where to look or what to do. "Shall I fetch your robe Lauren?" she finally squeaked out the question.

Lauren grudgingly rose from the snug haven of Devlin's embrace as he released her. She ushered the confused woman into her room, giving him a full display of her very feminine curves in the clinging gown.

"I thought they had skulked into the house to take you." Ellie tried to support her outcry. "I didn't realize your opinion of the lord had changed."

Lauren tried to shush her over loud voice. "It's all right Ellie. I had a bad dream last night and was frightened. Devlin woke me. He took me to his bed and held me throughout the night."

Ellie raised an eyebrow at the statement.

"Really!" Lauren said at the woman's dubious look. "He was a gentleman...and it was nice.

She remembered the sense of security she had felt in his strong arms, the warmth of his body, and the smell of the bed linens that held his masculine scent. Altogether she had to admit that it was an enjoyable night, and one she would be willing to try again, minus the nightmare.

* * *

Devlin invited Lauren to ride with him as he visited the tenants. The estate was divided into acres of land that were rented to the families that had lived for generations in the shadow of Barwick Castle. Lauren was greeted warmly by the people she had known all her life, and the years apart meant little to them as they were reacquainted. They expounded on their good fortune as they shared their bounty with her when they stopped their chores to chat. A glass of wine or ale was offered, or a slice of buttered bread and cheese, all accepted so as not to insult the families. They were eager to show her their improved lot under the new lord.

"Hallow Miss," they commented and would then relive a treasured memory of Lauren from her childhood as she and her pony, Clover, would range the land unsupervised and impervious to propriety. They told Devlin how she would stop and stay for lunch or play with their children, now grown and farming their own parcels of land.

At the Patterson farm, Devlin noted the old man sweating in the heat of the day as he chopped at logs of wood, hacking them into smaller sticks for the winter cordage. Dismounting, he removed his coat, pulled his shirt over his head, and threw it over the saddle.

"Give the axe over Mr. Patterson," he cajoled as he reached for the tool.

"Nay my lord. It's a 'ot day to be sure 'an I wouldna want ta be seein' ya work ta ease my lot."

"Where are your sons?" Devlin questioned, taking the handle from the man's grudging hands.

"Out markin' the rams for castration come the cool weather," he mumbled, casting a quick glance at Lauren. He wondered if she would be upset with the talk of farm life because she had become a fine lady.

Lauren noted his words and smiled at the old farmer. "Keeping only the best, I assume Mr. Patterson?"

"Aye Ma'am, Lord Barwick and Master James' givin' us a right good menterin' on that ta be sure. It's not a hard choice ta make now that we have some fine bloodlines ta choose from."

An aged woman came from the neatly tended cottage wiping her hands on her well-worn apron. "Will ya be comin' down from your horse ta sit a spell with me Mistress? I've a cool glass of milk sittin' in the well."

Dolly Patterson chatted merrily on about how over the past few years, Devlin had arrived and immediately began to improve the lives of the farmers and that he or James continued to visit often to see if any changes needed to be made to continue building on their good fortune.

Lauren sipped the cool milk and watched the play of the rippling muscles on her husband's broad back as he swung the axe and stacked the wood for the old farmer.

Dolly noted the soft gaze of Lady Barwick and smiled, feeling that the lord who had done so much for his people was content in the love of his lady. When they left, each farmer and their wives commented on the attractive couple and considered their good luck after years of toiling in poverty under the old lord.

Devlin was irritated that the Hartford family had lost another couple of sheep to the nighttime marauder, who had boldly come too close for comfort to the animals housed in a field near the farmhouse. Lauren noted a tightening of his jaw as Devlin was advised of the discovery. He took to heart the losses felt by the tenants under his watch and vowed that he and James would do their utmost to see to the culprit's identity and bring him to justice. It was also noted that the Harford family suffered substantially more loss than the other farmers, and Devlin suggested that it might be wise to split their herd and have them graze in neighbouring fields.

The hired watchers had been unable to locate the culprit, so extra lookouts might prove fruitful. The waste was unfathomable as the animals were never taken. Devlin could understand someone trying to feed an impoverished family, but this was just malicious destruction.

Devlin held the Arabian in check when the horse longed to stretch his muscles and eat up the ground in a frustrated gallop. Daniyal tried Devlin's patience as the horse attempted to impress the flashy mare Willow. Under the steady hand of his master, the Arabian pranced a few jarring sidesteps and tossed his head against the bit. Instead of the butt of Devlin's crop on the top of the horse's head, he held the reins in a firm grip, leaned forward in the saddle to whisper calmly in Daniyal's ear and soothed the beast with a soft hand, guiding him with the pressure of his legs. He commiserated with the romantic yearnings of the horse to impress the mare as he felt the same emotion regarding his wife. Devlin eventually led Daniyal to the realization that his displays of prowess would best be suited to the moments when his rider was not present.

Lauren showed a serene composure as she watched both horse and man flaunt their masculine propensity to the accompanying femininity. She was pleased with Devlin's patience and gentle manner in handling the amorous bend of the rowdy horse.

"How are the tenants who were unwilling to put their shoulders to the wheel faring after you and James worked with them?" she questioned. "I have been staying clear of their lands lately and wonder if I should ride over that way to see if I could offer any more help to the wives."

"Most have come around to our way of thinking. At least they are trying. All except the Harrington farm. He has not, and I've rarely seen a more slovenly man. James has been trying without much success to direct him on improving his lot, but so long as he can produce barely enough for their use, he refuses to accept any help which may lead to more work on his part. He has ordered James to stay away."

"It was much the same when my father was lord. I was always afraid to go near their plot of land. Mrs. Harrington refused the few gifts I tried to press into her hand in the village. I believe she was frightened of accepting charity and suffering the wrath of her husband."

"He's obstinate and lifted an axe threatening James when he's tried to help. He is seriously delinquent in his rents, and soon there will be nothing else to do but revoke his lease to the land."

"I wonder what will become of his wife and Penny if he is forced out."

"It's not the ideal situation. If there were a way to help them, I would see them away from him. He's a brute, and I've caught him abusing them on more than one occasion."

"His wife was always very quiet and barely had the nerve to raise her eyes from the ground, even years ago if I recall correctly. I don't know how she has tolerated him."

"I suppose she's learned to be timid, for I fear that it would be her undoing if she voiced any opposition to him. Unfortunately, the law is on his side where his family is concerned."

As they meandered their way through the forest back to the house, they came upon the refreshing pond where Lauren had found Devlin swimming. "Would you like to go for a swim before we return?" he invited.

"I think not, my lord." she answered primly, "the last time I was atop Willow, I didn't enjoy my swim."

# *Chapter Thirteen*

The autumn equinox heralded a temperature drop and increased the foraging of wild animals. Squirrels hopped from branch to branch, searching for nuts and seeds to stow away for their hibernation in leafy nests. The winds blew a little stronger and colder. Soon the gathering flocks of swallows, swifts and nightingales would migrate to southern climes, and the whooper swans and waxwings would arrive for their winter visits.

As Lauren dressed for bed, she contemplated the past twenty-four hours. Waking from the terrible dream to being held in Devlin's strong arms and carried into his bed, where she felt safe and protected, allaying all her fears. The day had been bright and sunny in both weather and mood as she accompanied him on his ride. She had renewed acquaintances and met new tenants who had taken up residence on the empty tracts of land. She had gained more confidence in her riding abilities with Devlin by her side, and he had carefully lifted her down from Willow at their stops and then helped her back into the saddle.

She was fully aware of his hungering gaze as he looked at her, and a molten warmth flowed through her veins at the attention he had bestowed on her throughout the day. She once again counted the blessings on how her life had changed since that day years ago when she had become his wife by a few spoken, barely understood words in a small office. She considered the time spent at the abbey to learn her lessons and where she would no longer have to consider herself an ignorant child. She had an appreciation of the talents she had discovered over the years and the fine clothes she now wore. She felt contentment in the family she was a part of and the kindness shown to her by the Cavanaugh family, especially the humour and dignity of his mother, the dowager.

She was pleased with her life, she realized. She was content with Devlin and the attention he gave her. She was aware that without him, she would have been alone and unable to cope when her father passed. The estate would be an empty ruin, the tenants gone, and the land wasted. Instead, he had forced new life into all around her. The castle was as grand as it had ever been. She was educated and accepted into society, the land was fruitful, and tenants were content. So much depended on one man, Devlin, her husband, mate for life and all of eternity, sealed by vows spoken by a child who had no idea what life would hold.

To that end, she came to the decision. She had no choice but to fulfill her vows and take him fully as her husband. She would freely give what was hers and bend to his will. How she would do so with cool detachment as she had been instructed, she did not know, for she burned where he touched and owed him all that she had. She prayed that her decision was right and that he would continue to forsake all others for her, because she felt her heart would stop beating if he took another.

When Lauren heard Devlin move about his room, she dismissed Ellie for the night. With halting steps, she followed where her heart led, to his door.

"My lord…Devlin," she whispered softly as he turned slowly to find her in the doorway.

He was dressed only in his trousers, having removed his shirt for the night. She noted again the muscular chest and deeply bronzed skin. She understood how he had come by the tanned colouring. He was no fop with soft hands and weak muscles like Lord Emory. Devlin bent his back to help the labours of those in his care as though he were one of them. The daily outdoor hours giving them aid to chop wood, riding Daniyal and sparring with James had produced the rippling muscles of this man of supposed leisure.

Her hair was unbound, softly curling across her shoulders in waves of silken tassels. She wore a diaphanous deep violet nightdress that matched the colour of her shining eyes. Thin straps held the lace that covered her breasts, and a deeper purple ribbon was tied below those mounds as the material flowed in undulating creases to the floor. The material made a slight whispering sound as she floated hesitantly toward him.

Devlin's heart pounded in his chest as he saw her image and watched her progression as she moved. He remained rooted in his spot, considering that she came haltingly like a fawn questing after an apparition, and at the slightest movement, would bolt and be gone.

"I give you what is mine to give my lord, and I bend to your will to become your wife in fact and deed," she purred a soft sigh of seduction.

"I would have waited an eternity for you Lauren," he responded huskily, thankful and amazed that she was here. "You are all that I desire."

He reached for her hair, and lifting it, laid it over her shoulder revealing the soft creamy flesh. His strong hand was gentle, reaching through her hair to pull her face up for a tender, fleeting kiss. Bending to her, their lips met as she moved against him, and he felt the full force of a caressing bombardment of emotion as her breasts touched his chest and she moulded herself to his form.

He brushed the strap of her gown down her arm as his hand followed, feeling the silky smoothness of her skin. His tongue traced a path around her ear and moved down her throat, over her shoulder and traced a weaving path across her breasts as she leaned back against his muscular arm holding her erect. Surely she would swoon from the feelings wafting over her in thrilling waves. Lauren was startled when her gown puddled to the floor at her feet, and she stood before him in all her naked splendour.

"Lauren," he whispered huskily, "You are so beautiful, and I ache for you."

Unnerved and vulnerable, she moved her arms to cover herself. He halted her attempt and lifted her in his arms to carry her to the bed, placing her on its covers. The mattress dipped to his weight as Devlin joined her. He continued his kisses until he felt her relax. Her fingers reached into the long hair at the back of his head, grasping him to her as he suckled and traced with his tongue over the pink crests of her breasts, pulling with his mouth and teasing into hard peaks her softness. His hands cupped their fullness, kneading them gently.

He moved lower, tracing kisses along her ribs, her soft flat belly reaching with his cool fingers to touch her most intimate place, the hot slickness between her legs. Lauren gasped in lustful surprise as his fingers entered her ever so smoothly. She wanted to let loose the wild urges she felt coursing through her. She felt desire and desired. Where he touched, she burned. But in the back of her head rose the warnings of the religious order.

'*Be a lady in all manner, especially during the intimate moments with your spouse.*' Oh, how was it possible?

'*Enter into the duties reluctantly.*' His touch was thrilling.

'*Give little, give seldom, give grudgingly*. He is a master at this game, she thought.

'*Unbridled passion is a dangerous thing, and must be avoided at all costs.*'

The words pounded into her brain though she tried to shut them out.

Lauren was aghast as she realized her bottom was quivering with his touch. She forced herself to remain still, but the heat, the touch, the thrill, everything he was doing to her with his magical lips and fingers was beyond anything she had henceforth experienced.

The words kept a static drumbeat in her brain.

The nuns had taught her to be respectable.

To be an honour to her husband.

Perhaps they were right, and she had to control herself.

Good Heavens! What would he think of her?

Devlin was absorbed in exploring the ravishing seductress beneath him. She was made for love, his love. Her body was a perfect temple he wished to worship at. Her skin was as smooth as the silk gowns she wore, soft and pliant beneath his questing hand and mouth.

Discarding his trousers, he moved her legs, bending her knees and drawing them aside as he positioned himself above her and between her thighs. Entering, he eased into her tightness in slow progression as she opened to him, feeling the warmth and smoothness of her innermost heat as the tight walls constricted and released around him. Little by little, he entered her fully, taking his sweet torturous time, enjoying the intimacy of the moment. He felt the barrier of her maidenhead and whispered words of love and seduction into her ear before rendering the obstacle in his path.

Lauren released a cry of pain that was covered by his mouth as he kissed her deeply, reaching into her mouth and tasting her with his tongue. His heart beat wildly in his chest, pounding with each slick stroke and the movement of his hips as they flexed and released. He felt a building of tension from the muscular contractions at the sensitive tip of his shaft, and he gazed at the burning blue flames of Lauren's eyes as she looked up into his face.

When their eyes met, she forced herself to be still lest he think ill of her. His eyes were intense, his face hard. What was he thinking? Did she disappoint him? She struggled to remain detached, motionless to the mounting waves that were trying to send her to a cumulative height. She squeezed her eyes tightly closed, and he felt a change in her response. He was too close to the end of his throbbing tension. Like pulling the string tight against the bend of a bow until the arrow is let loose, soaring to its target, so did he feel the pulsating release as he flowed into her.

She lay still and quiet beneath him. He knew that she had not reached the zenith of her climax and wondered if it was because it was her first time, and there had been the pain of her rendered maidenhead.

He remained above her, inside her, resting his weight on his arms on either side of her and saw her turn her face away from him. She would not look at him, did not touch him as he rolled off her and lay with his hands behind his head, staring at the ceiling, wondering how it could feel so amazing for him and not for her.

He had enough experience to know that he had been able to share the intricacies and joys of lovemaking with other partners. Yet here, with this woman, the one he desired and wanted to please above all others, she was unsatisfied. Lauren rolled onto her side, presenting her back to him. Her dismissal of him was complete.

"Lauren, did I hurt you?" he queried, hoping for some response from the dismissive back she presented to him.

"No my lord. Nothing I couldn't bear," she hoped he would stop talking to her.

She was upset and confused by her body's reaction. Would she face the years of their marriage studying the coffered ceiling during their lovemaking? Counting the seconds of blissful torture to remain aloof under the administrations of his knowledgeable touch? Would planning menus and contemplating chores take her mind to a safer place? She needed to set her thoughts to other areas instead of feeling the molten passion of her body trembling under him, and forcing herself to remain still.

Haltingly, Lauren sat up on the edge of the bed and reached for her nightgown to draw it over her head. She was embarrassed beyond words by her response to their play.

When she felt Devlin reach for her, she quickly stood, glancing fleetingly in his direction. She mumbled, "I would rather sleep in my bed," and fled the room.

Confused by the sudden departure after so intimate a moment, Devlin considered going after her, but the click of the lock, sounding from her door, negated that idea. He leaned back on the pillow and pressed the palms of his hands against his eyes, wondering how he would ever be able to keep his hands off his cold wife. It was apparent she did not enjoy the intimate moments of married life, and his heart grew heavy.

Lauren curled into the covers of her bed like a cocoon. She was sure Devlin would consider her a low-born trollop who could not control her emotions. She came to the firm conviction that no matter what the nuns had painstakingly taught her, nor how many years she had been sent away to learn proper decorum...it wasn't nearly enough!

* * *

Lauren cowardly hid herself in her painting room with the door locked to any casual intrusion. The day, like her mood, was dark and gloomy. Wind-whipped rain pellets struck the windows, forming runnels of water gushing down the panes. The night had been spent tossing and turning, fretting over her licentious behaviour in the solitude of her lonely bed. As she applied paint with masterful strokes, colouring in the background to the large canvas, she tried to focus all her attention on the piece before her. Her betraying mind would slip from her task to the splendid moments of the night before. Perplexed, she tried to make sense of her feelings compared to her teachings. That exercise became a muddle of confusion between the proper Victorian values, and how her body could betray her so. She was, however, confident of one thing. She could not bring herself to face Lord Barwick in her present state of duress.

Devlin was equally confused as he sat at his desk studying the row of figures that tallied the current investment numbers. After months of being solicitous to the care of Lauren and applying his patience to the hilt, once the bird had been brought to hand and he experienced the pleasure of what, he had assumed, would be wedded bliss, he now found himself in more turmoil than before.

Women! Sometimes a man couldn't understand their sense of reasoning. But therein lay the problem. Their emotions always got in the way of common sense, and common sense to him, regarding their joining last night, was that the time spent was ideal, perfect in every regard, except for her response. Not at the beginning, but the ending left much to be desired. She had left him to lock herself in her bedroom, and now she was locked in the room she used to paint.

There was no denying that his wife was a beautiful woman, a treasure he realized with each day's passing, holding more value than anything else he could lay ownership of. She was pleasing to the eye and the hand. She possessed grace and showed kindness to others. She had a dry sense of humour that he would occasionally glimpse when she let her guard down. It was her damn propensity to be worried about convention and what other people thought that concerned him.

To hell with propriety!

There had to be someone between the wild child of her youth and the haughty proper woman who graced his home. He wanted a wife who would come to him with joy, not one who performed the intimacies of married life as a chore. Lauren was perfect to him in every way, but this most important one.

She avoided him for the entire day, seeking solitude and taking her meals in her studio, stating she was busy and could not be disturbed. When he went to her that night, she feigned sleep, the covers clutched tightly in her fist below her chin.

He stood regarding his unapproachable ice queen. Not willing to brook an argument at a late hour, he kissed her on the cheek and went to his lonely bed.

The sun did its best the next day to drive the fog from the land and dry the dripping leaves as they hung heavy in the trees. Devlin was already about his day when Lauren decided to take Willow for a ride. She refused the stable boy's offer to go with her since she would stay in close proximity to the house and only venture on Barwick land.

In order to placate her great-aunt, Margaret had ridden the roadways, hills and valleys for the past week in the hope of *casually* coming across Devlin. Stopping in a forest glen, she allowed her old horse to drink deeply in the stream and dismounted from the poor example of horseflesh to wet her kerchief and cool her sweating face. A downed log lay near the bank that she could use to mount the steed again after she rested her sore behind from being in the saddle since early morning. The horse she borrowed from Agnes' stable was well-used, providing a disjointed trot as its old bones rattled below the skin that held the animal together. Shaded from the view of the roadway by thick brush, her ears pricked at the clip-clop of an approaching horse. Finally, she thought. Her hunted prey was nigh.

Margaret almost stepped from her hidden bower, until, instead of the one she had been searching for, there, atop a pretty high-stepping thoroughbred, was the woman who had sent her plans scattered to the wind, and induced the wrath of Agnes towards her. Her anger flared as she saw the straight-backed posture and experienced gloved hands holding the reins of an impressive chestnut with a flashy blaze.

She felt her temper rise with the heat of her fury. Not only did this interloper take Devlin from her, but she was showered with all of his riches. The gowns she wore, the things she could purchase, the horse she rode. It was infuriating that she had all that and Margaret had nothing. Rage, fear and humiliation, all the components of jealousy, roiled in her chest.

With physical force, Margaret stopped herself from confronting Lauren and quickly devised another form of attack. Retreating, she reached into the stream for a smooth heavy rock. If she timed it just right, she could do enough damage to remove this obstacle from the path she had set for herself to bring Devlin to heel. All she had to do was wait until the pair was close enough, so aiming the heavy weight in her hand would hit the target.

The road travelled through the wooded copse to the next open field. Lauren could hear the babbling brook on her left as she rode through the sweet-smelling foliage. Without warning, Willow screamed in pain, shied to the right, and with a mighty lunge, reared, lifting her forelegs high into the air while tossing her head wildly.

Lauren lost the reins as they were wrenched from her fingers. She grasped Willow's mane and leaned forward, pressing hard with her left foot in the stirrup, while at the same time, tightening her right knee against the pommel to keep her seat.

The horse's forelegs hit the ground hard, knocking the breath from Lauren's chest. Willow dropped her head low to the ground, flipping the loose reins over her head, before rising with a wild toss. The horse pranced in a dizzying display to escape the burning pain before she took flight with a jolting leap.

She raced the wind as if the dogs of Hell were on their heels. Without the reins to guide the horse, all Lauren could do was try to remain in the saddle. She grabbed two handfuls of mane and matched her movements to the terrified horse watching the ground speeding by. She lost her hat and the pins that held her hair in a neat coil. The heavy mass was whipped by the passing wind from the wild racing horse. Through fields and over hills they flew with alarming haste as Lauren did her best to hang on.

At this speed, her life depended upon remaining seated. She was too frightened to try to control the animal with her leg, fearing pressure on only one side would send Willow into a turn, and Lauren would find herself continuing in a straight trajectory without a horse beneath her. Surely, at this pace, a fall would cause serious damage. Lauren could only wait for the horse to tire and slow of its own accord.

Margaret stood in the roadway and cursed her luck that the weighty rock had not travelled the distance she had hoped, and instead of contacting with Lauren's round head, had smacked into the horse's hindquarters with a solid sickening thud. All may not be lost, she sneered to herself. Miss High and Mighty could still break her neck.

Devlin was returning from town when a streak of red caught his attention through the trees. He wheeled Daniyal around and kicked him into an earth-eating gallop to race after Lauren. He grew fearful that she would fall before he reached her and noted the reins flapping around Willow's chest and legs. Picking up his master's anxiety and seeing the chestnut mare racing before him, Daniyal stretched his great muscles into the chase, gaining ground as the tiring mare lacked his speed and endurance.

It seemed like an eternity before Devlin could grasp for Willow's bridle, and he brought them to an ever slower pace until it was safe to stop. He jumped from the Arabian, and sliding under the neck of the mare, reached for Lauren, grabbing her firmly to set her to ground. He shook her by the shoulders, angry from the scare she had caused him.

"Are you mad woman! To race like that with your experience could have caused you serious harm. How did you lose your grip on the reins?"

Eyes filled with tears of relief were immediately turned to spitting fires of anger as she pushed against his chest. "I didn't kick her into a gallop. What kind of fool do you think I am? Willow was startled by something in the forest, all I could do was hold on for my life."

Devlin brought the reins over the mare's head. His temper cooled quickly at his mistaken chastisement of his wife. "I'm sorry," he corrected. "I'm relieved you are not hurt."

He leaned on the mare and turned to look at Lauren. His brow furrowed, he added, "I'll admit that your riding has improved for you to stay astride during that crazed dash, but could you not repeat it? My heart can't stand the fright."

"That bit of advice will be taken under advisement most assuredly Devlin. I wouldn't want to upset you," she mocked.

After her legs stopped shaking and Willow had cooled, Devlin assisted her onto the mare's back. Stepping behind her to reach Daniyal, Devlin ran his hand along the mare's hindquarters when he felt the swollen bruise. The horse performed a sidestep to remove herself from the soreness of his touch.

"What's this?" he asked in a soothing voice to the mare. "Hold her tight Lauren. She has a swelling here the size of my hand." He examined Willow's flanks for more injuries and asked, "Did she hit anything when you were riding?"

"No my lord, nothing. We were enjoying a nice stroll when all of a sudden, she reared and bolted. I have no idea why."

"Something caused this. She's hurt. Carl will have liniment to help with the pain and swelling, but it's curious as to how it happened. There's no puncture or bleeding, just this swollen bump."

On the sedate walk home, they both avoided Lauren's previous day of absence. Lauren was pleased with the diversion, as they instead discussed the upcoming visit by the Cavanaugh family for the Halloween celebration, and plans for the Harvest Festival that would be held in town after the crops were brought in. It would signal a time of less work for all, as winter settled on the land to nip at fingers and toes. The land would lay fallow, and energy would be placed inside the barns and homes, in an attempt to keep everyone warm.

That night when he came into her room, Lauren was frightened that he would bring up the subject of their intimacy. It wasn't long before her prediction came true.

Devlin saw her as the only woman who had captured his heart. He would lay all that he had at her feet, for her pliant willingness to live fully as his wife.

"Will you give up this room and share mine?" he broached the existing turmoil.

She looked at his image in her mirror, laying the brush she held on the table. She tried to think of a myriad of topics to subtly change the direction of their conversation, but none seemed appropriate.

"Lauren, you need to settle yourself about the facts of marriage." he continued in the ensuing silence.

"I can't do this," she whispered forlornly. A tear escaped and trailed down her cheek.

"We need to talk about this." He knelt beside her, taking her hands into his, and with his thumb, brushed the tear that slid down her cheek. "I'm trying to have a serious conversation with you."

"I understand that my lord, and I'm trying to avoid it," she chastised.

"Come," he said, rising and pulling her from her chair. He led her through the water closet into his room and set her in one of the tall backed chairs before the fireplace. He handed her a small libation of whiskey from the bedside table to soothe her nerves, before helping himself to a larger one, taking a seat near her.

He stared into the crackling orange flames. "I never felt a need to share my life with any one woman." he ventured. At her quick look, he added, "Until you recently came back into my life.

You must know that I want you. Over these past few months, I have shown you that no other woman holds my interest. I want always to find you in our home, see you in the gardens where you like to sit. I want us to bring forth children together, and watch them grow, to be happy and healthy under our guidance. I want to prosper and live our lives to the end of our days together."

She took a sip of the whiskey, muffled a delicate cough as it burned down her throat and looked dubiously into the amber fluid as he continued.

"What is the point in gathering wealth and improving this estate without the possibility of passing it down to the generations that will follow us? Lauren," he lamented, "I can't do this alone. I need you. I hunger for your touch."

She heard the pain in his voice. "My lord. This is difficult for me. I want to hear the laughter of children in this house as well. A dearth of that sound has been ringing against these walls for generations. I crave a family I can love and care for. This is something I have yearned for all of my life."

Her face was growing hot with a blush. How could she tell him that she also wanted his touch? She wanted the feelings he aroused in her, but was afraid of her response. "I don't want you to think ill of me," she whispered with difficulty.

"How?" he asked, incredulous "What could you do that would cause me to think that?"

Lauren couldn't see a way out of directly answering him. "I can't seem to respond to you in the proper way Devlin. When you touch me, I quiver. It's not right, and I can't stop it from happening."

Of all the answers he had prepared for, this was not one of them. "Exactly how do you think you're supposed to act?" he was intrigued, waiting for her answer.

Lauren looked directly into his surprised countenance. "Why, like a lady, of course!"

Devlin laughed at her stunned look. "Who told you these things?"

Lauren was miffed that he found humour in her confusion. "The nuns did! Sister Mary Divine to be exact."

Devlin thought for a moment and considered the unamused face of his confounded wife. Holding back a smile, for she considered this discussion very serious business.

"Lauren, when the nuns taught you French and German, could they speak the languages fluently?"

"Of course they did; they were proficient in it," she answered.

"And when they taught you to play the piano, were they gifted with the knowledge of the instrument."

She again agreed in the affirmative.

"Have any of them been married or been with a man before entering cloister?"

She looked aghast. "No, none of them have! They entered in their early teens."

"Then, my dear wife, why would you believe that what they were teaching in this regard was the truth? Did they expound on the beliefs of the church? That the marital bed is for procreation and not recreation?"

Devlin could see that she was carefully considering his statement and pressed his point. "I want to honour you with my body, to care for you and no other. Will you see the truth in my words?"

Warm blue eyes gazed deeply into his heated green.

"I don't want you to act like a lady in my bed if you think that means you must lay still and allow me to do to you what I want. I am devoted to you and want to share the joy of becoming one. Believe these words to be fact Madam, that your participation in the act would not cause me undo reason to think ill of you." He smiled, and she realized that he teased her.

"You don't speak of love, my lord. Will I be a plaything for a time? Will you someday make some other woman your mistress?" she questioned earnestly.

Devlin thought for the briefest moment before he answered. "I cherish every day that we have together. Love doesn't arrive on butterfly wings when the sun rises daily or when the world is merry and perfect. It comes in everyday moments of life. It grows with laughter and shared sorrow. It is giving trust, respect and support and binds us in riches or poverty. Whatever life sends our way Lauren, I said the vows to stay at your side, through good and bad, until the end of my days. I give you my promise that I want no other, only you, and when the time comes, that the good Lord calls me home, yours will be the name I cry out in sorrow, when I must leave you and this earthly bond."

He sat quietly while his words swirled in Lauren's head. What more could she ask of him? He proclaimed his devotion to her. He had proven his fidelity. He wanted her, and she wanted him. A dark veil was being lifted from seeing a brighter future. She felt wonder in her acceptance of his statements, of their union and the consuming pleasure that she need not hide. He truly was charming, in all that he was, what he did, and how he spoke tender words.

The snap and crackle of the logs in the fireplace broke the silence of the room. Rising, Lauren hesitantly reached for Devlin's hand. He rose to stand before her as their eyes met. His showing a craving for her acceptance of his words, hers a dawning of what being his wife would mean. He lowered his head as his lips brushed her waiting mouth. He tasted the sweetness of her response as her lips parted. A timid tongue touched his. Their kiss, beginning soft and gentle, turned to heat and passion.

Her robe dropped to her feet. Bending to lift her in his arms, he carried her to the bed. Their bed, laying her softly as his muscles flexed. He tossed his robe onto a chair as she took in the full display of his raging emotions. Once again, she was amazed at his rippling muscles, the washboard indentations of his belly, powerful broad chest, and muscular arms that could wield a heavy axe or carry her gently.

He came to her then. The bed dipped, and she assisted him in removing her gown, watching the diaphanous material as it floated over his shoulder to land on the floor. His lips drank the honeyed nectar of her mouth as warm hands roamed over her soft silken flesh. Lauren explored the hardness of his body. Where she was soft, he was like smooth polished wood, warm and firm with dense solid muscle. He tasted her body, his lips moving from her face to her breasts, lowering to kiss the soft belly and roaming lower still. His caress grew bold as he fingered the soft folds of her innermost being. Touching a spot that nearly drove her wild in his quest to delve into the depths of her narrow canal. He rose above her and eased between her thighs as she opened to him.

Reaching between them, she enfolded his heat with her soft cool hands as he groaned above her. She guided him to her and felt the hilt of his bold blade touch her with delicious intent. Her body yielded to his hardness, and a soft sigh escaped her lips as he filled her. Soft to hard, yielding to taking. She enveloped him as they became one, uniting them in the universal play of making love, man to woman, like many others before them but utterly unique in their own way.

He moved with care at first, teasing and gentle, burying himself in her womanly softness, building the flames of desire with expert attention to her movements beneath him. Her knees raised higher as she contracted against him. She felt the muscles flexing in his buttocks as they moved against her hand, entering and withdrawing. She felt the waves cresting as she writhed in the swirling tides of desire, their bodies straining to reach the crescendo of passion together. She cried out for him as she felt a bolt of lightning go through her body. Wave after wave of delicious tingles coursed through her veins. He joined her ecstasy as he buried and released himself in her. He lowered himself to rest on his arms, teasing her breasts with his furred chest and kissed the base of her throat, her cheeks, and her eyes. They held each other, with the glistening film of sweat on them mingling, bringing with it the fragrant scent of their lovemaking. They lay entwined, her head against his shoulder, his arms wrapped around her cooling body.

"Will you stay with me tonight and evermore Lauren." he ventured in the darkened room. His words slipped off his tongue like a husky whisper in the fire-lit room.

She tilted her head to look up at him. "I must," she gave him a smile that melted his heart before adding, "because I don't have the strength at the moment to move, nor the will to leave you ever again."

He pulled the light blanket over them, and in each other's embrace, they drifted into dreamless sleep.

# *Chapter Fourteen*

The entire household noticed a change in the behaviour of the lord and lady of the house. Their ease in each other's company, the offering and acceptance of a hand, a coquettish look by the lady was met with a willing sensual reply from the lord.

When Devlin was with James or touring his land, Lauren would retire to her studio, and with determined dedication, work on the painting she had started after the fox hunt. The precision she applied to the piece showed her dedication to completing the canvas to the best of her abilities.

The cooling weather had the effect of producing a friskier step to Daniyal's gait as they traversed the roadway between the castle and town. Devlin was in a lighthearted mood as he headed to a distant farm to bargain for a particular purchase he was planning to gift Lauren at Christmas.

A feminine figure on a tired nag stepped out from behind a grouping of trees, and he was startled to see the calculated look on Margaret Edward's face as she prettily displayed a winsome smile.

"What a pleasant surprise to see you today Devlin," she warbled as she dug her heels into the reluctant horse's flank to force him to move.

"You're a fair distance from home Margaret. What brings you so far afield?" he tipped his hat politely as Daniyal did an impressive sidestep at the intrusion.

"I'm spending some time with my dear aunt. She lives not far from here, and I decided it was a bright, glorious day for a ride," She tilted her head and fluttered her eyes, stifling a sniff as her nose was about to run from the cold. "May I join you? I have been looking forward to seeing you again, since we are in the same vicinity."

Devlin did not want word returning to Lauren that he had been seen in the company of this adversarial woman. "I apologize, Margaret, I cannot spare the time, as I have a long way to go. I must be off if I hope to return home before dark."

Margaret had not expected an outright denial. What was the matter with this man that she had not been able to have him smitten with her? She could hold the attention of any number of swains who vied for her affection, though most of them were old and friends of John Marlow who had only one thing on their minds.

"Will you be at the festival?" she attempted to hold his interest.

"My wife is looking forward to attending."

Margaret gave him a tight smile. "I understand there will be musicians and dancing. You know that I love to dance, especially with you. Perhaps you will see me there."

"Perhaps," he wondered how he could excuse himself from the conversation. He had miles to travel and was eager to see to his purchase.

Margaret could tell that he was intent on leaving and fought for a way to hold him in her company. "Devlin, I want you, only you. I know I can make you more happy than that simpering wife of yours. You can't possibly deny me!" she begged.

Devlin eyed her warily. This would not do. He had to make her understand, once and for all, that he would not accept her in any way. "Margaret, I've told you numerous times that I am obligated to another. You knew that from the beginning, and now Lauren is home. I am married. Happily so. I bid you to look elsewhere for a mate. What you feel for me is not love, but an attraction that I never encouraged and one that I do not reciprocate."

A fire burned in Margaret's eyes as she insisted, unable to accept that she could not endear herself to any man, especially one so rich. Even without a wedding vow, he could keep her in luxury.

"I could have others! I am considered quite popular. But Devlin, I do not want them. It is you I will gladly give myself to. I don't care about your wife. Nor do I care about your marriage. I will have you any way that I can."

Devlin was infuriated by her cheap display and angry that she would not see reason. He had never encouraged her to believe that there could be anything between them, nor did he have any desire to be with her. The rumours of her soiled reputation in London were rife, and he wanted no part of her then or now. He had tried to extricate himself from her company, but like a moth to a flame, she had grasped at him at every opportunity. He was done with being a gentleman if she would not act like a lady.

"Be off with you Margaret. I have a wife that I care deeply for, and I want no other woman. Take this advice I freely offer you. Have more care for your reputation and seek your father's guidance to see you matched with a proper suitor. I am unavailable, and it is best that we never see each other again, here or in London." Dismissively, he kicked Daniyal's sides and left her in the dust of the road staring after him.

* * *

Mid-October brought the beginning of the harvest season as leaves changed from green to the red and gold of fall. Lauren and Devlin would ride the countryside, enjoying the changing landscape. Before the weather turned too chilly, he had enticed her to join him at the pond for a swim and had laughed as the cold water elicited a grimace from her before he took her into his arms to warm her in more ways than one.

After the leaves dropped in a swaying descent from the trees, the brown flora lay on the ground crunching below the hooves of the horses. The smell of autumn, rich and earthy, filled the air before being swept away by the blowing winds that swirled the leaves in a riotous eddy.

Halloween celebrations were planned and with great expectations. Lauren and Devlin counted the days that would see the Cavanaugh family return to Barwick Castle.

The excited chatter of the children could be heard from the second coach as the conveyances trotted up the drive. Greetings were hailed by the adults as the children ran about them in abandon when they were released from the confines of their quarters and the stern hand of Nanny Grace.

Overworked from being cooped up in a carriage with the four children, the woman was released from her duties and led away by Ellie to her favourite spot in the kitchen as they renewed their friendship and enjoyed the tea and treats offered by an accommodating and commiserating Mrs. Osmond.

A young woman with flaming red hair also stepped out of the children's coach. She was slim with a smattering of freckles over her nose and wore the garments of the Camber staff. Lauren noted how quickly James McCormack stood a little taller and smiled a little broader at the sight of her.

"We brought Ivy along with us this time to help with the children," Marian explained, giving Lauren an intense look.

"That will be no trouble at all," she quickly replied, believing that there was an ulterior motive to the invitation of this pretty girl. Lauren addressed the dowager as she made her way forward, "I hope your journey was smoother than the last time you arrived Mama." She leaned in to kiss her mother-in-law on the cheek. "We have your favourite brandy warming beside a chair in the parlour."

"Keep this up my dear, and you'll become my favourite child," she proclaimed, winking at Marian, who they all knew, doted on her.

After dinner, once the children and the dowager had gone to their beds, Marian explained the relationship between Ivy and James McCormack.

"He has been madly in love with her for years," she announced, "but because of their age difference, her father wouldn't allow her to accompany James here when he moved with Devlin. She's been miserable since and refused any other offers her father received for her hand."

"Has he relented, or are you risking a matchmaking scheme that could go wrong?"

"Oh, he's relented. She was breaking his heart and vowed she would have no other but James." If her father wanted to see her happy, he had to give his blessing. She's very talented at doing hair and mending clothes should she still want to work after they marry. I don't believe I'm getting ahead of myself because I'm sure he'll propose."

"That may work out well. I've been concerned with Ellie lately. She's been by my side all my life, and though her duties here aren't pressing, she looks tired lately and prefers to spend her time in a rocking chair in the kitchen. It may be time for her to retire."

"It's the most difficult thing to do, to decide when a servant cannot keep up with the job."

"I don't know how I will broach the subject with her. I don't want her to think I don't appreciate her. She's been more than a paid companion. She has been my only family, but she should have the time to stop tending to me and enjoy her remaining days.

"It's hard when they get old. Will you pension her off?"

"I couldn't possibly send her on her way. She would be alone, which would be such a betrayal, considering she never left me when I needed her."

"Mama was also concerned once Trevor and Devlin were too old for Nanny Grace. Father Tremont found work for her with a cousin who was in need of an extra nanny since the poor woman kept having twins, and then a set of triplets. Her household was so full of little people, that she couldn't turn around without her skirts hitting a child. I'm sure you and Devlin will do what is best for her."

"I don't know if Ellie has it in her to be a nanny anymore. She was never really a disciplinarian," Lauren smiled, thinking of her childhood escapades.

"Nanny Grace does grumble about the children, but I think we are all happy that she's back at Camber Hall. She is excellent at managing my four, and at times still acts like a regimental Sergeant Major."

"Have none of them learned the way of their uncle to get on her good side?" Lauren smiled.

"Thankfully no. When Mama is spending the night, I hear her and Nanny laughing in the drawing room, recalling old memories of Trevor and how Devlin tortured all of them."

They were joined by the brothers and spoke of the coming days of parties, guests and scheduled events. It did not go unnoticed by the older couple, the closeness that had developed in their absence between the younger brother and his wife. There was a softness in their gaze and a willingness in their touch, that had not been there when they were in London or even during the Glorious Twelfth. Then, they had acted more aloof and polite in each other's company. All was well in this household, and they expected that soon, an announcement would be forthcoming of more grandchildren for the dowager to enjoy.

Halloween arrived. The day that the veil between the worlds of the living and the dead was at its finest, and the spirits of the deceased could wander the halls of the manse. It was believed that they could foretell future events, and particular attention was paid to what was said and done. Carl assisted George,

Violet, Rose and Thomas to climb the ladder to the loft of the stables to stuff the black-clad effigy of a witch with hay. Later she could be burned in a blazing bonfire as the children hooted at the scourge and danced about. Devlin and Trevor gathered the children in the yard so they could bob for apples out of a steel trough filled with water. Thomas came up sputtering and blowing water out of his nose as he gave up the attempt and was handed the one George had earlier grasped with his teeth. The children giggled and laughed, shouting words of encouragement as Marian and Trevor; Lauren and Devlin chewed on a string with a raisin in its centre, each trying to reach the coveted fruit, only to ignore it when they reached the centre, instead to kiss and cause the girls to giggle in their enthusiasm and the boys to groan their despair.

Late in the afternoon, tenants arrived to dance and make mischief with some dressed in costumes of animals and ghouls. Lauren wore a tattered black garment that streamed out behind her as it dragged on the ground and the pointed hat of a witch with a long black veil tied around its brim to hang down her back.

True to his name, Devlin wore a red Devil costume complete with a pointed tail. Trevor and Marian were vampires with long black capes, while the dowager Countess proclaimed that as an old woman, she was frightening enough and required no embellishments. The children joined with those of the tenants and scampered about in black costumes with a skeleton painted by Lauren on the material.

A wide table held huge platters of succulent roast turkeys, bowls of stuffing and gravy provided by the house, and an assortment of the donated dishes that had arrived with the tenants. The staff was encouraged to join in the merriment. After a parade around the grounds culminating in the witch being set ablaze at dusk, the people formed into groups to sing an All Hallows' Eve-appropriate song to the occupants of the manor:

*The undead from their eternal sleep*
*Deep in the night, they prowl and creep*
*As falling leaves their limbs to bare*
*A wicked wind is in the air*

*The shadow of death is drawing near*
*Days to come are full of fear*

*A shiver crawls up the spine*
*Hold tight to that, which is thine*
*Brave men tremble, as thunder rumbles*
*Beware your mount, less you take a tumble!*

*The shadow of death is drawing near*
*Days to come are full of fear*

Lauren and Devlin showed appreciation for their talents and for taking time from their busy schedules to join in the fun. They handed out coins and food wrapped in cloth before their guests returned to their homes. Their melodic voices continued on their way by cart or foot, pleased with the day and generosity of their lord.

Wiping their sticky mouths from the candied apples Mrs. Osmond and her staff had provided for all the youth, the

Cavanaugh children were bathed and in their nightgowns, sitting before the fire in the library as a tale unfolded.

The lights were lit low, and shadows filled the corners of the room as they, with rapt attention, listened to the words their father spoke.

He set the scene of a small family, weary of travel through the Valley of the Rock Monster, he who would devour all that passed. Trevor lowered his voice to an eerie level, and held the children enthralled as he spoke haltingly.

"With a looming storm upon them, they searched for a haven of rest from the wind and darkening sky that threatened rain and hail. They came upon a large circular structure, with two upper, shuttered windows, and an oval entry with an open doorway set above ground level. The father secured the horses and rushed his family into the shelter as great drops of rain fell on them. It was barren of even the meanest piece of furniture, and therein was a heavy, pungent odour, stinking to the nose."

"Ewww," cried the children.

"But the haven was the best they could find," Trevor continued.

Violet and Rose moved closer together and wrapped their arms around each other's shoulders. Trevor's voice lowered menacingly.

"The howling cold winds entered through the open doorway, followed by a warmer column of air that breezed past the family to exit the portal." He paused and glared at each child to heighten their anxiety.

"Thinking to increase his family's comfort, the father left them huddled in the centre of the room and went to the cart to retrieve blankets to cover the door. Gathering their belongings, he turned towards the structure with an armful of blankets."

Trevor built the story to a crescendo and raised his arms to signify the events. "To his horrified eyes, he sees the howling wind throw open the upper shutters, revealing glowing orbs in each window that became evil eyes as the doorway groaned and began to close shut...the father, in dreadful panic, ran to beat on the door that locked him out in his desperate efforts to reach his family."

Sadly, he ended the tale. "He despaired of his lost loved ones, his wife and helpless children captive in the bowels of the monster. The solitary father falls to the ground and cries his anguish to the howling wind."

The children sat quietly, eyes large and round as they considered the demise of the poor wife and children gobbled up by the evil Rock Monster. Violet ran to her Grandmother to sit in her lap to be assured by a cuddle as Rose began to cry and George attempted to soothe his sister. With all the frightened commotion by the girls, Thomas couldn't contain himself and rocked back against where he sat at Devlin's feet and laughed out loud at their reaction.

"You will be getting up with the girls when they have bad dreams tonight," Marian admonished her husband.

At nine o'clock, a grand procession of the staff made an elaborate display of carrying a fruitcake into the room and handed the dowager, as the oldest in residence, a sharp knife to slice the cake into equal pieces to be handed about. Not a word was spoken. According to tradition, the first word uttered would predict the coming year. Ellie and Nanny Grace stationed themselves at either end of the children to try to coral their movement and excitement.

Baked into the cake were five objects: a ring, coin, button, key and a thimble. The silence lengthened as the cakes were chewed in silence. Darting eyes cast about the room to see who would speak first and who would find the trinkets.

A footman held up a key, encouraged by the meaning that he would be going on a journey the following year. The dowager grimaced when she pulled a thimble from her mouth and made a great show of disappointment that she would be an old maid. Devlin's coin prophesied wealth as he smiled at Lauren, believing he already had that precious gift.

Lauren and Marian could not have planned better when James' button foretold that he would meet his love, and Ivy's ring predicted that she would marry within the year.

The silence was broken when a quicksilver mouse nearly scurried up Ellie's dress, and she shrieked without thinking, "Get away you, evil beastie," immediately clasping her hands over her mouth, realizing that her words had been the first spoken.

The gathered staff exchanged worried comments as wide suspicious eyes darted from one to the other. Had she, in her fright, bought evil to the house? There was much made of the outburst as the staff crossed themselves in a religious furor, hoping to negate the spoken words. After so lovely a day, the servants moved with trepidation to their rooms as the household quieted for the night.

Lauren was settling beneath the covers waiting for Devlin to return from the bathing chamber. She glanced up from smoothing the coverlet as she heard his approach and giggled at his sport. He strode towards her, in all his naked glory except for a mask covering his eyes.

"That is truly a masquerade of the first rank my lord, but without a doubt, I do recognize you."

* * *

One less traveller departed from the castle when the Cavanaugh family left for home. James McCormack proposed to Ivy, and after the banns had been read in the ancient medieval church in town, they had a quiet ceremony followed by a celebratory reception hosted by Lauren and Devlin. They were showered with gifts that would turn James' sparsely furnished bachelor cottage into a homey, comfortable living space that would please any new bride.

Ivy offered her services to act as Lauren's maid, and Ellie had been happy with the help. Lauren was relieved that the old woman proved eager to instruct the younger Ivy and impart her knowledge, if not her odd descriptive phrases, to the willing participant.

They packed away the lightweight summer gowns into the huge chests and hung the warmer clothing in the large closet. Before they could be worn, the women saw to the steaming of the gowns, to remove the wrinkles that had set since they had been packed away in France last spring.

The household was busy preparing the inside of the castle for the cooler weather. Lighter window coverings were removed, washed and stored. The heavier velvet curtains were first aired outdoors and then hung in their place to ward off the coming winter chill. The extra tapestries that Devlin had purchased in

London, were placed on the walls to insulate them from the cold that would seep through the ancient stones.

The day of the festival dawned cool and crisp, with a light frost lying on the ground. Lauren requested a warm green and blue tartan gown, and a dark wool mantle for the day. She felt an odd weariness and wondered why she should feel so, but laid the blame on the amorous play of the night before. Devlin had woken her with a bold caress and the night had been lengthened considerably by their play.

She pulled on leather gloves to protect her hands from the cold, a saucy hat sat tilted on her head, and with sturdy walking shoes, she was ready to spend hours outdoors.

The cobbled street of the town was laden with tables grouped end to end, so only foot traffic could pass through. Lauren held the arm of Devlin for support in the jostling crowd as they moved from one produce-laden table to the next admiring the bounty and handmade items on display.

The town folk along with Mrs. Osmond and her collection of girls were filling baskets for the kitchens. Max Ferguson, the local merchant, was bargaining with the sellers to make arrangements to stock his shelves with the tastier preserves, baked goods and sundry items.

He was a friendly sort who had long been married to a plump, cheerful woman. Alas, she had passed away while Lauren and Ellie were in France. Lauren had often heard Ellie speak glowingly of the similar nature of the charming couple. Thus, to see Ellie following in his wake, attempting to look inconspicuous as her eyes often darted to the kindly gentleman, was no surprise to Lauren.

At the midday meal, the tavern was crowded as the throng of attendees jostled their way into the establishment to warm themselves with a hot meal and a chance to get out of the wind. A group of young men tipped their hats to Lauren and offered the lord and his lady their spot at a table. It was gladly accepted as the occupants, and those who had offered their places were compensated when Devlin heartily called for a round of ale to be served. Lauren's stomach did a little flip with the smells of the place. A heavy stench of the ale and cooking odours permeated the room, but she was unwilling to ask Devlin to take her outdoors when it was a jovial group who gathered, as the tankards were filled by the generous lord more than a thrice of times before they left the establishment.

On the outskirts of town, pens were set up to contain some of the stock produced that year. A competition was organized with awards to be presented to the owner of the best animals shown in their category. Before judging commenced, Lauren noticed Penny Harrington timidly standing near Josh Hartford, the youngest son of that family, and his gaggle of honking geese.

The poor girl looked half frozen as she crossed her arms to hug herself under the thin blanket that covered her shoulders, and with adoring eyes, shook her head at him when he offered her his coat. She was a plain girl with straight scraggly hair that hung down her back. Lauren surmised that she could be quite pretty if only she were not the offspring of Todd Harrington and lived in squalid conditions. He continued to refuse any help that he considered charity and did not allow the gifts Lauren tried to give his family through various means. He had sent the Barwick maids running when they approached and threw anything offered to his family from neighbours into the dirt. The best dresses Penny had, looked like filthy rags and the luxury to spare coin for the purchase of a bar of soap would not be considered.

Devlin was in the midst of a conversation with a pair of farmers asking him to provide an assessment of the qualities of their sheep.

"I ask you, my lord, is this not the finest wool you've felt?" one queried

"It's hardly fair to bring a sheep you've dipped in lanolin," replied the other with laughing good nature.

Devlin was saved from a reply as an angry shout rent the air. All eyes turned to the rage-filled face of Todd Harrington as he marched towards his daughter.

"What do ya think yer doin' here when there's chores ta be done ta home ya nasty chit!" he bellowed, spinning the girl around and cuffing her on the side of her head, with enough force to knock her to the ground.

While the crowd stood agape, shocked at the scene unfolding before them, Devlin rushed forward and grasped the man's arm before he could lay another blow on the grovelling girl. He held it in a vice-like grip, and with sheer force, drew it down and turned the man so they were nose to nose.

In a low voice, Devlin commanded, "Cease this display of your foul temper. Can the girl not, for a moment, be excused from her endless toil to attend the festival and have even the slightest enjoyment of her day?"

For all of his burly bulk, Todd Harrington could not break the iron grip Devlin had on him. "I'll ask you not ta intrude on how I raise my kin…my lord," he sneered the title like an insult, displaying contempt at the well-bred gentleman who had the unexpected power to hold him at bay.

Harrington looked around at the townsfolk and tenants who were witness to the unbreakable hold Devlin had on him, and his ire grew. He could see by their smug looks that they were pleased with what they were witnessing. He was known as one who got his way by his mean, determined temperament and his propensity for using force. Yet here he was being shamed by a gentleman who should have the soft hands and easy life of leisure.

Devlin broke his grip with a backward shove. "Be warned that when you are in sight of the good men of this town, you had best be mindful of the treatment of your women."

Harrington did a quick prancing step to regain his balance and reached with a mighty fist to collect his daughter from behind Josh Hartford, who had helped her rise. Todd shoved Josh out of his way and roughly led her from the area, throwing a noxious glare at Devlin as he cursed under his breath, the wind blowing the words away so none could hear what he spoke.

The afternoon continued more pleasantly as the judging occurred. Ribbons were awarded, and new tools were handed out as prizes to the farmers for the animals with the best conformation, girth or coat. Lauren's mind stayed on the shabby state of Penny and worried about what her punishment would be. It was a tricky affair to decide what she could do to help the girl and her mother without Todd Harrington being aware of the assistance.

With the coming dusk, temperatures dropped, and the crowds thinned. The packing was well underway when Lauren and Devlin gathered Ellie from Max Ferguson's shop. They sought the comfort of their coach and left the little town to head home, looking forward to the warmth of a fire.

Lauren's toes had felt like icicles even after dinner, and she had not been able to completely warm herself until she was immersed in the liquid heat of a steaming bath. She considered her excessive tiredness from the activities of the day and her heightened sense of smell. She placed her hands on her stomach and counted the days since her last course, smiling with the inner knowledge of the seed that had been planted and now grew inside her. Devlin entered and watched as bubbles danced around her. The mounds of her breasts formed perfect slippery islands in the water. Her hair was piled on top of her head, exposing her exquisite slim neck as he grasped the sides of the tub and leaned towards her for a deep kiss.

"Would you care for company, my sweet?"

Lauren chuckled, "Only if you want to be attended by Ellie. She'll be returning soon."

Devlin groaned in mock frustration. "There is always someone about when my most fervent desire is to see you all to myself."

"You would make a terrible lady's maid Devlin. I would forever be undressed." she rejoined saucily.

"Exactly," he murmured huskily.

He removed his shirt and went to the washstand. Lifting the pitcher, he filled it with hot water from the tub faucet and poured it into the bowl. Lauren appreciated her view of his rippling muscles as he lowered his head into the water, shaking it as he rose, flicking wet droplets into the air.

"James and I are going to be taking some of the shifts to watch for the person responsible for killing the animals," he said, "will you miss me in your lonely bed when I'm not there?"

A prickling of worry slid up her spine. "I will miss your warmth on the cold nights when I have no arms wrapped around me to keep me nice and toasty. But I'm more concerned for your safety. You will be careful Devlin."

"Always my love," he drawled. "Especially when I have you to come home to."

Ellie entered with towels and cast him a glance as he towelled his hair dry. "My lord, can you please see to my delicate nature and not parade yourself half naked until I've seen to my girl," she huffed.

"Does an honest bit of skin ruffle you so much Mrs. Butterfield?" he asked, leaning his hip against the washstand to address her.

"Nay my lord, you'd make a stuffed bird laugh if what you display is called a little bit of skin."

Devlin's attention was drawn from the vexed maid to Lauren as she rose shimmering in the tub and reached for a towel. The sight of her in all her naked splendour stirred more than his mind. The fact that she had forsaken her moral dilemma, and come to the appreciation that their honest desire for each other was a quest to be enjoyed, was a relief beyond comprehension. He saw before him years of pleasure in her company, and contentment filled his being.

"My toes will turn into prunes if you keep arguing Ellie."

The little woman helped Lauren from the tub and towelled her back. She held the pink nightgown for her to slide over her head as Devlin turned to finish his ablutions for the night, hoping the maid would hurry and be on her way.

When they were alone, Lauren came behind him and ran her hands along his broad back, drawing the edge of her nails up his sides, beyond where the muscles flexed outward like the hood of a cobra.

"Are you playing with me, Lauren?"

"Ticklish, my lord?" she sighed.

He turned, scooping her into his arms. He carried her from the room to their bed.

"In one particular spot," he assured.

# *Chapter Fifteen*

The late afternoon heralded a bitingly cold north wind. Small white flakes fell from the grey clouds that obscured a timid sun. The reds and golds of autumn were replaced with brown. Bare trees, placated the sky with outstretched arms, beseeching the gods for the warmth of the past days, dreading the frigid temperatures and blowing snow that would soon be upon them. The horses were frisky in the cold weather, eager to be on their way to warm their bodies with activity.

Lauren stood in the open doorway wrapped in a shawl to wave to Devlin as he and James rode out of sight. She watched long after their figures were obscured, dreading the danger they could face as they ventured into the cold night to search for the raider. She had been told not to wait for his return. That they most likely would not be back until the next morning, though if he did arrive in the night, she made him promise that he would wake her.

The tenant families had been dividing their time guarding the land. However, their numbers had dwindled with the extra work that needed to be done before winter. This had provided an increased opportunity for the one who created mischief, to be more proficient at his cause. The waste was placing an extra burden on the hardworking tenants and growing frustration at their inability to capture the evading culprit.

The crescent moon in the cloudy sky provided meagre light, as Devlin and James rode along the paths and hedgerows. They were often plunged into total darkness when the heavy clouds obscured the moon. The land was still and quiet, except for the occasional bleating sheep or mooing cow. Their voices were subdued in the gloaming night.

The horses perked their heads up when a shot echoed across the fields. Taking their bearing, the pair kicked their mounts into a gallop in the direction of the report. They crested a hill, and below them saw the crumpled form of Josh Hartford. The sheep had scattered to the far end of the field.

Josh moaned as they approached, attempting to pull himself into a seated position. He swayed slightly, hanging his head until the ground stopped revolving below him. James knelt on one knee to lend him support as the younger man rested his back against the bent leg. Blood streamed down his face as James felt for the wound.

"Ahhh," Josh grunted, spying friendly faces instead of foes. "I didn't hear the blighter coming and must have nodded off for a few minutes. I was hit from behind, and it's my own damn fault."

"We heard a gunshot, where are you struck?"

"Nay, no other wound, just this bash on my noggin,"' he woozily replied, lifting his ancient weapon. "I must have squeezed the trigger when I was hit. I should be glad I didn't blow my leg off." He reached for his limb to ensure that part was still intact.

"You're in no condition to remain here tonight," Devlin commented, seeing the boy sway against his agent's leg. "James will see you safely home."

"Da's gonna be mad if we lose any more animals," he groaned, holding his sore head.

Devlin and James exchanged looks, controlling the upward curve of their threatening smiles, that the lad was wary that his father would feel more concerned about the safety of the livestock, than his son.

"I'll stay and keep watch. James can join me once he sees to getting you home. In your condition, I wouldn't want you to end up lying frozen and unconscious in a field overnight."

James grasped the boy's arm and pulled as Devlin hoisted the dizzy lad behind the cantle and bid him hold tight onto James' jacket lest he fall.

"Tis a bleedin' cold night milord. I thank you for mindin' to my duties."

Devlin waved the lad's concern away and watched them leave as the youth wobbled on his precarious seat. He turned his attention to the field where the sheep lowed their subdued calls, ever watching for the one who had failed in his mission to attack the sheep and had instead harmed the boy. Devlin noticed a fleeting movement in the woods, as the slight light caught a dim shimmer of a barely shining object. He watched for a moment more and saw again the darting pass of a shadow.

In a bound, he leapt onto Daniyal's back, and as one, they flew towards the copse. Entering the thickly littered underbrush, the Arabian picked his way over vines and sticks as Devlin raised the grabbing branches out of their way. Though he was sure this was the spot where he had seen movement, Devlin wondered if his eyes had not played tricks on him in the sparse light. Surely no human could easily pass this way or wish to retreat in the encompassing thicket. Yet he could think of no animal that would be able to glow in the dark.

The further they entered the copse, the way became easier to traverse. The dense brush gave way to darker woods with scattered low growth. Able to sit taller in the saddle, they progressed through the gloom. Devlin heard the report the moment the force of the blow hit him. It was like being struck by a heavy slag hammer wielded by the Rock Giant Trevor had spoken of, and it knocked him back in the saddle.

He felt the quiver of the horse below him, as Daniyal lunged forward. He felt the searing heat of the bullet that sliced through his skin and muscle high on his chest. It grazed off the shattered bone of his rib, bursting out his back, leaving a gaping hole, draining a gush of blood from the wound.

Devlin struggled to pull hard the reins to the right and kicked the trembling sides of the horse, sending him crashing through the growth. Each jarring step reverberated through his aching body. The world spun before him as he leaned forward in his seat, laying low on Daniyal's neck. His arm hung loosely down the animal, as his draining blood coursed down his limb and the side of the horse. They progressed into the deep woods, propelled by the noise of the pursuer who followed stealthily.

Devlin's brain was foggy as he forced himself to think about their escape. The pain pulsated with each step of the horse, each breath of the man. The dim light turned darker, and his view was through a closing tunnel as he felt himself unable to hold his seat. He ceased to acknowledge consciousness as he toppled from the Arabian's back to lay unseeing on the cold hard turf.

Daniyal paused as he felt Devlin fall from the saddle. He quivered at the unaccustomed discharge of his master and worried at the ground where he lay, pawing at the uneven turf, nuzzling at Devlin's hand for a soothing touch. He gently prod the human face with his velvet nose, willing the man to rise so they could return to his warm barn. No response came from the prone form. Daniyal lifted his elegant head and pricked his ears forward, listening into the woods at the sound of breaking twigs. He nudged his still master again. The heavy iron smell of blood filled his nostrils. Danger was about. The horse felt it in his tense muscles. He felt the helplessness of the man who guided him. He sensed that to stay would bring more peril, and with a final snort, Daniyal stepped carefully away, leading the one who followed from the spot where Devlin lay.

The freezing temperatures brought brief moments of consciousness. His head ached from hitting the ground, his neck was stiff and sore, and the pain from his wound seared through every fibre of his being. He was weak from the copious loss of blood. Trying to rise, he collapsed as the trees spun in stomach-turning revolutions, and he couldn't draw his legs under him. He pushed himself under the thicket, covering himself with leaves, branches, and anything he could reach that would provide a measure of warmth to his shaking frame. He attempted to assess his wound and touched the hole on his chest, sticky with blood. The searing pain blocked out the light as the clawing fists of Morpheus overtook him.

James returned to the field and scanned the area for Devlin. He waited anxiously for his return, searching for any movement.

When Graham Hartford left Josh in the care of his mother and arrived to relieve James, they discussed the absent lord in the dark still night.

"He wouldn't leave when he said he would stay and watch," James insisted.

"I'll keep my eyes open for him for the rest of the night, but in the morning. I'll be seeing about my chores, so must return home."

James rode the outskirts of the field, searching for any sign of Devlin. He entered the brush and could find no way of passage. He tried again and again in the dark to see the sign of a path Devlin could have taken. With the first streaks of dawn showing in the sky, he kicked his horse into a fast gallop for the castle.

As the dawning sun peeked over the horizon, Lauren fretted that Devlin had not returned in the night. She noted that his side of the bed was unruffled and had not been slept in as she rose and pulled a robe over her nightdress. She was still buttoning the gown as she ran down the stairs and into the dining room to see if he was there. Her route took her to his study, which was still dark, with curtains drawn and shutters closed. The maids were starting their day when Winslow arrived, listening to her questions on Devlin's whereabouts.

"He did say that he might not arrive home until this morning, but the wind was blowing so hard, and with the freezing temperature, I didn't think they would be staying out all night."

"James did not return either, my lady, so they are together," ventured Ivy when she joined the group.

Lauren felt a slight amount of relief that both men had remained on watch throughout the night. "They'll be cold when they arrive home," she addressed Mrs. Park. "Could you have the maids take some blankets to the kitchen and warm them in the oven? I'm sure the men will appreciate being wrapped in the hot covers when they return."

As she finished speaking, she could see Carl through the library windows as he raced to the front door and burst into the house.

"My lady," he rushed to speak, undecided on which question to ask first. "Is his lordship hurt bad? Should I send a lad for the doctor?"

Lauren drew in a deep breath. Stinging pricks of fear crawled up her back. "Why would you ask that?" she gasped.

The household drew near in anxious worry as Carl looked from one to the other. "Dani Ma'am, he come bangin' on the tack door stampin' an tossin' his head in a fit of rage," he paused, unwilling to impart his knowledge at her look of concern. "He's covered in blood Mistress."

Ellie wrung her hands in anxious trepidation, and her superstitious nature reached a crescendo. She had prophesied this when she spoke first after eating the fortune cake. She moaned in despair that she had brought evil to the house, all because of her fear of a silly mouse.

The door banged against the wall as James entered. With a cry of relief, Ivy flew to his side. His arms went around her as he looked at the gathering, concluding that Devlin had not returned.

"He's not here then?" he questioned, seeing the worried faces. "We were separated when I took Josh Hartford home. The lad was hit from behind on his head. When I returned to the field, there was no sight of Devlin, so I stayed the night waiting for him. When I hadn't found him by morning, I came home hoping he was here, and if not, to gather men to search for him."

"Dani's come to the stables covered in blood. It didn't come from the horse, he's no wound I can see, so it has ta be from his lordship." Carl offered, casting a quick peek at the worry he saw in Lauren's face.

James took charge. "Gather the stable hands and any footman who can sit a horse. It's as cold as a witch's tit." He glanced apologetically at Lauren, "There's snow threatening, so we must find him soon."

Lauren dashed upstairs lifting the skirt of her robe, not caring that her legs flashed for all to see, calling out, "Saddle Willow for me Carl. I won't sit here if I can help look for Devlin."

The staff scurried to do what they could. Mrs. Park glanced at Winslow. He was always in command of himself, and she drew her strength from his stately presence. This time, he shook his head sadly. "Be prepared as best you can Annie. Set out the medicines and anything that may be required should they bring him home badly injured."

James held Ivy from him. "Help your lady. I have to go back out to find Devlin."

Before he was finished speaking, Ivy had already turned and ran to follow Lauren up the stairs.

A fretful Ellie looked at him with wide tear-filled eyes. Though she had kept her opinion of Lord Barwick cool, having yet to fully forgive him for casting them from their home, she knew he had found a place in Lauren's heart that had been empty all her life. She despaired that tender organ would surely break if Devlin were not found.

"Find my lord, and bring him safely home," she whispered to James forlornly, clamping her back teeth together to stop herself from wailing. She turned to make her slow progression up the stairs.

# *Chapter Sixteen*

The cold north wind whipped at her skirts as Lauren and Willow roamed the hills and vales near where James had last seen Devlin. More than a score of men from the house searched for him. They were joined as word spread, by the farmers who left their fields, animals and chores, to hunt for their lord in the forests surrounding the open areas. The biting cold left cheeks stiff and noses red, but they vowed not to give up until they found Lord Barwick.

Late in the afternoon, Lauren noted a horse and well-dressed rider passing along the hedgerow of the field a short distance from her. She nudged closer for a better look at the individual as the grass and wind muffled her approach. John Marlow leaned far over the side of his horse, studying the ground for any telltale sign of passage for the one he sought.

"John Marlow!" Lauren called out, surprised to see her step-uncle on the search.

He straightened and looked around in surprise. "Lauren," he said, "It's a miserable day for a ride to be sure. What brings you out in this weather?"

Lauren wondered that he had yet to notice the others in the area searching for Devlin and that he was not part of their group. "What were you looking at?" she asked, suspicious of everything this man did.

His posture was menacing as he stared into her face. She saw the fleeting look of a foul temper that she dared to question him. The last thing he wanted to do was have anyone aware of his presence. That could lead to suspicion of any involvement he may have had, with what he only hoped, was a dead Viscount. He decided to admit part of the truth.

"A friend and I were hunting game and wounded a buck," he smirked, "I was looking for a blood trail."

Before she could reply, a shout came from behind, drawing her attention. She turned without giving Marlow a further thought and sped Willow to the farmer frantically waving his arms.

John Marlow watched her go. They would find out soon enough if Harrington had been successful. Considering the man did the least work possible, John would not be surprised if he had failed to kill Devlin Cavanaugh and could imagine his mother's rage if the man still lived.

When Lauren arrived, four men gingerly carried Devlin's unconscious form from the undergrowth. His head hung limp, and the front of his coat was soaked red with dried blood. They laid him in the back of the rough cart and covered him with blankets. Lauren was lifted beside him and glanced about to find the one she sought. She directed Carl to ride into town to fetch the doctor.

Yanking hard on the reins, there was an audible thump as his heels kicked the flanks of his horse in rarely-used reckless abandon. Carl further dispersed the animal with a whip to fly the roadway to town.

Lauren held Devlin's head in her lap, alarmed at the ashen colour of his face. She considered the harsh treatment Carl had applied to his horse, experiencing her own fright as she held her husband. Pulling his shirt aside to assess the damage, she stared agape, alarmed at the round wound on his chest.

James stood at the side of the cart as Lauren settled herself and secured Devlin for the ride home. "T'was a bullet that passed through him. The exit wound is far worse. He's most likely alive because of the frigid temperature." At Lauren's unspoken question, he continued. "The cold slowed the bleeding." He stepped back and tapped his hand against the side of the cart, "Take it easy driving him home lads."

With every jostle of the cart, a low moan escaped Devlin's pale lips, and with each one, Lauren blanched. His lips were blue, and his lashes looked dark against the green cast to his face. She held his cold, blood-stained hand in hers, and her fear mounted at seeing this robust and virile man laid prone and unmoving. She closed her eyes, bowed her head and sent a silent prayer on his behalf, as she was sure he stood before St. Peter at heaven's pearly gates.

When they arrived home, Devlin was lifted by the four footmen and carefully carried upstairs. Ellie laid thick towels on the white sheets before he was placed on the bed. James helped to remove his clothes, accepting scissors from Ivy so he could cut them off his body. Warm water arrived, and Lauren received clean cloths to wipe the blood from his chest. She felt the lump on the side of his head, tenderly feeling for a gash, but found only a small cut. When James rolled Devlin so she could administer to his back, Lauren pulled her lip between her teeth at the sight of the gaping hole on his shoulder that still dribbled blood.

"Buck up my girl," Ellie insisted, helping Lauren attend the injured man. "Now is no time for theatrics or swooning. We've work to do!"

Doctor Wilson arrived, puffing up the stairs in haste to reach his patient. He probed the wound as Devlin unconsciously twisted away from the painful invasion. He removed broken pieces of bone, dirt, and bits of Devlin's coat from the gaping wounds. The doctor packed the holes from the front and back in a zigzag motion with a long string of boiled gauze that had cooled. He wound a bandage around Devlin's chest, up and over his shoulder, tying it tightly.

"Let us hope that a fever doesn't take him. There was a considerable amount of dirt in there," he mumbled. "Once he warms up and he comes around, give him a few drops of laudanum to ease the pain," he directed Lauren, placing a brown bottle on the night table. "Give him as much fluids as he'll take. There's no point bleeding him since there's not much blood left in him. I'll drop by again in a few days, but send word if you need me before then. There's naught to do. Keep him as still as possible so he doesn't start to bleed again."

James placed a chair beside the bed for Lauren. She sat and brushed the ever-present wisp of hair from Devlin's forehead and covered his hand with two of her own, pledging to stay by his side until she was assured that he would wake.

She lifted her face to look at the stark doleful gaze of James. His weariness showed in the lines of his sad face and the droop of his shoulders.

"Ivy, take James home and look after him," she softly commanded."

They left the room as Lauren turned her attention to Devlin, watching for any sign of life.

Ellie entered with the warm blankets from the oven and a light meal for Lauren. After covering Devlin's deathly still form, she left the darkening room, having no words of encouragement to offer her worrying mistress. She returned later and noted the uneaten meal where she had left it. Lauren had not moved from her position, sitting forward in the chair watching for any sign of movement, her brow creased as she stared into Devlin's face.

"I've laid out your night dress in the other room. Go, get yourself out of your riding habit. You've been sitting in it all day. Clean yourself up, wash your face and get comfortable. It will be a long night for you sitting here with his lordship." At a defiant look from Lauren, the old woman continued. "I'll stay and watch while you're gone. You won't be but a few minutes." she gave the girl a gentle push towards the spare room.

Ellie took the moments of Lauren's absence to beseech God to take pity on them and send his healing angels to lift the shadow of death from Lord Barwick. She placed a small bag with pigeon feathers under the mattress to hold Devlin's spirit to its earthly bonds.

When Lauren returned, she curled herself in the chair, and Ellie drew a blanket over her. "Will you not lay beside him and spend the night in comfort?"

"I'm afraid that any movement will cause him more pain. I'll be fine here. It's been a long, horrible day Ellie. Go find your own rest."

Throughout the night, Lauren caught only brief moments of sleep, caring for the man she had considered strong and vigorous. She had believed there was naught that could lay her powerful husband low. Now he lay near death, still and vulnerable, and she was afraid for him. She longed to see his teasing grin, the smiles he had casually tossed her way, and the smouldering depths that shone in his beautiful emerald eyes when he undressed and made love to her. She reached under the covers to lay her palm on Devlin's chest to assess his temperature. He had been brought to the house stiff and cold. He shivered, moaning and twisting his head from side to side, and warm blankets that had been heating on the back of chairs before the fire, were placed gently on top of him.

The colour returned to his face and then grew pink. A film of perspiration covered his body as his temperature rose. Lauren removed the extra blankets and now fought a battle to cool the heat rising from him. She wet cloths, and laying one across his forehead, used another to bathe his body, drawing the fabric down his arms; along his taut stomach.

Ellie and Mrs. Park took over the duties the next day after removing Lauren from his side. Ellie darkened the smaller room Lauren first used, pulled the blankets over Lauren's shoulders and ordered the girl to rest. "Just stay here for an hour and let

Mrs. Park and I care for his lordship. You'll do no good making yourself sick from worry."

"Wake me as soon as the hour passes, or if Devlin needs me," she wearily mumbled.

At the back door of the house, tenants arrived in a steady stream to inquire on the lord, only to turn away with heads bowed when no good news was forthcoming. In the kitchen, Mrs. Osmond sent a maid into the yard to butcher a plump chicken and prepared a hearty soup, hoping that a healing broth would quicken the master's return to health. Simple fare was prepared for the staff and Lauren as she had requested nothing special be made for her while Devlin lay abed.

The house was muted as all went quietly about their duties. There was no chatter as voices were subdued, expectantly waiting for any word.

Lauren woke from her nap and jumped from the bed to pull on her wrap. She felt refreshed and ready to face another night caring for Devlin. She didn't have the heart to condemn Ellie for letting her sleep longer than expected when she saw the two women busily bending over Devlin to tend him. But her heart dropped when she saw the writhing body and wild glazed eyes that stared without seeing. He twisted and spoke unintelligible words as they continued to rinse the hot cloths in the water and apply them over and over again in an attempt to cool his raging fever.

"Why didn't you call me," she forced through trembling lips.

"You needed the rest, and there's nothing more you could do for him that we are not seeing to. Everyone is worried enough about Lord Barwick. If you're planning on caring for him day and night, we'll be adding you to our prayers should you drop from exhaustion."

Lauren took the cloth from Mrs. Park when she stood to press her fists on her lower back easing the pain from bending over the bed.

"Should we call for the doctor?" Lauren asked.

"I think we are doing all that can be done for him, my lady. Doctor Wilson can mend a broken limb and clean a wound, but he's still of the old opinion that a good bloodletting is the answer to most other ailments, and I'd just as soon see Lord Barwick get through this misery without those ministrations," Annie Park said uneasily.

Winslow volunteered to stay with Lauren during the night, in case a strong arm was required to hold Devlin, as he thrashed in the bed to the unknown horrors that swirled in the delirious mind of the fevered man. Dawn arrived, showing signs of a blood-red sky, before he lay still. Winslow and Lauren were physically spent when Ellie returned carrying the breakfast tray.

"Thank you for staying with me." Lauren spoke to Winslow, "I could not have endured the night alone." She was too exhausted to do little more than offer him a grimace of a smile, but, laying a hand on his arm, she stood on her tiptoes to kiss his cheek.

"I am at your service, my lady. As I have mentioned to you before, I will be here anytime you require me." he bowed stiffly, turning before she saw him swipe at his damp eyes.

"Will you take yourself to bed Lauren?" Ellie puttered around the room, noting Devlin wore a better colour from the red-flushed face of the day before.

"No, I'll just sit here and wait. He seems greatly improved, don't you think," she asked, hoping for encouragement.

"Aye. His fever has broken. There's prayers aplenty being said for him in this old house and all over the estate."

Ellie waited for a comment and looked at Lauren, seated in the oversized chair. Her head rested on the outstretched wings of the back while her legs were curled beneath her. Her delicate hands lay limp in her lap as a deep breath was drawn in slumber. Aye, Ellie thought, the little miss was spent, using all her energy for the care of the husband she had said she would steel her heart from. It was plain to see in the past few months that Lauren felt she belonged. She was part of a family with the Cavanaugh clan, pleased with all she had around her, and ready to build a life with Devlin. Gone was the feeling of being alone and unwanted. She was definitely in love with Lord Barwick, and if Lauren felt he was a good match for her, then Ellie would accept him as well.

With that thought in mind, Ellie resolved to do all in her power to care for Devlin and set herself to that task.

# *Chapter Seventeen*

Devlin woke with a pounding head that ached for days and a numbing pain in his shoulder and chest every time he moved. Eventually, the goose egg swelling on the side of his head shrunk in size. He gladly accepted Lauren's ministrations when she rubbed the back of his neck and laid cool cloths on his forehead. He was still too weak to dismiss the fawning of Ellie and Mrs. Park and bore their attention with grudgingly poor humour.

As the days passed, he knew he was feeling better when more than just his spirits rose, when his preferred nursemaid came to him and lay along his side. She curled against him and gingerly rested her hand on his chest throughout the night, feeling his heart beating strong and steady.

The bandages were removed and refreshed daily as new strips of clean linen were woven into the gaping wounds on his chest and back, gently pushed by a queasy Lauren and Ellie, who bit their lips to perform the task and hold back their bile. The healing process had to be done from the inside out, so there would be no abscess infection in the wounds.

Gradually Devlin was up and returned to light duties that could be performed in the manse. He was in his study, a glass of whiskey set before him to ease the still gnawing ache in his chest, after a fresh change of bandages. Ellie came to timidly knock on his door asking for an audience. Devlin was curious about her intentions as she usually spoke to Lauren about any matter of importance.

"My lord," she ventured, "I think that I'm no longer an asset to your house, and I should make my own way," she announced, staring at the floor and refusing to meet his eyes.

She gained his full attention as Devlin considered the years the woman had dedicated to his wife. "Have you spoken to Lauren about this?" he queried, unsure why the little maid would want to leave.

"No my lord," she replied, unable to hold back tears.

He saw her trembling and rose, moving to take her plump old hand and guide her to a chair. He poured her a draft of whiskey, ever at a loss to a woman's tears.

"Then what has brought this sudden decision?"

She took a hearty swallow and squared her shoulders as she continued. "It's my fault you were laid low."

Devlin sat at his desk and leaned back in his chair, moving his hands to the back of his head, elbows jutting out on bent arms, feeling the tug on his chest, but unwilling to pander to it. He lifted his leg to rest his ankle on the opposite knee and prepared himself for what he expected would be the wild explanation to come.

"If you are the one who fired the shot, then you are an excellent markswoman. I wouldn't have imagined that."

She gave him a queer look. "I brought it on by the fortune cake," she said wretchedly, wiping at her tears.

Devlin considered the odd assumption of the woman's superstitious nature and leaned forward again. By her woeful expression, she considered this a very serious discussion.

"Ellie," he said, using the less formal address. "Did you put the bag of feathers under the bed for me?"

"I did. Since it was my fault that the evil deed was done to you, I felt it was my duty to help save your life by any and all means. The talisman was to keep you grounded in this life."

He smiled gently at her. "Then I have you to thank for doing so, do I not?" he tried to ease her mind and sway her from believing that she had conjured the misfortune that had befallen him. "I believe the person responsible for trying to kill me was here before we arrived from London. That was long before you ate the cake and were frightened. You are a trusted member of this house, and I am indebted to you for your care of Lauren throughout the years."

"Do you think I'm an old fool for my beliefs?"

"I daresay you're not the only one who has these superstitions, but Ellie, I know you wouldn't harm anyone here, so rest assured that if you want to resume your duties, you are free to continue. If you would like to take a step back from your responsibilities, you can also do that. The choice is yours."

"My wish has always been to stay with Lauren."

"We can offer you a little cottage of your own to spend your days in, or you can choose any room in this house to decorate as you desire. My lady would not want to see you leave. You served Lauren faithfully and stayed with her when you both had nothing. Your value to us is beyond measure. You were the only one who cared for her in her youth. You are more like her family than a maid, and you may also consider yourself a part of my family as well."

Ellie had not considered that her offer to leave his employment would lead to her being considered a family member.

"I would be lonely off by myself, so if I could, I'd prefer staying here," she said, adding, "I've made great friends with the kitchen girls, and I didn't really want to leave Lauren, or you Lord Barwick," she added quickly with a timid smile.

"Fine, it's settled then," he rose to usher her out of his study, handing her the half-finished glass to see her on her way. "Go pick out a room of your choosing and let the carpenters know what you would like done to it. Lauren can help you furnish it, and there's no more need for you to climb the steps up to the servant's rooms any longer."

Ellie downed the whiskey in one gulp, handed the empty glass to Devlin, as though she were already a family member and he her subordinate, and merrily left to choose the room beside Lauren's art studio, rushing to tell the girl about her good fortune.

As Lauren joined Devlin in bed that night, she considered the kind gesture he had offered to her lifetime companion. She lay against his good side and ran her fingers over the tight bandages.

Ellie told me what you did for her today."

"Hmmm"

"That was very kind of you. She was so excited to be given a room on our floor."

"She's not too close to our bedroom, is she?" Devlin asked quickly.

Lauren laughed at his concerned look. "No, she's beside the studio."

"Good. I wouldn't want her bursting in here if she heard your amorous squeals," he chided.

She raised on an elbow and feigned anger. "I don't squeal!"

He placed his hand on her back and pulled her towards him. Before his lips touched hers, he replied, "No, you don't, but you do purr."

He kissed her deeply, slanting his mouth on hers. She was amazed at how quickly he could be aroused.

"Devlin, you're in no condition for this activity," she pulled away from him.

"Would you like a riding lesson?" he responded wickedly, pulling her knee over his legs so she straddled him. He reached between them to her moist, tender spot slipping his fingers inside as she arched her back from the delicious feel of his stroking touch.

He lifted her hips and held her poised on the tip of his hard shaft as she lowered herself in indulgent degrees of exquisite torture. She watched his face, feeling a triumph that she could ride him to heights of pleasure with her movements slow and steady or quickening them to cause robust sensations of intense fervour. She constricted around him and gasped as the *petite mort* of her release pulsated, sending her spiralling to the clouds. He came, his seed flowing into her as he watched the changing expressions on her face. This beautiful woman was made even more so by the powerful emotion of his love for her. He did love her, he realized as she collapsed against his chest, their ardour spent. He loved everything about her, this gentle woman he had sent away and returned to him, perfect in every sense.

He revealed his thoughts to her as he whispered the words against her ear. "I love you, Lauren. You bring me joy beyond any bond I could imagine. You've stolen my heart, and I gladly give you all I have."

"I think you just proved that my lord," she winked, giving him a seductive smile.

"Though I tried to harden my emotions from you to protect myself, I have fallen madly in love with you as well. I am ever willing to please you, for you give me pleasure in return. I feel safe in your arms, and I bend willingly to all your desires."

They lay together, murmuring words of love, planning a lifetime to hold it.

* * *

The four candles of the Advent wreath had been lit one after the other each Sunday. The windows facing the front lawn held short white candles that glowed as a sign to weary travellers, that food and shelter could be found within during this season of giving. Snow lay wet and heavy on the land. Fires were stoked in the manse, which brought a cold draft sliding along the floors to escape up the chimneys.

Winter clothes and woollen mantles were the order of the day, and soft, warm slippers kept toes from the chill. A planned Christmas trip to Camber Hall had to be cancelled as Devlin's wounds had not yet fully healed, but they would see the family again after the winter snows gave way to the warmer season.

As Devlin's strength grew apace with each passing day, James regularly visited with him to keep him informed of the comings and goings in the district. There had been no further mischief since Devlin's wounding. The farmers breathed a sigh of relief that the miscreant had gone to ground with the frigid temperatures, and their lord had survived the attack.

During one visit, James imparted particularly good news that Devlin held close, waiting for Christmas morning to surprise Lauren.

"Your package arrived this morning," he announced.

"Take exceptional care of it and make sure it's hidden away from Lauren's view. See if you can find a nice ribbon for it, and anything else you can think of to make it a special gift."

* * *

The kitchen staff was busy baking ornaments for the enormous trees that had been cut and set on either side of the front staircase. White candles were tied to the branches, and gay red ribbons were woven through the boughs. Lauren fought a dizziness as she slipped a thread through a painted ornament. She was exhausted one day and had a burst of energy the next. Her stomach was often queasy, and she carried a piece of dried bread to chew on to settle her misery. It was becoming increasingly difficult to keep her secret from Devlin and the rest of the household. She counted the days to Christmas morning when she could share her joy.

Lauren put the finishing touches on another gift for Devlin that she had been working on for months. She made arrangements for its placement on Christmas Eve, so she could surprise him in the morning. She had also ordered a special gift for Ellie that Devlin had instructed her to purchase, and she marvelled that he was so considerate of the old woman.

Ivy had taken over many of Ellie's duties while the older woman, secure in her newfound position, spent most of her days in her favourite spot in the kitchen. It being the warmest room in the house that bustled with good humour, tasty treats and no more mice as Ellie's lap held her new friend, the kitten that had turned into a fat grey cat.

There was a stillness to the land on Christmas Eve as the snow fell softly from the dark sky. Lauren was tucked in Devlin's arms, with her feet curled under her as she lay against his solid frame on the settee in the library. In the glow of candlelight, he read from Dicken's Christmas Carol. In the distance, the soft melody of carolling rose through the house, sung by the staff celebrating below stairs. Now and then, they could hear Ellie's strident off-key note, when she attempted to reach for the soprano parts of a hymn, before wisely dropping down the scale to sing alto.

Her mind strayed from the story as she considered the idyllic mood and peaceful surroundings. Smiling to herself, her thoughts turned to the Christmas they would share next year with their first child. She remembered Christmases past, when Ellie had vainly tried to make the season a joyous one. None could compare with the contentment that now filled her.

Devlin stopped her below the mistletoe hanging in the doorway, and tilted her head with his finger below her chin, kissing her long, slow and passionately. "We need to get to bed so St. Nicholas can deliver his gifts," he whispered with boyish enthusiasm.

To Lauren, the evening was perfect as they passed the decorated trees, stopping to touch the animal-shaped Dresden ornaments and being careful not to have her wide skirt tip the potted poinsettias that filled the back of the landing by the wall.

She came to him with a willingness, soft and tender as the night had been and revelled in the consummate joy of their passion as they showed their need for each other. Their joining was as precious as giving and receiving, which made their union special in its own way, as Lauren's soft moans and muffled cries of passion drifted in the seclusion of the dark room.

"Merry Christmas, my love," Devlin whispered when Lauren opened her eyes the following day. He was propped up on his side; arm bent with his head resting in his hand.

Lauren stretched like a pampered kitten and blinked sleepy blue eyes at him. "Merry Christmas to you, husband," she purred.

Devlin reached behind him to his nightstand to retrieve a long, gaily wrapped box and handed it to her.

Sitting up with her back against the plumped pillows, Lauren untied the ribbon holding the paper that surrounded the gift. She took her time to reveal the contents, prolonging the pleasure she was experiencing. Resting on a bed of black velvet was a long gold necklace with an oval cut sapphire circled with diamonds, matching earrings and a ring that Lauren gently lifted from the box and slipped on her right ring finger. She admired the sparkling blue gem and dancing diamond lights that surrounded it.

She rewarded Devlin with a kiss as he commented, "I love the colour of your eyes, and the jewellery matches their beauty. But even its brilliance doesn't compare with yours."

Lauren sighed warmly. "Oh Devlin, don't ever lose your charming phrases. You melt my heart with your pleasing words. I won't ever take this ring off."

"I speak only the truth, Madam. I wouldn't fill your pretty head with lies," he avowed as he turned and bounced out of bed, grimacing only slightly at the pull on his shoulder by the quick motion. "Let us be about our day. There are more surprises to follow."

"Indeed there are," she smiled, eager for her special secret to be announced.

Heading down the stairs, Lauren stopped on the landing and motioned for Devlin to remove the draping on a sizeable hanging canvas that faced the entryway below. It revealed the painting she had diligently been working on since the fox hunt and had commissioned Winslow to have it hung after they retired for the night. The colourful artistry showed Trevor and Devlin on their mounts as they cleared a hedgerow with the foxhounds in hot pursuit of their prey. It was an excellent rendition showing movement in the musculature of the dogs, horses, and men.

"It's magnificent! I knew you were talented, but this is amazing. The motion is obvious, the background detailed," he marvelled at the likeness and studied the brushwork more closely. "Trevor will be pleased you made him look years younger."

Ellie joined them for breakfast at their request and stammered her thanks when Devlin pressed a small box into her hands. She was awed by the diamond-studded earrings and shook her head from side to side so they could admire them placed in her ears.

"My thanks, Lord Barwick. I never dreamed I'd ever own anything so lovely."

"Could you also start calling me Devlin, Ellie?" at her look of surprise, he added, "We are family, are we not?" he raised an eyebrow expectantly.

"Aye Devlin, we are. Somewhat." She teased, giving him a quick peck on his cheek before heading to the kitchen to show her present to her friends.

Lauren fingered her new necklace as it lay on the white lace overlay that covered the rich blue velvet of her gown and admired her handsome husband.

Devlin called for their coats and bent to help Lauren exchange her slippers for walking boots.

"Where are you taking me?"

"I have another small surprise for you."

They kicked the snow out of their way, marking a path to the stables as they progressed around the house.

"Not another horse? I have enough problems with Willow," she exclaimed.

"Be patient, Lauren. This gift is special."

They entered the warm stable to see Carl at the far end of the walkway, who nodded his head and couldn't suppress a broad smile as he spied them. He turned to pull open the door of a stall, disappearing inside. The jingling of clappers against metal rang in the open doorway when he reappeared, leading a sturdy little brown cob whose round hooves clicked on the hard surface of the floor. Bells hung around its neck on a leather strap with a giant red bow tied on top. The pony's copious blonde mane, tail and leg feathers were brushed to silky smoothness while a shaggy coat covered its sturdy body. Atop its thick neck, a heavy head and deep brown eyes looked at the approaching couple. The horse gave a high-pitched whinny and stamped a little hoof.

Lauren gasped, "Devlin," she whispered in surprise, "Is she...is that?" Tears sprang to her eyes, and she ran to the little pony. "Clover, is it you?" Lauren wrapped her arms around the cob's neck. "I thought you were lost to me forever." She turned a tear-streaked face to Devlin as he approached. "How did you find her? Where was she? Oh Devlin, thank you." She covered his face with kisses.

"James did a fair amount of research to find where she had been sold, and I was able to talk the farmer into selling her back to you. She's quite sturdy, so you may still be able to ride her."

Lauren took his broad hand and rested it on her slight belly. "No my love, she will belong to someone else, who we will meet later this summer."

Devlin chuckled. "And I thought my gift would be the best surprise." He enfolded her in his arms and lifting her against him, spun her in dizzying circles as they laughed in pure enjoyment of the moment. Lauren clung to him when he set her feet on the floor. She looked into his summer green eyes and pushed the ever-stray drift of hair from his forehead as he gazed deeply into her mesmerizing blue depths. Joyfully, their lips met in a warm caress of love.

A light snow fell softly from puffy clouds as the couple returned to the warmth of the manse. Arm in arm, they spoke quietly of their devotion and the perfect day that had produced the best Christmas they had ever experienced.

# *Chapter Eighteen*

Boxing Day saw Devlin and Lauren attend the staff dining room with boxed gifts for the household. In hearty good nature, the lord and his lady attempted to serve breakfast to those gathered around the table. Lauren stirred a huge bowl of cracked eggs, while Devlin heated lard in a giant pan atop the cookstove. Mrs. Osmond gave direction to the inept cooks as best she could while the rest of the serving crew laughed at the over-emphasized difficulty shown by the owners of the manse. Burnt toast and runny eggs were pushed around plates until Devlin and Lauren were ushered back up the stairs.

"I believe we made enough of a proper mess that they won't expect us to do that again," Devlin laughed.

They were joined by the local gentry during the holiday season and visited others who opened their homes for merriment. It was a grand time to speed along the short days and long nights of winter. Devlin's wounds healed completely, and his former strength returned. He and James moved their outdoor fencing practice into the roomy ballroom, while Lauren and Ivy tended the greenery that struggled for survival in the observatory. There, they could watch the strategy of the men's movements and their rippling muscles.

Lauren found herself in moments of utter exhaustion. While reading a book, it would drop slowly into her lap, and her eyes closed for a long afternoon nap. Someone would eventually notice her and cover her with a warm blanket.

Sitting at her desk, engrossed in her correspondence to Marian and Devlin's mother, she felt the fluttering movement of their child for the first time. She became still, waiting expectantly for another bubbling ripple of the miracle in her womb.

Winslow broke her concentration to announce, "My lady, Margaret Edwards is here to see you."

Lauren grimaced, and laying down her pen, was reluctant to stand from her seat. Since Winslow stood waiting for her direction, she was forced to relent.

"I will see her here," she advised.

"Shall I call for refreshments?" he queried.

"No. She won't be staying long."

Margaret entered, her wet boots leaving a trail of water in her wake. She pulled off her gloves, tossed them onto a freshly polished table and sank into a chair before being invited. "You look well Lauren, but then why wouldn't you?" she derided.

"What can I do for you, Margaret?" Lauren prodded, hoping the woman would get to the point so she could usher her on her way.

"No niceties? I thought you would have been better schooled in the social graces," she snarled.

Lauren took a deep breath. The nerve of this woman, to enter her home and insult her. "I ask you again Margaret, before I have you physically escorted out of the house. What do you want?"

"I want your husband," she unabashedly proclaimed.

Lauren was taken aback. She glared at the woman before she answered. "You are almost six years too late. He was not available when you hung about his neck in London, and he is exceedingly unavailable now."

"You left, and I was here with him. Everyone knows he was forced into marriage with you and did not call you back to England. He was mine while you were out of sight and out of mind. I fell in love with him while you were away."

"I daresay that you have fallen in love with many men in and out of London. There was talk that it was you who spread the nasty rumours of an impending divorce between Devlin and I. You told a lie, and it was that falsehood that preempted my return to England, so for that, I thank you. You have no one to blame for my return except yourself. Devlin never had any intention to nullify our marriage. Not for you or any other woman who tried to secure a place with him."

Margaret looked at her with malicious intent. "I'm with child!" she blurted bitterly, "I carrying Devlin's seed and will spread that bit of information far and wide. Then he will have to do right by me and set you aside."

Lauren felt like she had been punched in the stomach. Outwardly, she remained cool and calm as she faced her adversary. She considered all she had learned and experienced with Devlin over the past few months, from the unfortunate first meeting to the present. She concluded that she believed him to be honourable. She believed the words he spoke to her when they were alone at night. She believed in her love for him and his for her.

"We are in a similar state," she placed a hand protectively over her growing bump and without feeling so, she calmly continued. "You foolish girl," she paused, considering her next words, and spoke with conviction. "I know not who has gotten you in this condition, but I am certain it was not Devlin. So, spread another lie and destroy your reputation. Devlin has power, influence, and an honourable standing in the community, and I will be at his side to decry your libel. Do you think that your word will be believed over ours?"

Margaret saw Lauren through a haze of red rage. Her hands formed into fists, and she launched herself out of the seat to attack the slight woman who spoke the truth that sent daggers of harsh pain through her, refuting her quest to obtain what she desired.

Lauren stepped away from the onslaught as Margaret's tightly swung fist brushed against the side of her brow. Instinctively, Lauren's right arm lifted in a wide arch, and her flat palm smacked into Margaret's cheek with a resounding whack as Devlin, with Winslow in hot pursuit, entered at a run.

"Cease!" Devlin bellowed, striding with long steps to Lauren to assess any damage.

Margaret held a hand to her stinging face. She was astonished by the quick reaction of her adversary. "You'll pay for this. All of you!" she insisted, noting the room filling with servants.

"Be gone, Margaret. Your lies will never be accepted here," Lauren declared.

"I will have you," she glared at Devlin, "or I will bring ruin to this house!" She stretched out her arm and pointed to Lauren. "I will see an end to you, grand lady!" she sneered.

Margaret took her gloves and stomped from the room, pushing a petite maid out of her path. She opened the outer door without expecting or waiting for it to be opened for her, and giving it a mighty heave, spitefully slammed it shut. She dreaded the confrontation she would face with Agnes Etherington more than the one just passed. She had been sure that Lauren would have accused Devlin of the indiscretion, and an unbreakable rift would have formed between the couple.

When the servants dispersed, Lauren sat in Devlin's lap with her hands clasped behind his neck. She looked deeply into his eyes. "I love you, and I apologize to you now for what I am about to ask. But I need to hear it from your lips, though I feel it with every fibre of my being. Tell me you did not lay with Margaret and get her with child."

"I tell you truly that I had neither the time nor the inclination to do so. Ever. Even before you arrived." He held her against him. "How is it that you have completely put aside your distrust in me to the point when confronted with this accusation, you sprung to my defence and believed her not?"

Lauren thought for a moment, evaluating her emotions. "Because I love you." She continued, "I give you my trust. I give you my heart to hold and see to its tender care. Should I be jealous of women who want you but can not have you? Would that not lessen the love and trust I place in you?" she challenged, wise beyond her years. "Would you be jealous of other men if they approached me? Would you not trust that I would spurn any and all of them because of my feelings for you? Jealousy has no place in our marriage because we have trust, and what is love without it?"

Devlin marvelled at the mature wisdom in this slip of a girl and felt the truth in her words. She could tutor several men and women who felt an overwhelming fear regarding their relationships. For is that not what jealousy is? Fear?

* * *

Margaret returned to the manse and went straight upstairs to avoid Agnes. She careened into John's bedroom in a high rage and spying him, ran to pummel his chest with her fists, venting her anger and frustration. He backhanded her, his fist striking against the side of her head, knocking her to the ground.

"What the hell has gotten into you?" he roared.

"You foul, stinking ass," she ground, sitting where she had fallen. "I'm pregnant by your seed."

John stared at her, feeling an evil sense of pride that his sperm had reached fertile ground but similarly dismayed at the prospect of what it would mean. He felt a tightening in his trousers and rubbed at his groin. "You stupid bitch, do you not know ways to avoid that?"

She came at him again, scratching and clawing at his face. Her strength was no match for the wiry man as he grabbed her wrists in a painful, vice-like grip and forced her to the floor. Pushing her back against its cold boards and throwing her skirts over her head, he grabbed for her flesh. She fought and kicked at him as he roughly shoved his fingers into her. Her anger and gyrations excited him to hurt her further and make her cry out. The thick lips of his mouth replaced his fingers as he bent his head between her thighs, sucking and biting at her vulva and clitoris, pinching her labia between his teeth and forcing his tongue into her void. Her movements turned from flight and anger to writhing passion at the assault.

He turned her onto her stomach on the cold hard floor, spitting onto his finger, he rubbed it against her anus to lubricate the entrance. Swiftly and painfully, he penetrated her with his engorged organ as her muffled guttural screams tore from a harsh throat. She sobbed and begged him to stop, ignoring her pleas as he thrust into her until his release. His weight toppled onto her back, crushing her against the unforgiving wooden planks.

"You won't get pregnant that way," he grunted into her ear.

"Get off me, you pig," she rasped, fighting for breath.

She rose painfully and felt a rush of moisture run down the back of her legs. Whether it was blood or his ejaculate, she knew not nor cared.

"What am I to do?" she sobbed. She would face ruin. Her father would abandon her for sure. She would have to do what many women did in her situation and ply her body on the streets for what little sustenance could be gained there. She would not only have to support herself but a brat as well. Looking into his cruel, unconcerned face, she came to the only option open to her. "You are going to have to marry me," she declared.

John stared at her, incredulous. "I have other plans, and they do not include being saddled with the likes of you," he growled coldly.

Her lip curled in contempt before he continued. "I'll see that your condition is remedied. No one will be the wiser, and you can continue to play at being a virgin multiple times," he laughed at her impotent rage.

A week hence, John returned from a ramshackle hovel in a far-off woods. He had paid an old crone to conjure an herbal remedy of pennyroyal, mugwort, parsley and other plants. He added it to a cup of morning tea laced with rum, which did little to erase the smell or taste of the concoction. He waited until Margaret had downed the noxious drink and then left her alone. He was unwilling to witness the effect, as she spent an agonizing day and night with severe cramps, dizziness and nausea.

She writhed on the bed, her body and hair sticky from her sweat. When John finally crept into her room the following day to see for himself the success of the brew, he was disappointed with the results.

"This isn't working. Help me," she beseeched him weakly, her eyes rimmed red in a pale face.

"What do you expect me to do? You have yourself to blame for the state you are in," he accused. "Drink more of the tea," he growled, handing her another cup of the foul liquid, forcing her to drink it.

She violently spewed the contents from her stomach on his trousers and shoes before he could move away from the bed.

Disgusted, he snarled, "For God's sake Margaret, this isn't going to work. I'll see what else there is to be done." He curled his lip as he closed the door behind him, ignoring her pleas and cries.

John halted a passing servant in the hallway. He kicked his shoes off and peeled the soiled pants from his legs, shoving the soaking garments into the maid's arms. "Get these cleaned and returned to me within the hour, or you'll be sorry," he commanded, moving down the hall on his bandy grey-haired legs.

Returning from a second jaunt to visit the crone, John forced Margaret's reluctant mouth open with a hand squeezing her puffy cheeks. He dropped the oil of savin from the pretty aqua blue bottle onto her tongue, using more than prescribed to see the job over and done with.

Alas, there was little progress. The fetus within her body continued to grow as Margaret's health weakened. Her already depleted body descended further into spasms of torture, and a fever rose from the toxins he had induced into her system. She saw figures that were not present and began to shake violently, causing her damp mattress, with its soiled coverings, to shake beneath her.

Agnes' curiosity grew when Margaret was absent from the dining table for a score of days. Reluctantly, John was forced to disclose the process taking place.

"You fool!" she chastised her son. "Get her to London and see to an abortionist. That stupid girl will cause us nothing but trouble. Marry you? Her whims swing wildly from any man with a cock between his legs."

"What will you tell Fiona?"

"The truth," she chortled snidely, "almost the truth," she corrected. "I will tell her Margaret found a rich bachelor in London and leave it at that until she can be returned home. Then she can stay there, under Edward's thumb, for all I care."

John hauled Margaret down the back stairs, her feet dragging on the steps, as he descended to the back of the house. A timid maid pressed herself against an indented doorway as they crossed the hall, doing her best to hide herself from their view. She watched the slow, awkward procession as the master and his cousin stumbled along the back corridor. They had both used her against her will on more occasions than she wanted to remember. The ill woman was mercilessly ushered out the back door along with a lingering scent of rotting flesh, like discarded offal hanging in the air where they passed.

John propped Margaret into the corner of his coach as she uttered a miserable cry. She was deathly ill and slept the days it took for the coach to arrive in London. The meagre throw tossed onto her body for the journey often slipped aside, and the freezing temperatures did little to ease her fever. Her face had become a sickly grey-green, and her mouth sagged open. Fluid-filled bags hung below dull, half-opened eyes, and her skin hung on her like melting wax. He dragged her along a dismal, stinking alley crawling with rats in the slums of London. The snow here fell grey as ash, and the stench of excrement and urine hung in the air. Cutthroats and bawdy harlots hawking their wares lingered in open doorways.

John pushed her into a disgusting dark hovel. The stench inside was worse than in the alley, permeating the air as he dropped her heavy body on a splintered wood table. A malevolent bulk of humanity, with a vacant stare, joined John to hold Margaret's limbs as a withered old woman with dirt-encrusted fingers applied a long sweeping hook into the depths of her womb amid Margaret's screams of pain and violation.

John hauled her up the stairs to his flat, half dragging her as she stumbled beside him. He threw her onto the soiled bed covers, leaving her to lay in her blood-soaked petticoats. She curled into a fetal position as agony in every part of her worn body enveloped her. Margaret refused food or drink. She felt more wretched than at any other time in her life. She worried deeply about her continued existence. In grief and sickness, she was unable to lift her head from the sweat-dampened pillow as she drifted in and out of consciousness.

In a delirium, she ran through a flower-strewn meadow, her breath wheezing in her chest, the sun beating down on her fair skin, blistering the pale flesh. She paused her flight and watched in frozen horror as a poisonous black adder twined around her legs, winding and constricting up her sore body, lengthening its thick coils as it slithered around her waist, causing her to cry out in pain and fear as its evil tongue flicked out between its fangs to touch her very centre. The flat head rose to face her. She stared into its cold, dead eyes, certain of her doom.

John spent as much time as possible away from his London flat, unable to cope with Margaret's deranged mad ramblings. When he could stand no more of her, he hauled her used, worn body back to the abortionist and left her in their dubious care.

She weakly begged him in an elusive moment of clarity, "I'm dying John. Please don't leave me here."

John ignored her plea and left her with a feeling of relief from the responsibilities of Margaret and her incessant whining. He made the rounds with his friends, entertaining himself by gaming and drinking at a local pub where he fondled the serving wenches and took advantage of what they would offer for a price.

Days later, when he assumed Margaret had enough time to recover from her misadventure. He placed the necessary coin into grimy, outstretched hands before he was offered the still body of his cousin wrapped in a thin, dirty covering. He stared at the dead grey face that peered at him with dry, dull eyes. He cursed his bad luck and railed against Margaret that she had not survived their care. Her inconsiderate demise placed him in the awkward dilemma of finding an option for disposing of her body.

He sought the advice of the curs and unsavoury found in a dank waterfront tavern and made the arrangements for her removal. In the late night hours, when no one was about, except for those whose intentions were as ill-conceived as his own, he stealthily moved her body in a borrowed cart. The horse's hooves thumped on the frozen manure-filled road as he made his way out of the city toward the mouth of the Thames.

He struggled to lift her dead weight to the bank of the river, his grunting breath showing in great bursts of steam in the early morning air. The river passed slowly, thick and muddy on its journey away from the filth of London. John stood upright and kicked the body of his cousin down the steep embankment. Margaret slid over the wet snow and dumped into the depths of the waterway with the barest splash. John watched it float away, mingling along the channel with other pieces of sewage and floating rubbish to join the multiple lost and murdered souls of London that had gone before her. He saw her shroud dip and sway in the current as she was carried out on the tide. The sun rose yellow and bright over the North Sea, heralding a pleasant day to come.

# *Chapter Nineteen*

Lauren and Devlin waited anxiously for the backlash from Margaret's threat. As the weeks passed and they heard no word of condemnation, they put her visit from their minds, deciding to face the consequences when and if they appeared.

They turned their attention to Lauren's growing belly and marvelled at the kicks that were felt when they lay quietly in the night. In the security of Devlin's love, with his large hand resting on her rounding stomach and the child growing safely within her, Lauren was content and happy with her world.

In the dead of winter, Lauren bundled in a fox fur hat that matched the collar of her light brown coat. The luxurious fur extended down the front and flowed around the bottom hem so a draft of cold air could not reach inside along the buttons. Ellie had retrieved a pottery bottle from the kitchen filled with hot boiled water to keep her booted toes warm. She handed it to Devlin in a cloth drawstring bag to keep his fingers from being burned. Lauren tucked her hands into a fur-lined muff to keep them warm as she and Devlin made their way in a sleigh cutter to the frozen pond.

While discussing the day's skating party plans, Devlin had refused to allow Lauren to join in the fun, "If you fall, you could hurt more than just yourself my love, and your cargo is far too precious to risk injury," he exclaimed.

Seeing her disappointment, he drafted a sled that he could push along the frozen surface and then personally saw to its construction. It held two curved runners that would slide along the ice, a comfortable seat for Lauren and a board for her feet to rest on, with a handle reaching behind the seat for Devlin to push the unit before him. On the morning of the outing, he presented the chariot, painted a bright red, to her great surprise.

Ivy and James joined them on skates and held hands as they sailed along the surface. Lauren had slid on the ice wearing her old boots in her youth, but it did not compare to the speed that could be obtained with the blade of steel strapped to the shoes of her companions. A thick robe lay about her lap to protect her from the icy weather as Devlin sped along the top of the solid surface, spinning her in a dizzying circle to her squeals of terror and joy.

"Oh Devlin, thank you for thinking of this." She gleamed, breathless from the excitement, "I was beginning to feel like an old woman forced to sit at home on a rocker like Ellie while others have fun."

Devlin laughed at the joy on her face, "When that time comes my love, I will join you on a rocker, and we will sit and look over our lives and all that we have accomplished."

Late in the afternoon, the couples returned to the castle and held mugs of steaming hot chocolate served by Ellie, who bristled at the folly of spending a day outdoors in the freezing temperatures. James and Ivy remained for dinner and chatted well into the evening in shared conversation huddled near the burning fire. A companionship was formed that went beyond the lord and lady of the manse with the young estate manager and his lively wife.

* * *

Spring approached, and there was a seasonal battle as winter desperately tried to keep its grip on the land. The flowing brooks eventually broke through the ice, and dams formed in narrow gaps or against a fallen tree. As the sun grew bolder, the water ran a little faster, and birds sent their chiff chaff calls into the warming air. Soon to appear would be the house martins, who searched the skies for their winged treats.

After a light shower, April rainbows sent their arch of colour across the sky. Leaves peeled back their hard coverings to open, and grass turned from dull to fresh verdant. Tulips and daffodils peeked their heads above ground in waves of yellow, pink and red as they swayed against the music of the breeze and pointed their colourful faces toward the sun. White and pink petals of the ripening blooms of the apple and cherry blossoms would soon shed their flowers to lay on the ground, in much the same way as the snow had done, creating a blanket of colour below the trees.

Amid the rebirth of nature, Lauren grew apace with the budding flora and active fauna, as long-legged fawns in the forests picked a delicate path to follow their mothers or hid in the underbrush waiting for their return. Calves and lambs were welcomed on the farms, and the planting season saw the tenants hitching their plows to turn the ground, sending the earthy scent into the air. Bertha and Bess were in constant demand as their straining muscles tilled the fields for those farmers who required the help of their lord.

Carl sat atop the carriage in front of the castle, waiting for Lauren and Ellie to venture into the bright day. A quick trip to town was planned to purchase yarn, soft lawn and quilting material to begin preparations for the new arrival. It also became apparent that Lauren would need more clothing. She had recently chosen a couple of simple ready-made designs in the mercantile, a size or two larger than she usually wore, but even those were becoming far too tight. The new dresses would have to see her through to the end of her pregnancy with plenty of room in the waist to grow into.

It was a pleasant trip with Ellie, who was excited to be included in purchasing items for the baby and another chance to see Max Ferguson.

"Pick out a yellow material, and I'll be happy to smock a little dressing gown and hat for the baby. Also, a fine bit of soft yarn for a wee sweater." Ellie was especially eager with the prospect of the new arrival and that her sewing and knitting talents would be well used. "If I'm to spend my days sitting in the kitchen rocking chair with nothing else to do, I may just as well keep my hands busy and out of Mrs. Osmond's cookie jar."

"I saw the thick pad you sewed to soften the seat," Lauren chided. "That must make the chair more comfortable for you."

"It does, but I've also added a bit of padding to my arse with all the treats to be found in the kitchen. If I don't find something else to take my mind off all the goodies, I soon won't be fitting between the arms of the chair."

Lauren hugged the old woman. "You are perfect Ellie. If there is a little bit more of you, it will simply give us more to love."

They stopped before the large front display window and entered the dark interior. Max bobbed a quick hello and offered Ellie a bright smile when he spotted her from behind the long front counter. One had to look carefully to find him behind the huge red coffee grinder, shiny metal scales and elaborate gold-coloured cash register in the dimly lit space. Behind him was the apothecary section, well represented with medicine, remedies, toiletries, and elixirs.

Lauren noted a twinkle appear in his eyes as he welcomed them. He was a short man, just a little taller than Ellie. Bald with white hair ringing along the sides and back of his head. He had a barrel chest and a ready smile. His cheery disposition suited his occupation as owner of the mercantile, as the shop offered not only a place to purchase the goods that the townsfolk required, but a meeting place to socialize, as neighbours stopped in to learn the latest gossip, inquire on letters, or post their mail.

The emporium was crowded with shelving along every wall. The floor was scattered with wood shavings and crammed with boxes, crates, and barrels full of brine and pickles. There were tables holding tea, coffee beans, dry goods, hard candy, flour and spices, to name but a few of the things one could find there. It was a jumble of sights and smells, with everything stored in its proper place.

"Good day ladies," Max Ferguson called out.

"Good day to you," the ladies replied in unison.

"And how are you this fine day Mr. Ferguson?" Ellie greeted. She considered Max Ferguson to be a wonderful gentleman indeed.

"Well, the day has become brighter the moment you walked into my shop Ellie Butterfield," he smoothly replied.

Lauren was intrigued by the slow courtship of the elderly couple. "You stay here and have a nice chat with Mr. Ferguson Ellie, and order what dresses you think I will need. I'll go and get the things for the baby."

The second floor held the material Lauren sought, and Ellie was just as happy to stay and flirt with Max Ferguson. Lauren moved along the narrow aisles, searching among the bolts of cloth, buttons, pins, needles and thread. She chose the items she would need to make the baby dresses and bonnets, imagining the designs and how she would stitch the garments. She suddenly stopped short as she recognized the shape of Agnes Etherington eyeing her from the back of the shop.

"What a surprise to see you Lauren," Agnes mewled, staring at the extended girth of the younger woman. "I expected to have received some word from you since we last spoke."

Lauren took an unconscious step back from her malicious step-grandmother. "Mrs. Etherington, I am sorry not to have sent you a note regarding my intentions."

Agnes narrowed piggish eyes. "Your attitude shows a definite lack of a proper upbringing, but what else can we expect from Phillip Berwyke's get."

Lauren squared her shoulders and faced the adversary straight on with what courage she could muster. If Agnes was going to show a lack of courtesy, Lauren might just as well get straight to the point.

"I wish you no ill will, but I am not inclined to have a relationship with you or your son."

"How you can dare to turn down my heartfelt advances towards you proves that you are no wiser than your useless father."

Lauren held few fond memories of her sire, but it was not this woman's place to pass judgment on the man. She pulled herself upright and answered in kind.

"Madam, I find you both malevolent beyond the extreme and want nothing to do with either of you. I would forever be grateful if we never spoke again."

"Be careful with how you speak to me," the matron advanced, "I will not tolerate you to besmirch me or mine."

Lauren held her ground. She would not be cowed by this woman yet again. "Your dissertation proves my point, Madam. I cannot fathom being in your presence and feeling any form of ease."

"You are an ungrateful child." Her eyes narrowed, and her hands formed claws. "You left me waiting and hoping, and you spurned my honest offer to be a part of your life."

Lauren felt the familiar quivering fear in the woman's presence but pushed back against it. "I find no joy in any meeting between us. Not now, not before, and not in the future," she stubbornly declared.

"You always were a stupid girl. You turn away the chance to have a part of your grandfather's heritage," Agnes disdained with a smirk curling her lip.

"I regret that I did not know my mother or my grandfather. However, I doubt whether I would gain any knowledge of them through you." Lauren pledged.

"You think that because you possess a title, you are better than I? Do not consider yourself above my station, dear Lauren," the crone said with a noxious air.

Lauren gave a rueful laugh, amazed at the statement. "It is not by means of a title, Mrs. Etherington."

"You and the rest of the nobility in this land think you can look down your aristocratic noses on anyone who is not a part of the gentry. You make and enforce rules to keep the common folk down and will not allow entry into elite society. One day, we will see the lot of you take note of us."

"It is your manners, Madam, or lack thereof, that would cause the aristocracy to shun you. As for the common folk, my husband and I take great store in the tenants and families on our land. We value them greatly."

Agnes grabbed a firm hold of her temper. To be spoken thusly by this child, whom she had long despised, was beyond contempt. To value tenants more than her. It was ridiculous in the extreme. "One day, sweet Lauren, I will see you show due respect and honour me."

"You are not my family, and you do not represent them in any way. I have seen no reason why I should show you any respect. The Etherington side of my family was ever lost to me when my mother died. Therefore, I do not acknowledge you as any kin I must honour. There is no blood tie that would bind us in that way."

"There is the bond of my marriage to your grandfather. By that vow, I demand it of you."

Lauren's heart was pounding in her chest. She was sure that Agnes would notice the rapid tattoo against her bodice. She would not let herself be cowered by this woman and had to escape the situation.

"It is my wish that we will never meet again, Madam. You made your opinion of my father and me quite plain years ago, and it seems you have not changed that judgment. Rest assured, whatever consideration I had of you as a child remains the same now as then."

Lauren turned and made her way down the creaking stairs, making a concerted effort to keep her steps sedate, measured and not flee in panicking haste to be away.

"Mr. Ferguson, please add these to my order for the new gowns," Lauren laid the baby items on the counter and waited anxiously for him to wrap the purchases in paper before slipping them into a cloth bag.

Lauren's eyes darted to the stairs to see if Agnes would be descending them. "I'll take this home now," she said. "Send the rest to the castle along with anything Ellie has chosen," Lauren directed shortly, wanting desperately to get out of the shop.

"The dresses should arrive by the end of the month, my lady," he replied, always happy for large orders and wondering about the abrupt instructions from the lady of the manse, who always stayed to smile and chat in a friendly way.

Lauren grasped Ellie's arm with shaking fingers and ushered her out of the mercantile without bidding Max Ferguson a good day.

"What's your hurry girl?" Ellie questioned. She was highly enamoured of Max Ferguson and was enjoying his courtship, though she instigated many of their meetings.

Lauren held her tongue, not wanting to upset the older woman with her confrontation, in case Ellie decided to head straight back into the emporium to confront Agnes Etherington. "I'm just tired Ellie. My feet and ankles are swollen; I feel woozy and want to go home."

"Aye, being with child can make a mess of you," Ellie commented. "Do you think the fly-rink on Mister Ferguson's head shines because he polishes it?" she giggled. "He's a lovely man, so attentive to his customers, and he has a charming smile on him." Ellie chatted happily about her intended beau, adding her unique phrases.

As they extended the distance from the village and Agnes Etherington, Lauren began to relax. She considered her unpleasant conversation an irritation to her morning that she could put aside and take enjoyment with the remainder of the day.

Devlin returned from a meeting late in the afternoon. He had discussed with the tenants the possibility of the right for them to vote. The previous Parliamentary year saw the electorate extend the option to landowners. Still, the current session would have the lords voting on an act allowing all eligible men in the city to receive the right to choose their representation for the first time, provided they could prove a fifty-pound savings qualification or paid ten pounds in rent.

Devlin and Trevor were more progressive in their thinking, believing that the people deserved the right to govern themselves by the power of the ballot box. However, they were in the minority of the gentry who believed that the status quo worked fine. The majority of the lords feared a loss of their influence. They lamented and complained that only 'respectable' working men, those of morality, skilled, sober and thrifty, should be allowed the vote. They excluded unskilled workers, the feckless and the poor. Rural men, which included the tenants of both the Barwick and Camber estates, would not be eligible under the current restrictions. Devlin had assured them that he and a few others were working towards the goal of having all men included. Perhaps in some distant future, even women would be allowed to vote. Devlin surmised that a brave man would have to introduce that bit of legislation. He was sure the idea would be laughed at and heckled through the grand halls of the Parliament building by the stodgy old representatives.

"Would you like to take Willow for a ride tomorrow?" he asked Lauren, arriving to find her reading in the library. "You may not have much opportunity to ride her in the next few months between your rounding little belly and that Willow is also in the same tender condition as yourself."

Lauren laughed. "How amazing that my horse and I are both expectant mothers. If our offspring should arrive on the same day, where will we find the lord of the manse," she gave him a saucy look. "In his own breeding or the expected filly in the barn, he has been so looking forward to?"

Devlin raised his eyes to the ceiling, "Could I have a few moments to ponder on my response," he paused. "The foal will be a fine example of the Anglo-Arabian bloodlines. He should be well-formed, powerful, and with a good gait. He'll make an excellent sport horse but won't carry the refined look of his sire." Devlin knelt on one knee before her, taking her hands in his. A half smile curled his lips, "Now, when I consider our breeding, there's no comparison. First, the actual breeding was far more enjoyable, and unlike when we bred Daniyal to Willow, not for a moment did I think I would get my teeth kicked out." He smiled and became more serious. "A boy or girl, it matters not. I would have a daughter, the image of my precious wife that I can spoil and protect, or a son that carries the beautiful blue eyes of his mother, so I can see her in him every time I gaze upon his cherubic face. In all things, I will choose you." He then teased, "Carl will keep me updated on the mare's progression."

Lauren laughed at his play, "Do you intend to visit with the tenants, or will we be free to go our merry way? I fear if we must stop and I'm offered food and drink at every home, I won't last the length of the journey."

Devlin considered her delicate nature and the numerous trips to the bathing chamber to use the commode. "We have a day to ourselves to wander where we will." he declared.

The following day saw them astride their mounts, meandering along the forest trails. Mrs. Osmond packed a lunch so they could stop at the waterfall, where Devlin laid a blanket on the ground. They ate and discussed family and friends, sharing moments of their day, dreams, and their wishes.

Lauren suggested names for the baby. "If she is a girl, we could name her after our mothers. Diana Elizabeth, or do you prefer Elizabeth Diana?"

"The way Ellie is puttering about and into every discussion or comment on the little one, do you think she expects her name to be used as well?" he asked.

"The child could have the lengthy names of royalty if we included everyone. Diana Elizabeth Marian Ellen. Where would we stop?"

Devlin rolled onto his back and used his hands to pillow his head as he gazed at the blue sky. "Would giving the baby its own name not be safer?" The light shone in his eyes, "Gertrude has a nice ring to it."

"Really Devlin," Lauren asked, a knot of worry showing on her otherwise smooth brow.

"No my love," Devlin joked, then suggested the more outlandish, "Brunhilda?"

"You are no help at all!"

"Let's go for a swim," he changed the subject.

"Devlin, the water is still cold."

"I can keep you warm," he glanced deeply into her eyes with a sure promise.

Devlin coerced Lauren into shedding her clothes and joining him in the pond. With only a slight concern that someone would come upon them in this secluded area, they splashed and played in the brisk water. The birds and the bees saw things best left to lovers as they lay on a blanket, waiting for their bodies to dry before donning their garments once more.

They were making their way home when a shadow slipped into the woods beside the trail. Devlin halted their horses and pushed Daniyal to step in front of Willow before he called out, "You there, step out from the trees and show yourself."

Stealthy figures moved from the dark undergrowth. Josh Hartford led the timid Penny Harrington by the hand, shielding her from view as best he could. "It's Josh, Lord Barwick, and Penny." He exhaled a sigh of relief that it was not Penny's father who had happened upon them in the woods.

"Please sir, don't tell my Pa that you seen me!" Penny whimpered, her nervousness apparent in her downcast eyes and the plucking of her threadbare skirt.

Devlin noted the slight figure of the girl and the protective stance of the young man. "My dealings with your father are far removed from congenial conversation Penny, fear not. I need not warn you that your meeting with Josh should be taken with great care." Penny nodded her ascent. "Your sire was unhappy at the fall festival in town when you were surrounded by other people. He would not take it well if he were to find you two alone."

"We are aware my lord," Josh offered. "My intentions are honourable sir. I want us to be married, but her father will not release her and refuses to let me call on her properly at her home. We see no other way but to meet here to spend time together."

"Devlin," Lauren whispered, "could they not see each other closer to the castle? Todd Harrington would not dare come near our home. There are places in the garden they could sit and talk. It would be quite proper with the gardeners working nearby should anyone raise a concern, and the staff could be cautioned to be discrete in spreading any tales."

Devlin was torn between granting his wife her plea to help the young couple and concern over the impending doom if her father discovered the relationship. He noted the expectant look on the smiling face of Josh and reluctantly relented.

"See Carl in the stables when you first arrive. He'll find a spot for you to meet and try to be careful so no one follows you."

"Thank you, Lord Barwick," Penny gasped, unaccustomed to kindness in anyone other than Josh.

The chance for the young lovers to meet were few and far between as Penny was confined to working with her mother most of the day, and Josh had his duties on the farm. The times when the staff did notice their presence among the hedges, they turned their eyes away to give the young couple privacy for moments of whispered dreams and stolen kisses.

It had become a habit that Ivy and James joined Lauren and Devlin on an evening each week. Occasionally, the parish minister Luke Reynolds and his wife Trudy, would also attend and enjoy the elaborate dinner provided for the guests, along with cards, parlour games or music to pass the time.

After dinner, while the men were enjoying a brandy, Luke was mesmerized as the rare treat of the amber liquid swirled in the cut crystal goblet, which brought to mind the subject of a missing delivery of wine for the church service.

"I don't understand what could have happened. The order should have arrived at the rectory a good month ago, and the barrel currently in use is well below a quarter full. I have had to order another, but I'm unsure if it will arrive in time."

"Several other deliveries have gone astray," James interjected. "It appears that we have exchanged one problem for another."

"Eh?" Vicar Reynolds asked, "what other problem has been about?"

"Last summer we were dealing with a miscreant who was killing stock and setting fires. It was more than a prank when the devil tried to kill Devlin."

"Yes, yes, I was aware of the grave injury to Lord Barwick as we were praying for him every Sunday, but not so of the fires and dead animals."

"It has stopped over the winter, much to the relief of the farmers who were losing their stock. Yours is not the only delivery that hasn't reached its destination. Max Ferguson has missed two shipments, one of farm implements that had been ordered and paid for and a second of household items. Some things destined for the kitchen here have been delayed and had to be reordered," offered Devlin.

"Perhaps the time has come for the county to hire a constable," offered James.

"I should have discussed implementing one years ago with the town council, but there hadn't been a need until now. With little to no crime, the '*every person powers*' has suited us well." He stood to look out the window into the darkening expanse. "I'll contact the police in London and see if any of the metropolitan force can be lured into the countryside. An experienced Bobbie will be better prepared to face our situation. Perhaps an older officer with a few years left before retirement would be willing to relocate."

Devlin turned back to his guests. "You may have a barrel of our wine for now, so you don't run short. I'll have the boys deliver it to you tomorrow." He concluded, "If you are ready gentlemen, let us leave off this discussion for now. Our wives and a pleasant evening await."

# *Chapter Twenty*

The planned trip to Camber Hall was scheduled to be taken by rail. This time, if Ellie wished to be invited along, the ensuing train ride would be a necessity. One minute, she was ready for the adventure, and the next, her nerves got the best of her. She cancelled, only to say that she wanted to go again. She was looking forward to a visit with Nanny Grace and discussing the plans for her expectant baby.

When the day arrived, Ellie bucked up her courage and joined Devlin and Lauren for the trip. From the beginning, she was awed by the Victorian Tudor-style Carlisle Station and gaped at the long grey stone building with three arches set to the side of a central clock.

"Goodness, but isn't this grand? You won't be losing track of me in this behemoth of a building, will you milord? There's such a large crowd of people daring to go on an adventure. I wouldn't have believed it. Don't let me be getting lost and having to find my own way about."

"You'll be fine Ellie," Lauren patted the nervous woman's hand. "Stay in sight though, and don't wander about gawking at everything you see."

Ellie did gawk as she stood on the platform beside Lauren, waiting for the train. Her mouth opened in amazement as she stared at the iron spans across the track that buttressed one side of the building to the other.

As the great steaming beast entered the station, spilling its white blast toward those gathered awaiting its arrival, the little woman rushed back and plastered herself against the wall.

"Come, Ellie," coaxed Devlin, leaving Lauren's side to usher the nervous woman into the cab of the train.

Devlin shook his head in disbelief as Lauren returned his bemusement with a tolerant smile. "Thank you," she mouthed.

With eyes closed and white knuckles clasped together, Ellie murmured her prayers as the train picked up speed.

"The Weather Viaduct is coming up Lauren," Devlin mentioned. "It spans six hundred and sixty feet, and we'll be one hundred feet above River Eden."

"May the Saints protect us," cried Ellie. "I'm not opening my eyes until we stop. How much longer must I suffer milord?"

"Not long Ellie, it will only be a few hours," he teased and added, "Don't forget there's the return trip also, so let's hope you come to like the ride by then."

Lauren shook her head and gave him a shaming look for frightening the maid.

* * *

Trevor sent the landau to meet them at Newcastle station. Lauren had to stop Ellie from bending down and kissing the ground when they were back on terra firma. She gently pushed her towards the waiting coach. "The carriage is more to your liking, Ellie, so can we please move along," she chided.

The pleasant ride through the country soothed Ellie's frayed nerves. They passed through the fortified perimeter of the medieval fortress with its arrow slots cut into the building. Large towers and battlements faced the rolling green hills. The coach rattled over the cobbled lane of a dry moat and whisked through a stone gatehouse into the sprawling courtyard. The circular drive wound around an island of flowers, with a central depiction of a warrior bearing shield and sword. A carpet of pretty bluebells circled the outer perimeter of the garden, their delicate purple flowers laying low among the colourful rising flower bed and imposing statue. This ancient castle had been built to hold a garrison of hundreds of knights and serfs. The outer wall and the living areas were laid with thick, impenetrable stone layers.

Marian and Trevor greeted them warmly, immediately noticing Lauren's rounder form as Devlin assisted her down from the coach. "When is the baby due?" laughed Marian.

"Either late June or the beginning of July, I'm not quite sure."

The children streamed out of the open doorway as the chattering girls squealed in delight at seeing Lauren. "Auntie, may we come and help you take care of the baby?" chimed Violet and Rose, who then began a heated discussion on who would hold the baby first and who would hold the baby the longest.

Nanny Grace followed in their wake, greeting Ellie. "Did you enjoy your first trip on the train?" she queried curiously.

"Good lord, no!" Ellie cautioned, "Don't let them get you on one of those iron beasties. It was travelling so fast. I'm sure I left my stomach somewhere on the west coast."

"The Countess and I have already discussed the train. We agree that a human body was never meant to travel at the horrendous speeds they reach," replied an agreeing Nanny Grace.

"Perhaps if we tell Mother that the rails are much smoother than her coach, she will take pity on Frederick and leave the driving to the train engineers," suggested Devlin to his brother.

"You are welcome to try," replied Trevor. "I have given up. You know how stubborn and set in her ways she is. Besides, if she can't grumble at the coachman, that leaves only me for her to chirp away at."

They entered the cool dark interior of the great hall, where Lauren was amazed at the number of paintings on the high walls. Groupings of families, young boys, girls, Countesses and Earls in ancient costumes standing, and on horseback. It was a picture book of ancestry on display, and Lauren studied each and every one.

"Do you know if our common ancestor is here?" she asked Devlin.

"I'm not sure. Growing up in this house, these paintings have been an everyday sight. Mother will know; you can ask her when she comes."

Devlin studied a painting of a Renaissance woman with alabaster skin. In flowing gown and golden girdle, a long pointed headdress circled with a trailing lace veil, sat back on her head, and with the barest smile, spoke of wise things unknown to the observer. With Lauren at his side, he took note of the members of his family who had lived and died in his childhood home. They studied members of Queen Elizabeth's court with both men and women in their high ruffled collars and puffy sleeves. The ladies wore bejewelled bodices and elaborate skirts, while the men had short and equally roomy garments that ended high on the legs and were encased in white stockings. Beside those elaborate costumes, Devlin pointed to his grandparents, who had lived in the Regency period with simple high waist fashions.

Marian and Trevor led them from the gallery wing to the library, with its chocolate brown walls and books from floor to ceiling. All the while, the children chattered excitedly at the visitors.

"We will have a spot of tea, and then you can go and refresh yourselves before dinner," Marian advised, scattering the children out of her way as she cleared a path for Devlin and Lauren.

The days were spent much the same as when the family enjoyed time together in London and at Barwick Castle in the fall. They played games with the children, and Devlin borrowed a phaeton to take Lauren for a ride around the estate.

"I would make it this far from home before my pony would buck me off and head back to the barn," Devlin reminisced. "He was a cantankerous, ill-natured beast who enjoyed nothing more than nipping at Father's prized Arabians and pushing what little weight he had around the barn."

Lauren laughed at his description. "Clover could be naughty as well. Though she allowed me to stay on her back, she would take unkindly to stray dogs who would bark at her. It was rather fun to watch them tuck their tails and run when she lowered her head and went after them."

They came to a deep azure pool surrounded by massive swaying willow branches. "This is where I stole my first kiss from a young miss, who was also in her seventh year. It was a summer of pure bliss and romantic love as we swung from the branches into the water." He jeered at her, "If you are the slightest bit unsure of my devotion to you, I could kiss you now and ease your mind. Perhaps I could talk you into taking a moonlight dip with me this evening? No one will know what we do, but the stars."

"No one will know in our bedroom either, and I won't have the midgies nipping at my bare bottom there," she laughed.

The dowager gave Lauren a lesson on the family history, pointing out the 2nd Earl of Camber Hall, one Sterling Caomh, the ancestor that both Devlin and Lauren's line descended from. Devlin was a direct descendent from the firstborn from that house, while Lauren's ancestry wound a path from the younger daughter of another ancestor Diana pointed to.

Lauren sketched a drawing of the warrior as he sat atop his white charger and held his helm in the crook of his arm. She asked Diana to sit in the garden with the children as they leaned against her chair. She drew their portrait among the flowering vine that clung to the castle wall. Later, she would add her and Devlin's baby onto the Dowager's lap once she knew what he or she would look like. This would be her present to Diana the following Christmas.

On the last day of the visit, as Lauren prepared to change for afternoon tea, Marian and Ellie came into her bedroom carrying a large wardrobe box.

"Devlin sent a message before you arrived telling me that you were having difficulty finding maternity dresses, and bade me pick a certain outfit for you in Newcastle. The dress has finally arrived, and he would like to see you wear it this evening." Marian could not stop the corners of her lips from forming a mysterious smile.

Ellie pulled the dark violet lace dress from the box and held it up for Lauren's perusal. The bodice had a V-neck design with pink embroidered roses over the breasts. The flower design reached up to the shoulders and down the sleeve to end in a circle around the wrist. A wide, pink satin ribbon tied just under her breasts, ended in a bow at the back and trailed down to rest on the train that would drag along the floor in her wake. The skirt was full and flowing with a similar pattern over handmade lace that sighed as it flowed along the ground when she moved.

"This is lovely and so light and pretty. You have excellent taste Marian."

"I would love to take credit Lauren, but Devlin was implicit in what he wanted to be made for you. I believe he said the colour would make the violet in your eyes dance."

Ellie left Lauren's hair pulled from her face, hanging down her back the way Devlin preferred it and wove a bouquet of purple and pink flowers atop her head with ribbons flowing down the curls.

"My goodness, but we're being a bit extravagant for tea, are we not?" Lauren asked.

Ellie stood back and admired her creation. "If you aren't the jammiest bit of jam Lauren, then I don't know who is. Even in your present state of motherhood, you shine like the prettiest star in the heavens." Lauren noticed Ellie's eyes fill with tears before Ellie hurried from the room. "There's to be a nanty narking time tonight, so hurry downstairs."

Great fun? Lauren considered the past few days in the company of Devlin's family always to be great fun. She descended the stone stairs to find Master George waiting for her at the bottom.

"Auntie, would you care to accompany me for a stroll before our tea?" he politely questioned.

Lauren smiled at the gentleman-in-training and accepted his arm. He walked her outside, moving across the courtyard to the chapel entrance. Lauren could hear the giggling voices of Violet and Rose as they peeked out from a sliver of open door to disappear quickly inside.

Red-jacketed footmen opened the doors, revealing the long aisle of the chapel. On the alter, a vestment-robed Vicar stood facing Lauren, with Devlin standing at attention on his left. Beside Devlin, Trevor held Thomas's hand to keep him in place, and Marian smiled at Lauren from the opposite side.

Ellie, Nanny Grace, the dowager and her dear friend Lady Eleanore Benson turned to the back of the church as Violet and Rose started walking down the aisle, dropping petals of early spring flowers from the white baskets they carried.

George attempted to move forward, but Lauren's feet refused to take a step. The scene before her finally dawned in her mind, and she realized that Devlin had arranged a renewal ceremony for their vows. Those barely understood words, once spoken long ago, under duress by an angry man and frightened child.

Lauren smiled, and turning her astonished countenance to George, nodded her approval and had to stop herself from skipping to the front of the chapel.

Devlin looked into her eyes as she spoke the words her heart sang out. "I love you."

"That indeed is a relief," he replied, winking at her, "otherwise, this whole affair would have been a colossal waste of time and planning."

The minister conducted the solemn vows as Devlin slipped a diamond ring on Lauren's finger, resting it beside the gold band he had given her in London. Their vow was sealed with a kiss.

Before they turned to the family, Devlin whispered, "Do you recall the date Lauren?"

"Besides the happiest one, my love?"

"Today is the sixth anniversary of our first attempt at saying our vows. This time, I hope I have honoured the day and promise to make you happy for the rest of our lives.

"If I had known how you make me feel loved, I would have made my way over the English Channel on a raft to reach you." she pulled his head down for a long lingering meeting of their lips.

She came to him that night without reserve. The man who filled her heart and mind with his presence. His gentle consideration of her in all things. A Madonna, in the full ripeness of womanhood.

As they lay whispering words of love, their hands and mouths searched and discovered. She joyfully opened to his quest, taking him to her and revelling in their coupling. They danced the waltz of love, rebirth, and renewal. They reached unattainable heights to float among the gods. They felt immortal, forever basking in their togetherness. They descended back to earth, spent and glorifying in the moment of satiation, feeling tired and exhilarated all at once. They spoke the language of lovers, partners, of the future and the excitement it would hold.

# *Chapter Twenty-One*

Todd Harrington was in more of a foul mood than his usual frame of mind. His wife and Penny were hiding something from him, and he felt the rage growing in him. The sun was setting on the horizon, casting long shadows into the gloomy interior. The shanty bore the bare necessities. A pot crane was bolted to the side of a cracked brick fireplace, and before it squat a rough table, the top chipped and stained with many a questionable meal. Three chairs that rocked unevenly when sat upon, hid under the table as if embarrassed by their humble appearance. Behind a wearily hung curtain, an unmade bed with dirty sheets and threadbare cover sagged against its rope supports. On the far wall, a slatted ladder led to the upper bunk, under the tight confines of the roof, where Penny slept against the eaves.

Todd sat hunched at the table, grasping a pottery cup like an erstwhile treasure that held the dark contents of a rough brew. He watched through rummy glazed eyes, as mother and daughter cast furtive glances between them. They silently went about the room, stirring the pot over the fire and filled his plate with the meal. It slid towards him over the rough planks as they did their utmost to stay out of his reach. Penny had already felt the bite of his temper when she nervously dropped his bread onto the filthy floor. A purple bruise under her quickly closing eye had been her reward.

"Sit and eat," he ordered them. "Do ya think yer too good ta be sittin' at table with me? I can't abide yer fussin' an fidgety movements when I'm tryin' ta enjoy me supper."

"Aye Todd, we'll sit." simpered his wife, instructing Penny to do the same as they took their places opposite him.

The tension was thick in the room as he plied his spoon from dish to mouth, dribbling the juices of the stew into his unkempt beard. His licking tongue passed repeatedly over his thick lips with each spoonful. He eyed them suspiciously, ever watchful of the nervous movements of his wife and especially his muted daughter, who cast guilty fleeting glimpses from her plate to her father to judge his simmering mood. As he often did when he was well into his cups, he wondered how a robust and virile brute of a man like himself could sire only one child, and she a timid, fearful girl. He left off his musings as his addled brain returned to the issue of the moment.

"There be somethin' afoot in this house," he bellowed drunkenly. "I'll be hearin' it now."

"It's nothing Todd, yer scarin' us is all."

Todd lifted his plate and threw it into his wife's face. "Don't you lie to me woman! Yer as skittish as a pair of mice caught in a trap by their tails."

Sadie Harrington didn't dare move. When Todd slammed his fists on the table and kicked back his chair to fetch another bottle of rum, she quietly lifted a shaking hand to wipe the bits of meat and vegetables from her hair. She could feel the trembling of Penny beside her. Todd could handle the copious amounts of ale he drank, but when he could afford rum, it was another matter entirely. He was a mean drunk, more cruel and uncaring than was his habit. Sadie didn't know where he found the coins that jingled in his pocket, but that fact bode ill for them until he had it spent.

He came from behind them and pushed his face between mother and daughter, catching them around the back of their necks. He squeezed his course rough hands to inflict pain and panic as they flinched and tightened their muscles for the coming onslaught.

He belched loud and wet, sending the stink of rot-gut rum and half-digested meat into their turned faces. "You'll tell me what it is yer hidin', or I'll beat the pair of ye within an inch of yer miserable lives."

"Please, Pa," Penny whispered, desperate for her and her mother's continued existence.

"Please what? Are ya out sniffing around some boy? Are ya liftin' yer skirts ta let 'im 'ave his way whit ya? I have a way of findin' things out, and I won't have it. Yer needed here ta help yer mudder whit the chores that need doin'. I'll see ya an old maid, withered like yer Ma before I'll let some good fer nothin' take ya from here."

Penny was desperate to appease her father with an answer as she felt his fingers digging into her neck. "No Pa," she lied.

Todd released his grip but noticed the quick sidelong glance Penny gave her mother. He raised his mighty arm and cuffed Sadie alongside her head, knocking her off her chair onto the floor. As he approached the prone form of his wife, though dazed and alarmed, Sadie knew what was coming from the years of abuse she had suffered at Todd's hand. She would take the beating to save her daughter.

She screamed at her child before the onslaught began, her voice rising in panic, "Get out Penny! Run!"

Todd stumbled over Sadie's kicking feet as Penny jumped from the tipping chair to throw open the door and run for her life. Her heartbeat pounded in her ears, along with her huffing breath, as she stumbled over the refuse littering their yard and ran through the field, seeking shelter in the brush. She continued her mad dash until the pain in her side forced her to stop. Leaning onto the gnarly bark of a tree, she turned to scour the area for any movement of her father. She was alone, but her relief was short-lived when she considered her mother's fate. She knew the morrow would see Sadie with a broken face and swollen eyes, and she ground her fist against her lips to still the cry of anguish she felt.

Penny followed the trail through the woods, then took the roadway to the Hartford farm to knock timidly at their door. Martha pulled the door open to find the frightened, scraggly girl on her stoop.

"What are you wanting at this hour Penny? Is your Ma sick?

"No Mrs. Hartford, not sick. Is Josh home?"

Martha correctly judged that Todd was on another of his rampages, and the girl had evaded his clutches to hide out for a spell before returning home.

"Do you want to come in and sit for a while? Josh is spending the night at Rachel's farm, and we're not expecting him back until morn. His sister was feeling poorly, and he went to give her some aid in looking after the little ones. You can come inside. We've got a nice warm fire," she coaxed.

Penny shook her head, not wanting to risk her father finding her here and causing trouble for the family. "No, thank you. Can you tell Josh I'll be waiting to speak with him when he comes back?"

"Of course dear, will you be home?"

"No, that's not a good idea right now; Josh'll know," was all she said.

Mr. Hartford joined Martha at the door as the girl headed onto the road. They watched until her silhouette faded into the gloom of the night.

"Something needs to be done with Todd Harrington," Graham contended.

"Aye Da, he's ner' but a wastrel who does naught but abuse his womenfolk." agreed Jacob.

"My Ma says that Sadie was once a pretty girl until she took up with Todd and had ta marry up with him," offered a concerned Edith as she clung to Jacob's arm.

In a nearby tree, a cawing crow sent a shiver up Martha's spine. "There's a bad omen," she whispered as she crossed herself and shut the door on the dismal night.

* * *

After breakfast, Lauren picked up her book to sketch the fading spring blooms in the garden. Moving along the pathway to select a flowering plant, she noticed the sleeping form of Penny resting on the bench under the wooden arbour. Salty, dried streaks of tears could be seen on her sleeping face. Lauren touched her gently, shaking her shoulder, "Penny, wake up."

The tired girl sat up and rubbed her face, wincing as she touched her swollen eye.

"Have you been here all night?" Lauren asked.

"I had nowhere else to go."

Lauren put her arms around the dirty girl and led her into the kitchen. "Mrs. Osmond," she called, gaining the cook's startled attention. "Can we do something for Penny to see her cleaned up with something nicer to wear and a hearty breakfast?"

Ellie stood and immediately came to help the girl. "Did you get into the collie shangles with someone?" she uttered. "You've copped a wee mousie there," she said, pointing to the girl's black eye.

Penny hung her head and looked at the floor.

"Ah, don't get yourself all poked up girl," Ellie enticed kindly. "There's no need to get the morbs. You're among friends here. We'll be taking good care of you."

"Leanne," Mrs. Osmond called, taking charge of the situation, "heat some water and pull the wooden tub into the scullery and when you've finished that, get a new starched dress for the girl."

"I will leave her in your capable hands Mrs. Osmond." Lauren commiserated with the wounded girl and the hardships she faced. "Ellie, I'm sure you can do something to make her hair look nice?"

"We'll see her fixed up proper." Mrs. Osmond finished, leading the girl to a seat as Ellie nodded in agreement and plied a cool cloth to Penny's swollen eye.

* * *

Devlin and James could smell the acrid stench of smoke that clung in the air as they came upon the scorched side of the Hartford cottage. Buckets and other containers were lying on their sides on the trampled grass. The family was exhausted and resting under the shade of a tree as Graham rose to greet them.

"We had a visit from Todd Harrington last eve," the father said. "He would have burned the place to the ground with us sleeping inside. It's only due to Josh here that we escaped."

Martha patted her son's hand, "We consider it a blessing he returned home when he did. Otherwise, he would have been spending the night with his sister and her brood. Rachel was feeling poorly when he went there, but late in the evening, she was much improved, so he decided to come home." She looked fondly at Josh. "He saved us all."

"Aye," snarled Josh. "I saw Harrington against the flames as he was hightailing it away from here."

"This is deadly business," Devlin said, surveying the damage done to the cottage. The perpetrator would face severe repercussions for this deed. "Are you absolutely sure it was Harrington you saw?"

"It was him my lord. I'm positive. There's no mistaking the bulk of the man and the way he walks," Josh replied.

"Penny came here last night looking for Josh. If he thought she was here, this could have been our punishment for helping the girl," added Martha.

"Why he would set fire to the cottage if he thought his daughter was inside is beyond evil," accused James.

Josh rose and dusted off his trousers. "It took us most of the night to put out the fire. Penny said she would wait for me to find her, so I'm going there now. You know where she'll be milord," he waited for Lord Barwick's confirmation.

Devlin nodded in acknowledgement, "James and I will ride to the Harrington place and see him taken into custody to await a trial for this." He and James turned their horses as one and kicked their heels into the side of their mounts to force them into a gallop toward Todd Harrington's run-down cottage.

There was no sound or movement as they cautiously entered the yard. The door hung askew as if the last to leave hadn't bothered to secure it. A scrawny chicken exited the building and ambled away, scratching in the dry dust and ignoring the horses as if it lacked the simple courtesy to greet the visitors.

"See if anyone is in the outbuilding. I'll look in the house," directed Devlin.

He peered into the dark interior. No light showed through the oiled cloth that hung on the windows. Devlin smelled the contents of the burning pot that was hung over the embers of a fire. Metal plates and utensils were tossed onto the table and floor while upset broken chairs were pushed against the wall. Rounding the table edge, he saw Sadie curled on her side, her head lying in a pool of blood that had soaked into the dirt. Kneeling, he checked for a sign of life and was relieved when he heard her moan.

Devlin lifted her from the floor and carried her outside as James came from the barn.

"No sign of anyone there," he uttered, studying Sadie's injuries as Devlin carried her into the sunshine.

"She's been badly beaten and needs Doctor Wilson to stitch up some of these wounds."

"Hand her up to me. I can get her to town and see her looked after." James advised stepping into the stirrup and throwing his leg over the rump of his horse.

Devlin handed the frail, unconscious woman into James' waiting arms. "I'm returning home in case Todd decides to look there for Penny. I don't want him near Lauren. Josh will also be on his way there."

***

John Marlow heard the loud gurgling snores over the grunting pigs in the corner pen as soon as he entered the barn. Sprawled on top of a worn horse blanket in the corner of a manure-filled stall lay Todd Harrington. The useless barn boy was nowhere in sight. "You get what you pay for," grumbled John as he kicked at Todd's feet to rouse him. "Wake up, you sot."

Todd woke with a snort. "Here now! Take care Marlow. I don't appreciate being disrespected any more than the next man," he growled.

"You are hardly like any next man," John scoffed. "What brings you here? You've been given your orders, and we've already explained what is expected of you."

Todd stood, weaving slightly with the lingering effects of the full night of drinking. His stomach grumbled discontent as the last dregs of rum sloshed in his belly.

"I needed a warm place to hide out for a bit. Had me some trouble with the missus and me daughter," his watery eyes glazed as he focussed on John. "Caused a bit a' mischief over ta the Hartford place. That should be worth a few quid ta ya."

"The meagre problems you created for the tenants had little effect on their loyalty to Barwick. What we need now, more than ever, is the cash we can get from the merchandise we lift from the drummers. You've been falling behind and haven't made a delivery to the sellers in weeks. That is where you should be spending your dubious talents."

"I'm thinkin' if I'm doin' all the work and takin' the risk ta get the things ta sell, then why do I need you? I need ta find me own buyers, and then all the profit would be mine." He puffed out his chest in self-importance.

John contemplated the drunk's words, annoyed at any incident that necessitated a confrontation with the swine. He needed the man to continue to do the job that was required of him. Not known as one who would think a problem through, Harrington had been easily manipulated. With bulk and brawn and very little brain, Todd Harrington was perfect.

"I'm willing to increase your share of the profits and can give you a few more coins to tide you over." Seeing the dull look of concentration on the drunkard, he continued, "The people who buy our product wouldn't have you at their back door, so you need me just as much as I need you." Marlow stared at the vacant look Harrington returned.

"Come," he said, taking the man's silence for acquiescence. "You can have the money and get back to your own home. Don't come here again. The last thing we need right now is for anyone to see you even heading in this direction."

A dribble of spittle fell from the slack hanging mouth of Harrington as he squinted and shielded his eyes against the bright sunlight. Against his better judgement, Marlow entered the cool, dark interior, passing through the still, quiet house.

Todd's big head rolled from side to side as he saw all John Marlow possessed. Expensive carpets, fine furniture and possessions crowded on every flat surface of the big house. The current business venture didn't seem fair at all. That Marlow would own all of this while he was living in squalor. He slipped a china figurine of a dancing lady into his pocket as he passed a hall table.

They entered an excessively embellished room. Faded brown velvet curtains hung beside streaked windows, through which hanging vines could be seen trailing from above, obscuring any view. Ancient weaponry, shields, swords and pistols hung on the walls around the room. Mounted stag heads stared down at him in an accusatory fashion while a large grandfather clock ticked slowly in the stillness. Its elaborate pendulum bob and lyre swung on a long gold-coloured cable mechanism. Todd ran his hand on a globe standing at the entrance, spinning the world on its axis.

"What's this?" he questioned.

"The earth, you dolt!" John answered curtly, wondering at the ignorance of the man.

The hackles on the back of Todd's neck rose at the insolence in the other man's voice. He wandered about the room, peering into glass-enclosed cabinets, growing increasingly vexed at the opulence. He pursed his lips and started nodding his massive head in agreement with his inner thoughts. "Ain't right, 'ain't right at all," he muttered, lifting a brandy-filled decanter lid and sniffing the tantalizing brew.

"Put that down!" John scolded, heading towards a dainty desk in the corner where a small amount of change was kept. He sat his manly form on his mother's finely-legged chair and bent to retrieve a small purse from the lower drawer.

Todd sidled beside him to peer over his shoulder at the contents, and his wrath grew as he noted the miserly withdrawal of only a few of the silver coins. Instantly he grabbed for the purse, to have John snatch it back out of his grasping hands. John clutched the leather pouch to his chest with both hands and turned his upper body away from the stench of Todd, tipping the spindly chair whose legs were made to hold a more delicate figure.

Todd's anger peaked, and he pushed his adversary hard on the arm to see him topple over, chair and all. John's legs kicked the desk as he fell, sending it crashing to the floor along with himself. Todd was onto him in a moment as they thrashed between the broken desk, chair and window wall in the small space to gain purchase of the leather wallet. The fight dragged down the dusty velvet hangings that wrapped them in a vice as they struggled.

John felt the heavy weight of the man crushing him. He kicked his legs with all his might to raise Todd's body and heave out from under him. They rolled and twisted against the furniture and fabric, crashing and splintering the wood. Great heaving grunts were expelled from the pair as they struggled on the floor. Neither one was in superior strength to the other. John sank his teeth into the foul-smelling hand that held a significant portion of the prize and tasted blood.

With a bellow of pain, Todd released his grip on the purse and used both arms to unleash pounding, closed-fisted strikes onto his opponent, reaching upwards and outwards, swinging his arms in the motion of a great ape as he pummelled the man below him.

John felt stunned by the blows raining down on him and raised his arms to protect his head before he was knocked senseless. He was forced back onto the floor as Todd, released from the confines of the fabric, towered over him, beating whatever part of John's body his fists could connect. Marlow felt his cheek split and blood course down the side of his face into his ear. In another moment, he was sure Todd would get the best of him, and he was afraid he would lose more than the few coins the purse held.

Agnes, hearing the commotion, entered to find the combatants rolling behind the splinters of what remained of her desk. Searching the contents of the room for a weapon to help her son, she dismissed the full, heavy container of exquisite brandy in the expensive crystal decanter. She spied instead, the long letter opener lying on the carpet. She grasped the sharp implement and stealthily made her way behind Todd, treading silently so he would not detect her presence. She raised her arm and struck. Once on the base of his neck, pulling the blade out, grinding on the bones to plunge it again and again into the centre of his back, slipping the sharp point between the bones of his rib cage to puncture his heart, his lungs, whatever organ the slicing blade could penetrate.

The beating stopped. Todd stiffened with the first strike, raised his upper body and arched his back. His arms hung limply, and a look of stunned surprise marred his ugly face. His eyes glazed with the continued assault. He fell forward with a crushing weight to land onto John, knocking what little breath that one had left, out of his lungs.

John opened his eyes to the blood-splattered face of his mother, whose still raised arm held the dripping blade. "Get him off of me," he snarled.

Agnes tugged with rheumatic fingers, yanking on the filthy coat, as John wiggled out from under the twisted curtain and still body.

"What is he doing in my house!" she curled her lip at the blood-stained carpet.

"I found him in the barn this morning and tried to assuage his sense of outrage with a few coins," he scowled. "Dammit, Mother, what are we going to do now. Not only do I have to figure out what to do with another body, but who will we get to seize the merchandise from the drummers and do the other work we are unwilling to do ourselves."

"What do you mean another body?" she challenged before waving away an answer. She straightened and paced the room. Staring at the dead man, a wicked glint shone in her eyes as she faced her son. "Feed him to the pigs," she chuckled evilly, "they're cannibals. Like eating like."

Moving as quickly as her old body would allow, Agnes spread the ruined curtain and helped John roll Todd's lifeless body into the covering. Her assistance with the body ended there as she morosely examined a broken fingernail. Agnes ordered the few staff members in attendance to the nether reaches of the house while John struggled with the corpse. Pushing and pulling at the dead weight, he was sweating profusely as he performed the gruesome task of hauling Todd out of the house. His grunts and curses filled the air as he dragged Harrington into the barn and pitched the body over the sty wall.

For the first time in many years, Agnes retrieved a bucket of cold water and sponges, diligently working over the marred carpet to remove any last traces of blood stains from the rug. By the time she was finished, her old gnarled hands were cold and sore, and her back ached. She decried her abuse and railed against the stupidity of John for bringing that piece of trash into her home. She straightened her desk, growing more angry at the broken drawers and spilled contents. Moving to sit at the chair that now tilted to one side from a bent metal leg, she adjusted her posture and drummed her fingers on the worn surface. John was the blood of her blood, but sometimes he did not think.

It might actually cause her concern if she had to deal harshly with him to protect herself. She was an old woman, miffed that he had caused her to expend what precious little energy she had. She depended on him to see her plans met, but should the occasion arise where she felt threatened by his carelessness, well, there were ways to get rid of a husband that would work equally well on a son. He would do best to mind that he did not cause her more problems in the future.

The pigs did their duty with squealing excitement as they chewed the fresh meat and ground the bones. They made short work of obliterating the warm corpse. The dainty figurine in Harrington's pocket danced her way out of the bloody, chewed, and torn jacket. It lay broken and shattered as tiny bits of china melded into the soiled straw and manure of the sty.

# *Chapter Twenty-Two*

Penny gratefully accepted employment at the castle, where she could stay out of harm's way and her father's reach. Her light brown hair was clean and pulled back, artfully arranged by a doting Ellie, who offered her services to style the thin strands and show the girl how she could do the same with little fuss. She wore well-stitched clothes for the first time in her life and took great pleasure in being taught the everyday process of washing and staying clean.

Devlin informed her of her mother's condition and that she would stay with Doctor Wilson, who had offered her room and board for light cleaning duties when she was ready to be up and about.

Josh came most evenings to be with Penny, and though he had fallen in love with the shy, quiet girl regardless of how she first appeared, he was even more proud of her once she was clean and presentable. Her black eye gradually faded, and she presented a pretty face with a light smattering of freckles over her nose. Her smile came more frequently, and as the days passed, she made friends with the other staff members through her willingness to lend a hand to help when she was finished with her tasks.

Flowers blossomed into ripe forms, as did Lauren. Her belly cleared a path, and she waddled rather than walked through the house. Devlin was heading to the Hartford farm in the few days he had before leaving for London. The process of rebuilding their home was taking on a life of its own. The simple cottage had become a sizeable imposing farmhouse, with Devlin and James lending a hand in its design and construction. James and Ivy had left to join the work crew as Devlin progressed more leisurely with his precious cargo in the open landau. Lauren had begged to accompany him since her forays into town had ceased, along with her expanding waistline.

In the dappled shade of the forest, Lauren asked him to halt the horses as a pair of haughty swans ushered their fluffy cygnets across the road. The pen appeared weak and depleted after spending more than a month strictly adhering to the attention of her eggs. The cygnets called and pecked at the gravel of the road, unconcerned with the parental calls to move along. The cob stood to attention and raised his wings in a protective stance in case there was a threat from the motionless horses.

Devlin held the pair of Friesians to their place as his wife watched the scene of domesticity unfold. His gaze was held by her look of merriment as she watched the little newborns tumbling and tottering over the grass, following the swans to the water's edge. The fuzzy grey balls wobbled into the water, trilling loudly at the excitement of their first swim, exploring the surface and pecking at all manner of floating plants and insects. When they were in need of respite, they finally jumped onto their parent's backs to float along with them.

Lauren dragged her eyes from the pool of water and looked into the soft gaze of Devlin. She loved that he had paused from his busy schedule to stop and let her view the family of swans. Smiling, she tucked her hands around his solid arm and leaned her head against his shoulder as he clicked to the horses, and they left the happy family dozing on the bank of the stream.

Construction was well underway. The burned side of the building had been removed, and a large extension was being added for Jacob and his wife Edith to have more privacy in the home. One day, Jacob, as the oldest son, would take over farming the Harrington plot of land. Saw horses were set up to hold massive planks, and shavings gathered in mounds underneath to send the fresh scent of the cut wood into the air as men bent their backs to their labour.

"I never considered the good luck a fire would bring to us, Lord Barwick," Jacob called. "The house will be double the size it had been and offer us the chance to increase the family without having to tuck sleeping babies into wardrobes. It's darn inconvenient to have someone come along to close the drawers and have us forget where we put them." Jacob winked at Lauren.

"If only it were that easy," Devlin rebuffed, "I think my brother would have locked his children away each night during their first year to save his ears from their constant cries."

He turned to help Lauren down from the open carriage and settled her among the women who were sewing curtains at a table under a large oak tree.

"There's still no sightings of Harrington," James mentioned when Devlin removed his shirt to help the men saw long strips of wood for the floor.

"Aye milord, the house is sitting empty. I've passed it a few times in the past weeks. No one is about," Josh responded.

"He's gone to ground for the evil he's done, but we'll keep a close watch for him. One never knows when he could pop up again and be about causing serious trouble," added Graham Hartford. "I've known the man all my life, and he's never been able to avoid causing mayhem."

Martha listened to her husband speak of Todd Harrington. His words rang true, but Martha remembered a young boy whose father ignored him after the death of his mother. She considered Harrington's fate and then the castle's gentle mistress sitting beside her. Lauren was treated poorly after her mother's death and did not have the childhood of a grand lady. Yet, like the branches of a willow swaying in the breeze, she did not break and become mean and bitter. She had grown gentle and steadfast, most likely with help from the dear Ellie Butterfield and the gentle nature of her mother's side of her family.

"Penny is getting along nicely and has made friends at the house," Lauren said, puckering her brow as she pushed the needle through the thick material, trying not to puncture her thumb in the process.

"Whatever she has to do now is probably nothing like the work she was forced to do at home. The poor girl rarely had a moment of peace," returned Edith.

"She's a good worker and does more than her share, often helping the other girls with their chores," added Lauren as she pulled the thread successfully through.

"Mrs. Osmond has taken her under her wing and is teaching her how to cook. She says Penny has a right good knack for it," added Ivy, emphasizing her benefit to any prospective mother-in-law.

Lauren could see the direction of the conversation and continued, "She's cleaned up nicely and is quite pretty. My Ellie is proud of the transformation and has offered to teach her everything she knows about sewing and whatnot."

Martha Hartford lay her sewing in her lap and gawked at her guests before bursting into a laugh. "Well, I'm sold. Now we just have to get Josh to propose to her!"

The men stopped their work at Martha's outburst, then turned eyes expectantly to Josh, who blushed a glorious shade of red.

* * *

A month before Lauren's expectant date of the baby's arrival, life was not idyllic. Her back ached, her balance was askew, and she felt as though she carried a pumpkin wherever she went. Devlin assured her of his love with his tender care of her person, and at Ellie's insistence, he rubbed a lavender-scented lotion over Lauren's blossoming midsection.

"I had Mr. Ferguson order it special. It's highly rated by a very knowledgeable midwife in London, that the local ladies rave about. So mind their words and perform the task, for my girl won't let me do it for her," she complained to Devlin.

Considering his wife's burgeoning condition, this was one of the few chances he had to run his hands over her smooth skin. Though he still thought her beautiful, perhaps even more so with the miracle of his growing child inside her, she did not feel attractive. She could find no rest during the night as she tossed and turned, attempting to find a comfortable position. In deference to her encumbered state, he had not pressed her for more intimate moments.

In their bed, she leaned heavily against him as he supported her weight. She tilted her head back to look at Devlin.

"I grow weary of this pregnancy and am eager to meet the little interloper dancing the cancan on my bladder."

"You have seen the cancan?" he asked in amazement, eyeing her dubiously.

"Yes," she smiled, "on a trip to Paris. A few of the older girls from the convent talked me into slipping away from the watchful eyes of the nuns."

"And here I thought you were a prim and proper young lady who would do no wrong. Do you remember the steps? Perhaps in a few months, you could show them to me," he chuckled.

"It was the most scandalous thing we had ever seen," Lauren winked at him, lowering her voice to a whisper, "they wore nothing under their skirts!"

"I will look forward to the performance," he leered.

"I am sure the baby knows all the steps to the high-kicking chorus line and can amuse you instead."

Devlin kissed her at the base of her long, slim throat. "I'm more interested in you lifting your skirts, my love."

Devlin put off being in London for the opening of Parliament, where he would attend the House of Lords to provide his vote. The conservative government would soon be introducing the Second Reform Act, and as the days passed, he could delay no further. He assured Lauren that he would not stay in the city long and would provide proxy votes on the necessary legislation so he could return in time for the birth. If not for the vote and important planned discussions on abolishing public executions and stopping the transportation of criminals to Australia, he would have stayed absent from the session altogether.

Devlin kissed Lauren's neck when they lay in their bed and murmured softly spoken words into her ear.

"I will miss you Devlin," she sighed, "please hurry home to me as soon as you are able."

"I won't stay a moment longer than necessary my love. You can keep yourself busy finishing the nursery, and you will find that I'm back before you have the chance to miss me."

Daylight brought Carl and the Friesians around the front of the house. Lauren stood on the drive to wave goodbye to Devlin. She watched with a feeling of melancholy as the carriage disappeared over the hill to deliver him to the train station. It was difficult for her to believe that a little over a year ago, she had been forced by an article read in a distant land to take her life in a different direction. She had prepared herself for a confrontation with a mate she was certain she would despise. Instead, here she was, full of life and love, holding back tears that threatened to fall as the man who filled her heart, travelled away from her.

"Come along Lauren," Ellie encouraged, "Your emotions are getting the best of you, so let's get the day started. We've plenty to keep ourselves busy preparing for the wee one, and your fine gent will be back before you know it."

Lauren threw herself into a hectic schedule with a burst of energy. The time spent helped to ease her loneliness, though how she felt that way in a house full of people made her appreciate her love for Devlin all the more.

When she sat, her hands were busy sewing the finer details into a gown for the baby. She painted a whimsical forest scene on the nursery walls, often stopping to sit and review her work as her back ached from standing for too long. She considered starting a small painting of the dowager to gift Devlin as a birthday present but decided her aching back wouldn't tolerate the hours of standing before a canvas. She wondered if she would have the time to complete the larger painting for the dowager's Christmas gift after the baby was born.

The local constable arrived with his family and was given accommodation in a townhouse in the little village. Paul Moriarty's uniform consisted of a black bowler hat, a long coat with brass buttons, black trousers and black boots.

The job would not have suited a young, ambitious man. The one who had applied and accepted the position jumped at the chance to get out of the foul-smelling city, to return to the peaceful countryside he had enjoyed as a boy. He was reaching retirement age and was more than willing to integrate into the quiet life.

His wife, Jean, joined the local social scene and was welcomed into the sewing circles, church functions and gossipy groups with open arms. The village ladies were happy that they could rehash stories of old to a new audience and learn of the exciting lives of the city folk. The sons, Ben and William, who arrived with their father, would be taught the profession and take over the duties when the time came for their parent to retire. Until then, the single Bobbie swung a long cudgel in multiple patterns that entertained the children as he roamed through town at odd times of the day and evening. He performed an exemplary job of providing protection from the odd stray cow and barking dog.

* * *

Devlin joined Trevor and his family in the London townhouse. Though he had spent the last few years in their company and made the rounds of London's high society functions with a sense of pleasure, this year, it lacked the bustle and thrill of excitement it had in the past. He accepted the children's demand for his attention, but when left to himself, he became morose and thoughtful, missing his wife's quiet grace and humour. He was amazed at how quickly he had become accustomed to her presence and the enjoyment of sharing moments with her. More often than not, instead of attending the many invitations presented to him, he stayed at the townhouse reading over the lengthy legal briefs that required the assembly's attention.

"Can you imagine the laws we could pass and the progression of the common man, if only the House of Commons and the rest of the lords would leave their families at home and set their minds to improving society instead of gaming and attending balls?" Devlin asked as he perused the current laws to transport desperate criminals to Australia for stealing a loaf of bread to feed their starving families.

"I don't know about you, but my eyes are ready to cross," answered his brother as he removed his glasses and pinched the top of his nose where they had dug into his skin. "Would it hurt overmuch if we stepped out this evening?"

The family felt obliged to attend the Ferndale ball that was taking place at their London home. It wasn't until they arrived, that they discovered the night had been organized as an Egyptian experience. Three hundred guests would have an opportunity to peel back the wrappings of a genuine mummy until it was fully exposed.

"I'm sure we can make our excuses to leave before the grand climax of the evening," Marian hoped.

Devlin glanced wryly at his sister-in-law, "What an odd fascination with the macabre we have developed."

"Do we not believe it to be a crime and have installed iron cages over our own deceased, so the resurrection men cannot extract the bodies to sell to the universities," she declared in outraged annoyance.

"We feel it is a gross infringement of decency when it comes to protecting our own," chimed Trevor, "yet have no problem with plundering the Egyptian ruins to transport mummified remains thousands of miles for our entertainment."

Nicholas Emory rushed past them, greeting a quick hello on his way to the viewing. Isn't it thrilling to see the sarcophagus?" he chimed, holding a lace handkerchief to his nose. "I hear the ones made of limestone can reduce flesh to dust."

Marian shivered at the prospect of gazing at the sight of the gruesome, deathly grimace the unwrapped mummy would reveal.

Fiona Edwards, a plump bundle of energy, searched the crowd pausing only to ask her singular question as she swept the room from one end to the other.

My dear Lords, Lady Cavanaugh," she warbled as she spied the family. "How lovely to see you here this evening. Have you seen my Margaret at any of the balls?"

"I have not," replied Trevor, "but then we have not been to many of the affairs held this season."

Fiona turned concerned eyes to Marian, "Any function? Anywhere at all? The shops, a tea house, a concert perhaps?"

"I am sorry Baroness, she has not been present at any of the places I have visited or been invited to, but I will watch for her and if I see her, let her know you are concerned."

Devlin took pity on the frightened woman. He considered that Margaret had not told her parent of her state and that she could have taken herself off to deliver the child she had accused him of siring. If Margaret had not discussed this with her mother, he certainly would not broach the subject.

"She was staying with an aunt near Barwick Castle last fall. Perhaps she can ease your worry and is apprized of her whereabouts," he remarked kindly.

Fiona blanched. "Thank you Lord Barwick," she contemplated his answer, feeling a prickling of fear that Agnes would be involved with her daughter's disappearance.

More than a few of the unhappy, bored wives of the aristocracy noted Devlin's appearance in London. Word spread quickly that the newly arrived wife was not in attendance and stayed home in the country. Where before Devlin had been amused by the flirting attention he had once received, now it seemed sordid. Wives of prominent lords slyly offered trysts or flagrantly mentioned their wants in a more direct manner.

"Lord Barwick," chimed one such Countess, "I see you are once again unattended by your wife and how quickly it has become so," she fluttered her eyelashes at him coquettishly. "My dear husband is seated in the card room and is more inclined to wagering instead of dancing with me. Perhaps you would be so kind?" She offered her hand to him.

"Of course, Lady Rowbothom, I am honoured," he politely replied, thinking he was committing to only a dance.

"Randolf will be away tomorrow, and I have no pressing engagements," she murmured, moulding herself far too intimately against him.

Devlin attempted to hold her at arm's length as they danced the light steps of the waltz. "What a privilege it is for you to enjoy private times," he attempted to sway the conversation.

"I will be spending the time alone," she came abruptly to her intention. "I don't really enjoy being totally alone," she winked suggestively.

"Marian will be attending the concert in the park. I'm sure if you ask, she would enjoy your company."

"I think not," she persisted. Did Barwick not understand what she was offering? "I don't care for the park. In fact, I prefer the indoors. If you are lonely, perhaps we can enjoy each other's company," she stated with a smile.

Devlin thought of the woman waiting for him at home. Though they had not recently enjoyed the loving relationship that existed between them and would not for some weeks after the birth of the baby, he considered that his abstinence would assuredly prevail. There wasn't the remotest chance he would accept what was brazenly offered. He would gladly wait for the one he desired. Lauren could easily trump any immediate release he would achieve with another.

"Thank you for the offer, but no," he firmly stated without further explanation.

In the middle of the dance floor, with other swirling couples around them, the Countess suddenly stopped, and in a high rage of offence, stomped off the floor. She was followed by a smiling

Lord Barwick, who cheerfully greeted the curious guests with a friendly smile.

Devlin attended a few of the affairs due to courtesy but found himself, more often than not, with the older gentlemen in the smoke-filled rooms playing cards. He was anxious for the discussions and voting proxies to be finalized so he could make his way home.

Receiving an elaborately scrolled calling card from the butler, Trevor found Devlin in his study. "Bertie has sent a request that would be difficult for you to turn down."

Devlin chuckled, "His mother is probably furious with him again. Though I think she has been in that state since he was a lad."

"It's not as though he doesn't give her good reason," Trevor recalled the many instances of outrageous behaviour.

"What else does he have to do? He has completed his current duty by providing an heir and a spare, and until such time that the Queen departs her mortal coil, his is nothing but a waiting game." Devlin tossed the sheaf of papers he was reading onto his brother's desk.

"I believe that Victoria considers him a complete and abject failure and won't entrust even the slightest matter of state into his hands," replied Trevor. "Lord knows he has given her multiple reasons to feel this way."

Devlin looked expectantly at his brother, "I cannot refuse to attend and would appreciate your coming along. Considering the company that will be there, you might want to leave Marian at home."

Trevor and Devlin entered Marlborough House, stepping beyond the four outdoor columns and red-bricked entry into the front hall, already brimming with guests. Princess Alexandra, a lovely dignified woman who was affectionate and jolly in private, welcomed the brothers as they bent to kiss her extended hand.

"I see that your wives are not joining us this evening. A fine pair of rogues wandering about these halls are usually the norm, and there are many distractions to be found." She nodded towards a group of eligible and unattended women, most likely special guests of Bertie.

"My wife is home expecting our first child Alix, and Marian was unable to attend."

"Ah, so there will be no gossip this year on your adventures with the lovely Lauren," the princess smiled lazily. "Whenever there is talk of another's misadventure, Bertie gets a reprieve from the wagging tongues."

The princess moved away from them to greet a Duke and his Duchess, walking haltingly with the limp her bout of rheumatic fever had left her with. The charming woman welcomed both fellow royalty and her husband's mistresses alike. Most assumed that she appreciated the relief those women gave her from the overburdened duties of the insatiable Prince of Wales.

Bertie was found in the smoking room puffing deeply on a cigar and motioned for the brothers to join him. He led them to a quiet corner.

"Charles Mordaunt has lost his mind," he regaled. "Harriet is so young and gay. He shouldn't expect her to linger alone in the house while he's out hunting with his old cronies. I merely went to see the fair lady for a friendly visit."

Neither Trevor nor Devlin dare spoke a word, already aware of the tilt of the conversation and the ensuing scandal, especially when Bertie was involved. Harriet and Charles had only been married for six months, and the prince was already causing problems in their marriage.

"We were not really alone," he said with a lopsided smirk.

"That was wise," Trevor admitted, noting Devlin's doubtfully raised eyebrows.

"We were out riding two white ponies when Charles came upon us in a rage."

"Are you implying that the ponies were your escort?" doubted Devlin.

"Well, if they were not there, we would have been alone." The prince smirked. "When Charles found us, I assumed that discretion was in order and left the couple to their private discussion." He inhaled from his cigar, blowing a cloud of smoke into the air. "That, of course, was after I was ordered out of his sight! I felt it was the best thing to do." Bertie cast about to ensure no one could overhear their conversation.

Devlin wondered how a man with the reputation of the prince could be so popular in stuffy old England. If not for his cavalier, charming and generous personality, he could easily be the most despised. Yet everyone loved him. Everyone, that is, except his own mother.

Bertie continued in a low voice. "I hear Charles shot the ponies in front of Harriet for spite. You don't suppose he will aim his gun at either her or me in the future, do you?"

"Bertie, why don't you take your wife on a nice trip to Ireland for a while until things cool down here?" Devlin suggested.

"Excellent idea. Excellent," he agreed, snuffing out his cigar. "England has lost its appeal at the moment. That arrogant Brown won't leave my Mother's side and refuses my admittance into her company. Can you imagine him calling the Queen of

England 'Woman! The insult! Her perpetual mourning hangs over me like a storm cloud, and Alix is devoted to spending as much time as possible with the children even though the youngest is already four months old."

"Ireland sounds like an excellent idea," Trevor agreed with his brother, attempting to coax the recalcitrant prince to mend his ways.

The prince pulled another cigar from his coat, lit it, and after a deep inhalation, flicked the ash onto the floor as he considered the trip. "Ireland. It reminds me of my dear Nellie Clifden," he whispered so no word could be overheard and relayed to his wife. "I've tasted the fine talents of the local aristocracy," he quickly assured them, "except, of course, your excellent wives." He noted the slight hardening in his confidante's eyes and appeased, "Fear not, my fine gents, I am well aware of your marksmanship and propensity for fencing. I am well outmatched in either sport, and I have no wish to risk a puncture from either of your weapons, be they blade or pistol. Your friendship is worth more than a toss with any woman, fine though they may be. I respect your wives as much as I respect each of you." He pondered upon his choice before stating, "Mayhap I will take a trip to Paris. I understand they have some of the finest whorehouses in all of Europe."

# *Chapter Twenty-Three*

Devlin threw his luggage into the back of the cart that waited for him at the station and collected Daniyal, who had accompanied them. He raced the lathered horse up the lane to find a laughing Lauren waiting for him on the front lawn. Slapping Daniyal on the rump to send him to the stables, Devlin rushed to kiss Lauren's happy face and rest his large hand on her belly.

"What have you here? Are we expecting one baby or a litter?" he teased.

"I'm huge, and considering the size of the sire, there had better only be one inside of me!"

As they walked to the house, she leaned her head against the arm she held. "I have news," she smiled prettily when he looked down into her upturned face, "James and Ivy are expecting a child as well."

"That is good news. This ensures that whoever is hiding inside you will have an estate manager as wise and as good a friend as James has been to me."

"They will need a bigger house. His little cottage is barely large enough for the two of them."

"Most estate managers have a large manor. We will have to get busy designing one for him and have it ready for their growing family. I don't believe they will be stopping at one either," he smirked, wondering if this was an appropriate subject to bring up when she was already heavily burdened with a child.

Lauren pushed the stray hair from his forehead. "Either?" came her velvet reply, "It is an injustice to have only one child. With only one, we will know who to blame when the child gets into mischief!"

"Are we not assuming that our child will be perfect?"

Lauren laughed, "With the stories Nanny Grace has told me about you?" She became more pensive, "I lived a solitary life, and I certainly would not want that for our son or daughter. If only you could have the next one, it would make my life much easier."

She walked with him to the stables and sat on a bale of hay, playing with a kitten as he curried Daniyal and inspected Willow.

"How was London? Did you attend many parties?"

Devlin's lips curled into a smile. "Not many. I was devoted to completing the necessary tasks so I could return home to you."

"Good. Let the young misses find themselves another beau. You have definitely been taken off the marriage market," she laughed.

Devlin was reminded of the concern Baroness Edwards had for her absent daughter.

"Margaret is missing. Her mother was looking all over London for her. No one has seen her since last winter when she came here."

"Would that be unusual, Devlin? She would certainly not want to be seen if she was unmarried and expecting a child. She must be in a safe place waiting for the birth and surely will be back in the social scene before too long."

"She was visiting an aunt in the area. Do you know of any relative of hers near here?"

"That would be a surprise to me. I can think of no one related to the Edwards locally."

"I'm sure she'll turn up soon. She always does."

* * *

Devlin was touring the land with James when Lauren felt the first twinge of a contraction. Long moments passed as she waited for another, and when it didn't appear, she put it out of her mind and continued painting the last fairy on the woodland scene in the nursery. When she finished, she rocked the wooden horse that had once belonged to Devlin, which Diana had insisted he take home for the baby. The clothes were neatly arranged in drawers, and a thick pad had been placed on a dresser containing lotions and powders that would soon find their way onto a tiny bottom. A stack of soft white absorbent cotton nappies were folded into small rectangles awaiting the one who would see them well used.

Ellie had been enamoured with an elaborate brass canopied bassinette draped with a cream-coloured lace curtain. A pewter hawk stood guard on a massive base with the swinging bed supported on wooden lyre-shaped rods that looked more like a Viking ship than a baby's cradle. The design had seemed totally impractical to Lauren. However, to appease the older woman, Devlin had seen to its purchase.

When Devlin returned home, Lauren tried to heave herself out of the library chair only to find her bottom on the edge, her back above the seat, and her head resting on the back. She could not bend at the waist to get herself up and was held in that position no matter how she twisted and turned.

Devlin entered the room as she begged for help. "Devlin, I'm stuck," she cried.

Laughing, he lifted her into his arms and let her legs slide down his own until her feet were firmly on the floor. "Have you been stuck for long? Shall I have Ivy sit with you when I am not home so we don't find you rolling on the floor like a turtle on his back trying to turn over?"

Lauren pouted at him and childishly stuck out her tongue. "You have done this to me. I once was a proud and graceful lady, and look at me now. I cannot see my feet and must waddle like a duck and look like a hippopotamus."

"Hardly a hippopotamus, my love. More like a beautiful woman swollen with the product of our love. It shouldn't be long before he will be out, and you will just be yourself again." He touched the tip of her pert nose as she scrunched it at him.

"He, Devlin? Do you wish for a boy?"

"As long as the baby is healthy, happy, and has your eye colour, I don't care. A mere slip of the tongue. I wouldn't want to insult him, or her, by calling our baby 'it' any longer and anxiously await the day for the arrival."

Lauren awoke in the early morning hours as Devlin dressed for the day. She lay in bed admiring him as he reached for his clothing. His tight buttocks flexed and indented on the sides as he lifted his leg to slide into his trousers, hoisting them up to button the front and removing from her view what she was enticed to witness.

She felt a tightening in her lower belly and wondered if her time would ever come. She was anxious to see this pregnancy to its end.

The contractions came throughout the day. They were mild and irregular, and Lauren was sure her time was nigh. This would be easy. There was nothing to it. A little twinge here, a tightening there. She would see this day through and at the end of it, gift Devlin with a beautiful babe held in her arms while she sat in bed, wearing a modest frilly nightgown, hair styled, and cheeks pinched to show a healthy glow.

The day progressed, but Lauren did not. This was proving to be a test of emotional stamina as she waited for the baby. She tossed and turned, trying to be comfortable during the night. No sooner would she fall asleep, than she was awakened as her muscles tightened, and she curled into a fetal position to relieve the stress of her muscles.

By daybreak, she fell into an exhausted slumber as Devlin quietly left the bedroom to begin his day. He and James were helping to put the finishing touches on the Hartford home. The farmhouse continued growing as the original wing addition was now a large brick structure that dwarfed the cottage. There were rooms on the main level for Graham and Martha and a second addition on the side for Jacob, Edith and their family. With all the added wings and changes, the building process had taken longer to complete, but the finished structure would be a sign of the prosperity the tenants had achieved in the past few years and those they expected to reap in the future.

Lauren took herself to the studio to pace the length of the room away from prying eyes. Forward and back again, she moved in front of the windows, grabbing with white-knuckled fingers to hold the back of a chair, the ledge of a window or her easel when the pains intensified. She kept track of the time.

First, the contractions came every ten minutes, then seven. Now, they were every five minutes and were lasting up to one minute in length.

As the hours progressed, Lauren's idea of an uncomplicated, easy birth waned as reality set in. This would not only be a test of emotional stamina but one of physical endurance as well.

Ellie appeared to bring her a light lunch. As she opened the door, she saw Lauren bent forward, holding onto the chair and her lower belly. Ellie dropped the tray on a nearby table, sending the contents askew, spilling tea and sandwich pieces among the tipped pottery.

"What are you thinking to be hiding yourself away in this condition? Are you daft girl? Take my hand, and we'll get you into your room."

Ellie called for Ivy, her voice rising an octave as she bade the girl hurry. Fresh linens were laid thickly on the bed as the house was set into a frenzy of motion. Lauren was stripped of her clothes and dressed in one of her old, voluminous cotton nightgowns.

"I daresay you won't need to be wearing any of those fancy nightdresses his lordship purchased for his pleasure," the old woman declared with an abrupt nod of her grey head.

"I haven't been able to wear them for months Ellie. They are all of them too small." A sudden gush of fluid splashed onto the floor, soaking the newly donned gown. Lauren looked at Ellie in surprise. "Oh my! I'm relieved that didn't happen when I was alone."

"Aye," the maid scurried to find a dry gown. "For all your high flown education, you should have been wiser than shutting yourself away!"

Lauren settled into bed and groaned aloud as the pain came hard upon her.

"When is Devlin expected back?" she asked.

"We'll be sending word to him. He'll be hightailing it home as soon as he can. Now think of yourself and try to relax between contractions."

Lauren considered Ellie's take-charge attitude. "How is it that you seem to know what to do, Ellie?"

The old woman considered the nervous look of her mistress and assured her, "What do you think I was learning when you were in your lessons at the abbey?"

At Lauren's shrug, she continued, "There was another part of the convent that you young ladies were ignorant of. There was a hospital ward outside the big stone wall where the nuns took in unmarried girls who had gotten themselves into trouble. We ladies' maids received instruction there on how to take care of you when your time came. I helped deliver many babies and watched over the poor young girls desperate for any show of affection." She shook her head sadly, "Many of them were turned from their homes by angry parents, and their prospects were awful."

"You never told me this."

"Well, it's not for innocent ears. Now breathe through the pains."

***

The fast clip of a racing horse sounded among the hammering of the boards on the roof of the large farmhouse. Inside, Devlin cursed as he adjusted the hinges on a cupboard door to have it hang properly for the third time.

He heard the whoop and cry of the men as Carl bound into the structure. "Lord Barwick, get yourself home! The baby's comin'!"

Devlin released his grip on the door and left it hanging askew as he ran outside and jumped across Daniyal's rump to land in the saddle, not bothering to waste the time using the stirrup to mount the startled horse. His hair blew in the wind as the pair sped their way homeward. He jumped from the prancing steed as they reached the front of the house and slapped Daniyal on his flank to send the lathered horse to the barn where the stable boys would find him and see to his care. He took the stairs three at a time, slowing before the door to his bedroom, taking a deep breath, and preparing himself to show an outward calm before entering.

The room was full of women. Mrs. Park wet cool cloths to place on Lauren's forehead as maids scurried in and out of the chamber to fetch clean towels. Ivy held Lauren's hand, counting the seconds of a contraction, and for once, Ellie was relaxed as she sedately rocked in a chair, watching the proceedings, confident that when needed, she would be ready to help her lady.

Lauren relaxed when Ivy reached the count of one hundred and ten. "Oh, that was a long one," the maid said.

Lauren raised a hand to Devlin as he approached and took the offered member. When Devlin appeared, her idea of a graceful presence had vanished hours ago as her excitement waned and the reality of labour progressed. Her hair was matted, and she felt sticky with sweat as she strained to bring forth their child.

The contractions came every two or three minutes and lasted less than two minutes. The constant, unceasing barrage of pain was drawing on Lauren's reserves. She was tired and frustrated with the slow progress, irritated with the clamour around her one minute and cold and shaking, appreciating their help the next.

Devlin stayed at her side throughout the hours, blanching with every moan and shiver of his wife. To see her in agony was almost more than he could bear. When he was in the way and ordered away from Lauren, he walked from the bed to the door and back again, not knowing how to ease his tension and fear as the process droned on. Ellie had enough of his pacing and questions. When the time came, she would be busy with Lauren and have no time for a pale, prostrate lord lying on the floor. They would be otherwise occupied, and she had no inclination to take care of him when Lauren was her priority.

She reached up to turn his solid form and pushed him towards the door, "Go make yourself arf'arf'an'arf," Ellie declared. He stared dumbly at her, unable to comprehend what she was trying to convey. "Go and make yourself busy elsewhere, Devlin, preferably with a middlin' amount of whiskey to see you through the delivery!" she gave his broad shoulders a push that ushered him out of the room, closing the door firmly behind him.

James and Winslow were in the parlour, unabashedly partaking of his excellent brandy. They handed a hearty draught to Devlin, and the gentlemen saluted each other as the hours passed.

"How much longer Ellie? I can't take more of this."

"An hour, maybe two," she spoke with authority, then murmured, "easier to get it in than out, eh," and immediately had the good sense to remove herself from Lauren's angry look and most unladylike comment.

Lauren transitioned from the twisting agony of contractions to an intense desire to push, to bear down as the pressure mounted. Ivy positioned herself behind Lauren to help her sit forward. Strips of linen were tied to the foot of the bed for Lauren to grasp and apply pressure as she leaned into her pain to expel her child from her body. Ellie was waiting and ready to ease the baby into the new day.

"Don't be holding the tension in you. Push for all you're worth and use your energy to bring this baby into the world," Ellie instructed.

Everyone was involved with the exhausted woman. They either held their breath or breathed along with Lauren as she strained to deliver her child. The head came through as a guttural grunt spilled from Lauren's throat. A moment of pause and a mighty final push was followed by a slick rush as the rest of the newly born babe was delivered.

"A grand boy Lauren. You've done a fine job, and you're a bricky girl, my pet. You faced the trial of every woman with courage and didn't scream the roof down. I'm proud of you for delivering our little chuckaboo," Ellie said as she caught the baby with a firm grasp and laid him on Lauren's stomach.

Lauren was engrossed with the sight of her child. He was perfect in every way. Like every mother before her and those who would come after, she counted his fingers and toes. He sported light brown hair and opened blue eyes to quizzically examine her as well. When offered, he took her breast in a greedy display of taking what was his without question.

"He'll be conquering the world this one. He takes what is given to him without a fuss and enjoys his demands," Ellie said as the baby made little gulping noises.

He was returned to Lauren after being cleaned and swaddled when Devlin entered the room. "You have your son," Lauren tiredly murmured.

Devlin lay on the bed beside her to look at the wizened face of his firstborn. "We won't be able to call him Brunhilda," he smiled. "Do you have any other suggestions?"

Lauren reached up to push back the hair from Devlin's forehead. "I was thinking of Sterling. To name him after our common ancestor and start anew."

"Sterling Cavanaugh. I like it."

"Sterling Devlin Tremont Phillip Cavanaugh. A great man will need an impressive moniker," she whispered as her eyes closed and she drifted to sleep.

Devlin lifted the baby from her arms and settled him beside his sleeping wife, who, with an instinct born of motherhood throughout the ages, turned toward him to circle him in her protective arms.

* * *

Sterling Cavanaugh woke the sleeping house early the next morning with a lusty cry that was soon quieted as he received succour from his demands. He assumed that the world revolved around him and his wants, and he was correct. His mother doted on him, and his father, for the first time he could remember, ignored his duties, as their attention was focused on the child they had brought forth with their love.

Whenever he was laid in the elaborate bassinet, he would soon find himself picked up by Ellie, who had waited patiently for her turn to hold the child. Therefore, he felt loved and spoiled as his every whim and those beyond his ken were seen to.

"You're a Saturday child who's to work hard for a living," Ellie warned him as she rocked the babe in Lauren and Devlin's bedroom. "So you had best take your leisure now and sleep so you can grow big and strong like your father. You're under the sign of Cancer and you will be a good person with grand ideas." She rubbed her old fingers along his soft baby cheek. "You will be a hearty, brave soul and take up any challenge you encounter."

Sterling studied the old woman's wrinkled face and appeared to be deep in thought as he considered Ellie's words.

"That's right young Sterling, heed my words, for you will be an ambitious lad. By your hand, we will see Barwick Castle prosper into a new century."

Lauren giggled as Ellie spoke of the responsibilities the baby would face. "Shouldn't we be telling him that all we expect of him right now is to sleep through the night and sit up on his own at some point?"

"Aye, you're to do that as well, Master Barwick," Ellie agreed.

# *Chapter Twenty-Four*

Fiona attended every soiree, concert, ball and dinner party the city offered during the summer season. While other guests were gay and frivolous, her mood was dark and gloomy. She asked everyone she knew, those she only had a passing acquaintance and others she had only noticed at the various events, if they had seen Margaret. She was frustrated and annoyed with their flippant comments.

"Margaret who?" some asked, looking down their haughty noses.

"The girl throwing herself at Lord Barwick last season?" challenged others with a similar lofty air.

Even those of their own class, the prissy daughters of Barons and their nattering mothers, had plainly stated that she had not been noticed…or missed they snidely murmured to one another. Their attitude infuriated Fiona. They had nothing to do but play and party their meaningless lives away while she hunted for her lost child.

She saw London as a dirty, soot-covered city. She saw the streets filled with the excrement of the fine horses that rode the thoroughfares and she cursed the idea that the social scene had offered a chance to improve Margaret's standing. They had attempted to climb the social ladder and have Margaret accepted beyond her level to make a marriage contract with an Earl or perhaps, even to have a Marquis or Duke take her to wife. The barriers had proved impenetrable. One would be extremely lucky, or had to be extraordinary, to climb the social ladder. She gnashed her teeth in frustration, not knowing where her child was or what had become of her.

Fiona attended a lesser affair, one not associated with the higher class of families. She saw lords, not with their wives, but attending with mistresses and well-dressed harlots. The music was as fast as the women were flagrant, knowing their duty was strictly for the enjoyment of the men they accompanied. They were outwardly fondled in public, and an exposed breast was flaunted rather than quickly concealed. Turning down a hallway, Fiona saw a woman pressed against a wall with her legs wrapped around a stocky lord. His trousers were pooled around his ankles as he thrust into her, banging the trollop repeatedly against the tapestry. Lord Nicholas Emory emitted a high-pitched giggle as he led a young lord and maid into a bedroom.

Fiona was desperate in her search. To be in this situation, at a party of ill repute, seeking her daughter was beyond what she considered proper. She could stand no more of the sights and sounds she heard. Determined to leave, she made her way through the crowds to the front door when she spied John Marlow entering. On his arm was a tall, gaudy woman that belonged on the streets of the city, instead of in a fine home.

"John," Fiona pulled at his sleeve, "I have been searching everywhere for you."

John gaped at her in surprise. "What brings you to his party? I would have thought these diversions were beyond your liking."

Panic was in her reply. "John, have you seen Margaret? I have searched everywhere for her."

A glint of steel shone briefly in his eyes. He pushed the whore into the room as he bade her. "Find something interesting to do. I won't be long." He turned to Fiona, and grasping her arm, led her out of the house. Standing on the pavement, he hailed a cab.

"John," Fiona gasped as her tears flowed. "I have learned that Margaret was with Agnes months ago. That was the last time anyone saw her. I am desperate. I need to find her, and she is not in London. I have looked everywhere."

"Have you spoken to Devlin Cavanaugh?" he questioned, attempting to place the blame on Barwick. "She was at Barwick Castle to speak to them about some matter. I don't think that she has been seen since."

Fiona stared at him incredulously. "If she has been missing since then, why didn't you or Agnes send me word? Why didn't you go to Barwick and confront him about this? She's my baby. She's gone, and you did nothing?"

"If you hadn't raised a flighty social-climbing adventurer, perhaps we would have. She comes and goes on a whim. Should Mother and I be responsible for your whelp?"

"My whelp is your cousin!" she exclaimed, incensed with his attitude.

"Do you question our loyalty to family? If I were you, I would seek answers from Barwick."

She had to think. Was Lord Barwick involved in Margaret's disappearance? Had he tried to focus the blame on Agnes when he mentioned she had been visiting an aunt near his home? Were John and Agnes to be trusted? Fiona's head was spinning with multiple thoughts, all of which were dreadful.

John pushed her into the rented conveyance and tossed a few coins at the driver to see her away. Fiona's option was to go to Agnes, regardless of the fear she felt in the presence of her horrid aunt. The answer to Margaret's disappearance began there.

* * *

Mid-summer, Lord and Lady Ferndale hosted the Glorious 12th as the families gathered for their special celebration. The children were invited along with their families and attended their own events under the watchful eyes of their nannies. George and Thomas gave the newest family member a cursory glance and went off to join the other boys practising archery. Violet and Rose spent much of their time vying for a chance to carry Sterling along the garden path. They sat in a swing, holding him securely as they gently pushed themselves on the wooden board, keeping their feet on the ground, being especially quiet and careful as he slept in their arms.

Diana watched, amused. She noted the proud display in Devlin's eyes whenever he looked at Lauren and the baby. She was pleased he had settled down to married life and was assured he was content in his role of husband and father.

"Sterling looks exactly like Devlin," she exclaimed the first time she looked at her new grandson. She winked at Lauren, "Are you sure you're his mother?"

"I know," Lauren laughed, "how unfair that I carried him for nine months and worked so hard to bring him forth, to find that he doesn't look even a little bit like me."

"It was the same with Trevor and Devlin. They take after their father. That wisp of hair that always falls down Devlin's brow, that comes from me. If my lady's maid didn't force it to behave, my hair would constantly be in my eyes."

"I am forever smoothing it back from Devlin's forehead. I think I now do it unconsciously." She gazed at her sleeping child. "It adds to his roguish good looks, and since Sterling is the image of his father, we are fairly confident that he will be a handsome devil and a source of great pleasure to the young misses he comes across," she smiled into Devlin's bemused face.

"As long as he keeps his blue eyes. That will be your claim upon his good looks."

That night, Nanny Grace tucked the children into their beds as Ellie laid Sterling into his cot.

"He seems like a good baby and is happy no matter who is holding him," commented Nanny Grace.

"Aye, he already has lovely manners this one, and it doesn't hurt that everyone in the house takes their turn with the young lord. Even our stuffy Winslow has been seen bouncing him around the castle."

"Considering his sire, I hope, for your sake, that he keeps those manners. With everyone holding him, he'll soon be a spoiled young master."

"Can you spoil a baby by loving him? He will be big and strong like Devlin, but I can see a gentle, easy-going nature more like Lauren. He's very patient for a wee one. He lets us know what he wants and waits to see if his demands will be catered to before he raises the roof if we don't see to his need soon enough."

They closed the door on the sleeping children and joined the other nannies in their common room. There, they discussed the discipline required to quell the antic of their charges and boasted of raising the future lords and ladies of England.

The shoot followed the fox hunt. Lauren partook in neither, as other women joined both of the events. Willow was left at home eating double her allowance of hay and oats as she grew the foal inside her.

Marian and the girls sat with Lauren in the shade of the manse as she discretely nursed Sterling. Violet and Rose giggled when his eyes darted over her breast from one to the other.

"He favours looking at me," chided Violet.

"Mother, can we get a baby too?" begged Rose.

"Go ask your Father," Marian replied, rolling her eyes as the child scampered off to find her father in a group of men.

Trevor and Devlin stood in a circle of hunters, dressed in their gear and deep in discussion on the excellent game to be found in the area. They stood relaxed, resting their weight on one leg with their guns leaning on their shoulders or in the crook of their arms, preparing for the excursion onto the field.

"Father," Rose's strident voice demanded attention among the gruff voices of the gentlemen. She skipped into their circle, her ringlets bobbing, skirt swishing, as she placed herself in their midst. With her attention directed at her father, Rose was unconcerned that all male eyes focused on her in their very masculine group.

"Mother wants a new baby, and so do I," came her piercing, high-pitched voice.

Conversation ceased as everyone raised their eyes from the child to Trevor. Devlin waited expectantly for a response from his brother, who smirked and took his daughter by the hand.

"Here," he said, pushing his shotgun into Devlin's hand, "Hold this! I have more important things to see to!"

* * *

The stables were quiet as the men leaned against the open door of Willow's stall, speaking in muted tones, waiting and watching. The wheat straw had been laid thickly on the ground in preparation for the foal's birth. Willow's braided tail flagged as she stirred with mild contractions. Colostrum dripped from her teats while she continued with her favourite pastime of late, reaching into the feed bin and taking her fill of the extra rations she had been given.

Every once in a while, she would turn to look at her backside and give a soft grunt as another contraction tightened her muscles. She would lie down, only to be up the next moment. A slight bulge appeared, round and fluid-filled, as a tiny hoof poked out and remained. Willow seemed unconcerned with the protrusion as she snuffled in the hay. She remained relaxed, standing or laying on her side, raising her big heaving sides to bear down on her attempts to deliver the sac.

When the face appeared, Devlin broke the membrane, expelling the fluid onto the straw. Willow whinnied and gave seven strong pushes that saw the new birth enter the day. Willow turned to look, unsure of what she had done, while the foal filled its lungs with air and lifted its bobbing head.

Willow touched her nose to her baby and licked its tiny nose. She stood and reached into her grain bucket again, not appearing particularly interested in her new stall mate. The foal made several attempts to stand. Its jerky motions cheered on quietly as the men gave encouragement. Observing that the foal was getting the admiration of her handlers, Willow took hold of motherhood and gave her full attention to the foal, who finally stood with legs spread wide to balance himself. His stance was that of a drunken sailor; if only he had a gas lamp post to lean on in his stupor, he would be fine.

He gave himself a little shake from nose to tail and immediately fell back into the straw. This time, he was quicker to rise and went in search of his mother's teats. Willow accepted her role and pulled her face from the feed bucket to thoroughly lick and welcome her newborn.

When Lauren ventured into the stables, the long-legged foal wobbled more assuredly in the thick bedding. Standing next to Devlin, who appeared almost as proud of the Anglo-Arabian as he had been of Sterling, she viewed mother and baby.

"Not you too Willow," she exclaimed when she saw a miniature version of Daniyal.

"Strong genes," smiled Devlin.

"Do you have a name picked out for him yet?"

"I was thinking of Abbi. It means elder son in Arabic." Devlin turned to her and rested his head on his hand as he leaned his elbow on the open stall door. "What do you think of that?"

"If he's part English and part Arabian, he should be Lord Abbi," she smiled and leaned in for a kiss. "Shall I expect you to return to the house sometime today, or will you stay in the barn?"

"I've seen what I wanted to here. There are more appealing sights in the house," he nudged her towards the door.

* * *

The tenants, servants at Barwick Castle, and the families in town were invited to the Hartford farm to celebrate the completed home and witness the wedding of Josh and Penny. Todd Harrington had not returned from wherever he had ventured, and all considered his absence a blessing. Lauren gifted the girl with a new rust-coloured gown. It was the first dress the girl owned that had not been worn by another, causing tears to gather in her eyes.

"Tears may be good luck on a wedding day, but don't be getting a case of the morbs, my girl," Ellie argued as she arranged Penny's hair, circling her crown with the autumn flowers the gardeners had arranged.

Devlin and James had seen to the cleaning and repair of the old cottage the Harringtons had farmed. The women in the castle sewed new curtains and bedding for the place, while carpenters laid a new floor and fashioned stylish furniture for the couple. In Todd's absence, James had posted a notice in the papers legally stating his forfeiture of the land through unpaid rent. Josh and Penny would hereafter own the lease to farm the land.

Lauren leaned against Devlin's side as he held Sterling throughout the ceremony, presided over by Minister Reynolds. The long-winded Vicar went through what seemed like every one of the psalms that related to marriage. He finally concluded his seemingly endless sermon as Josh shifted his weight from one foot to the other, anticipating the moment when they would be pronounced husband and wife, and he could finally kiss Penny and know that she was his. With the words finally spoken, Penny fairly jumped into Josh's arms as a cheer roared through the crowd of onlookers.

A longboard was set on saw horses and piled with dishes contributed by all the families. A pig roasted on a spit, turning crispy and brown, sending its delicious fragrance wafting into the air. The local musicians brought out their instruments and set a lively pace for the rest of the evening.

Max Ferguson sat with Ellie during the meal and kept her dancing throughout the night. When they tired, he brought her ale to sip while they chatted among the stars. Joining the older couple, Lauren and Devlin seated themselves at their table. To impress Ellie with his manners, Max excused himself to scurry off to fetch Lauren a glass of wine.

"Mr. Ferguson's asked me to go walking with him when he can get away from his shop," Ellie whispered, leaning towards Lauren, "and before the evening's out, we'll surely be doin' the bear."

"Doing what?" Devlin asked.

"There my sauce box goes again, speaking in tongues so you can't understand a word I'm saying, milord. Can you not speak the Queen's good English?"

Devlin shook his head at his dressing down. "I always thought I could until you came into my life Ellie." He turned to Lauren, "Can you understand what she's saying?"

"Not always," Lauren smiled, "but I believe she thinks there will be some cuddling between her and Max Ferguson."

"Why don't you just say that Ellie?" Devlin quizzed, "Please don't teach Sterling your phrases. I'd like to understand what my son is trying to tell me in the future." He turned again to Lauren. "When you finish drinking your wine, I'd like to do the bear with you, too," he leaned towards her for a quick kiss.

Lauren cooed and sang softly to Sterling, waiting for him to fall asleep in her arms before laying him in his cot. Devlin leaned casually against the doorframe with his legs crossed at the ankles, watching the homey scene. Lauren noted the hungering look he gave her before approaching them. He leaned over and kissed his son on the forehead before raising his attention to the lad's mother.

"I won't be long Devlin," she promised.

"I'll take a bath and draw one for you when I finish. I'll be waiting," he winked, pushing the errant curl from his forehead.

Devlin was sleeping soundly by the time Lauren completed her toilette. Sterling had been in a playful mood, and it took a while for him to settle from the excitement of the day when he had been passed from pillar to post among the gathering. Lauren felt saucy and fresh from the bath. It had been a long time since she enjoyed the attention of her husband.

The bed moved slightly as she lifted her knees onto it to crawl across the space. Her slumbering mate lasted in that state only a breath of time when she reached under the covers to grasp him with her cool fingers, touching and fondling his manhood, who, like a proper English gentleman, rose to the occasion.

A smile turned the corners of Devlin's lips while his eyes remained closed. "I must be dreaming of a wood nymph that has come to me to steal more than kisses."

"We can start with kisses," Lauren murmured, leaning toward his waiting lips.

Devlin pulled her head towards him and drank deeply of her desire. He rose above her, taking her back upon the bed. His starved affections bid him hurry, yet he slowed his quest, making the sexual desire burning in him wait its due course.

He basked in his love, that complex emotion, for the woman who opened herself to him and only him. He kissed the sides of her breasts, her flat stomach and moved lower still. He pulled her legs up, spreading them as he kissed her inner thigh, listening to her moans and gasps of pleasure. He opened the lips to her secret place and kissed her there.

Lauren gasped as his lips and tongue touched, tasted, and flicked her private place. He worshipped her body, building a yearning that aroused an urgency in her tense muscles that drove her spiralling to heights. It felt as though red hot flashes of burning flame devoured her. She twisted and cried out his name as waves crashed upon heavenly waves of intense, absorbing, lustful feelings of desire. The physical indulgence filled her with surprise and excitement as Devlin rose above her. She saw the green light shining in his eyes and an intense look on his face.

"I see eternity in your eyes, and I am yours forever," she whispered seductively.

Lauren reached for him and guided him back to where he had recently played, feeling the heat of his solid shaft as it smoothly entered and filled her. She contracted her muscles around him, and he groaned with the pleasure of her tight passageway. Her arms encircled his back, feeling the hard muscles, and her hand lowered as she grasped his thrusting hips.

He moved in her, stroking, filling, and pulling back as they revelled in the overpowering emotions to bring the other to the pinnacle of sexual passion and release. It was spiritual and reciprocal, she caring for his, he caring for her pleasure and enjoyment in their love play, asking for nothing, receiving everything. The molten heat of their passion dissolved around them in an explosion of ecstasy as they reached their heights. She moaned her pleasure in soft gasps of breath as he filled her with his love.

In the afterglow of their joining, as they lay facing one another, hands clasped between them, Devlin kissed the back of her fingers. Raising his warm gaze to her face, he spoke intensely, "There will be times when I am forced to leave you Lauren, but I will count the minutes in anticipation until I can return to your side. I have found in you, all I could ever wish for. You are perfect for me and for our child. You are my life, and you make it complete in every way possible."

"Even when you were in London, I felt your love and knew you were steadfastly mine," she answered softly.

"I speak the truth Lauren, when I say that you are the only woman I have ever loved. I would not want to survive if you were ever taken from me. I would be a broken man."

She smiled up at him in response, reached behind him to thread her fingers through his long hair, and pulled him towards her for a long, luxurious kiss that ended in a mutually enjoyable continuation of their love.

# *Chapter Twenty-Five*

Fiona entered the iron gate of the Etherington estate, its rusty bars sagging against a weed-strewn garden. She had not been here for years and noticed the change that had come over the place. A once elegant manor, had now the appearance of a gothic haunt.

"What brings you here Fiona?" Agnes demanded, not pleased to see her dumpy niece.

"I want to know what has happened to Margaret. She was last seen here. What did you do with her?" she challenged, fear for her daughter making her brave.

"Are you blaming me for the flighty girl?" Agnes came to stand over her niece, "Do not condemn me of a malicious act if you know what is good for you," she snarled indignantly.

"I have searched all over London. She has not been there. John told me himself that she was here."

"You are the one who has lost contact with your only child!" Agnes accused. "You come here and demand to know where she is when you misplaced the girl?"

Fiona felt cowered by the awesome presence of her aunt. She had been a force in her life that saw her lifted from poverty as a young girl. Agnes had scooped her from drudgery, dressed her in fine clothes and searched for a wealthy husband for her. The future Baron Edwards was a prime target. Spurned by the love of his life, Agnes had sent Fiona into his path as often as possible. On a rebound, a relationship of convenience grew. Fiona knew that the baron didn't love her, nor did she love him. He was her chance for a life of ease. She was available, while his true love was naught. Succumbing to pressure from his parents, who were demanding he settle down with a wife, and at that point, any wife. Agnes had generously supplied a dowry and a story with a respectable background, expecting a healthy reward in return. Lawrence Edwards had proven wiser than any of Agnes' other victims, and Fiona was not nearly as evil as her aunt. Thus, Agnes' plan failed, and the contempt for the wasted funds she had spent on Fiona grew over time. She had little use for weak people, and her niece was no exception.

"I suggest you speak with Barwick or his wife. They are the ones who saw Margaret last." She placed the blame on others, knowing full well that John had taken the girl to London on her advice to seek an abortionist. She contemplated that the trip may have had something to do with the comment John made when Todd Harrington's body had required disposal. John had mentioned then that he had another body that he would have to deal with. At the time, Agnes had not probed into the meaning of his statement, but she had her suspicions and would speak to him when he returned.

* * *

Sterling lay on his blanket, reaching for a stitched doll that Devlin held just out of his reach. He gurgled his baby noises and smiled at his father, pumping his fat little legs to the tune Lauren was playing on the piano. It was the heart-melting smile that earned Sterling the prize from his doting father, which was quickly brought to his mouth for a taste.

"Sterling likes the music you are playing. Either that, or he's dancing a jig. I think he may be out of step," Devlin laughed at his son.

Lauren ceased the music and came to sit on the floor with her husband and son. "He's a clever young gentleman. All he has to do is blow a bubble, and everyone remarks on his genius.

The rapid banging on the front door was followed by the tattoo of heavy steps and the dignified harumph of Winslow as he followed a blustering Fiona into the parlour.

"My apologies," he stammered, "this woman barged into the house before I could halt her."

"Thank you Winslow," Devlin put the flustered butler at ease. "What can we do for you, Baroness?" He ambled to his feet to formally greet the woman.

"It has come to my attention that you are the last people who saw Margaret," she outright accused. "I want to know what you have done with my daughter."

Lauren came to her feet and bent to retrieve a pouting Sterling, who was growing upset at the angry voice and emanating fury of the stranger who had barged into his happy world. Lauren patted his bottom to soothe the baby and responded in a hard-won calmness, "Margaret left our home with no more than a stinging cheek after she struck me."

"She would not!" barked Fiona.

"She most certainly did," accused Winslow, who had not left the room and felt justified to add his comments to the outrage. "Half the servants in the house saw the aftermath of her abuse of my lady, and she pushed young Sally out of her way to exit the manse."

Devlin was mildly surprised at the bristling butler whose decorum had always been impeccable. At the moment, his face was red with indignant anger at the intrusion and uproar caused by Fiona Edwards. Devlin saw Winslow to the door, speaking to him in a low voice as he ushered him from the room, then turned his attention to Fiona.

"I would not wish to bring this subject to your ears Madam and upset you further, however, I feel you have the right to know that when Margaret came here last winter, she bore the news that she was expecting a child."

"It's impossible!" she declared, wide-eyed at the shocking insinuation that her daughter was in such a state. "She's a good girl. She would never be active in that way."

Lauren took pity on the upset woman. "Sometimes a young girl cannot control the situation she may find herself in. Margaret seemed as though she were desperate to find love. Perhaps she became overwhelmed with a gentleman. Do you know of anyone she had set her cap to?"

"Only you Lord Barwick. You led my girl by the nose and had your way with her. You got her in that state and then abandoned her," she accused.

"I did not." Devlin spoke levelly and looked directly at Fiona, "As you are well aware. You pushed her in my path for months and knew there could never have been any commitment in that regard."

"You were with her at many functions. You were seen together by all of society last year," she railed.

"Madam, do not confuse cool politeness with any form of affection. "

"Margaret would speak of you and no one else after attending the balls. What am I supposed to think?"

Devlin was becoming frustrated that the woman would not accept the simple fact that he had not desired her daughter. Not before Lauren returned home and especially not afterwards. "Margaret was told on many of those occasions that nothing could come of her wish to be with me. Though Lauren was not in England, I was still a married man, and it was exceedingly difficult to extract myself from her presence!"

"There was the gossip article in the newspaper. It hinted at a divorce and suggested that you would set Lauren aside and take up with Margaret." Fiona was desperate and near tears.

"Fiona," Lauren prodded, seeing the exasperating subject turning in on itself, "it is rumoured that Margaret herself set tongues to wagging on that score and spoke to the gossip columnist. My maid told me that girls in situations, such as Margaret was facing, would go into a convent to have their babies away from the prying eyes of neighbours and friends. Take heart that she is safely ensconced in such a place and will someday return."

Devlin escorted the stunned Fiona to her carriage and closed the door on both the landau and their conversation. "There was never anything between Margaret and I. Though she did voice her feelings to me, they could not be returned. I hope she comes home to you soon."

Devlin returned to the parlour, seeing the pensive frown on Lauren's face, held out his arms so that she could step into his embrace.

"Now that I am a mother, I can understand how frightened Fiona is. It must be dreadful for her not knowing where Margaret has gone or if she is hurting and alone. I feel sorry for both of them. For Margaret wanting what she could not have, and now for Fiona, desperate and searching for her daughter."

* * *

Agnes entered John's bedroom, quietly closing the door behind her. Turning, she noticed the maid pushed against the wall with his questing hand reaching under the girl's skirt.

"Leave off!" she barked as John quickly searched the room at the sound of his mother's voice. Agnes squawked at the frightened maid, "Get out, you slut and be about your regular chores instead of this one." She turned to her son as he adjusted his trousers, "I am not paying the servants to see to your whims. Every time you play your games, they are unable to perform their duties for days afterwards."

"What do you want Mother?" he snarled as the bulge in his pants remained pronounced.

"Where is Margaret?"

John grunted and lifted a hand to rub his forehead. "She's gone."

"Answer me boy! Gone where? Gone to church? Gone to the country?" her strident voice pricked his nerves.

"Gone to Hell, more like," he glared.

Agnes threw her arms into the air, "Can you do nothing right? I told you where to take her."

"Your friend in London wanted more than I was willing to spend to perform the deed. I found another," he rebuked.

"Another? Cheaper! Filthy! Less capable I'll wager. So, she's dead! That's what you meant when Harrington was killed, and you said you had to take care of another body! What did you do with her?"

"Never fear Mother, she won't be found," he insisted, "she's either somewhere in the fiords of Norway or heading to the Arctic Ocean."

"You are a heartless bastard!" she railed.

"I was taught well, Mother. Why are you so concerned with Margaret now? You didn't care about her when she was alive unless you wanted her to do something for you?"

"Fiona is here. What am I to tell her? She knows that Margaret was in our company and hasn't been seen since." Agnes paced the room. "She could cause us trouble if she suspects we had anything to do with Margaret's absence."

"I will handle her."

Agnes looked into her son's cold eyes. She had raised him in her image. Had he exceeded her in cruelty? She surmised that he had and would be careful, lest he saw no need for her continued good health.

"You do that and be careful. We don't need yet another body to dispose of."

"There will be one more at any rate, Mother. Barwick is still alive."

Agnes nodded at John, giving him an evil smile. He was just like her. At this very moment, at least, she believed him to be a good son.

John spoke at length to Fiona, advising her on the accusations to be levelled at Barwick. She was to speak of Margaret and Barwick's ongoing intimacy over the past few years and the abuse she had suffered at his hand. That he had impregnated her, and when she had gathered the courage to confront him, she was never seen again.

At his insistence, she found herself standing before the home of the local constable in the pretty little town. Rows of neat townhouses lined the brick street. Children played in the cool afternoon on the small plots of grass, chasing after coloured butterflies as wispy clouds tumbled across the azure sky. Baby carriages were parked in the dappled shade of leafy oak trees, holding sleeping little ones who continued to dream despite the chaos of the excited children.

She looked longingly at the little tykes who enjoyed the day without a care, remembering a pretty blonde girl with ringlets tied in bright ribbons bouncing on her father's lap. Lawrence had loved her then, before Margaret grew up and began scheming with Fiona. The girl heeded the ministrations of her mother and sneered at her father's title, ignoring the Baron's wishes and advice. He had tried for years to have them listen to reason, to guide them to accept their station and not set their sights on the unattainable. He loved his daughter, but knew her limitations. Reality would see her married if she would listen to him. No duke in the land would take a plain Baron's child over the wealthy, noble-titled beauties one could find in society. Perhaps it could have been different if it was not her lot to take after the well-proportioned figure and facial image of her mother, more and more as the years passed.

Fiona stood quietly, wringing her hands, waiting. The door was opened by the tall, uniformed constable. Paul Moriarty removed the napkin tied around his neck, protecting the front of his impeccable jacket, and wiped the luncheon crumbs from his chin.

"May I be of service Madam?" he quipped.

"I would like to report that my daughter, Margaret Edwards, was last reported in the company of Lord and Lady Barwick this winter past and has not been seen since." The words spoken to the law had a finality to them and unleashed a torrent of sobs as the constable led the distraught woman into the privacy of his home.

Paul Moriarty, the no-nonsense officer that Devlin and the town council had sought and hired, stood in the front entrance hall of Barwick Castle with his hat in his hand.

"Lord Barwick, if there were some other way to handle this matter, I surely would see to it. But allegations have been levelled against you sir, and it is my duty to place you under arrest pending further investigation."

"This is ridiculous!" Devlin stubbornly declared. "I had nothing to do with Margaret's disappearance, and she may very well be safe and sound in some abbey delivering her child."

"Well sir, there is that accusation as well. There's talk that you were the father of her babe and may have done her in to save your reputation and marriage."

"Who speaks such slander?" quipped Lauren as she descended the stairs, sparkling flashes of blue flame igniting in her eyes.

Moriarty had heard talk of the Lady of Barwick Castle. He had assumed that the townsfolk had been enamoured of the late lord's daughter, and their loyalty spurred their glowing reports. He had heard of her easy-going nature, which he currently saw little of, as she stomped towards him.

"Well, Ma'am, John Marlow and his mother, a Mrs. Agnes Etherington, have come forward to corroborate Baroness Edwards's claims."

"I shouldn't be surprised. They are my step-family. I have learned long ago that they are not to be trusted." Lauren insisted.

"I'm only doing the job I was hired to do. I have to assume that you, Lord Barwick, are a threat to the peace of this area, and I have to hold you in custody until your name can be cleared or we find evidence to prosecute."

"There is no gaol in town. Where do you propose to keep me?" Devlin challenged.

"There hasn't been a need to build one as yet, so I thought we could hold you in a bedroom in my house. The missus is pretty excited to have you stay for a spell. As soon as she heard I had to arrest you, she went shopping for special ingredients to make you a fine meal," he answered wryly.

Devlin quirked a half smile at Lauren's angry face. "I'll be home soon. Rest assured that it will not take long to get this sorted out."

"It makes no sense Devlin. She left our home that day. She was seen leaving by our staff," she argued, reluctant to see him taken from her.

"You have my word that this will receive the best investigative knowledge that I have, Lady Barwick," Moriarty declared.

"You will excuse me, sir, if I have not noticed that ability as of yet," Lauren rejoined snidely.

Devlin was held in an upstairs bedroom overlooking the street. If he had wanted, he could easily have escaped through the window, shinnied down the drainpipe, and reached the front garden. For now, he would stay in the room that was not much larger than his and Lauren's bed at home. It contained a cot with a flat pillow, a homespun quilt, a chest of drawers and a wash bowl.

Ben and William Moriarty visited with Devlin often in his secluded 'prison'. Stories of the high court, current laws, world events and agriculture management entertained the young lads. No matter what topic they broached, Lord Barwick seemed to have knowledge that he could impart on the subject, and they increased their interest in the varied questions they put to the agreeable lord.

Their mother, Jean, was excited to have Lord Barwick as a houseguest. Of course, she would not even consider calling him a prisoner. He was excessively handsome and flagrantly masculine, and though she was in the later years of life and loved her husband completely, she could still appreciate a magnificent specimen of humanity. The ladies in the village were agog that Devlin Cavanaugh was in the custody of the constable and queried Jean anxiously for any tidbit of information she could expound upon.

They worried that the kind gentleman who had improved all about them would be found guilty of a heinous crime against a young woman. They wondered what their beloved Lauren would do, if such came to pass. They could see with their own eyes and gossiped over fences, how much she loved the lord, and he, the father of their own precious recently born child.

Through their talk, they became his judge and jury and with firm conviction, decided that it could not be. He was innocent of the charges, and throughout the day, they sought to improve the condition of his imprisonment. The townspeople dropped off sundries for his use. A rug was added, baked goods, a standing mirror, feather tick for the bed, assorted linens and pillows were delivered to his room to see to their lord's comfort.

* * *

Fiona stumbled around the Etherington manse as one locked in a nightmare. She wept and cried, and the occupants of the house found their patience at an end with her constant drudgery.

"She's dead," Fiona sobbed, "I feel it in my bones that my baby is gone."

"You will have your revenge when they hang Barwick," Agnes crowed.

"We can drink champagne and watch his neck stretch," John jeered.

"It won't bring my Margaret back," she looked at John and accused, "When she was here, why did you not protect her? Why did you not immediately see him brought to justice and accuse him of killing her? Perhaps it did not happen immediately, and he kept her locked in the castle."

"Why did you let her come?" he growled. "Blame yourself for not keeping Margaret in check."

Fiona's imagination ran amuck. "What if he kept her as his plaything and abused my darling?" She glared at her aunt and cousin. "You might have been able to save her. Did you know she was with child?"

Agnes glanced at John, and Fiona saw the slightest glint of guilt in the furtive expression. The old witch was losing some of the bravado that had seen her through her years. Fiona felt that there was more to the disappearance of Margaret, than what she had been led to believe.

John threw his hands in the air and stomped to his feet. He marched his corrupt bulk across the room to glare at Fiona. "I have had enough of you trying to blame us for Margaret. If she gave herself to a man and found herself expecting a brat, then that falls to you and your teachings. Content yourself that Barwick is being held for her disappearance, and you will shut your mouth on blaming Mother and me any further, or I will shut it for you."

Fiona gripped the arms of her chair until her knuckles turned white. She stared with wide, fearful eyes at the evil menace of John Marlow as he towered over her. She felt the heat of his body emanating from him to encompass her like a physical weight, forcing her back into her seat.

"From now on, it is Cavanaugh you will swear harmed Margaret, and no other." He raised his hand and cuffed Fiona on the side of the head to slam the point into her brain. "Do I make myself clear?"

She was stunned by his outburst and too frightened to do anything but nod her head in agreement. She held her breath until he moved away from her, releasing it in a long slow sigh. Though John had left the room, she still felt in danger, with Agnes tapping her fingers on the poorly repaired desk.

"You will mind his words, Fiona," Agnes spoke low and menacingly. "We will hear no more of you questioning what we did or did not do when Margaret was here. Settle yourself to the fact that she is gone. We expect you to see that Barwick is found guilty and hanged." Agnes picked up the long gold letter opener and sliced through the wax that sealed a note. "You are dismissed to go to your room," she bade Fiona.

Agnes scanned the missive and slammed the paper onto the desk. She sat but for a moment before she went in search of John.

"Barwick will be the death of me!" she railed. "I received word from the senior Emory that Cavanaugh has been snooping around London. He commissioned a detective from Scotland Yard to look into our past. He has located the children of my first husband. They are spinning a tale that puts us in grave danger. If the police find out about the others," she let the statement hang in the air like a beady-eyed bat hanging from a dank, dark cave.

"You mean that it puts you in grave danger of being a black widow," John smirked. "How many in total did you do away with Mother? I fear I have lost count."

"Mind yourself John," Agnes narrowed her watery old eyes at her son, "You too will fall, should they discover my secrets. There is a tail on the detective to stop him, but a letter was sent to Barwick Castle. That should have arrived around the same time I received my letter. You must find and destroy it before there is a chance it will fall into the hands of Devlin Cavanaugh."

# *Chapter Twenty-Six*

Late in the cold evening, James and Vicar Reynolds unloaded another barrel of Barwick's fine wine into the parsonage. Their breaths expelled in a misty haze as they laboured to remove the heavy weight from the cart. Once on the ground, they could jimmy the heavy barrel along the damp grass towards the stairs, that would see it safely stored into the cellar.

"This is a far better vintage than we normally have for the parishioners," Luke insisted. "I'll admit, that Trudy pours a glass for herself when she's cooking dinner and a couple for me afterwards. Lord Barwick, and the Good Lord above are spoiling us."

A distant retort of gunfire echoing through the hills stopped the easy camaraderie between the friends. They halted their work and stared into the dark, waiting for another shot. When two more followed, they propped the barrel against the church and in unison, hopped into the cart, shaking the reigns against Bertha's back to begin a search of the vicinity. Turning a sharp corner, they noted two dead bodies in the roadway.

The minister knelt to assure himself that the souls had indeed departed and bent his head in prayer. "This man tried to defend himself. His old gun was underneath him, still held in his hand."

James laid his hand on the vicar's shoulder. "We'll load them into the wagon and take them to town. Look," he said, pointing to the dusty roadway, "there's a trail we can follow to find who did this. It could prove dangerous, so I'll continue alone if you want to return home."

"I knew these men," the vicar spoke sadly. "They would come to service when they were in the area. They were devout men. They worked long hours, delivering goods to towns far and wide, and often told me of their families." He added with conviction not generally found in a man of God, "I'm coming with you."

They followed the easily laid trail left on the road by the cart that had been heavily loaded with supplies to replenish the merchant's stocks along the coast. Passing near the summit of Cardunnock and the large mound of stones where an old chieftain was laid to rest with his war axe and spear beside him, they finally came upon an abandoned farmhouse in the distance. The pair of weary travellers pulled Bertha into the shadows of a copse of trees to view a scurry of activity as merchandise from the cart was unloaded into a tumble-down barn. A farmhouse missing part of its roof stood a good distance away, and they noted a shadowy figure pass by a window, signalling more thieves were about than those who could be seen at the barn.

"There's too many of them for just the two of us," ventured the nervous vicar.

"I'm afraid you are correct. It would be foolhardy to go near," agreed James. "At least we know where their lair is, and it looks like they will be here for a while. We can get Constable Moriarty and some villagers to apprehend these criminals."

"We can also see these poor souls in the cart returned to their loved ones," added Luke.

* * *

Lauren found it difficult to seek her rest without the warm form of Devlin beside her in bed. She had seen Sterling fed, in a clean nappy, and settled in his cot for what she hoped would be the remainder of the night as she moved through the dark house. A bit of Diana Cavanaugh's balm might help her find the sleep she needed to face another day of worry over Devlin's absence.

There was an eerie quiet about the place. Lauren's lamp cast a small circle of light that did not extend beyond a feeble attempt against the dark gloom and shuttered windows. Her soft slippers were silent against the cold, solid wood of the floor. Only her dressing gown made a soft swish that brushed the doorway as she entered Devlin's office.

She was almost on top of him before she noticed John Marlow reach out to grab her. He caught the tilting lamp before it fell and set it hard on the table, clamping his hand roughly over her mouth while she was taking a startled breath to scream. Every muscle in her body tensed at the shock to find him in her home while Devlin was not, and the servants were tucked safely in their beds many floors above them.

"What a pretty gift you are, my lady," he grumbled into her ear, sliding his free hand to clutch her throat. "Should I leave you here to scream the house down upon my head, or take you with me for my pleasure?"

Lauren struggled in his embrace. The last thing she wanted was to be taken from her home by this depraved man. John Marlow, who had always made her feel sick in her stomach and frightened. She kicked at his legs and fought against him as he tightly squeezed her throat. He moved the hand covering her mouth until it also covered her nose. She could not breathe, could not draw air into her burning lungs. She was being suffocated by his course hands. Her chest hurt, and her struggles became weak against his hold on her. Sparks of lights danced in her eyes before being snuffed out by darkness, and she lay limp in his embrace.

John slid the letter he had found lying on top of the desk into his pocket and lifted Lauren, throwing her weight over his shoulder. He exited the manse as quickly as he had entered.

* * *

The first streaks of red highlighted the thick grey clouds in the morning sky when James pulled the cart to a stop before the Moriarty rowhouse. Birds, freshly awake, attempted to sing their morning songs, but at the sight of the dawn's gloomy day, they soon gave up the effort. They ruffled their feathers and settled in the bower to await the storm. Bertha sighed a tired flap of her lips and turned an accusatory glare at James for keeping her away from her warm barn overnight. He patted her neck in appreciation of the work she had done, feeling as exhausted as the horse. Luke raised his tired arm to rap on the constable's door.

"Come in, come in." Jean cheerily invited the visitors. "What brings the two of you to our door this early morning hour?" Adding before they could speak, "Stamp the mud from your feet and join us to breakfast. Paul and his lordship are already seated."

Jean was pleased that she could regale the neighbours with more juicy gossip. She had become the most sought-after woman in the village by the other ladies as they stopped her wherever she went to learn the news of the day.

"We've more food than we know what to do with since Lord Barwick has arrived," she informed, placing full plates of ham, eggs, blood sausages and thick pieces of toasted bread before them as they sat around the crowded table.

Putting an end to her cheerful banter, James broke into the conversation. "We discovered where the stolen merchandise is being stored. With enough men, we can capture those involved and see an end to this mayhem."

"There are two drivers' bodies in the back of the cart. They must be taken to the mortician and prepared for their return to the families," added Luke.

Paul stared momentarily at James and Luke before reacting to their words. "Ben," he directed to his oldest son, "see to the dead men, will you?"

"Bertha and the cart can stay at the smithy." James continued. "She's done more than her share this night. As for myself, if I can rest for a few moments while you gather more men, I can lead you back towards Cardunnock."

"I'll volunteer as well," chimed Devlin. "Daniyal is in the stables, and we could both do with an outing."

The officer shook his head at Devlin, "I'm sorry Lord Barwick, I can't have that. You are a prisoner here."

"You need men, and I'm doing nothing," he chafed, frustrated with his incarceration.

"Well, that may be so, but the law is the law, and I can't let you go free right yet."

"You take Daniyal then," Devlin directed James.

"Thanks, but no. Your horse and I have never seen eye to eye, and I value my hide too much to ride him. I'll borrow one from the livery."

Paul and Ben gathered the volunteers, primarily young men, anxious for a chance to prove their worth and stop the thieving that placed a hardship on the community. James felt somewhat refreshed after a quick nap, and Luke took himself home to write letters of condolence to the families of the slain men.

Later that morning, the constable's brigade stealthily approached the dilapidated farmhouse, slinking from tree to tree, aware that a watchman could herald their presence at any moment. They entered to hear snores of the sleeping robbers, who had spent the night moving cargo and celebrating expected earnings with the wine they had pilfered from the parsonage and a stolen cask of brandy. Not a shot was fired, to the disappointment of the eager volunteers, who had hoped for an exciting end to their adventure.

They kicked at the sleeping sots, who were still too well into their cups, to form much of a defence. They booted them in the rear, sending them stumbling out the front of the house. It was decided that hog-tying them together, to make the ride back to the village as uncomfortable as possible, was a suitable punishment for the time being.

Lord Nicholas Emory brushed the dirt from his trousers. As he rose from a bench in the barn, he damned his father for sending him on this mission to see that they received their fair share of the loot. He examined the dust on his shoes and disdained that they had ever taken up with Marlow and the crone Agnes Etherington in their ventures. Marlow had let slip the plans they had for the Barwick estate, and he was sure that he could portray a hero of sorts, in the near future, to foil those plans.

Once they saw to the demise of the current Lord Barwick, he would sweep the delectable Lauren from their grip. He would gallantly offer her his protection from the pair. In his mind, she would gladly accept; they would marry happily, and he would replace Lord Barwick with her undying gratitude and rich inheritance.

That power could set his family free from debt and allow them to once again be essential members of society. It would also give him the opportunity to attend the expensive and exclusive brothels recently opened in London on Cleveland Street or join Bertie on his excursions to Paris. Marriage would be no reason to end the hedonistic lifestyle he enjoyed. Invitations to the snobbiest class of the aristocracy during the past season had not been as plentiful as before, and with Bertie temporarily out of the country, Emory's social status had dropped considerably.

Emory felt a sickening in his stomach as the cold steel pressed against his temple. He heard the chamber rotate and realized that the components of the gun would line up to see a bullet enter his perfectly coifed head. As Paul Moriarty locked the hammer on his pistol, the click was enough to cause beads of sweat to pop out on Emory's forehead.

"Do not move a muscle, lest this gun discharges, ending your miserable life," Moriarty warned.

Bravado fled Lord Nicholas Emory, as quickly as his bowels.

# *Chapter Twenty-Seven*

Ellie was dreaming of years long ago. The castle was in ill repair as she strode purposefully from her bed to seek the crying baby Lauren. She searched her charges room to find her where she had last left her, in the white cot. She pulled open the drawers to the dressers and could find no crying child. Ellie lay still in the dawning day, realizing she was awake and no longer dreaming, yet the squalls continued. It was not baby Lauren crying, but Sterling. She expected the muffled wails to stop when he was soothed by Lauren, yet they did not.

She rose from the warm bed, feeling her age, as stiff old muscles took their time to loosen each morning. She slipped on the knit slippers she had finished the day before, pulled on her quilted robe, and tied the sash around her thickening waist, thinking for the hundredth time that today she would not overindulge in any of the sweet treats Mrs. Osmond offered.

Sterling's cries became loud and angry as Ellie padded her way down the long hall and around the corner into his room.

She glanced into Lauren's rumpled and empty bed before attending to the young master.

"Where's your mother, lad?" she questioned the screaming, red-faced baby. "Nay, hold your wee temper, and we'll get you fixed up quick and find her."

Sterling brought his fists to his mouth, making loud smacking noises as Ellie changed his nappy, fit him into a fresh, clean gown, bundled him, and went searching for Lauren. The maids were opening the curtains and shutters to let in the light, and their shaking heads answered Ellie's question as to the location of the mistress. The scullery girls, carrying their ash buckets from room to room, could also give her no clue as to Lauren's whereabouts.

The plump baby was getting heavy, not to mention fussy at wanting his breakfast, and nothing was forthcoming. He mewled and whimpered in Ellie's arms as she headed to the kitchen to find something to tide the lad over. When she found Lauren, it was in her mind to give the girl a dressing down over her lack of care for the boy. This was simply not like her, and the lapse of judgment was most unusual.

"Mrs. Osmond," Ellie called, plopping down into her chair and setting Sterling more comfortably in her lap. "Have you something to feed this young lad? I have no idea where Lauren has gotten herself off to, and he's fairly starving."

Mrs. Osmond thought for a brief moment until she found an answer to their dilemma.

"I was wondering what I'd do with these cans of milk I purchased from the emporium," she said, searching the cupboards, "let me warm some of the milk. I'll add tiny bits of bread to it so we can spoon it into him. Mayhap he can handle that."

"Are you not off with Max Ferguson today," the cook queried as Sterling smacked his lips, sucking on the small wet morsels of nourishment. "I've the fixings of a basket for your big adventure."

"Oh, I almost forgot, and here I've been looking forward to the day since he asked me to go walking with him!" Ellie blushed. "May I leave Sterling in your care while I go find Lauren?" she asked.

Ellie searched high and low. She scanned the gardens from the second floor at the back of the house, sides and front. She had not wanted to cause a ruckus the way she had months ago after Agnes Etherington's first visit to the castle, when she had entered Lauren's bed-chamber and found her missing. But where was the girl? With mounting trepidation, the maids were told to stop their duties and look for the lady of the house. Footmen were sent to the stables and returned with no sighting of Lady Barwick.

Winslow presided over another orderly search of the castle that saw every door, on every floor, opened, with all the rooms completely examined. Ellie's misgivings were released in a panic, and the entire staff were in an uproar when Max Ferguson arrived holding a bouquet of late flowers in his hand. He was dressed in his Sunday best and had spent particular attention to his starched collar and neatly tied bow.

"She's gone!" Ellie cried as Max attempted to hand her the flowers. "I don't know where she is, or if she's lying injured somewhere. She wouldn't just leave the baby."

Ellie's face turned pale as death. She was as sure of Lauren's absence as she could possibly be. There was no denying the truth. She turned to Winslow, her eyes wide and wild. She grabbed hold of his starched shirt in both of her chubby fists, crying, "She's been taken. She has to have been!"

"Now, Ellie," Winslow soothed, "our lady must be here somewhere."

"No! You don't understand! They've come for her because they know Devlin is away. They're a scheming ne'r do well pair. The old bat and her minion. They tried to snatch her when she was a babe." She turned to Max. "Sterling! We must hide him in case they come back for him."

"Sally," Mrs. Park called, feeling the effect of Ellie's concern shiver up her back, "collect clothes and necessities for the young master and pack them in a bag. Be quick," she insisted.

Ellie ran as fast as her legs could carry her down to the kitchen. Sterling was being bounced on Mrs. Osmond's lap as Ellie hustled into the room and searched for the cans of milk she had seen earlier. She tossed them into a basket and wrapped the loaf of bread in a cloth.

"This will have to do for now. I hope he took it well enough."

"Yes, he gobbled it right up," agreed Mrs. Osmond, becoming alarmed at the hustling motions of the ordinarily sedate woman. "Where are you taking him?" she queried as Ellie pulled Sterling into the safety of her arms.

"Where Agnes Etherington and John Marlow can't find him!"

* * *

Lauren opened her eyes, surveying the room she was in. The ceiling was soot-stained a dark grey, and the bed she lay on had a dusty smell. Wallpaper was just beginning to curl near the ceiling, and she wondered if she were in an abandoned room of the castle that had not, as yet, received the attention of the carpenters and cleaning staff.

Her throat felt bruised and sore, and she became aware that her dry mouth held a cloth tied tightly with a knot at the back of her neck. She struggled upright and felt a wave of nausea envelope her. Her movements were slow and sluggish as she pulled at the cloth, picking weakly at untying the knot. She felt the room spin with any amount of exertion to move her body.

Fiona cracked her bedroom door open the tiniest sliver to spy on the furtive movements of Agnes. The old woman peered down the hallway from side to side, assuring herself she was not being watched. Fiona held her breath so she would not be noticed peering out from her room. The grate of a key unlocked a door, and it swung open with a grinding creak.

"How nice of you to visit us," she heard Agnes say. "Your stay will be long and joyful, I'm sure."

Fiona heard the words she spoke before the door was closed behind Agnes. She wondered, hopefully, if it were possible that Margaret was in the locked room. She tiptoed down the hall and pressed her ear against the panel to hear the muffled voice. She could hear only Agnes speaking and picked out the name she said, "Lauren." It was not Margaret. They had Lady Barwick in the manse.

A maid stumbled out of John's bedroom. She sported a black closed eye, and blood flowed from a swollen cut lip. Fiona could not return to her room without being seen. The maid tilted her good eye towards her, and attempted to turn away to flee in the opposite direction. Fiona moved quickly and grabbed the girl by the arm, pulling her into her room. Shutting the door firmly behind them, she locked it to avoid any intrusion. She wet a cloth from the pitcher and handed it to the frightened maid.

"Speak softly so we cannot be overheard," she whispered furtively. "Do you know who I am?" At the maid's nod, she continued her questioning. "Do you know my daughter, Margaret Edwards?" Again her query was met with an affirmative nod.

She could see the timid maid was frightened by the trembling that overtook her body. The poor little maid had several cuts with varying degrees of healing on her face and bruising on her arms in shades from yellow to deep purple.

"Has Marlow abused you?" she asked the girl kindly.

The maid shook her head no and darted her eyes from side to side looking for an escape. She needed the work, regardless of the terrors that were inflicted on her. Her employers had promised to send her wages directly to her parents, who were living in the slums of London. They had nothing but what she could send to them and her starving siblings. She kept nothing back for herself since she had been told that her needs would be met in the household accounts, by providing the clothes she wore and the food she ate. Madam Etherington had personally guaranteed to have her wages sent, as she did with others in her employ.

Fiona took the cloth and rinsed it, handing it back to the girl. "Hold this on your eye. You say no, but my own eyes tell me the truth," she prodded. "I desperately need to know what happened to Margaret. Can you tell me anything?"

The maid remained mute.

"I will find a way to take you from here. My husband, Baron Edwards, can offer you employment. You will be treated properly if you help me," Fiona begged for a reply. "What is your name?"

"Lucy," came the timid response, "but they call all the servants here Mary." She hoped the lady would stand by her word and take her from this life of torture. She gritted her teeth and recalled, "I saw the master take your daughter from the house. She was in a bad way."

"Tell me all you know," Fiona urged.

"Whenever Miss Edwards was here, the master left me alone 'cause he had her to play his games on.

"He forced himself on Margaret?" Fiona clutched a fist to her breast, terrified of the possibility.

"Oh no Ma'am. She weren't like me," Lucy answered truthfully, "She enjoyed it and gave as good as she got. They sometimes had me watch. The master said she was to teach me to be more like her. But I never did like what they did."

Fiona put her hand to her pale forehead as the blood drained from her face. She struggled to understand all that was being said about her daughter. Finally, she came to realize that her idea of Margaret and the reality of her child was a myth. She did not know Margaret at all. "Is there more?" she asked, feeling ill and unsure that she wanted to hear anything further.

"She was expecting a baby."

"Because of Lord Barwick?"

"Lord Barwick?" Lucy questioned. "No Ma'am. It was John Marlow's get. 'Course, he tried to do away with it. That's why Miss Edwards was so sick and poorly."

"You saw her ill?"

"She was ill, all right. He had to drag her out of the house 'cause she could barely walk. There was a terrible smell of death to her."

"Do you know where he took her?" Fiona anxiously asked.

"I do. I overheard him talking to Mrs. Etherington. It's illegal what they done," she whispered, lowering her voice so Fiona could barely hear what she said. "He took her to London, and things didn't go well for her there." Lucy looked into the drawn face of the Baroness and blurted out the facts as she knew them. "He didn't take her to the abortionist the Madam told him about. He took her elsewhere, and your daughter died. The Master chucked her into the sea."

* * *

Carl raced the lathered Friesians into town as folks on the street scattered out of his way to gawk wide-eyed at the heaving team. While pulling hard on the reigns, he stood on the brake to stop them in front of the home where Devlin was being held prisoner. Jumping from the carriage, he pounded on the door and yelled for admittance, gathering a curious crowd.

"Where is Lord Barwick?" he commanded as Jean opened the door, wiping her hands on the apron tied around her waist.

"He's having a cup o' tea in the kitchen at the moment," she spoke, overwhelmed that the driver pushed his way past her to run down the hallway before being invited to enter and remove his soiled boots.

Devlin was up and moving towards the door as he heard the urgency in Carl's voice.

"Your wife, my lord, we can't find her anywhere."

"Is Sterling with her? Does she have the baby?"

"No. Ellie found him alone in his room this morning, and the household has been searching for Lady Barwick since," he continued with difficulty, "Ellie thinks Lady Barwick's relatives have her."

Devlin nodded slowly. Since Lauren's reaction to her first encounter with her step-grandmother, Devlin had looked into the actions of Agnes and John Marlow. A private investigator had sent him preliminary findings of past indiscretions and possible evil wrongdoings. A grim look came upon his face.

"Spread the word throughout the estate to watch for her and look anywhere you think she could have walked in case there is a simple explanation to her disappearance, and Ellie is overreacting. I'll get Daniyal and pay a visit to Etherington and Marlow. If she's there, I will find her and bring her home.

Devlin returned to the kitchen and slipped a sharp knife, the only available weapon, into his boot top as a modicum of protection. He and Carl headed toward the door to find their way blocked by Jean Moriarty.

"Lord Barwick, you are a prisoner of my husband, and I cannot allow you to leave this house!"

Devlin picked the woman up by her arms and turned to set her down gently behind him in the narrow hallway. "My wife is missing, and I am going to find her. You can tell your husband he can arrest me again when I know she is safe."

# *Chapter Twenty-Eight*

Pulled by one grudging pony, the cart took a winding path through the fields to arrive behind the emporium unseen. Max unhitched Clover and pushed the recalcitrant cob into the lean-to at the back of his shop. He grabbed the basket and case of baby necessities from the cart, leading Ellie into the storage area at the back of the mercantile. Sterling remained blissfully asleep, unaware of the clandestine events.

"Thank heavens the lad is so accustomed to being handled by everyone in the castle, so he's not frightened by strangers. He's a good little darling and will sleep in anyone's arms," Ellie stated as she gave her weary arms a rest, placing the baby in Max's care.

"Poor mite. We will see him safe, Ellie. Never fear," Max spoke with conviction.

The room was filled from floor to ceiling with boxes and crates of merchandise. They entered his humble abode at the back of his shop through a curtained doorway. A fireplace dominated the main room, with two cozy seats facing its warmth. A small table and counter space to prepare his lonely meals delineated the kitchen area. He gently laid Sterling in the centre of his bed and excused himself to find an empty crate. Laying a thick blanket on the bottom, he draped another over that to soften the sides and set it beside his bed in the room at the back. Ellie placed Sterling into the makeshift cot as Max entered his closed mercantile to arm himself with a long, evil-looking knife and a large cricket bat to protect Ellie and the baby.

What had been planned as a pleasant excursion into the country with a lively companion had turned into warfare. He was prepared to lay down his life to see to their safety. Ellie was mightily impressed with the bravery and care that Max was extending to her and Sterling. Their concern was to keep the child happy and quiet throughout the day and the coming night. No one could be made aware of their whereabouts in the empty closed shop. She had to see to Sterling's good health and assumed that Devlin would see to Lauren, and until that time, they would remain hidden. It warmed her heart that Max had risen to the challenge of their welfare, and she was assured that those who faced an adversary as strong and forceful as Devlin Cavanaugh, would find a warrior of old in their midst.

She wouldn't mind one bit if their blood were shed! In fact, it was long overdue!

* * *

John Marlow approached the drugged woman as she lay on the dusty coverlet. Her beverage had been laced with laudanum to keep her quiet, and it provided an unobstructed chance for him to view her ample assets without causing too much of a fuss. Although, a good fight by an unwilling partner was not necessarily without its merits. He leaned over her and plucked open the buttons holding her robe together, one by anticipated one. He viewed the swell of her ripe breasts beneath the diaphanous pink material and saluted Devlin Cavanaugh for his excellent taste in women. His hands reached for her full breasts, and a drop of milk leaked from the nipple. Pushing the garment aside, he lowered his head for a taste of the mothering brew.

Lauren fought against the suffocating waves of inertia, struggling upwards from the depths of intoxication. She felt her breasts pawed roughly and viciously suckled. She cried out and pushed at the man whose body held hers imprisoned on the bed.

"Get accustomed to my presence, sweet Lauren. What you give to your child, you will now give to me. More, in fact, for me and less for your whelp. I will become more important for your well-being than any other, and if you deny me, your child will suffer."

Lauren's mind whirled at the implication of his chatter. Did they have Sterling? She struggled against him, pushing at him weakly as she tried to clear her brain from the fog. Tears leaked from her eyes as she considered what might have happened to her baby and the loss of her freedom. The thought that they were at the mercy of Agnes and John gripped her in terror. She fought and twisted away from the groping paws as Agnes entered the room.

Seeing John's prostrate form on the unwilling captive, she barked, "You rut like a filthy boar. Is that all you ever think of?"

John lifted himself from Lauren and wiped at his lips, closing his eyes to grit his teeth at this intrusion at a most inopportune moment. Lauren's mind cleared briefly and with his attention diverted from her, she formed her hand into a tight fist and reaching upwards, struck at the side of Marlow's head with all her might. With its sharp diamond setting, her sapphire ring caught on the fold of a wrinkle by his eye and tore at the thin skin to split the tissue apart.

Blood dripped from his wound as he jerked his head to the side. He raised his arm to strike before glaring at his mother, who cackled in wry humour.

The old woman gave her son sage advice at the unexpected look of surprise on John's face. "She has spirit this one, and you'll do well to remember that. She's not a timid maid who has to take your abuse. Mayhap, she will prove more of a handful than you are accustomed to."

Lauren curled into a fetal position, pulling the robe closed around her. She felt dirty and repulsed. If only she could think clearly and rise from the bed to flee. Her worse fears were realized as she found herself caught in the web of Agnes Etherington.

"Come into my parlour," said the spider to her son. "We need to make plans for our future...and our move to Barwick castle. I have dreamed of this moment for a quarter of a century, and it is finally within my grasp."

She came close to the bed and looked at Lauren, "Your husband will be hanged when they find him guilty of murdering poor dear Margaret," she condemned.

"No," Lauren replied, struggling to rise from the effects of the drug, "he did not."

"Who will be there to say so, dear Lauren? You will remain here, and the constable will believe us when we tell him that you have fled a murderer. That you feared he would take your life as well."

John wiped at the blood running down his cheek. "You will pay for this wounding, my pet. Once we are married, you belong to me."

"Never!" she whimpered.

"Think you so? Not even for the life of your child?"

Lauren sobbed and shook her head negatively. The fog in her brain overtook her as she listened to their words drift in and out of her consciousness.

"We will raise your son as our own. I have done a fine job raising John and look forward to rearing another."

"We will manipulate him to care for us, and he will grow in our image to do our bidding."

Their evil words continued, shouted in her ear one moment, close and hurtful, while from a distance the next, barely heard, yet each word caused her fear to mount. Physical pain pounded in her head as they droned on, nattering at her, forcing her to listen to their vile thoughts and plans.

"After your husband is hung for murder, he will be nothing but a sweet, brief memory. Content yourself that John will marry you. He will finally become Lord Barwick, and we will have control over you, the land and its tenants. But most importantly, the wealth that comes with it."

"Until then, my future wife, you will remain in this room, drugged and held in our custody. We don't want you to be able to stand with his family and present a defence for your dear husband." John lowered his hand and gripped Lauren's face, squeezing her soft flesh, forcing her eyes to open and look at him. "Don't expect the luxury of drugs to keep you unfeeling and unresponsive after our union." He rejoined snidely, "You will be mine then, to do with as I please."

A cloud of darkness overtook Lauren, and she felt herself falling into the silence and forgetfulness of a dark void, akin to the nightmare she had dreamed of long ago. Only this was no dreamed nightmare, but her truth.

* * *

The wind whipped the trees, sending the gold and red leaves scattering in whirling eddies before horse and rider. Heavy drops of rain were unleashed from the swirling dark clouds as the door swung open at Devlin's approach.

John Marlow pointed a flintlock duelling pistol at his guest's chest. Devlin stared down the long heavy cylindrical barrel of the gun and judged it to be of ancient design. There was no spur on the trigger guard to improve the shooter's grip, not that it would matter much at close range. The lead shot would produce the same, if not a worse wound than the one he had suffered the previous year.

"You surprise me, Barwick," Marlow sneered, "I expected you to be hung shortly."

"For what crime Marlow? Margaret left my home alive and well. It was only after she returned here that she was never seen again. I believe she was your cousin?"

"A distant cousin. No matter, we were very close."

"I can imagine." Devlin sneered.

Marlow lifted his shoulders in a shrug. Soon it wouldn't matter what the lord knew. "Step inside Lord Barwick," he emphasized the title, "my mother is anxious to greet you."

Devlin noticed a furtive movement in the gloom at the top of the stairs. Fiona saw the weapon pointed at Lord Barwick and stepped back quickly from view.

They entered the parlour, where Agnes sat like a queen in her chair. Three windows were covered with brown velvet curtains, and one was bare. The hanging vines ticked against the window as sheets of rain were unleashed to run in streams down the panes. Agnes held the head of her raven cane and clicked the fingernail of her right hand on its crystal unseeing eye.

"Lord Barwick. Welcome to my home," she greeted and gave a piercing laugh. "John, are we not amused that Barwick has decided to finally visit us!"

Marlow's lips turned up in an evil grimace and moved closer to the lord.

"I'm sure you realize this is not a social visit," Devlin cooly replied.

"Always the gentleman," she mewled. "You and your kind put manners above all else."

"Not always," Devlin smiled. "Where is my wife?"

"Put away for the moment. Regardless, you will never see her again," the crone cackled.

John lifted his booted leg and kicked the back of Devlin's left calf causing his knee to drop hard to the floor. He maintained his footing with his right foot, bending it at the knee to half kneel before Agnes.

"Let's see if the lord will beg for mercy," Marlow growled.

Devlin remained mute and glared at Agnes.

"It wouldn't have mattered who married Lauren," Agnes explained, "I had schemed to get that estate before she was born."

"It should have been ours shortly after we forced Elizabeth to marry Phillip, but that didn't work out as planned," Marlow added to the tale. "She died before we could do away with the old lord. If she had survived, I would have been the next master of Barwick Castle by my marriage to Elizabeth."

"Yes," Agnes agreed, "the meddling solicitor hadn't yet talked Phillip into writing a will. The land and title would have passed on to Elizabeth and her new husband."

"So you see, Barwick," John challenged, "you took a title I almost had."

"It seems that if you have wanted the land for that long, you are deucedly bad at plots and deception," Devlin challenged.

"Under Phillip's management it wasn't worth the effort," Agnes crowed. "The castle was worthless, and the land even more so."

"And you were foiled by a little old maid who hid a child from you!" Devlin chuckled. "Should I be so concerned if Ellie Butterfield outmaneuvered you?"

Agnes leaned forward to look directly into Devlin's face with trembling rage. "Butterfield will feel my wrath for stepping into my plans and protecting Lauren when she was a child, and you, sir, are hardly in a position at the moment to be so cocky!"

"We really should thank you, Barwick. You have made the land prosperous, and the improvements to the castle were done with excellent taste. I was able to see it when I snatched your wife. The value has increased beyond measure. When we add the delicious Lauren into its worth, it is simply too good to pass up the chance to have it," Marlow taunted, stepping closer to Barwick.

Devlin felt the bore of the gun press against his temple. He knew the standard weapon would have a noticeable delay between pulling the trigger and releasing the bullet. However, he wasted no time ducking his head and drew the knife from his boot in a fluid motion.

A slash from his outstretched hand cut tendons and veins in Marlow's wrist as he squeezed the trigger. The errant shot barely missed the back of Devlin's head, digging deeply into the worn wood of the floor. Marlow screamed in pain, grasping his bleeding appendage.

Devlin flipped the blade, spinning in a quick, mesmerizing circle before he grabbed it up again to have it face backwards in his fist. He plunged the knife into Marlow's thigh to have it lodged against the bone. Marlow screamed at a higher pitch and hastily retreated from the lord's reach.

Devlin grabbed the cane from the crone's grip and landed a heavy blow against the retreating man's temple, knocking his head sideways. Marlow careened off balance as he pulled the blade from his leg and, gaining purchase, rushed forward as though his life depended on the next few moments…which it most certainly did. Marlow felt the metal raven's head smack under his chin. He heard the solid thunk of his teeth slamming shut and felt the force that knocked him backwards against the wall, momentarily dazing him.

Agnes made a hasty retreat to search for a weapon and save her son yet again.

In a dizzying rage, Marlow scanned the walls, eyeing the shields and armour that hung there. He grabbed the first handy sword. It was pitted with rust and dull as a butter knife, but it would have to do. With his left hand, he swung it in an awkward vicious arch, as Devlin stepped back, easily avoiding the blade.

Marlow's blood oozed in a steady flow from the wounds while he staggered and advanced on Devlin.

"You will not prevail here," he claimed with false bravado approaching with the raised weapon. "You were an easy target in the forest for Harrington's aim to find you. We would have finished you off then, had we not lost you."

"Your tracking skills need much improvement," Devlin rejoined, taunting his adversary. "Your minion was outsmarted by a horse who was intelligent enough to lead him away from me, and I can only assume you were not clever enough to find me before I was discovered by the searchers."

Marlow stumbled. He held the awkward blade in his left hand, lunging forward as it waved unsteadily toward his target. The dull blade glanced off the cane as Devlin flicked the raven's head up and around the sword, knocking it from Marlow's clumsy grip.

Marlow stared dumbly at Devlin, who had easily gained the advantage. A flicker of motion caught his eye, and with evil intent, he held Devlin's attention as he waited for his mother to sneak up behind him, as she had done with Harrington. Fiona stood in the open doorway behind his mother, levelling a gun at the back of Barwick's head. Though beaten and bloody, victory was imminently theirs.

"Your kind always thinks that they have right on their side, and that good prevails over evil," he narrowed his eyes at the man before him. "If you think you have bested us, Barwick, you will be sorely disappointed."

Agnes was a few silent steps behind Devlin as Marlow spoke to him. She raised her arm to strike when a loud retort and a blinding flash of lightning simultaneously filled the room. Agnes was focused on the task at hand and was blissfully unaware of the shot that pounded through the side of her head, dislodging the frontal lobe of her brain onto the prized possessions she had achieved throughout her life by dubious means. The bullet obliterated half her face after it plowed through her brain. Her legs crumpled as she folded to the floor with a heavy thud in a mass of black silk from the stylish gown she wore.

John screamed a horrifying rent that mixed with the crack of thunder from without, to cause the window panes to shudder. With a slack jaw and horrified eyes, he saw the smoking gun held by Fiona.

"You damned fool!" he screeched. "You missed Barwick and killed my mother!"

"I missed no one, John." Fiona answered calmly to turn the pistol on him, "You killed my daughter, not Lord Barwick. You lied to me, and I know the sordid truth. I know everything you did to Margaret."

Marlow reached for the sword and heaved it ineffectually at Fiona as the full force of Devlin hit him around his protruding middle, carrying them backwards to fall crashing to the floor. Marlow's breath was jolted from him at the impact. Devlin lifted him by his neatly tied cravat, and with pounding force, knocked his fist into John's face, breaking his teeth, his nose and blackening his eyes. From the corner of his rage-hazed eyes, he saw Fiona pointing her gun at Marlow's bloody head.

Sanity replaced his rage. "Fiona," Devlin said, rising and taking the weapon from her hand. "Let the law have its day to deal with him."

Fiona stared stupidly at Devlin as John curled into a ball, sobbing. The blood from his wounds joined the puddle moving across the floor that seeped from his mother's grotesque wound.

Lucy stood in the doorway with a smile on her face as she glared at John Marlow. Servants gathered in the hallway, and none were disappointed in the day's outcome.

"Lord Barwick," Lucy ventured, "your lady sir, I can take you to her."

Devlin ordered the butler to bind Marlow before hastening up the stairs with the maid. Lauren was curled on the bed and would not rouse from her stupor.

"They've been giving her laudanum to keep her asleep. The effects should wear off," Lucy promised. "I've stayed as close to her room as possible while she was here. She was not harshly abused, my lord, the master put his hands on her, but the old mistress stopped him from doing any worse."

Devlin's jaw hardened at the thought of Marlow touching or harming his wife in any way. In due course, he would use all the power he could wield to see that Marlow would never beset his evil ways on any living being again.

"Lord Barwick?" Lucy questioned, "The rest of the staff and I are grateful for what you've done. This is an evil home to work in, but we have nowhere else to go. That's why we have stayed here. But what will we do now, sir? Your wife is related to this house. Will you take charge of this place?"

"I have to see to Lauren," he pledged, "we will address your concerns, rest assured."

Devlin lifted Lauren and carried her down the stairs. Fiona rushed forward to open the door for him.

"I want to apologize, Lord Barwick. For everything." A tear rolled down Fiona's cheek "Margaret, and I were unfairly cruel to you and Lauren."

Devlin nodded briefly before leaving the house. Fiona had suffered much and was most likely used by Marlow and his mother. At the moment, he could not completely forgive her while he held his unconscious wife in his arms.

Though Devlin protected Lauren from the weather, the cold sheets of driving rain that hit them allowed her to regain her senses by the time they reached the castle. Tears filled her eyes and streamed along with the rain down her face. Her hair was wet and clinging to her cheeks.

"Hold me tight Devlin," she sobbed into his chest, "Keep me safe from those awful people. It was a nightmare come to life."

Devlin held her tighter. "You're safe Lauren. They will never bother you again."

She was miserable as Devlin felt her body trembling in his arms. "Where is Sterling?" she cried. "Was anything done to him?

"He is with Ellie. When she couldn't find you, she roused the house for a thorough search of the place, and when she realized you were gone, she knew who had taken you, and she disappeared with him," he spoke tenderly, assuring her of the baby's safety. "She and Max Ferguson are protecting him. We can go there straight away to get him."

"Ellie will see to him for now. I want to wash the stench of that house and Marlow off me first."

# *Epilogue*

**Barwick Castle**
**April 17, 1870**

"There'll be a right benjo going on in the castle this day," Ellie quipped

"Translation, please Lauren," queried Devlin as he entered the library.

Lauren stood Sterling on the floor before her and smiled as the baby tottered off in search of his toys.

"She's talking about her wedding to Mr. Ferguson and saying it will be a grand noisy holiday." She furrowed her brow and tilted her head at her old companion, "That's right, isn't it Ellie?"

"It is, and don't I just look like butter on bacon in all my finery?" she twirled in a girlish circle, stopping when she lost her balance on one rotation. Ellie formed a dizzy expression on her face that caused Sterling to laugh his boisterous toddler giggles at her play and topple over.

Lauren watched the silk of Devlin's shirt stretch taught over his broad back. Her admiring gaze shifted to his tight buttocks as he bent to lift Sterling and toss him into the air. She noted how his bulging biceps flexed before catching the sturdy baby and sighed at how lucky she was to have such a fine loving husband and father to their child.

"You know Devlin," Ellie blushed haltingly, "I've never been married, and I was wondering if you would escort me down the aisle in case I faint."

"If you are asking me to give you away Ellie, it would be my greatest joy and honour," he teasingly winked at her.

Long tables were set up near the castle on the front lawn, and an array of dishes were being hustled onto it before the girls could cease their labours and attend the wedding. Mrs. Osmond was putting the finishing touches on an elaborate multi-tiered wedding cake that had been well-soaked in brandy.

In the distance, Willow and Daniyal watched Abbi race along the fence, kicking his hooves into the air. The garden was lit with the colours of the spring flowers, as guests assembled on the bright warm day. The Hartford's were present with their brood of grandchildren, and Josh was ever mindful of Penny. Old man Patterson and his wife Dolly had become particularly good friends with Ellie and Max, and were seated in a place of honour where they could stand up for the couple as they spoke their vows.

The Cavanaugh family was in attendance, having finally talked Diana into the ease of rail travel. It was apparent that Rose's wish to have a new baby join the family was in full fruition, as Trevor aided his massively pregnant wife into a chair. Nanny Grace had the children under control and sitting primly in their seats, awaiting the service to begin.

After the demise of Agnes Etherington and the conviction and subsequent hanging of John Marlow, who had to be dragged to the gallows by a group of stalwart men, Charles Kearney paid a visit to Lauren. He advised her of the inheritance as the only surviving member of her grandfather's estate. The house sat on twenty acres and was offered to Ivy and James to purchase. They had moved in at once, and it was hard-won progress to turn the dull gothic building into the pride of ownership it currently possessed. The servants had gladly stayed in service to their new employers, and with Ivy's departure, Lauren found herself with Sally as her new lady's maid though she preferred Devlin as her helping hand to dress and undress. He was measurably better at performing the latter.

Ivy pushed a fashionable perambulator that held their twin boys, who remained fast asleep.

"Devlin, we could use your help with a few repairs to the manse," James hailed. "Surprisingly, Ivy is not a fan of the ivy that covers the bricks."

"It's not the plant I dislike as much as the spiders it holds." She shivered at the thought of the evil arachnids that had been so like the former mistress of the estate. "It must be trimmed from the doorways and windows to brighten the interior."

Max arrived in jovial spirit, placing himself before Parson Reynolds, while Devlin excused himself to find Ellie. Max had told her to pick out whichever wedding gown she desired from a catalogue from a top designer in London. He had ordered it wholesale through the mercantile, to Ellie's thrifty propensity. It was made of cream silk, and with the happiest smile beaming on her chubby face, the bride fairly sparkled in the shimmering dress.

"Are you ready Ellie?" Devlin questioned as he came towards her and offered his arm.

"If Max loves me half as much as you love my Lauren, then I'm as ready as I'll ever be," she admitted.

Ellie linked her arm through Devlin's, and he attempted to walk her down the flower-strewn pathway as she stopped to greet every person on the way to her Max. Devlin offered the necessary vow that he was responsible for giving away the aged bride.

Returning to Lauren's side, he took Sterling from her arms. He shifted the boy so he could see the events, and also find the most important person in his young life, his mother, who stood holding Devlin's other arm.

Lauren smiled into his face as he viewed her beauty, shining with her love for Ellie, him, and their son. She was pleased with her life. Happy that their family and friends were sharing the joy of the day and prospering under Devlin's careful administration.

As the minister's words echoed in the garden, Devlin bent his head to hear his wife.

"I love you," she whispered softly. "You are my life, my home. My heart is lonely no more, because I am yours."

# *About the Author*

Cathrine started her career as a secretary until she realized her first dream; to become a wife, mother and now grandmother. Her second dream came about when she opened a kennel, breeding Champion Labrador Retrievers under the Embrace prefix. At the time, she wrote an Owner's Manual for those who purchased her puppies, providing them with knowledge of the stages a dog will go through and training tips that should be incorporated at that time. Her artistic nature led her to dream number three; to become a professional artist. She then designed and had built a log home where she and her husband ran a successful Bed and Breakfast business welcoming guests from around the world.

For almost 50 years, she knew she could compose more than consistent in-depth grocery lists and Christmas letters, which led her to write her debut novel, Embrace the Lonely Heart.

Splitting her time between their home in Ontario and winter residence in Florida, Cathrine is working on her next novel. Stay tuned for Embrace the Captive Heart and never give up your own dreams.

If you enjoyed this book
please consider leaving a review
on Amazon ♡

Manufactured by Amazon.ca
Bolton, ON

39512823R00240